Praise for Ir

"The narrative crackles with suspense all the way
through its surprising conclusion."
Publishers Weekly on *Into the Fire*

"A compelling mystery with a palpable love story."
Booklist on *Into the Fire*

"This author never disappoints."
Interviews & Reviews on *Into the Fire*

"A suspenseful whodunit to the end."
Evangelical Church Library Association on *Body of Evidence*

"One of the best offerings by master of
romantic suspense Hannon."
Library Journal starred review on *Labyrinth of Lies*

"Hannon's winning inspirational thriller
will please fans and newcomers alike."
Publishers Weekly on *Labyrinth of Lies*

"Riveting suspense."
Relz Reviewz on *Point of Danger*

OVER THE EDGE

BOOKS BY IRENE HANNON

HEROES OF QUANTICO

Against All Odds

An Eye for an Eye

In Harm's Way

GUARDIANS OF JUSTICE

Fatal Judgment

Deadly Pursuit

Lethal Legacy

PRIVATE JUSTICE

Vanished

Trapped

Deceived

MEN OF VALOR

Buried Secrets

Thin Ice

Tangled Webs

CODE OF HONOR

Dangerous Illusions

Hidden Peril

Dark Ambitions

TRIPLE THREAT

Point of Danger

Labyrinth of Lies

Body of Evidence

UNDAUNTED COURAGE

Into the Fire

Over the Edge

HOPE HARBOR

Hope Harbor

Sea Rose Lane

Sandpiper Cove

Pelican Point

Driftwood Bay

Starfish Pier

Blackberry Beach

Sea Glass Cottage

Windswept Way

Sandcastle Inn

STANDALONE NOVELS

That Certain Summer

One Perfect Spring

OVER THE EDGE

IRENE HANNON

Revell

a division of Baker Publishing Group
Grand Rapids, Michigan

Published by Revell
a division of Baker Publishing Group
Grand Rapids, Michigan
RevellBooks.com

Printed in the United States of America

Library of Congress Cataloging-in-Publication Data
Names: Hannon, Irene, author.
Title: Over the edge / Irene Hannon.
Description: Grand Rapids, Michigan : Revell, a division of Baker Publishing
    Group, 2024. | Series: Undaunted courage ; #2
Identifiers: LCCN 2024005993 | ISBN 9780800741891 (paperback) | ISBN
    9780800746391 (cloth) | ISBN 9781493447206 (ebook)
Subjects: LCGFT: Christian fiction. | Thrillers (Fiction) | Novels.
Classification: LCC PS3558.A4793 O94 2024 | DDC 813/.54—dc23/eng/20240214
LC record available at https://lccn.loc.gov/2024005993

Cover design: James Iacobelli

Baker Publishing Group publications use paper produced from sustainable for-
estry practices and postconsumer waste whenever possible.

24 25 26 27 28 29 30   7 6 5 4 3 2 1

To my husband, Tom,
as we celebrate our 35th anniversary.

Though many years have passed since we said I do,
you will always be my handsome groom . . .
the man who stole my heart with his kindness,
integrity, generosity, and honor—
not to mention the bluest eyes this side of
the Lakes of Killarney.

Thank you for walking with me during good times and bad.
For supporting my dreams and cheering me on.
For being my partner . . . my hero . . . my friend.

I treasure our happy yesterdays,
and I look forward to all the beautiful tomorrows
we have yet to share.

Three dot. Forever and a day.

ONE

THAT WAS ODD.

As Lindsey Barnes guided her car up the long drive that led to her client's upscale house, she eased back on the gas pedal and surveyed the empty bay in the three-car garage. The spot where the female half of the power couple always parked.

If Heidi Robertson had gone out, why hadn't she closed the door?

Whatever the reason, her absence was welcome news. It should be simple to dash in and grab the knife roll she'd left yesterday, with no one the wiser.

Unless the other half of the couple was home.

But according to Heidi, James lived at the office. From what Lindsey had gleaned during her interview for the personal chef position four months ago, running a commercial real estate development firm was a 24/7 occupation.

So odds were this would be a quick in-and-out.

Nevertheless, she continued toward the concrete pad out of sight behind the garage, where the help parked. If her client happened to return during this brief visit, she wouldn't be happy to discover an out-of-place car. The lady of the house liked her instructions followed to a T—a lesson learned via a taut email after the new personal chef forgot to use the woman's preferred font on the heating instructions for each dish.

Rolling her eyes, Lindsey rounded the garage.

At least she didn't have to deal with Heidi beyond their menu planning emails. All she had to do was slip into the kitchen once a week, do her thing, and leave. Plus, the Robertsons paid their bill promptly—an important consideration if you were still establishing your business and cash flow was sometimes an issue.

Lindsey tucked her older-model Focus next to a pickup truck bearing the name Allen Construction.

Chad must be on the premises.

Good for him.

He deserved every plum job he could get after all the hardships he'd endured.

Lindsey set the brake, pulled out her phone, and called Heidi's number.

Like her first attempt more than thirty minutes ago, the call rolled to voicemail.

But Heidi had told her to let herself in whenever she came—and she needed those knives. Besides, the woman had assured her that neither of the Robertsons hung around in the kitchen.

After stowing her phone, she opened the door and slid from behind the wheel. The faint sound of contemporary music came from the vicinity of the pool house, the driving beat pulsing through the unseasonably cold early November air.

That must be Chad's work site for the day.

Shoving her hands into the pockets of the puffy, quilted coat that hit her midthigh, Lindsey lengthened her stride. The bright noontime sun hadn't put much of a dent in the St. Louis pre-winter chill, and after years in more temperate South Carolina, she was going to need longer than eighteen months to adjust to the harsher fall and winter temperatures here.

At the back door, she dug out her key, inserted it in the lock, and prepared to tap in the security code.

But the high-pitched *beep, beep, beep* that always sounded was absent as she twisted the knob and stepped inside.

Huh.

Was someone home after all?

She paused on the threshold. Listened.

All was quiet.

Maybe Heidi had forgotten to activate the security system. Or she could have left it off, if Chad was scheduled to do a job in the house too.

No matter. All she had to do was grab her knife roll and make a fast exit.

Mentally running through the recipes she'd be preparing for her afternoon client, she hurried through the large mudroom, past the half bath, and into the spacious kitchen replete with granite countertops and high-end appliances. All for show rather than utility, though. From what she'd gathered, the only real cooking that happened here occurred on the days she came.

Except . . .

She paused. Sniffed.

The distinctive smell of charred bread—along with another faint scent, indistinct as it mingled with the stronger odor— suggested someone had used a toaster very recently.

She glanced across the center island, toward the sink.

Yep. A crumb-filled plate stood on the counter beside it.

But cleanup in the Robertsons' kitchen wasn't on her agenda today.

Lindsey continued to the island, where she always did her mise en place. And there'd been a ton of it yesterday, thanks to the complicated menu Heidi had selected. But chopping, cutting, peeling, slicing, and grating all the ingredients up front was super efficient.

One of the many valuable lessons she'd learned in culinary school.

She scanned the long island that ran parallel to the sink.

No knife roll.

Propping her hands on her hips, Lindsey gave the large room a once-over.

Ah. There it was. Over on the coffee bar in the far corner, past the second island with stools that faced into the kitchen and doubled as an eat-in counter. She must have put it there while she was cleaning up.

Sport shoes noiseless on the tile floor, she hurried across the room. If a chef without her knife roll wasn't akin to a surgeon without a scalpel, she'd have skipped this unplanned detour. Wedging it in after shopping for today's ingredients had cut into her afternoon cooking schedule.

She rounded the corner of the second island, strode toward the coffee bar—and jerked to a stop as a scream bubbled up in her throat.

Between the main island and the sink, a man lay sprawled on his stomach on the floor, his vacant pupils aimed her direction. Beneath his center mass, a crimson pool stained the white tile. A half-eaten bagel lay beside him.

It was James Robertson, based on the photos she'd found of him on the internet while researching the couple after securing this chef gig.

And he was dead.

Even worse?

The location of the blood suggested he hadn't died of natural causes.

Lindsey grabbed the edge of the island to steady herself. Tried to suck in air.

She had to call 911.

And she would. As soon as the room stopped spinning and she could—

The toilet in the guest bathroom flushed.

As her brain did the math, another shock wave rolled through her.

The person responsible for James's demise was still here.

And the murderer was between her and the back door.

Heart stuttering, she gave the room a frantic sweep.

Could she make a run toward the front of the house? Try to—

The knob on the bathroom door rattled, and panic squeezed the oxygen from her lungs.

Too late.

She was trapped.

Letting her instincts take over, she dropped to her knees, edged the last two stools closer together, and tucked herself under the island.

Please, God, don't let whoever is in here find me!

As that plea for deliverance looped through her mind, she crouched lower and peeked through the shelving between the end of the cabinetry and the decorative column that held up the granite slab on top of the island.

A figure entered the kitchen, but a long coat, ski mask, latex gloves, and boots hid every identifying feature.

When the person walked her direction, Lindsey stopped breathing.

The murderer rounded the granite at the end of the other island. Halted when something clunked to the floor and skidded her direction.

It stopped sliding less than three feet from her, on the other side of the island where she'd taken refuge.

She froze as the killer walked toward her, bent down to grasp the sparkly item that lay almost within touching distance, then continued toward the dead man.

From her vantage point, only the person's jeans-clad lower legs were visible as one of them nudged the body with the toe of a boot.

No reaction as James's lifeless eyes stared at her.

Every nerve in her body vibrating, Lindsey snaked a hand toward the shelves at the end of the island and curled her shaky fingers around the rim of the Daum crystal vase Heidi had pointed out during their tour of the kitchen. The one she'd said had cost more than $4,000.

But with her knives out of reach on the coffee bar, the pricey decorative piece was the sole weapon at hand. Better to risk her client's wrath if she broke it than certain death if the killer spotted her and she had no way to defend herself.

Best case, the murderer had finished what they'd come to do and would leave through the back door.

If they had more business to attend to in the house, however . . . if they walked past the island that was her refuge . . . they could spot her no matter how small she tried to make herself.

And if that happened, her career as a personal chef would likely come to a very sudden end.

Along with her life.

ST. LOUIS COUNTY DETECTIVE JACK TUCKER ducked under the yellow tape around the mega mansion that was now a crime scene and strode toward the responding officer who'd been the first to arrive.

Meyers swiveled toward him as he approached. "You got here fast."

"I was close when Sarge called." Unfortunately. Another half hour, he'd have been miles away from this tony neighborhood, racked out at home. And after putting in eighteen hours straight on a mall shooting that had left one dead and three injured, that was where he'd rather be.

But this job didn't come with a time clock.

"You inherited a big one."

No kidding.

The scrutiny could be intense at scenes that reeked of power and money. No doubt the media would descend at any moment.

"Fill me in."

He listened as the man gave him the basics and summarized the two reports he'd taken. One from the woman who'd called in the crime, the other from the workman who'd been on the premises.

"Where are they?"

"Woman's in my car. She's shook." He motioned toward his cruiser, parked along the circle drive that led to the sprawling contemporary structure. "The guy preferred to stay outside, despite the cold. He's on the patio. Also shook, but in a different way."

Jack's antennas went up. After more than two decades on the street, Meyers often had valuable people insights.

"Explain that."

The officer shrugged. "Spooked may be more accurate. I ran him, and he's clean. But he's got a major case of nerves. Could be a natural reaction to finding himself in the middle of a murder investigation, could be more. That determination is above my pay grade." He flashed a grin.

"Thanks for the input."

"Anytime. You want me to unlock the cruiser?" He pulled out his keys.

"Not yet. I'll do a quick walk-through first."

"Make it fast unless you want Hank to be all over you." He motioned to a Crime Scene Unit van as it took the corner up the street faster than was prudent, with a slight screech of tires.

Yeah, that was Hank. The cantankerous tech was the only CSU investigator who drove like the hounds of hell were after him. If he wasn't so skilled at what he did, he'd have been canned years ago for his tendency to ding up vehicles—and for his nonexistent people skills.

"I'm on it. Stall Hank if you can."

Meyers snorted. "I'll try, but don't hold your breath."

Jack took off for the house at a jog, stopping at the back door to slip a pair of booties over his shoes and snap on latex gloves.

The interior was quiet as he entered. No surprise. The responding officers congregated around the perimeter knew better than to traipse around inside and risk compromising a crime scene. Only two stood guard in the kitchen, conversing in low tones.

He acknowledged them with a dip of his head and circled the island.

The scene was exactly as Meyers had described it, and if the woman who'd reported the crime was correct, the victim was the homeowner. A wallet would help confirm that, but until someone from the medical examiner's office got here and Hank worked the scene, it was safer not to touch the body.

He pulled out his phone and did a quick Google search. Everyone had an internet presence these days. Especially the movers and shakers who tended to live on estates like this one.

Identity verified. The victim was James Robertson.

He edged closer to the body. No murder weapon had been left in plain sight, but the location and quantity of blood suggested either a knife or bullet wound to the front midsection.

After giving the rest of the kitchen a fast perusal, he signaled one of the officers to join him and did a quick walk-through of the house.

Nothing but the bedroom raised red flags. In the master suite, dresser drawers were pulled out, a few pieces of clothing lay puddled on the floor, and the walk-in closet door was ajar.

Jack crossed to it.

The doors of a free-standing jewelry armoire were open, and many of the hooks inside were empty.

It was possible the homeowner had interrupted a robbery, and—

Voices spoke in the vicinity of the kitchen, and Jack retraced his steps.

Hank glared at him as he entered. "I hope you're not mucking up my crime scene."

"Perish the thought. I have booties and gloves." He lifted his foot and wiggled his fingers.

"Hmph." Hank pulled a baseball cap out of his kit and yanked it over his flyaway gray hair. "Lacey here yet?"

"I haven't seen her." But in light of past experience, the assistant ME wouldn't be far behind.

"I'll have to work around the body."

"You could start in the bedroom at the end of the hall." Jack waved that direction. "There was activity there."

"We have a warrant yet?"

"In the works."

Hank hefted his kit and brushed past. "Get out as soon as you're done. I don't want any contamination in here. You too." He poked a finger in one officer's chest as he passed. "We don't need two of you hanging around."

The guy waited until Hank disappeared down the hall toward the bedroom before speaking to his colleague. "Guess I've been ousted. I'll take up a position outside the door if you want to follow Mr. Personality." He hooked a thumb in the direction the grouchy tech had disappeared.

"Thanks a lot."

"I'm leaving too." Jack walked toward the back door. "I have people to interview."

He exited, ditched his protective gear, and circled the house. After catching Meyers's attention, he signaled for the man to unlock his cruiser.

The officer beat him there.

The back door swung open, and Jack took a swift but thorough inventory as a thirtysomething woman emerged.

Slender, about eight inches shorter than his six-foot frame—and gorgeous. Not even her bleached complexion or the severe hairstyle that corralled her russet-colored hair into a barrette at her nape could take away from the delicate jawline, full lips, and high cheekbones that gave her a classic beauty.

She didn't look like any chef he'd ever met.

And she certainly didn't look like she belonged in the middle of a murder investigation.

But looks could be deceiving. So he'd approach her as he approached anyone at a crime scene—with a healthy dose of suspicion.

Hands buried in the pockets of her quilted coat, she waited for him by the cruiser.

As he drew close, Meyers backed off.

"Ms. Barnes, I'm Jack Tucker with the County Crimes Against Persons Bureau." He extended his hand.

Instead of grasping his fingers, her lips parted slightly, and she stared at him, her eyes going a tad glassy.

Aftershock?

Was she going to pass out?

"Why don't you sit again for a minute?" He moved forward to take her arm and help her back into the car.

"No." She scooted along the fender, toward the trunk—and out of his reach. "No. I'm f-fine."

That was a lie. Quivers rippled through her, and her pallor had worsened.

"I'd like to speak with you for a few minutes. Shall we find a warmer spot?"

"Here is fine. But I already told the officer everything I know."

At the chill in her voice, he scrutinized her. Fear . . . anxiety

. . . nervousness . . . all of those emotions were understandable in this situation.

But what had prompted her subtle animosity?

Once again, his antennas went up. "I'd like to hear it straight from you, if you don't mind." He pulled out a notebook and pen, reining in a shudder as a frigid gust of wind whooshed past. Man, it was way too early for this kind of cold. "Tell me why you were here and what happened after you arrived."

She burrowed deeper into her coat and repeated the same story Meyers had relayed.

He let her finish before speaking. "Was the open garage door unusual?"

"It seemed strange to me, but I haven't worked for the Robertsons long enough to know if it's that uncommon."

"Has it ever been open on any of your prior visits?"

"No."

"Same question about the deactivated security system."

"Same answer. But James Robertson was home. He must have turned it off."

Not necessarily. The murderer could have gained access prior to Robertson's arrival.

The question was how.

"Other than you and the owners, are you aware of anyone else who has the access code?"

"No. And mine was unique to me. To all users, I assume. Ms. Robertson was very clear that their system tracks the codes entered and they could find out if anyone visited without an invitation." Her shivering intensified. "Are we almost f-finished?"

"For now. But let's talk a little more about the person you saw in the kitchen."

"I don't have anything else to say. As I told the officer, they were covered head to toe. I gave him a description of the clothing."

"How tall would you say this person was?"

"I don't know." A puff of cold air materialized in front of her face as she blew out a shaky breath. "My view was from an odd angle, and I only saw the full figure for a handful of seconds."

"Best guess."

Twin furrows appeared on her brow. "Using the Sub-Zero fridge they passed as a gauge, maybe five nine or ten?"

On the tall side for a woman, but the perpetrator *could* have been female.

"Any hints about gender?"

"No. The coat was unisex and almost knee-length. The feet were kind of large"—her frown deepened—"but now that I think about it, the boots were more like overshoes rather than real boots. The kind some people wear to protect their shoes in bad weather."

Or to mask footprints at the scene of a crime.

And they tended to be bulky, so the size of the foot didn't provide much of a clue to gender, either.

"How long after the person came out of the bathroom and left through the back door did you call 911?"

"A couple of minutes. I wanted to make certain they were gone."

Jack flipped his notebook shut. "We're done for today."

"Would it be possible for me to get my knife roll? It's on the coffee bar in the kitchen. I have a client who's expecting me this afternoon."

Until the cause of death was determined, her knife roll wasn't going anywhere.

"Sorry. You'll have to do without the knives this afternoon. And you may want to reschedule your client."

"Why would I do that?" She brushed back a wind-whipped strand of hair that had escaped from her barrette.

Instead of responding, he shifted his attention to her hand.

She followed his gaze to her quivering fingers. Clenched

them into a fist. Let her hand drop to her side. "They're counting on me."

"In light of the extenuating circumstances, I doubt they'll mind eating pizza or takeout for a few nights."

"But I have all the ingredients in my car." Her chin rose a hair. "And I try not to let people down." Her comment lingered in the cold air as a shadow passed over her eyes.

What was that all about?

Since the answer to his question wasn't pertinent to the investigation, Jack moved on. "Speaking of your car—we'll need to look at it."

Her face went blank for a moment before shock replaced confusion. "Am I a suspect?"

"Anyone connected with a crime is a person of interest."

She groped behind her for the cruiser and sagged back against it. "This is surreal."

"I can get you out of here faster if you'll give us permission to examine your vehicle rather than make us wait for a search warrant."

"Have at it." She waved a hand toward the back of the house. "There's nothing incriminating in my car except the candy bar I splurged on for lunch and never got to finish."

"Would you like to wait in the cruiser again, out of the cold?"

She eyed it, her reluctance to spend any more time in the back of a police car obvious. But in the end she bowed to logic. "Yes. Thanks."

Jack signaled Meyers to rejoin them. "Ms. Barnes will borrow your backseat again while we check out her vehicle." As the man unlocked the door and pulled it open, Jack once more extended his hand toward the chef, whose manner remained as glacial as the air. "Thanks for your assistance."

"My hands are like ice. I wouldn't want to give you frostbite." She sidled away from his outstretched fingers and slid into the car.

Meyers closed the door behind her and turned to him. "What did you do to rankle her?"

"Nothing. I just asked the standard questions in my usual polite manner."

"Huh. Even though she was shook earlier, she wasn't unfriendly. Maybe the events of the day are catching up with her."

"Could be."

Yet as he walked back to the rear of the house, that explanation didn't ring true. While anyone would be upset after going through a life-threatening experience, that wasn't why Lindsey Barnes had frozen him out.

For whatever reason, she'd taken an instant dislike to him. Which didn't sit well.

Tamping down a surge of annoyance, he turned up the collar of his coat.

Why should he care what a stranger thought about him? He ought to put their encounter out of his mind and concentrate on the looming murder investigation. A man lay dead inside the walls of this high-end house, and finding the killer deserved his full focus.

If he'd rubbed Lindsey wrong, so be it. As long as she didn't end up a suspect, he never had to see her again.

Instead of giving him comfort, however, that notion left him feeling somehow disappointed.

Weird.

But that wasn't a subject worth pondering when he had vehicles to search, neighbors to talk to, security camera footage to review, and interviews to conduct—including one with the dead man's wife once she was located and the police chaplain broke the bad news.

A task that never got easier, even after more than a decade in law enforcement. And one he wasn't looking forward to on this cold November afternoon.

TWO

THE COP WHO HAD THE KEYS to the cruiser was heading her way.

Finally.

Lindsey drew a shaky breath and tried to suppress a shiver that had nothing to do with the cold wind whistling around the car. In here, it was toasty. But after everything else that had happened today, being confined in the back of a locked police car wasn't conducive to peace of mind. Nor was the whole crime scene experience.

Especially for someone with her history.

At least Jack Tucker hadn't returned to free her. If she never saw him again it would be too soon.

How ironic was it that he, of all people, would be assigned to handle this case?

At least he hadn't recognized her name. If Clair had mentioned her, she must have just used her first name.

The lock clicked, and a moment later the door swung open. Officer Meyers leaned down. "Ma'am? You're free to claim your car and leave."

"Thank you." She slid from the cruiser, bracing as a bitter gust buffeted her.

"Steady." His hand shot out as she wavered.

"I'm fine."

Not really.

But she would be, later. After she finished her work for the day, went home, locked her doors, took a hot bath—and prayed the nightmares she'd at last vanquished didn't return to disrupt her sleep.

If they did, though, she had Dr. Oliver's card and his personal cell number. She'd get through this, just like she'd gotten through the last trauma.

As she thanked the officer again, Heidi's red Tesla was waved through the police barricade on the street.

While it rolled down the drive, a man in clerical garb appeared at the front door, as if he'd been alerted to her arrival or had been watching for her.

Lindsey's throat tightened.

Heidi might not be her favorite client, but she wouldn't wish the woman's next few minutes on her worst enemy. Traumatic as her own day had been, she hadn't lost someone she loved.

The woman passed her and the officer, continued toward the main entrance, and alighted from the car. She glanced toward them, then let the cleric usher her inside.

Not until she disappeared through the door did Lindsey circle toward the back of the house to claim her car.

Unfortunately, Jack Tucker was between her and it.

She slowed . . . but when it became apparent he was waiting for her, she picked up her pace. The faster she got this encounter over with, the faster she could get out of here and try to forget the whole nightmare.

Including her upsetting encounter with a certain St. Louis County detective.

"Officer Meyers told me I was free to leave." She stopped several feet away from the clean-cut, sandy-haired man, whose toned physique and summer-sky-blue eyes would have been attractive under other circumstances.

24

"Yes. We're finished."

"I assume you didn't find anything incriminating."

"Only the remains of that candy bar." One side of his mouth rose a hair.

She dug out her keys, keeping her lips flat. "I have work to do." She attempted to walk past him, but he stepped in front of her.

"Are you certain you're up to driving?" He sent a pointed glance toward her white-knuckle grip on the keys.

"Yes. Please let me by."

After a couple of seconds, he extracted a card and held it out. "If you think of anything else that may be helpful, please give me a call." He waited until she took it before moving aside.

Card in hand, she continued to her car, past Chad's truck. His grilling either hadn't taken place yet or was in progress.

But neither of them were the culprits in the crime that had been committed in this house today. And it shouldn't take Detective Tucker long to figure that out, if he knew how to do his job.

As for the real killer?

Unless he or she had left clues behind, finding them could be a challenge.

That was Jack Tucker's problem, however. Not hers. She intended to put the past few hours out of her mind as soon as she drove off the property.

And pray today's ordeal didn't cause a major setback in her recovery from the other nightmare that had upended her life twenty-one long and stressful months ago.

"EARTH TO JACK. Come in, Jack."

At the summons, Jack swiveled away from Lindsey Barnes's disappearing taillights and toward the female voice.

Detective Cate Reilly-Sloan, arms crossed, long dark hair

pulled back into her usual high ponytail, stood beside the hedge of arborvitaes that hid the concrete pad behind the garage from the backyard.

Her amused expression was hard to decipher. But sometimes women were a mystery.

Like the one who'd just driven away.

"Sorry." He walked over to join her. "When did you get here?"

"A few minutes ago. I'm your reinforcement."

"Lucky you."

"TBD."

"Is Lacey here yet?"

"Yes. She's inside. The wife's on-site too. You want to bring me up to speed?"

He gave her a quick briefing. "I already spoke with Ms. Barnes. Chad Allen is up next. We can tag team it."

"Learn anything helpful from the witness?"

"Nothing other than the approximate height of the subject. She couldn't see much from her hiding place."

"Tough spot to find yourself in. She okay?"

"Claims to be. She was planning to pick up her work where she left off before we delayed her."

Cate's mouth bowed. "I think I like her." Then she sobered. "What do we know about Allen?"

"Nothing beyond the fact he doesn't have a record. Meyers ran him."

"Why?"

"Intuition."

"He has solid instincts."

"I know. Let's see if our impressions mesh with his. Allen's on the patio." He motioned toward the back of the house and followed Cate as she took the lead.

The man was sitting on a naked patio chair, its cushions relegated to post-season storage, but he shot to his feet the instant he caught sight of them. The officer waiting with him walked a discreet distance away as they approached.

Moving past Cate, Jack extended his hand and introduced himself as he assessed the man.

About five ten, thirtyish, dark brown hair, lean but muscular build, a touch of premature gray at his temples, eyes that looked as if they'd seen too much and were afraid they were about to see more.

Meyers was right.

The man had a tense, spooked air about him. Like someone who was waiting for the other shoe to drop.

As soon as he had a few minutes, he'd dig deeper into the guy's background.

Unlike Lindsey, Allen didn't hesitate to return his handshake. He also shook hands with Cate.

"We have a few questions, Mr. Allen, but we'd be happy to find a warmer spot." Jack motioned toward the house. "There may be a clear area inside we could use." If Hank was in a generous mood.

The man hesitated but in the end shook his head. "If you don't mind, I'd rather stay out here."

"Cate?" Jack deferred to her. From past experience working cases with her, she wasn't a fan of spending any more time than necessary outside in cold weather.

"Why don't we at least move closer to the house, under the covered portion of the patio and out of the wind?"

"That's fine." Allen walked over to a spot under the overhang, where bushes on either side served as a windbreak.

It was warmer, but not by much.

"Would you like to sit?" Jack indicated several chairs grouped around an outdoor fireplace, fighting the temptation to flip the gas burner that would send a modicum of warmth their direction.

"I don't mind standing, unless you expect this to take a while."

"Our preliminary discussion shouldn't hold you up long." He pulled out his notebook again, flexing his fingers to stimulate circulation. "I know you already gave a brief statement to the responding officer, but tell us again why you're here and what you've seen while you've been on the premises."

Allen slid his bare hands into his pockets. "I'm replacing a floor in the pool house. Or guest house. I think they use it for both." He indicated a structure farther back in the yard, on the other side of the large, winterized pool, accessed by a paved path from the patio. "I got here about nine, unloaded my supplies, and went to work. The next thing I knew, the cops were all over the place."

"Did you see anyone when you arrived, or afterward?"

"No."

"Were the garage doors open or shut?"

"Shut."

"How did you get into the pool house?"

"The owner said she'd leave the door open."

"Did you go into the main house?"

"No. I was planning to later, though. Ms. Robertson asked me to fix a sticking door. I told her I'd do it at the end of the day, but she said she'd leave the alarm off when she left in case I wanted to work on it earlier."

"Did you hear anything unusual this morning?"

"No. I play music while I work, and I crank up the volume."

Jack asked a few more questions, but it was clear Allen either didn't have anything to offer or wasn't telling everything he knew.

"Do you have any objection to us searching your truck? We can get a warrant, but you'll be out of here faster if you give us permission to proceed."

The man's forehead puckered. "I didn't have anything to do with what happened here today."

"Then you shouldn't mind if we take a look at your vehicle."

After a moment, he pulled out his keys and passed them over. "Fine. I'd like to leave sooner rather than later. I'll wait here."

"Cate." Jack motioned for her to join him.

She left the shelter of the overhang with obvious reluctance and fell in beside him. "I hate this Arctic weather. It shouldn't be this cold in early November."

"Why don't you move somewhere warmer?"

"I like being close to my sisters. Besides, my husband relocated here for me, and it wouldn't be fair to disrupt his career. What do you think about Allen?"

"He's nervous."

"Agreed. But that's not a red flag in and of itself. Most people who find themselves linked to a murder investigation are—" She squinted toward the privacy hedge that blocked their view of the concrete pad behind the garage. "I think we're being summoned."

Jack followed her line of sight. One of the officers was waving them over.

He hurried forward, Cate beside him.

"What's up?" He paused beside the uniformed man.

"One of our people spotted something." He led them around the hedge and motioned toward the running board on Allen's GMC Sierra.

Jack moved beside it and leaned down, catching a sparkle in one of the grooves.

On closer inspection, what appeared to be a diamond stud earring was wedged into one of the treads.

A search of the truck suddenly became high priority.

"We need to get Hank out here as soon as he's finished inside." Jack straightened up.

"He'll love that." Cate bent to examine the earring too. "He hates the cold as much as I do."

"Let's see what we can find while we wait." Jack pulled out another pair of latex gloves.

"Doesn't that strike you as a bit obvious?" Cate tugged on gloves too, tipping her head toward the stud.

"You think it's a plant?"

"I wouldn't rule out the possibility."

"I'm not. But criminals aren't always the brightest bulb in the chandelier. I was involved in an armed robbery case once where the clerk convinced the thief he couldn't open the cash drawer without running the guy's credit card. Believe it or not, he handed it over."

"We've all had a few of those. Let's do this."

For the next fifteen minutes, the two of them went over the truck. No jewelry emerged other than the earring they'd already photographed and bagged in an evidence envelope.

Cate was either right about the plant, or Allen had stashed the rest of his haul elsewhere for later retrieval.

Meaning a search of the residence grounds and the edge of the park that abutted the backyard would have to be done. If Allen was the killer, he couldn't have gone far to hide his bounty, since he was on-site when law enforcement arrived minutes after Lindsey's 911 call.

Jack finished inspecting the underside of the truck, scooted out, and stood. After handing the officer back his flashlight, he brushed off his slacks and addressed Cate. "Let's give Allen the bad news."

The man stopped pacing and swung toward them as they approached the patio where they'd left him. "Can I leave now?"

"Yes. But not with your truck." Jack stopped in front of him.

"Why not?"

"We found this." He angled his phone to display the photo he'd taken of the stuck stud before bagging it.

The man leaned closer. "What is that?"

"A diamond earring wedged in your running board. Any idea how it got there?"

Allen recoiled from the image, the color leeching from his complexion. "No."

Jack waited him out as an ice pellet stung his cheek, heralding the arrival of the sleet storm the meteorologists had predicted.

"Listen, I had nothing to do with what happened here today. I can't explain the earring, but I was in the pool house working until the cops arrived. That's the truth, even if there aren't any witnesses who can verify it."

The man appeared to be sincere. Yet the desolation in his eyes suggested he didn't think anyone would believe him.

What was this guy's story, anyway?

He'd find out later, after he talked to the next person on his list.

The victim's wife.

"If you don't want to wait for your vehicle, you're free to leave and come back later to pick it up. I can get someone to give you a ride home."

"No. I'll call my wife." He pulled out his cell, shoulders slumping. "She should be home from work by now."

"We'll be in touch if we have any more questions. And if you think of anything else you'd like to pass on, give me a call." Jack offered him a card.

The man took it, turned away, and trudged to the far side of the patio.

"I'm not getting guilty vibes." Cate watched him.

"Me neither. But I've been fooled before."

"I hear you. Want me to dig into his background while you talk to the victim's wife?"

"Or you could talk to her and I'll do the background dive."

"Sorry. You were tapped for the lead on this one. The dirty work lands on your desk."

"Thanks a lot."

"You'd do the same if the situation was reversed."

He couldn't argue with that. "Let's regroup after I'm finished. Where will you be?"

"Somewhere warm. I'll ask Hank to find me a spot inside where my fingers can thaw."

"Good luck with that. You know how protective he is of his crime scenes. I doubt he'd have let us in even to interview Allen."

"He and I have an understanding."

"Yeah? How'd you manage that?"

"We both have Greek blood. Plus, my sister makes the world's best baklava—and I sometimes share a few pieces with Hank."

"Bribery."

"Kindness."

"Hey. I'm nice to him too."

"Maybe. But you're not Greek, and you don't come bearing sweets." She took off for the house at a fast clip. "Let's go inside where it's warm."

Jack followed at a much slower pace.

Warmth was relative, and he'd had little of it today. Not from Mother Nature, and not from Lindsey Barnes.

Nor was the upcoming interview with a very recent widow likely to chase away the chill in the air.

And there was certainly no warmth in the hard-hearted killer who'd slain a man in his own kitchen and disappeared on this wintry day.

The best he could hope for was a break that would lead him to the culprit fast, before the trail grew cold.

But unless a solid clue surfaced, or Lindsey Barnes remembered a shock-suppressed detail about the killer, this case could be as difficult to resolve as the guilt that had plagued him for three long years . . . with no end in sight.

THREE

AS THE BLADE SLASHED across her finger, Lindsey let out a yelp, dropped the knife, and dashed toward the sink, leaving a trail of crimson dots on the wood floor.

Annoying as it was to admit, she should have followed Detective Tucker's advice and called it a day instead of trying to muscle through with her scheduled cooking session.

Sometimes there was a fine line between perseverance and stubbornness—and she'd crossed it today.

Lindsey twisted the faucet and stuck her left index finger under the spout. As water diluted the crimson stream, she pumped out hand soap from the dispenser beside the sink and washed the cut.

She could blame the accident on the unfamiliar knives, but why kid herself?

Her nerves were shot.

In fact, if anything, her shakiness had worsened over the course of the past few hours.

She rinsed her finger, dried it with a paper towel, and held it up to examine the cut.

No, not cut. It was more like a slice. Straight down, from

the outside of the middle knuckle to the one closest to her nail. Even elevated above her heart, it was already filling up again with blood.

There were bandages in her kit, though, along with other first-aid supplies. If she could get through this cooking session, she'd have the whole weekend to chill. All she had to do was take the remaining prep slower than usual and focus on pleasant thoughts while she worked, like her first therapist in South Carolina had taught her.

Lindsey pulled out antiseptic cream and bandages, doctored up the cut, and cleaned the blood off the floor and counter as she psyched herself up for the task at hand. At least her mise en place was finished, and today's clients had chosen familiar dishes that weren't difficult to prepare.

She could manage this. Especially since both halves of the couple were working late tonight, which would minimize interruptions and eliminate chitchat. Unlike Heidi Robertson, these clients liked to talk.

Calling up the calming memory of her last rowing session at Creve Coeur Lake before the abrupt cold front had descended, she moved at a measured, deliberate pace rather than charging ahead at her usual high-speed velocity. She made steady progress too—until her phone began to chirp.

At the sudden noise in the quiet kitchen, her hand jerked, sending two of the shrimp she was sautéing skidding out of the pan and across the floor.

Well, crud.

She needed that soothing music and relaxing hot bath.

Fast.

Continuing to stir the remaining shrimp with one hand, she tugged her tote bag across the counter, fished out her phone, and skimmed caller ID.

Madeleine Clark.

Perfect.

She could use a friendly voice about now, and Madeleine's more than qualified. If they hadn't met at church, and if Madeleine hadn't gone above and beyond to welcome a stranger in their midst—plus convinced that stranger to volunteer at the nonprofit she ran—the transition to both a new city and new career direction would have been much harder.

After removing the pan of shrimp from the burner, Lindsey put the phone to her ear. "Hi, Madeleine. What's up?"

"Praise the Lord! You're okay."

Lindsey frowned.

How could Madeleine know about—

Wait.

During their phone conversation last night about the six-week class she was teaching for Madeleine's Horizons organization, she'd mentioned the forgotten knife roll she had to retrieve today.

"You heard about the murder at the Robertson house." Lindsey pulled out a stool at the counter and sat.

"It's all over the news. Were you there?"

"Yes."

"Before or after?"

"After, but not by much." She gave her a quick recap of the day's events.

"Oh, Lindsey." Dismay and sympathy suffused Madeleine's inflection. "I'm sorry you have to deal with that on top of everything else."

"Me too. I'm beginning to feel like Job."

"Are you all right?"

"Physically, yes." Except for a persistent case of the shakes. "Mentally, we'll see."

"Go see that psychologist again if you need to."

"Trust me, I have his card at hand. Did the news story mention any suspects?"

"No. Do they have one?"

"Not as far as I know. I wasn't much help, even though I saw the person. I doubt Chad was able to offer anything either."

"Who?"

"Chad Allen, from church. He did some carpentry work at my condo a few months ago, and I recommended him to Heidi Robertson when she mentioned having trouble finding someone to do small projects. He was working in the pool house today."

"That's unfortunate, given his background."

True. A former homeless veteran who'd lived on the street for two years no doubt preferred to walk a wide circle around law enforcement.

"I hope the cops don't hassle him. From everything I've seen, he's got his act together now."

"I agree. But I expect the police will consider everyone a suspect until they find the real culprit."

"Let's hope that's soon. The killer didn't see me, but knowing they're still on the loose is more than a little unnerving."

"Understandable. You know, I think I'll call Dara. If I were Chad's wife, I'd be glad to have a friend reach out in support."

"I may call her too when I get home." After that hot bath.

"Aren't you there now?"

"No. I'm finishing up the cooking for my every-other-Friday client." She slid off the stool and put the pan of shrimp back on the burner.

"After everything that happened today, you should be home decompressing, not cooking."

"You sound like the detective who interviewed me." A man she was trying hard to forget. But Madeleine didn't know that story, and this wasn't the time to bring it up.

"Why didn't you listen to him? Your clients would have understood."

"I think you two compared notes." She shook the pan of shrimp with more force than necessary. "I know the world

36

wouldn't have ended if I'd slacked off, but that's not how I'm wired. Besides, it isn't professional to walk away from a job. This is a career, not a hobby."

"Hey. I'm not your mom." Madeleine's rebuke was gentle but firm. "You don't have to prove anything to me—or to her."

Lindsey drew in a slow, steadying breath. Madeleine was right. She was an established chef. A pro with American Culinary Academy and Le Cordon Bleu credentials. Her job was every bit as legitimate and important as the marketing VP position her mother held.

No matter what Mom thought.

"Thanks for the reminder. And as soon as I wrap up here, I'm going home—where I intend to hibernate and indulge for the entire weekend."

"I like that plan. Will you emerge for church on Sunday, assuming this sleet is short-lived?"

"Yes."

"In the meantime, call if you want to talk."

"Will do. Thanks for checking in."

Once they said goodbye, Lindsey plunged back into the task at hand, doing her best to ignore the throb in her finger. Thank goodness she was right-handed—and at least the cut hadn't bled through the bandage. She ought to be able to finish up here within the hour.

And barring any other glitches, she'd be in that hot bath surrounded by scented candles and soft music fifteen minutes after she walked through the door.

HEIDI ROBERTSON was a mess.

Jack paused on the threshold of the gargantuan living room and surveyed the woman with the bowed head and slumped shoulders who was sitting beside the chaplain.

Talking to grieving next of kin, forcing people in pain to

try to carry on a rational conversation, was the worst part of the job.

But it had to be done.

While it was possible the victim had surprised a robber and ended up dead, it was also possible this had been a deliberate crime with a specific target.

And if anyone would know about a man's enemies, it ought to be his wife.

The chaplain glanced his direction, touched the back of the new widow's hand, and spoke softly.

She met his gaze as he walked toward the duo, and he gave her a rapid but thorough perusal.

Chic outfit with designer written all over it. Highlighted hair cut into one of those complicated layered styles. Flawless manicure. Slender figure.

If not for the red-rimmed eyes and streaked mascara, she would have been photo-shoot ready.

He stopped three feet away, introduced himself, and took a seat across from her.

"I'll be nearby." The chaplain rose and exited.

"I'm sorry to have to disturb you further today, but I do have a few questions." Jack pulled out his notebook.

"I understand." She sniffed and dabbed at her nose with the tissue wadded in her fingers.

"Did the chaplain give you any details about what happened?"

Her irises began to shimmer. "Only the most important one. That James is g-gone. That someone k-killed him." A tear spilled over her lower lashes, and she wiped it away. "Do you have any idea who did it?"

"We're hoping you can help us answer that question. Let's start with what happened today from your perspective. What time did you leave the house, and where did you go?"

"I left about eleven for a salon appointment, then met a

friend for lunch in Kirkwood. After we finished, I stopped at a small boutique. I was there awhile, trying on several dresses. When I found one I liked, I bought it and came home."

"Do you usually leave your garage door open when you go out?"

"No, but sometimes I forget to close it. Why?"

"Lindsey Barnes said it was open when she arrived."

She rubbed at her temple, as if a headache was forming. "I saw her as I drove in. She wasn't supposed to be here today—but I did see two missed calls from her after I finished at the salon."

"She said she came by to get a knife roll she forgot."

"That's possible, I suppose. She was here yesterday. Did she see the person who did this?"

"Briefly. But their clothing masked their features and gender. Is your husband often home in the middle of the day, Ms. Robertson?"

"Only on days he has business trips. He was supposed to fly to Atlanta this afternoon. His pattern is to go to the office for a few hours, then swing by here for his luggage en route to the airport."

"Did anyone know he would be home around that time today?"

"Some of the people at his office, I suppose. I don't know why he would have told anyone else."

Giving credence to the theory that her husband had surprised a robber, who'd reacted by killing him.

But the obvious answer wasn't always the right one. That's why nothing in a case could be taken at face value.

Time to move on to the harder questions.

"Ms. Robertson, did your husband have any enemies?"

She stared at him. "You mean . . . someone who would want him dead?" She swallowed. Shook her head. "None I'm aware of. But he does work in a cutthroat business. He can be aggressive if a big deal is at stake, and I doubt his competitors are happy about losing out to him. But you don't kill someone because of that."

Maybe not in her world of lunches with friends and shopping and day spas, but big bucks could be at stake in commercial real estate.

"Any recent deals cause animosity?"

She dabbed at her nose again. "James did mention not long ago that one of his competitors was angry. The man thought James had plotted with a seller to raise the bids on a property my husband really didn't want in exchange for a deal on another property he *did* want. An apartment building, I believe."

"Was that the case?"

"I have no idea. My husband didn't often share details of his business dealings with me."

"Did this competitor threaten your husband?"

"Not that I know of."

"It would be helpful to have his name."

Heidi hesitated. "I hate to cause trouble for an innocent party."

"If they're innocent, they have nothing to worry about. And I'm sure you want us to find the perpetrator as soon as possible."

"Of course." She swiped the tissue under her lashes again. "I believe the man's name is Matthew Nolan."

"We'll have a conversation with him."

"Did the contractor who was working in the pool house see anything?"

"He says he didn't."

The woman bit her lip. "I hope it wasn't a mistake to hire him."

Jack's antennas went up. "Why do you say that?"

"I wouldn't normally hire someone with his background,

but Lindsey gave him such a glowing recommendation." She shrugged.

Lindsey knew Allen?

Why hadn't she mentioned that?

And what background was Robertson's widow referring to?

"What can you tell me about him?" Jack flipped to a new page in his notebook.

"Only what Lindsey passed on. That he'd had a rough stretch after his stint in the service and lived on the street until he got his act together. She knows him through her church, and he's done work for her. I thought it would be charitable to give him a few jobs here and there."

"What other work has he done for you?"

"Just one small job. He installed a chair rail in our bedroom before we repainted about a month ago."

So the man had been inside the main house, knew the layout, and had had the opportunity to poke around the master bedroom closet—and discover the jewelry armoire.

Jack asked a few more questions that provided no additional helpful information, then closed his notebook. "The only place we see evidence of activity beyond the kitchen is the master bedroom closet. It appears jewelry may have been stolen."

"Do you think this was a robbery? That James surprised the person?"

"That's one possibility. After we release the scene, I'll have someone walk with you through the house. Please let them know if you see anything else out of order. We'll also need a list of any items that are missing. Is there somewhere you can go until we're finished here, perhaps overnight?"

"I have a friend with a guest cottage."

"That would work." He gave her one of his cards, rose, and extended his hand. "My condolences on your loss. I promise we'll do our best to find whoever is behind what happened here today."

"Thank you." She stood too, unfolding her model-like frame as she placed her cold fingers in his and returned his squeeze. "I'll call my friend."

"Whenever you're ready to leave, I'll have someone walk with you to the bedroom so you can pack a bag." And keep her away from the kitchen, where Lacey was still at work. "I'll be in touch."

After leaving the room, he rounded up an officer to accompany her, then continued to the kitchen.

Lacey looked up from beside the body as he entered, her short, gray-streaked ebony curls barely contained by the cap she'd pulled over them. "Keep your distance or Hank will have your head." The twinkle in her eyes offset the warning.

"Duly noted. I'll stay on the threshold. What do you have?"

She pushed herself to her feet and stretched her back. "I'm getting too old for this kind of work."

"Never. The medical examiner's office would be lost without you."

"Everyone's replaceable. But thanks for the ego boost." She motioned to the victim. "I'm seeing two gunshot wounds to the chest as probable cause of death. To be confirmed by an autopsy, of course."

"You done here?" Hank bustled in.

"Yes." Lacey stripped off her gloves. "We're ready to transport the body."

"You don't have to hang around." Hank turned to him.

Jack edged toward the door. "Wasn't planning to. I want to talk to Cate."

"She's in the laundry room. Through there." He waved a hand toward a hallway, set his kit on the floor, and opened it.

"Talk to you soon, Lacey." Jack headed the direction Hank had indicated.

"Don't make it too soon. We're backed up. Be patient."

"As if," Hank muttered.

Jack sent him a dark look. Apparently everyone at County knew about his reputation for wanting answers yesterday. "I can be patient."

That drew a snort from Hank.

"I'm out of here." Jack turned to go.

"Good." Hank got to work.

With a wave at Lacey, Jack escaped to the laundry room.

Cate had claimed a straight-backed chair by the laundry-folding table, and her head was bent over her laptop. She motioned to a stool against the opposite wall as he entered. "Have a seat."

"Happy to oblige. I'm pushing twenty-four hours straight."

"Were you at the mall shooting?"

"Yeah."

"You should go home and crash after we're done here."

"I want to talk to a few neighbors."

"We can round up reinforcements to handle that."

True. And one of these days, he'd learn to delegate. To accept that he couldn't control everything. To trust other people to do what they were supposed to do.

But not today.

"I'll see."

"Uh-huh." Cate gave him an I'm-not-buying-that look and waved toward her screen. "Want to hear what I have on Allen?"

"Yes."

"Age thirty-one, decorated army hero who served in the Middle East. Awarded a Distinguished Service Cross."

Jack frowned.

Major disconnect.

How had a guy who'd been recognized for extraordinary heroism with the second-highest army military decoration ended up on the street?

"Heidi Robertson told me he was homeless for a while."

"Correct. He came back with PTSD, and his life spiraled

out of control. He lived on the street for two years. After he got his act together, he went to trade school, did a carpentry apprenticeship, and opened his own company. He got married a few months ago."

"How did you dig all that up?" In light of Allen's background, it wasn't likely the man would have much of a social media presence.

"I'm good at what I do." Cate smirked at him.

"Let me rephrase my question. *Where* did you dig all that up?"

"Well, if you want to get technical . . ." She angled the laptop toward him.

He scooted closer and leaned in, skimming a feature article about Allen in a church newsletter dated a few months back.

"Send me that link."

"Already done."

"How did you stumble on that?"

"The truth? Blind luck. I saw a bulletin from this church in Allen's truck while we were searching it and decided to browse through their website. This popped up while I was scanning their quarterly newsletters."

"I owe you."

"I'll take my payment in the form of a few of those phenomenal chocolate mint squares you brought to Mike's retirement party last spring. They don't beat my sister's baklava, but they're close."

"You got it."

"You want me to coordinate the neighborhood canvas while you go home and sleep?"

"I'll stick around for a while."

"That's what I figured." She shut down her laptop and stood. "Let's see if anyone spotted suspicious activity, or if any security cameras caught a helpful snippet of action. Maybe we'll get lucky."

"A few more clues would be welcome."

But as he turned up the collar of his coat, followed her out, and braced for another blast of frosty air, the gut instinct he'd learned to trust said this wasn't going to be a case with a fast resolution.

Even more disturbing?

That same instinct was telling him other people might get hurt—or worse—before it was over.

FOUR

AT THE SUDDEN RING of her cell phone, Dara Allen jerked. Dropped her fork.

It clattered to the table beside her plate of pushed-around food, striking a discordant note in the silent, tension-filled room.

"Let it roll." Her husband of nine months poked at a green bean on his plate, shoulders hunched, eyes bleak, stress oozing from his pores.

No wonder. The reporters who'd seen him drive away from the Robertson home after his truck was released two hours ago had been calling his phone nonstop.

"The news people don't have my number." She stood, crossed to the counter, and scanned caller ID. "It's Lindsey."

"I wonder if the press is bugging her too." Chad set his fork on the table and shoved his plate away. "What a mess."

Mess didn't come close to describing the sudden upheaval in their lives.

Wiping her palm on her slacks, Dara picked up the phone and greeted the woman who'd gone out of her way to be kind at church—and convinced her to sign up for the Creative Cooking on a Budget class she was teaching.

"Is this a bad time?" Lindsey's voice was laced with concern.

"No. We just finished dinner." What little they'd eaten of it.

"I won't keep you, but I wanted to see how you both were after everything that happened today. I don't know if Chad realized it, but I was at the Robertsons' too."

"He didn't know until Madeleine called me a little while ago. We're hanging in." Barely. "How are *you* doing?"

"Also hanging in. A hot bath helped."

"Have any reporters been bothering you?" Dara peeked at Chad, who remained at the table, brooding, his picked-apart meatloaf forgotten.

"No. Are they harassing you?"

"Yes. I guess they saw the logo on Chad's truck."

"I never thought about that. There were press people around when I left, but I drove away fast. I'm sorry they've been giving you grief."

"We'll survive." Maybe.

"If there's anything I can do to help, please let me know."

"Thank you."

Chad rose and began clearing the table.

"You'll be at class next Tuesday, won't you?"

"That's my plan." Dara cringed as Chad stacked the plates with more force than necessary.

"I'll see you there. Don't let the press get to you."

Easy advice to give—but Lindsey wasn't married to a man who'd been scarred by shattering trauma that had almost ruined his life. Who'd been conditioned to expect the worst in any situation.

"I'll try not to." She shifted aside as Chad deposited their plates on the counter. "Thank you for reaching out."

They said their goodbyes, and Dara set the phone on the table.

"Why did she call?" Chad put the stopper in the sink and twisted the faucet.

"To see if we were okay."

He squirted detergent into the water, posture stiff. Watched as bubbles began to multiply, covering the surface until the clear water was obscured. "There's one thing I didn't tell you earlier."

She braced, dread snaking through her.

Whatever he was about to say was why he'd been taut as a bowstring all afternoon. Why he'd relayed only the bare facts as she'd driven him home earlier, then shut down and buried himself in video games until she took him back to get his truck.

"Tell me now."

"The police found one of Heidi Robertson's earrings wedged in the running board of my truck."

Dara's pulse stuttered.

That was very bad news. No matter how it had ended up there, the police would take a hard look at the owner of the truck. Especially an owner with Chad's history.

"What did you tell them?"

"That I had no idea how it got there. I don't know if they believed me." He twisted off the faucet, and quiet descended in the room as he faced her. "Do *you* believe me, Dara?"

Pressure built in her throat, and she moved closer to him. Laid her hand on his arm. "Of course. The man I married isn't a thief."

His Adam's apple bobbed, and he eased away from her touch. "He was once, though. On the street, I . . . I stole food when I was hungry and warm clothes if I got cold."

A tingle of unease swept over her. "You told me you didn't have a record."

"I don't. I only got caught once, and the store didn't press charges."

"Why not?"

"I'd met Reverend Long by then, and I called him. He intervened for me."

"But why did you steal? Wouldn't homeless shelters have provided everything you needed, or pointed you to resources to get them?"

His jaw hardened. "My experience with shelters wasn't the best. Let's just say I felt safer on my own—until I ran into Reverend Long."

The man who'd convinced Chad he could turn his life around and hooked him up with counseling, training, and a place to live. She knew that part of the story.

Apparently there was a lot she didn't know.

"Why are you telling me this now?"

"I don't know what the reporters or cops will dig up about my past, and I don't want you to find out about anything bad from anyone but me."

She braced. "Is there more?"

"Yeah." He leaned back against the sink and wrapped his fingers around the edge. "I got into a fight once, on the street. A guy tried to take a coat I'd stolen. He jumped me from behind. I reacted on instinct, and my military training kicked in."

She tried to ignore the alarm bells beginning to clang in her mind. "Did you hurt him?"

"I beat him up pretty bad. If I'd had a weapon, I probably would have used it—and he might not have survived. I found out later he reported me to the cops."

"But . . . why would he do that if *he* was trying to rob *you*?"

"He claimed I jumped him. He knew my street name, and he gave that to them, along with my description. I assume it's still in a file somewhere." He massaged his forehead. "The cops are gonna dig deep into the background of every person connected to this murder. Especially people in possession of stolen jewelry. They could find some of this."

"Even if they do, it has nothing to do with today's crime."

Chad's lips flatlined. "If you were the cops and someone like me was in the mix, wouldn't you put me at the top of your suspect list? I don't have an alibi, Dara."

"They can't pin this on you without any evidence."

"The earring is evidence."

"It's circumstantial."

"I've worked inside that house. There could be finger-prints."

"You had a legitimate reason to be in there."

He dropped his chin and focused on the floor. "I don't feel good about any of this."

Neither did she.

But one of them had to remain positive.

"Why don't we put this in God's hands and trust him to see us through? I refuse to believe an innocent man will be persecuted."

He met her gaze. "The Bible tells us otherwise."

It was impossible to argue with that.

"Is there anything more I should know?"

He hesitated for a millisecond too long. "No." He pivoted back to the sink. "Let's get the dishes done."

Fighting back a wave of panic, Dara picked up a dish towel. Stared at his broad shoulders as the muscles beneath his T-shirt flexed while he scrubbed the dishes.

What wasn't he telling her?

Something important, if her intuition was sound.

An insidious niggle of doubt nicked away at the confidence and trust she'd always had in the man who'd stolen her heart during their whirlwind courtship.

For what if their fast-track romance had failed to reveal secrets that were now poised to not only come back and bite him but threaten the foundation of their brand-new marriage?

PROBLEM SOLVED—for the moment.

Eric Miller tipped back his beer as the anchor on the evening news continued to report on James Robertson's murder.

Not an ideal resolution, but it should buy him time to fix everything. With all the upheaval this would cause at Robertson Properties, routine audits should be low priority for a while.

Long enough for discrepancies to be addressed.

His phone rang, and he picked it up off the end table. Scanned the screen.

Nolan.

No surprise the man was checking in.

He muted the TV and put the phone to his ear. "I figured you'd—"

"The cops dropped by."

Not what he wanted to hear.

Eric set the beer can down and straightened up. "Why?"

"The wife gave them my name. Apparently she knew about my less-than-cordial relationship with her husband."

"You didn't tell them anything, did you?"

"Nothing incriminating. But I suggest you watch your back. I didn't expect them to finger me, so who knows where else they'll start digging? Depends how much the wife knows, or what the witness may have overheard."

Witness?

"Someone saw the murder?" Eric muted the TV.

"According to my contacts in law enforcement, their personal chef was on-site. It doesn't sound like she saw anything helpful or overheard Robertson's end of the unpleasant phone conversation he initiated with me around noon. But if they go through his cell log, the call will show up. And that's not a complication I need." He blew out a breath. "I assume succession planning at the firm is in the works?"

Eric forcibly switched gears. "The officers are having an emergency meeting tomorrow morning. An email went out to the staff ten minutes ago."

"Will you be there?"

He snorted. "A lowly accountant? Get real. Robertson never bothered to consult the peons who did the real work."

"You're not a lowly accountant. You're a CPA and a manager. Besides, you won't ever have to stew about Robertson's attitude again."

"True. So when is my payment coming?"

"After the smoke clears and I have the strip mall Robertson and I were both after. Until then, keep your ear to the ground in case the new management continues their former leader's shady tactics."

Eric frowned. "Transactions could be delayed because of what happened today, and I need that money."

"With Robertson out of the picture, you should have a window to refill the coffers. No one will be doing audits during a management transition."

"That wasn't our deal. You said I'd have the money by mid-month."

"You've only kept part of our bargain. As soon as I have the strip mall in hand, I'll pay up."

"What am I supposed to do if someone wants to review the books in the meantime?"

"Deflect and defer."

"Easier said than done. I'm not the boss."

"I'm sure you can find an excuse to drag out the process. It's not that much money in the big scheme of things."

Maybe not to Nolan, whose deals ran in the tens of millions. But if your bank balance was in the low four digits, fifty-thousand dollars was a fortune.

He forked his fingers through his hair.

High-end vacations, upscale restaurants three nights a

week, and those crazy expensive purses his wife favored would have to go.

"Auditors won't agree. They red-flag anything that doesn't balance. The amount is irrelevant."

"You'll have the replacement money before that happens as long as you do the rest of your job. Going forward, let's switch to burner phones in case the police keep me in their sights. Get one and call me with your number tomorrow night. I'll get one too. And keep your ear to the ground. Company grapevines can be a rich source of information."

The line went dead.

Slowly Eric lowered the cell and glanced back at the TV screen.

The evening news was still fixated on Robertson's death.

Not surprising, given the man's prominent position in the business community.

But he was no great loss. His methods were ruthless, and he didn't tolerate mistakes. Giving Farley the controller's job six months ago when the company's longtime financial chief retired, instead of to the person next in line—namely him—had stunk. All because of the small, easy-to-fix error he'd made on a quarterly report. His fifteen years of dedicated service should have counted for something to the man pulling the strings.

Except they hadn't.

So "borrowing" funds for an out-of-work brother who'd had major complications after an episode of anaphylactic shock put him in the ICU on a ventilator for a week had been a no-brainer. The money to pay the medical bills had to come from somewhere, and his sister-in-law needed every dime she could get her hands on to feed and house their three kids.

Besides, Robertson owed him after bypassing him for the position he'd deserved.

And with Nolan willing to pay handsomely for proprietary

information about upcoming deals after Robertson colluded to jack up the price on that apartment building he'd wanted, repaying the unofficial loan should have been a piece of cake.

Maybe the cat-and-mouse game those two business rivals played had accelerated beyond his comfort level . . . and maybe he had a few regrets about his part in it . . . but no innocent parties had been hurt.

The only one who'd run into trouble since he and Nolan had made their deal was Robertson, who was far from innocent.

And truth be told, the world was better off without him.

FIVE

"THANK YOU FOR EXTENDING your office hours to see me, Dr. Oliver." Lindsey rose as the psychologist, attired in his usual sport coat and open-necked shirt, greeted her from the waiting room doorway.

"I'm always happy to accommodate clients, especially in the aftermath of a trauma." He ushered her through the door. "Would you like water or another beverage?"

"I'd love coffee, but that won't help my sleeping problem. Water is fine."

"Make yourself comfortable while I get you a bottle."

He continued down the hall to the tiny kitchenette as she detoured to the familiar office where she'd spent countless hours over the past eighteen months. Though her visits had tapered off, having this resource to tap into after everything that had happened three days ago was a godsend.

"Here you go." Dr. Oliver rejoined her as she claimed her favorite seat—a comfortable, cushy wing chair that wrapped its comforting arms around her.

She took the water and twisted off the cap while he sat in the more modern chair angled toward hers in the cozy conversation nook. "I'm sorry to keep you so late." She motioned to the second-floor window that overlooked the tree-rimmed parking lot, where pole lights cast ghostly pools of illumination in the darkness. "That's not the best way to start the work week."

"I knew this wasn't a nine-to-five job when I signed on." His calm, welcoming manner imbued the room with tranquility.

The tension in her shoulders began to ease. She owed her therapist in South Carolina a huge debt for researching and recommending Dr. Oliver. Given his empathy, keen insights, and ability to guide without directing, it was amazing he hadn't had a long waiting list of potential clients.

"I promise not to take up too much of your evening."

"I'm in no hurry." As if to demonstrate that, he leaned back and crossed an ankle over a knee. "It sounds as if Friday's experience has set you back a bit."

"More than a bit, based on this weekend." She sipped her water and set it on the side table next to her. "Like I said on the phone, the nightmares are back."

"Are they disrupting your sleep?"

"Yes."

"How many hours have you clocked since Friday?"

"I don't know. Nine or ten, total? Once I wake up, I can't get back to sleep. None of my usual de-stressing techniques have worked—breathing exercises, progressive muscle relaxation, visualization."

"That's not surprising. Friday's incident is very fresh. Why don't you walk me through it, then we'll talk about what you've been experiencing in the aftermath, and end with a guided visualization. Sound like a plan?"

"All except the retelling of Friday's event."

"I understand your reluctance to revisit that, but to best help you I need to have a sense of what happened. You don't have to go into great detail. An overview of the situation would suffice."

"Okay. I'll try." Linking her fingers, Lindsey launched into a topline of the story she'd told Detective Tucker.

Dr. Oliver jotted a few notes as she talked but otherwise gave her his full attention, as usual.

"So you were in close physical proximity to the killer."

"Yes. At one point, three feet. All I could see was their legs, but I was terrified they'd s-spot me." An echo of the mind-numbing fear that had clutched her as she huddled under the island swept over her again. "I knew I could be seconds away from death."

"Like last time."

"Yes." She took a sip of water, holding the bottle with both hands. "I mean, how many people encounter one life-and-death situation, let alone two? The whole thing was surreal. Like lightning striking twice."

"Yet you survived both experiences."

"With major fallout."

"Aside from dealing with the lingering shock anyone would experience after the situation you described, tell me your biggest concern."

"I'm not certain." She chewed on her lower lip as she pondered the question. "I guess . . . I guess I'm scared because this person is still out there. What if they find out I was in the kitchen? That I saw them?"

"Have you been publicly named as a witness?"

"Not that I know of. But what if that information leaks?"

Dr. Oliver sat back and tapped his pen against the edge of his notebook. "Let's apply logic to this. From what you said, you weren't able to tell the police anything that would help them identify the person. Even if that person finds out you were there, they know their features were masked. Is it possible your concerns are overblown?"

As always, Dr. Oliver was the voice of reason.

"Yes. And the left side of my brain accepts that. The right side, however, isn't convinced."

"Then let's focus on the right side. Tell me about the dreams you've been having."

"They're strange and disjointed, with elements from both of the events I experienced."

"Again, not surprising. In the mind, trauma is trauma. Events that evoke similar emotions can meld together. Tell me how the dreams have played out."

Lindsey relayed the bizarre sequences that had kept sleep at bay for the past three nights. Shook her head. "I told you they don't make sense. I mean, why would I put the guy's scarred hand from the grocery store in South Carolina with the boots I saw at—" A vague image flashed through her mind, and she halted. Tried to bring the fuzzy picture into focus.

"What's wrong?"

"I don't know." She knitted her brow. "For a second, I thought I was remembering a detail about the killer's boots—or overshoes—but now it's gone."

"It wouldn't be unusual for details to begin to emerge as the initial shock subsides."

"That didn't happen with the South Carolina situation."

"Every case is different. Or it could be that what you think you're remembering is only part of your fabricated dream, with no basis in reality."

She forced up the corners of her mouth and tried for a teasing tone. "Are you telling me I'm beginning to imagine things?" That was a scary thought.

"No. I'm suggesting it's important to realize that trauma can mess with the brain." He set his notebook aside. "In times of turmoil, routine can restore a sense of normalcy. I'd recommend sticking with your usual schedule as much as possible for the immediate future. Are you still rowing twice a week?"

"Yes—weather permitting. I didn't row last week, but I'll keep going as long as I can until it gets too cold on a regular basis."

"And you're running?"

"Every day I don't row. But I didn't do either this weekend. Other than church, I stayed home and locked the door."

"Perfectly fine in the immediate aftermath of a frightening experience. A return to routine as soon as possible may be helpful, though."

"I intend to pick up the running again tomorrow and the rowing on Wednesday. And I'm not planning to cancel my Horizons cooking class on Tuesday."

"Excellent. Any concerns about going back to the scene of the crime for your job?"

"Some. I'm sure Chad Allen feels the same way."

"The handyman you mentioned, who was also on-site during the incident?"

"Yes. I know him and his wife from church. And his wife is taking a cooking class from me. Nice couple. Probably as much in need of encouragement as I am. I'm trying to stay in touch, but it's hard to offer reassurance when you're on shaky ground yourself."

"Then let's do our best to get you off that shaky ground. Why don't we schedule another session for Thursday and end today with the visualization I mentioned?"

"That works for me." She settled back in her chair.

"I know you like to use your morning row as a visualization when you do this on your own, but today let's travel to that white-sand beach you enjoyed on your trip to Antigua a few years ago." He tapped an app on the phone beside him, calling up soothing music. "Go ahead and close your eyes. Concentrate on filling your lungs. Slow and easy. Now let the air out, slow and easy. Picture the stress leaving your body along with your breath."

As Lindsey listened to his mellow baritone and followed his instructions—calling up an image of the turquoise sea, the taste of salt on her tongue, the caress of the warm breeze, the pliant sand squishing between her toes, the lulling cadence of the lapping waves—her tension melted away.

Fifteen minutes later, as Dr. Oliver brought her back to reality, the restless agitation that had plagued her had dissipated.

"Better?" He smiled at her.

"Much."

"I'll alert Margie you'll be calling tomorrow and tell her to work you in on Thursday." He rose. "Let me walk you out."

Bottle of water in hand, she followed him to the door that offered clients discreet access to the hall in the professional building. "Thank you again for going above and beyond."

"My pleasure. And remember I'm here anytime if you need to talk. Since the beach visualization worked well today, try it again tonight if you can't sleep."

"I will."

Hoisting her shoulder tote into position, Lindsey left his office behind and strode down the quiet corridor that led to the outside door, mulling over the session.

What Dr. Oliver had said about routine being helpful made sense.

So beginning tomorrow, she'd do her best to forget those terrifying minutes in the Robertson kitchen and stop worrying about the possible repercussions of sharing a room with a murderer.

After all, as her psychologist had pointed out, the perpetrator didn't know she'd been there. And if they did find out, she'd seen nothing that would incriminate them. They had no reason to target her.

She had to set aside foolish fears and get on with her life. She'd survived, and she was safe.

There was nothing to worry about.

"THANKS FOR BUMPING our dinner up a day, and sorry I'm late. A glitch at the scene delayed me, and I had a call while I was in the parking lot."

As a breathless Bri slid into the chair across from him at their favorite neighborhood eatery, Jack sized up his sister. The long hours she worked as an investigator with the St. Louis Regional Bomb & Arson Unit sometimes took a toll, but tonight she was animated and energetic despite the tiring rigor of poking through a fire scene and the aftereffects of a job-related near-death experience nine days ago.

"From the sparkle in your eyes and the flush on your cheeks, I presume the call in the parking lot was from the new boy-friend."

She waved his comment aside and picked up the menu. "You know better than to trust circumstantial evidence."

"A preponderance of circumstantial evidence is compelling. Like reading the menu you know by heart from the restaurant we come to every other Tuesday."

With a wry twist of her lips, she set the bill of fare down. "Fine. It was Marc. He said to tell you hello. You're lucky he doesn't hold that overprotective-brother act you pulled at your first meeting against you."

"We reached an understanding. Besides, after I saw him in action when that nutcase went after you, he got my stamp of approval."

"I'm sure he'll be relieved to hear that."

He ignored her droll tone. "You doing okay?"

"Yep. Other than a few bruises that are disappearing as we speak." She tapped her cheek, where the black-and-blue contusion was fading to yellow.

"Getting back to the new man in your life—I've been think-ing."

"Uh-oh. That could be dangerous."

"Ha-ha. I'm trying to be serious here."

She folded her hands on the table. "Lay it on me."

"Now that Marc's in the picture, maybe we should rethink our locked-in-stone every-other-Tuesday dinners. Be more flexible going forward."

She stared at him. "Why?"

"In case Marc wants to see you on one of those nights. I don't want to stand in the way of romance or alienate a potential future brother-in-law."

"Aren't you getting ahead of yourself? We just started dating."

"To borrow fire investigation lingo, I suspect this relationship will rapidly combust."

Her slow smile confirmed his take. "I have the same feeling." Then she grew more serious. "But I'm not throwing you and Cara over. Marc knows we're the Three Musketeers, and that will never change. So don't even think about trying to stand me up for our Tuesday dinners. Got it?"

Warmth filled him at her passionate declaration.

It was inevitable that marriage would eventually alter the dynamics in their small family circle, but it was heartening to know Bri would continue to consider the sibling relationship a priority and that Marc was on board with that.

"Got it."

"Good." She selected a roll from the basket on the table as the server arrived to take their orders, picking up the conversation after they were alone again. "I hear you're the lead on the Robertson case."

"Yeah."

"You landed a big one."

"Luck of the draw."

"Not buying. Your boss knows you're tenacious—and cool under fire. The latter is an important asset when the press comes to call. And they'll be all over this one."

"I don't talk to reporters."

"Excellent strategy." Surveying the dining room from the secluded corner table that offered an expansive view of the restaurant, she lowered her voice. "Any leads?"

"Nothing solid." In truth, nothing period. The killer seemed to have vanished into thin air.

"No one in the neighborhood or the park behind the house saw anything suspicious? Nothing on security cameras?"

"No. And the witness couldn't offer anything helpful, either."

Bri stopped chewing. "You have a witness?"

Whoops.

This was why he didn't talk to reporters. It was too easy to let important pieces of information slip that were well known to the detectives working the case but news to the public.

Except Bri wasn't public. She was one of them.

No harm done.

"That fact isn't for general consumption."

"My lips are sealed." She made a zipping motion across her mouth. "Someone saw the murder?"

"No. The perpetrator. After the victim was dead." He gave her the bare bones.

"Whoa. That had to be super scary for her. Was she a wreck?"

"I wouldn't go that far, but she was shook."

"Who wouldn't be?"

"True." He unfolded his napkin and draped it across his lap. "But she was also kind of . . . cool."

As the words tumbled out, he mashed his lips together.

Blast.

Why had he mentioned Lindsey Barnes's attitude? His perceptive sister wasn't likely to let that slide by or miss the nuance in his inflection.

Bri inspected him. "Cool as in composed, or cool as in unfriendly?"

His sister's ability to pick up subtle cues only got better with age.

"Closer to unfriendly."

"It's possible cops spook her. Did you run her?"

"Yes. She's clean. And she was nice to Meyers."

He stifled a groan. What was with his case of motormouth tonight? That wasn't information Bri needed to know.

"Did you rub her wrong? You can be off-putting in inter-rogation mode, you know. Ask Marc."

"I wasn't off-putting. I was nice."

"Hey, don't get all defensive. I'm on your side." She broke off a piece of her roll and swiped it through the pat of butter on her plate. "Why do you care about her attitude anyway?"

"I don't."

Too strong, Tucker. Dial it back.

Affecting nonchalance, he took a roll from the basket.

"Yeah, you do." She examined him the way she used to study the pieces of a puzzle she was trying to put together when she was a kid. "The question is why."

"Can we please eat our dinner and forget about work to-night?"

"How old is this woman?"

Apparently Bri wasn't in a forgetting mood.

"Thirtysomething."

"Pretty?"

"Yeah."

"Single?"

"Unknown. But she wasn't wearing a ring." Pretending he hadn't looked would only raise more red flags. Single guys did ring checks on attractive women.

"I can see why you'd be upset." She bit into her roll and chewed.

He gave her a cautious glance. "You can?"

"Sure. It's an ego thing with men. You like to think you're appealing to the opposite sex even if you have no interest in a particular woman. But in this case, I'm thinking you do have an interest."

"Wrong. I know very little about her."

"You don't have to know a lot about someone for sparks to fly." She hummed a few bars of "Some Enchanted Evening."

He snorted. "You're just seeing the world through rose-colored glasses now that romance has entered your life. And for the record, there were no sparks."

"I'll concede there may be a rosy hue in my lens at present." She slathered more butter on her roll with her knife. "But you haven't convinced me about the lack of sparks. We'll have to get Cara's unbiased input at our next Sunday get-together—unless she comes up from Cape Girardeau sooner than that."

"No, we do not have to get her input. In fact, you can't mention this conversation to anyone. The witness angle is being kept under wraps."

Bri made a face. "Spoil sport."

Their salads arrived, and as they dug in, Jack changed the subject. It was never hard to get Bri to chat about her smoke-jumper days, or to reminisce with him about the adventures the two of them had shared during his trips out west to visit her during her previous high-risk career.

By the time they finished their shared dessert and walked out to the parking lot, his case—and Lindsey Barnes—had fallen off Bri's radar.

Yet as he drove away on the unseasonably balmy night, both were front and center on his.

In terms of the case, they needed a break soon or it was going to go cold fast and the perpetrator could walk.

As for Lindsey Barnes, unless he could get a handle on why

her coolness bothered him beyond the ego ding Bri had suggested, he was going to be stuck with two unresolved issues that would eat at his gut until he had answers.

Which did not appear to be forthcoming on either front anytime in the immediate future.

SIX

WHERE WAS HER CAR?

Keys in hand, satchel of cooking supplies slung over her shoulder, Lindsey slowed her gait and scanned the parking lot outside the church hall where she'd conducted the fourth Creative Cooking on a Budget class in the current session.

None of the few remaining vehicles in the dimly lit lot were her blue Focus.

How could that be?

She peered again toward the basketball hoop farther down where she'd parked, the closest spot she could find to the hall door thanks to the large turnout for the church's Tuesday evening Bible study program.

But her Focus wasn't there now.

Fist on hip, she did a step-by-step replay of her arrival three hours ago.

She'd pulled into the lot. Circled it, hoping to find a spot closer to the door so she wouldn't have to lug her heavy bag as far. Parked under the basketball hoop. Not ideal, but tucking her car into the narrow spot had been preferable to hoofing it from the far end of the lot. She'd set the brake, eased the door open in the tight space, and squeezed through with her supplies.

Yet the car was nowhere to be—

Wait.

She frowned as a bizarre possibility flashed through her mind.

Could someone have stolen it?

But that made no sense. Who would want a ten-year-old Focus?

Yet what other explanation could there be?

Lindsey massaged her temple, where a headache was beginning to throb.

After everything that had happened last week, adding a stolen car to the mix was too much.

Moving back toward the well-lit doorway, she dug through her satchel until her fingers closed over her phone. Pulled it out and dialed 911 for the second time in four days.

The conversation with the dispatcher didn't take long, and the response was swift. A police cruiser swung into the lot within five minutes and drew up beside her.

An officer emerged. "Good evening, ma'am. You reported a missing vehicle?"

"Yes. Thanks for getting here so fast."

The man pulled out a notebook. Once she provided the contact information he requested, he moved on to the events of the evening. "Tell me what happened."

"I don't know. I parked over there about six thirty." She waved toward the basketball hoop. "When I came out ten minutes ago, my car was gone."

"Give me the make, model, and license plate number."

She provided the first two. "I don't know the plate number off the top of my head, but I may be able to find it on a document at home."

"Do you have your insurance card with you?"

"Yes." She pulled out her wallet and extracted it.

"I can find the plate number using the VIN." He took the

card, wrote down more information, and handed it back. "I'll get a BOLO alert issued on this and notify our auto theft unit. Did you notice anything suspicious when you parked?"

"No. The lot was pretty full then. There's a Bible study here on Tuesday nights. But as you can see, most of the cars are gone now."

"One of our detectives from Crimes Against Property will be in touch. Is there someone you can call for a ride home?"

Not really. Who had time to make friends while settling into a new city and establishing a business? Madeleine came closest, but it was too late in the evening to impose on anyone.

"I'm kind of new in town. I'll call a cab."

The officer's brow pinched as he gave the deserted lot a sweep. "That could take a while. Can you wait inside?"

"Yes. I have a key."

"That works. Be sure to notify your insurance company about this as soon as you can."

"I will. Thanks." She strode back to the church hall door, her mind processing next steps at warp speed. Beyond calling her insurance agent, renting a car was a high priority. With a career like hers, mobility was essential, however much it dented her budget. And if her car wasn't found, she'd be hunting for a replacement. A much bigger dent.

Sighing, she inserted the key into the lock, waved at the patrol officer who'd waited until she opened the door, and slipped inside.

What else could possibly go—

Her cell began to chime, and she jumped. Slammed a hand against her chest.

Good grief.

Given the state of her nerves, she'd need an appointment with Dr. Oliver sooner than Thursday.

She pulled out her phone. Skimmed the caller ID.

Madeleine.

Strange timing.

Lowering her satchel of supplies to the floor, she greeted the Horizons director. "I was just thinking about you."

"Pleasant thoughts, I hope."

"Always."

"How did tonight's session go?"

Lindsey pulled out a stool from the stainless steel prep counter and lowered herself onto it. May as well tell Madeleine what had happened. "The session went fine. Afterward, not so much. My car is missing."

A beat ticked by. "What do you mean, missing?"

She repeated the story she'd relayed to the officer. "I seem to have fallen into the rut of being in the wrong place at the wrong time."

"Are you still at the church?"

"Yes. I was getting ready to call a cab."

"Not necessary. Watch for me in twenty minutes." The line went dead.

Lindsey lowered the cell from her ear, weighing it in her hand. She ought to call Madeleine back and tell her not to bother. That would be the considerate thing to do.

But at this point, the thought of riding home in a cab with a stranger behind the wheel held no appeal. For once, why not go with the flow and try not to feel guilty about giving in to selfish impulses?

Eighteen minutes later, headlights swung across the parking lot through the window. After gathering up her belongings, Lindsey stepped outside and locked the door behind her.

Madeleine pushed the passenger door open as she approached.

"Thank you for doing this." Lindsey slid in, set her satchel at her feet, and buckled up.

"It's the least I could do after I strong-armed you into teaching this class." She put the car in gear and circled toward the exit.

"I was happy to do it."

"And this is how you get repaid." Madeleine shook her head. "I'm sorry, Lindsey. You've had a rough stretch. How can I help you?"

Her throat tightened at the woman's kindness. "Thanks for offering, but I'll be fine. My client tomorrow cancelled because the family's down with the flu. That will give me a chance to line up a rental car."

"Don't hesitate to let me know if there's anything I can do. Beyond me, the Martha's Guild at church is always available to assist."

"I'll keep that in mind. And I'll remind Dara about the guild too. It may be reassuring for her to know there's a support system in case any issues come up for her and Chad after last week."

"Did she attend class tonight?"

"Yes, but she was distracted. Not that I blame her. I asked a few questions, but it was obvious she didn't want to talk about what happened."

"Do you think the police are hassling Chad?"

"I hope not. He seems like a nice guy, and he's had more than enough trouble in his life."

"Has anyone from law enforcement been back in touch with you?"

An image of Jack Tucker appeared in her mind, but she erased it at once. "No, and I hope no one ever contacts me again. I want to put the whole horrible episode behind me."

"I hear you. Tell me about your class tonight."

For the remainder of the drive, Madeleine kept the conversation focused on more pleasant topics, and by the time she pulled up in front of the condo, the tension in Lindsey's shoulders had loosened.

"Thanks again for the lift, Madeleine."

"Happy to do it. I'll wait until you're inside."

Lindsey didn't dawdle on her trek to the door through the darkness. Once in the condo, she made a beeline for the kitchen and deactivated the security system she'd installed the week she'd moved in. After setting her satchel of supplies beside the counter, she filled a mug with milk, added the other ingredients for hot chocolate, and slid it in the microwave for a fast version of her favorite comfort drink.

While she waited for it to heat, she wandered over to the photo that had graced her fridge door for six years, taken on the trip she'd made to Antigua with Clair.

What an amazing vacation that had been, as their two smiling faces confirmed.

Vision misting, Lindsey adjusted the BFF magnet that held the snapshot in place.

How would she ever have gotten through the rough patches with her parents during her high school years if she hadn't had her best friend's support and friendship?

The kind of support and friendship that would also have helped her weather the stress that had been her lot for almost two years.

At a summons from the microwave, Lindsey retraced her steps and retrieved her hot chocolate.

The truth was, the hole left in her life by the loss of Clair's gentle spirit, fierce loyalty, kind heart, and deep well of compassion would never be filled.

What a tragedy that countless young people in desperate need of her special empathy had been deprived of the wonderful advice she would have offered in her role as a high school counselor.

Thanks to Jack Tucker.

Lindsey took a sip of the sweet, warm drink, trying without success to dispel the bitter taste on her tongue.

At least she shouldn't have to see him again. Her role in the murder investigation ought to be finished. She'd already told him everything she knew, except for whatever vague memory had tried to surface in Dr. Oliver's office. No doubt a minor detail that wasn't pertinent anyway. If she did remember it, she could always send an email to the address on the card he'd given her.

For now, though, she had other priorities.

Like finding transportation until her Focus turned up—or biting the bullet and buying a new used car if it didn't.

And praying no more adversity was lurking in her immediate future.

SLEEPING ALONE WHILE YOU were still technically a bride was the pits. And Chad's excuse for moving to the couch was losing its credibility. The cold he'd claimed was coming on since the day of the murder had never materialized beyond a few minor sniffles that didn't seem genuine.

Dara pulled the covers up to her chin and stared at the dark ceiling in the post-midnight hour, as she had for the past five nights.

Based on the half-moon shadows beneath Chad's lower lashes, and the thrashing sounds that often wafted down the hall from the living room to the bedroom, he wasn't sleeping any better than she was.

Instead of waiting for him to tell her what was going on, should she confront him about the excuse he was using to keep his distance?

But what if that backfired? What if he shut down more than he already had?

Pressure building behind her eyes, Dara threw back the covers, swung her feet to the floor, and began to pace.

How could a marriage that had started out with such love and trust and devotion take such a sudden, negative turn?

In the living room, Chad began to toss again—and all at once he cried out. As if he was in pain.

Heart pounding, Dara dashed out of the bedroom and down the hall.

At the door to the living room, she halted, taking in the scene in the glow from the lamp Chad must have forgotten to turn off.

The covers were in disarray, and the sleeve of Chad's T-shirt had ridden up to his shoulder as he grunted and writhed on the couch, arms flailing.

He was having a nightmare. Like the ones he'd had in the early days of their marriage that had slowly abated.

Now, they were back with a vengeance.

But it wasn't his bad dream that twisted her nerves into a knot.

It was the large black-and-blue bruise on his upper arm.

A bruise that hadn't been there when they'd last slept together on Thursday night.

She gripped the edge of the doorframe and held on tight as the floor shifted beneath her feet.

Had he gotten that the day of the Robertson murder? In a struggle of some kind?

Like with someone who was defending himself?

A wave of nausea swept over her, and she covered her mouth with her hand. Stumbled back down the hall. Climbed into bed and burrowed under the covers.

But the warmth of the blanket didn't stop the shudders rippling through her as she tried to corral the insidious suspicion snaking up her spine.

Chad couldn't have had anything to do with Friday's killing. It was impossible. The man she'd fallen in love with may have gone through a black period thanks to the PTSD he'd brought home from the Middle East, and he may have killed people in combat, but he wasn't a killer. That's why his experiences in the army had eaten at his gut and affected his mind. Why he'd needed counseling to help him deal with his demons and put them to rest.

If taken by surprise, though—as he had been the day the other homeless guy had tried to rob him of his coat—was he still capable of inflicting major damage? Of killing?

She wadded the blanket in her fingers.

No.

She refused to believe that.

Besides, from everything he'd told her, the police thought the killing had been prompted by a robbery. And why would Chad steal? The days when he'd taken blankets and food to stay warm and keep from starving were long gone.

The pieces didn't fit.

Yet the bruises were real.

Chad cried out again from the living room, and she curled into a ball on the bed.

What should she do?

Asking Chad about the bruises—and why he'd hidden them from her—could be a mistake. He might think she had doubts about his innocence. That she suspected him in the Robertson crime, as the police did.

If only she had someone to confide in who could offer her confidential and reasoned counsel.

Unfortunately, her dad back in Caruthersville wasn't a candidate for that role. He was still angry about her decision to move from the rural bootheel of the state to the big city. Aggravated by her unwillingness to marry a local farmer and spend her life worrying about whether the whims of the weather would determine if they ate macaroni and cheese or steak in any given year. Opposed to what he considered a too-hasty marriage to Chad.

Mom would have understood her desire for a different life if cancer hadn't taken her too young. Maybe a sister or brother would have too, if she'd had either. Or a close friend.

An image of Lindsey popped into her mind, but she snuffed it out. Despite the woman's empathy, and despite her efforts tonight at class to reach out, telling her about this could be a mistake. What if the police contacted her again and she let it slip? No matter Chad's explanation for the bruise, in light of his background the police could assume it was related to what had happened at the Robertson house.

The wind rattled the window, and she tunneled deeper under the covers. An acceptable refuge for tonight, but hiding wasn't going to solve anything. She had to come up with a plan about how to broach this to Chad without shutting him down.

Until she did, she'd continue to do everything she could to support him.

And ask the Almighty for guidance.

SEVEN

"YOU MUST NOT HAVE GOTTEN much sleep last night."

At the comment, Jack finished topping off his coffee from the community pot in the office breakroom and angled toward Cate. "Why do you say that?"

"You're drinking the department sludge that masquerades as java." She wrinkled her nose and pointed to his cup. "What happened to your usual Americano?"

"I had that two hours ago."

Cate arched an eyebrow. "You were at Starbucks at six in the morning?"

"I needed caffeine."

"I rest my case about sleep. I'm assuming your insomnia is related to the Robertson case. Any new leads?"

"No." He blew out a breath. "Nobody in the neighborhood or park saw anything. Hank didn't find a single piece of evidence that would help identify the killer. None of the stolen jewelry has turned up at any of the usual fencing sites. I'm still waiting for the preliminary autopsy results. Lacey promised she'd have them today."

"You think those will steer you to someone?"

"Every piece of information helps." Jack took a sip of his desperation brew. Grimaced.

"Speaking of information . . . I was talking to one of the property guys this morning. Your witness's name came up."

"Lindsey Barnes?"

"That would be her—unless there's someone else I don't know about. She called in to report a stolen car last night."

Jack did a double take.

What were the odds someone involved in a murder scene would have their car stolen four days later?

"That's weird."

"More like a case of being rattled, based on the outcome. The car was discovered early this morning in a spot down the street from where she says she last saw it."

Jack frowned. "She forgot where she parked it?"

"So our people have concluded, with much amusement, even though she claims that's not the case. But what other explanation could there be? It was locked, and there was no damage. It's unlikely anything is missing from inside. If someone wanted to steal contents, they could have done that on the lot where she says she parked it."

"I'm sticking with weird." He took another sip of coffee. "She didn't strike me as the flighty type."

"Stress can mess with the mind. Cause uncharacteristic behavior."

The coffee left a trail of acid down his throat.

So could a variety of other factors.

Like mental instability.

Dark memories began swirling through his mind, but he wrestled them back into the locked vault where they belonged. This conversation wasn't about the past. It was about the present.

And Lindsey Barnes hadn't shown any evidence of delusional tendencies or instability.

"I may give her a call. Now that a few days have passed, it's possible another conversation could prod loose a subliminal detail or two."

"Couldn't hurt." Cate pulled her phone out. Skimmed the screen. "Gotta run. Let me know if there's anything else you want me to do with the case. I'd be happy to do the follow-up with your witness."

"Thanks, but I can handle that."

Her lips twitched. "That's what I thought. Keep me in the loop." She disappeared out the door.

Jack huffed out a breath as the same vibes his sister had given off Monday night wafted his way. Bri may have been more vocal in her assessment of his interest in Lindsey, but it appeared Cate had come to the same conclusion.

Must be related to the fact that both women had romance on their mind—one in a new relationship, the other in a new marriage.

That didn't mean they were right, however. Bri's theory about his ego being bruised was likely the reason for his fixation on his witness.

Whatever the explanation, he ought to get over it. After all, Lindsey's attitude may not have been anything personal. It was possible he'd reminded her of someone she didn't like, and her response had been exacerbated by the stress of the situation. By now, she might be calmer and more cordial.

He returned to his office, called up his case notes, and tapped in her number.

Two rings in, she answered, greeting him in a cool tone.

So much for cordial. Whatever she'd had in her craw the day of the killing must still be there.

"Ms. Barnes, Detective Tucker." He infused as much friendliness as he could into his voice. "Do you have a minute?"

"Not much more than that. I'm about to walk out the door. I, uh, have to pick something up."

"Your car?"

A beat ticked by.

"Yes." Her tone was cautious. "How did you know about that?"

"A colleague told me." He leaned back in his chair. "Unless you already have a ride, I'd be happy to give you a lift there. I'd like to talk to you again about last Friday, anyway."

"I don't see any point in recounting the incident."

"It can be helpful. Sometimes witnesses recall useful details during a retelling. Even minor things that don't appear to be important can help in an investigation. And I'm cheaper than Uber." If he couldn't win her over with sociability, maybe he could appeal to her pecuniary instincts.

Silence.

Just as he resigned himself to a refusal, she acquiesced. "Okay. How soon can you be here?"

He tipped his chair forward and homed in on her address in the report. Calculated the drive time from headquarters to the close-in suburb. "Fifteen minutes."

"I'll watch for you."

The line went dead.

No thank-you for the offer of a ride.

Then again, he'd indicated he needed to talk with her. Suggested there was a business motive behind his generosity rather than positioning it as doing her a favor.

A deliberate choice, since she would have refused the latter.

Pocketing his cell, he strode toward the door.

No matter why she'd accepted, maybe another chat with her would help him figure out why he couldn't get their first encounter out of his mind—and why he'd rubbed her wrong.

It would also give him a chance to assess the mental state of his sole witness, who'd seemingly misplaced her car.

SHE SHOULD HAVE REFUSED the ride.

But why spend money for a cab or Uber if she could get a lift for free? Plus, she did have one small piece of information to pass on about the person she'd seen in the Robertson kitchen. Sending it via email, as she'd planned, would have been less grating, but in practical terms a buck was a buck.

As Lindsey watched through her living room window, a Taurus stopped in front of the small, two-story condo unit that was tucked into a cozy neighborhood of single-family modest homes with well-tended lawns. The relaxed, residential vibe had been a huge selling point as she'd shopped for a place to live.

Purse in hand, she armed her security system and let herself out the front door. She was halfway down the sidewalk before Jack Tucker emerged from his car.

He did, however, manage to circle the Taurus and open the passenger door before she reached the vehicle.

"Good morning." He offered her a winning smile, the warmth in his cobalt blue eyes chasing away the morning chill.

The man was good-looking, no question about it. It wasn't hard to see why Clair had fallen for him.

How sad that he hadn't been able to accept her as she was instead of pushing her to be someone else.

Like her parents had pushed *her*.

At least she'd survived.

"Morning." Steeling herself against his charm play, she edged past him and slid onto the seat.

After closing her door, he took his place behind the wheel. "The story I heard at the office was that you misplaced your car last night."

"No, I didn't." She gritted her teeth and sat up straighter. "I know where I parked it."

"Cars don't move by themselves."

Though his manner was conversational, his comment rankled.

"I realize that. But I have an excellent memory. And I don't imagine things."

"The kind of experience you went through on Friday can play games with the head."

She frowned as Dr. Oliver's comment from their Monday session replayed in her mind.

"Trauma can mess with the brain."

But that hadn't happened. She knew where she'd parked her car. Could recall the exact sequence of events that led up to claiming the less-than-desirable spot.

"My head is fine. Someone moved my car."

"Why?

The $64,000 question.

"I don't know."

"Is there anyone in town who might be inclined to play a practical joke on you?"

"No. I haven't been here long enough to make enemies."

"Your car was found locked and undamaged except for a partially shattered taillight."

"That was already there. Someone backed into me in a parking lot. I haven't gotten around to fixing it yet, since it still works."

"Was there anything inside worth stealing?" His tone remained mild as he maneuvered around a slower-moving SUV.

"No." She couldn't fault his logic. The whole scenario didn't make sense to her, either. "Look, I realize this sounds crazy, but I know what I know. I can't explain why someone would move my car. Nor do I have a clue how they did it. I had the key fob with me the entire evening."

"I can't answer the why, but I can offer a few thoughts on the how." He hung a right and accelerated onto the highway. "Does your car have keyless entry and push-button ignition?"

"Yes."

"What's the range on the fob?"

"I have no idea, but I've opened the car from fifty or sixty feet away."

"Then your car would be easy to steal."

"How?"

"With an electronic device anyone can buy on the internet. One person uses it to capture the signal from your fob and transmits it to another person standing by your vehicle. It's a relay system thieves use to steal locked cars from driveways at night. The first person gets close to the house, picks up the fob signal, and sends it to an accomplice. In your case, someone could have been waiting out of sight in the dark parking lot near the church entrance and picked up the signal as you walked by. In less than a minute, the person by your vehicle could open the door and drive away."

Lindsey stared at him. "The detective who called me never mentioned any of that."

"Probably because your situation had all the earmarks of a misplaced car. That happens a fair amount. People think their vehicle has been stolen at a mall, call the police, and realize they forgot where they parked after their car is found in a different part of the lot."

"I didn't forget where I parked."

"Are you certain?"

"Yes."

He gave her a sidelong glance . . . then changed the subject as he shifted his attention back to the road. "Let's talk about the Robertson case."

Lindsey considered him.

Should she continue trying to press her case that she hadn't been mistaken about her car?

No. Why bother? Let him believe whatever he wanted—

even if his doubts about her story bothered her for reasons she couldn't fathom.

"Fine." Now was the time to bring up the one new piece of information she could add to the case. "I did remember a minor fact. I doubt it's important."

"Like I said on the phone, what's trivial to you could matter to us. What is it?"

"A few days ago, a fuzzy detail about the overshoes drifted through my mind. It was gone before I could bring it into focus, but I saw it again last night, much sharper, in a dream." During a replay of the nightmare she'd told Dr. Oliver about, actually, which featured the scarred hand. "It was the brand name on the overshoes. Dunlop." When her chauffeur didn't react, she shrugged. "I told you it was trivial."

"You never know how a piece of information will fit into the puzzle. I'll add that to my case notes."

"Do you have any suspects?"

"We're still in investigation mode."

Not an answer. But it might be all he could officially offer.

"I hope you're not bothering Chad."

That earned her another look. "Why didn't you tell me last Friday that you knew him? I found out you were acquainted from the victim's wife."

"It wasn't relevant. I didn't see him that day. And it's not like we're close friends. We met through church, and his wife is taking my cooking class. They've only been married a few months. I know a bit of his history before that, but he's turned his life around. You can't have any grounds to suspect him."

"Everyone involved is a person of interest while the case is active."

Did that mean they *did* have grounds to doubt Chad's innocence, or was Tucker giving her a standard line?

His guarded expression suggested she wasn't going to get an answer to that question, either.

She exhaled, reining in her annoyance. "You're as close-mouthed as the detective who handled the case I was involved in back in South Carolina."

His head spun her direction. "What kind of case?"

Whoops.

Major slip.

Not that the South Carolina incident was a state secret, with all the media coverage it had gotten, but rehashing it held zero appeal.

"I got caught up in a grocery store shooting there twenty-one months ago."

"How were you involved?"

She shifted in her seat, fighting back a wave of the same clawing panic that had constricted her windpipe in the grocery store and again last Friday in the Robertson kitchen.

"Since that doesn't have any bearing on this case, I'd prefer not to talk about it."

He flipped on the blinker, edged into the exit lane, and thankfully took her cue. "Is there anything else from Friday that has come back to you?"

"Nothing but the brand on the overshoes."

"What about other clothing details? Or the person's posture or gait or mannerisms? Anything they did in the brief window you saw them that struck you as odd or quirky or distinctive?"

"No."

"If any other memory does pop up, please let me know. You have my card, right?"

"Yes."

He drove in silence for a couple of minutes, then turned onto the side street next to the church where the property detective had said her car was parked. She spotted it at once.

"There it is." She pointed ahead.

He pulled into the empty space behind it. "Why don't you verify that nothing is missing before I leave?"

The instant the Taurus came to a stop, she pushed the door open. "I can check, but there wasn't anything in there worth stealing."

While she scanned the contents of the trunk and glove compartment, he gave the neighborhood a once-over. "Not the best part of town."

"But the perfect place for a class about cooking on a budget." She closed the trunk. "Everything's here."

"Is there anyone around when you walk to your car after the class?"

"Once in a while. But I usually get here early and park next to the door by the church hall. Most nights it's a matter of a few steps to get to my car. I was running late on Tuesday, which is why I parked farther away."

"Do you carry pepper gel?"

"Yes." Thanks to South Carolina.

"Smart. You can't be too careful in today's world." He searched her face, his discerning eyes probing—and compassionate. "You doing okay?"

At the sudden crack in his professional persona, pressure built in Lindsey's throat.

Other than her new friend Madeleine, there was no one who cared about her day-to-day life. Oh, Mom made the obligatory check-in call periodically, but it wasn't as if they were confidantes. Even after the grocery store incident, there'd been nothing more than a brief spike in the frequency of her calls.

And while she'd made casual friends in college and during her years in South Carolina, relationships were hard to sustain over long distances.

Only Clair had been there for her on a consistent, day-in and day-out basis since her teenage years. Emails, phone calls, texts—they'd touched base every single day even after their jobs took them different directions.

Now she was gone, thanks at least in part to this man.

But you played a role too, Lindsey. You share a piece of the blame.

Her spirits tanked, as they always did when she faced that truth—and the guilt over her own culpability would plague her the rest of her life.

Now, however, wasn't the time to dwell on that.

She straightened her shoulders. "I'm fine. Thank you for the ride."

"Glad to be of assistance. I'll let you get back to your routine."

"My routine for the day is already shot." She tossed her purse onto the passenger seat of her car and slid behind the wheel. "I didn't get in my morning row."

He hiked up an eyebrow. "Rowing as in a boat, or with a rowing machine?"

"Boat. A scull, to be more precise. I was on the rowing team in college and started solo sculling six years ago." Enough about that. "I should go."

After a moment, he stepped back. "Drive safe."

"That's my plan." She closed and locked the door.

He returned to his car and followed her down the street to the corner, where he peeled off in the opposite direction.

As his Taurus disappeared in her rearview mirror, Lindsey took a slow, calming breath.

Loyalty to Clair alone would make her dislike him, but on top of that it was apparent he had doubts about her car story. That he questioned her memory—and perhaps her mental acuity.

That didn't sit well.

Letting his reservations upset her was crazy, though. He didn't know her, and the car situation was indeed strange. In his shoes, she'd be dubious too.

But she trusted her memory. Organization and accuracy

and precise recall were important in her job, and those skills carried over into her life.

She'd parked in the lot. There was zero doubt in her mind about that.

Which made the car situation not just bizarre, but very, very unsettling.

EIGHT

JAMES ROBERTSON'S AUTOPSY hadn't revealed any new clues.

Expelling a frustrated breath, Jack leaned forward in his desk chair and gave the material a second scan, homing in on the pertinent parts.

Cause of death—two gunshot wounds to the chest, with perforation of heart and lungs.

Manner of death—homicide.

Two small-caliber lead bullets had been recovered and sent to the crime lab, all of the tox screens from the accelerated testing were normal, and no trace evidence had been found.

Bottom line? The case was getting colder by the minute.

He sat back and stared at the wall in his office.

Six days in, and they had zip. Unless a clue surfaced soon, he'd have to—

His cell vibrated on his desk, and he glanced at the screen.

A call from the owner of one of the more legit pawnshops downtown, who'd provided helpful information on several past cases.

He put the phone to his ear. "Tucker."

"Dirk West here, Detective. One of those pieces of jewelry on the list you sent around over the weekend is in my shop."

His pulse picked up. Maybe the Robertson case wasn't dead after all.

"Do you know the person who brought it in?"

"No, but he's still here."

Even better.

Jack stood and snatched his jacket off the back of his chair. "Try to delay him. I'll have a city cop there in minutes. Whoever shows up will detain him until I arrive."

"You got it."

"I owe you."

"I'll collect."

"I have no doubt of that."

Jack ended the call and took off for the parking lot at a trot as he put in a call to one of his counterparts in the city who could get an officer there fast.

Once behind the wheel, he pushed the pedal as close to the floor as he dared without flicking on lights and siren and raced east.

Not one but two cruisers were parked in front of the shop as he pulled up fifteen minutes later.

Wearing a disgruntled look, Dirk met him at the front door and motioned to the vehicles. "Major overkill. Cop cars in front of my shop are bad for business."

"Sorry about that. Must have been a slow day. I'll take care of it. Where's the guy?"

Dirk tipped his head toward the back of the shop. "They escorted him to the office and gave him coffee. My coffee."

"Watch for a Starbucks card in the mail."

A smile creased the man's face. "I do like me those fancy drinks." He led the way to the counter and picked up a diamond-encrusted bracelet. "Here's what he brought."

Jack pulled out a clear evidence envelope and opened the top. "Drop it in here."

"Yeah, yeah, I know the routine." Dirk deposited it. "Now get rid of the cops."

Pocketing the envelope, Jack continued to the rear of the store, where he found one of the officers checking his phone while the other kept tabs on the guy who'd brought in the stolen bracelet.

A guy who didn't come anywhere close to fitting the stereotype of a thief who targeted high-end houses in ritzy areas of town.

The officer with the phone stood. "You want us to hang around?"

"No, I've got it. Thanks for the assist."

"Not a problem." He hooked a thumb toward the man. "He doesn't have any ID, and we could only get a first name. Goes by Pop."

As the two officers filed out, Jack positioned the extra chair in the office in front of the grizzled, gray-haired man with weathered, wrinkled skin and faded blue eyes, whose mishmash attire screamed street person.

Hard to estimate ages for people who'd lived a hard life, but this guy had to be at least seventy.

Jack introduced himself. "Is there more to your name than Pop?"

"Long ago. In a different life. I'm Pop now."

Rather than push for an ID, Jack pulled out the envelope and held it up. "I understand you were trying to sell this."

"Yep." The man picked up the ceramic mug beside him, wrapped his fingers around it, and blew on the dark brew.

"Where did you get it?"

"From a friend." He took a sip.

"This friend have a name?"

"Uh-huh."

"What is it?"

The man squinted at him. "I don't cause trouble for my friends."

"The friend who gave you this is causing *you* trouble. This bracelet was stolen last Friday."

Pop shook his head. "My friend doesn't steal."

"Then he or she won't be in trouble if you give me their name."

The man studied him, his expression suggesting he was trying to work through the logic of that but having difficulty. As if too many hard years had dulled his brainpower.

"I don't think I should do that."

A different tack was in order.

Jack returned the envelope to his pocket and leaned back, adopting a casual tone. "Where do you live, Pop?"

"Down by the river most days, unless it gets too cold and I have to go to a shelter. But I don't like shelters."

"Why not stay with this friend of yours on cold days?"

"Nope. Three's company, you know." He grinned, revealing a gap where his left lateral incisor should have been.

"Your friend is married?"

"Uh-huh."

"When did this friend give you the bracelet?"

"Yesterday. Not in person. Someone delivered it."

"Who?"

Pop took another chug of coffee. "Don't know his name. Another homeless guy who was passing through. He left this morning."

Dead end.

"How do you know the bracelet was from your friend?"

"There was a note with it."

"What did it say?"

"That I should bring it here and use the money to buy myself a warm coat and a pair of boots for winter."

"You still have the note?"

"Nope again. I was supposed to throw it away after I read it, so I did."

"Where?"

"I tore it up into little pieces." Pop pantomimed the motion. "Then I tossed it into the river."

In other words, the note was gone—assuming this whole story wasn't a fabrication.

Yet every instinct in Jack's body told him the man was being truthful.

Even if he wasn't the perpetrator of the robbery or the murder at the Robertson house, though, the bracelet said he had a connection to the killer.

On to plan B.

"You know, Pop, you're in possession of stolen jewelry. And you were trying to sell it."

"I didn't know it was stolen. My friend must not have known it was stolen, either."

"Where do you think your friend got it?"

"I don't know."

"Is your friend rich?"

He chortled. "Richer than me."

This was going nowhere.

Maybe if they could identify this guy, they could get a lead on his friend.

Jack stood. "At the moment, you're my prime suspect."

"I didn't do anything wrong."

"It would help if your friend confirmed that."

"I'd have to ask him if it was okay to tell you his name."

"Why don't you call him?" Jack pulled out his cell. "You can use my phone."

That earned him another gap-toothed grin. "I may be missing a few marbles, but I don't fall for too many tricks. If I call him, you'll have his number. I'll ask him next time I see him."

Frustrating as the man's answer was, it was hard to fault his loyalty.

"When will that be?"

"He comes around regular. You have a card? I could borrow a phone and call you after I talk to him."

"I'd rather talk to him myself."

"I'll tell him that."

Now what?

He could find grounds to take the guy in, but the man wasn't likely to be any more forthcoming at headquarters.

Jack flicked a glance at the almost-empty ceramic coffee mug on the desk.

Bingo.

There was no law against running prints from an item if the owner gave permission. Namely Dirk.

Identity problem solved—if Pop was in any of the databases.

As for the friend who'd sent him the bracelet? A job for the undercover crew. Cataloguing who showed up to talk to the man could be very helpful.

On to his next question.

"Where were you last Friday around noon?"

"Where I am most days at noon. Eating lunch at my favorite restaurant." He mentioned a charity that served daily meals to the homeless in the city.

"Can anyone verify that?"

"Sure. The volunteers all know me. I'm a regular." He picked up his coffee and drained the dregs.

"You mind if I take your picture?" He extracted his phone again. "So I can show it around at your lunch spot."

His face split into a smile again. "This mug could break a camera. But shoot away if you want. And try to make me look good."

Jack snapped several shots, put the phone away, and fished

out a card. "Remember . . . I'd like to talk to your friend as soon as possible."

"I'll pass that on." He tucked the card into one of the pockets of his beat-up coat. "Can I go?"

"Yes."

The man set the mug down and ambled out of the office, toward the front door.

As soon as he disappeared from sight, Jack snapped on a latex glove, pulled out another evidence bag, and sealed the mug inside. After filling out the chain of custody label on both items his trip to the pawn shop had produced, he returned to the front of the store.

"What's the story on your guy?" Dirk motioned toward the front door.

"I don't know yet." He hefted the bag with the mug. "I'd like to borrow this."

"Keep it. I have dozens of them. You gonna run his prints?"

"You have any issue with that?"

"No. The mug's yours now, anyway."

The bell over the door announced the arrival of a customer, and Jack pulled out his keys. "Watch for that Starbucks card. And thanks again for the call."

"Anytime, my friend."

Jack exited into the almost balmy weather. Quite a contrast to last week's sudden cold spell. But that was November in St. Louis for you. And according to the meteorologists, the warm spell was going to last for another few days.

Meaning Cara should have decent weather on Sunday during her drive up from Cape for their monthly family get-together.

That would be a pleasant interlude in what otherwise had been a frustrating week.

Maybe Pop's prints would provide helpful information. Or the man would follow through and talk to his friend. Or the undercover operative would observe a helpful interaction once he picked up Pop's tail at the man's favorite lunch spot.

But as Jack slid behind the wheel of his car and pointed it west, the mounting odds against solving this case didn't leave him feeling hopeful.

Nor did the unsettling sense that despite the murderer's apparently clean getaway, he or she was keeping tabs on this investigation and wouldn't hesitate to strike again if anyone got too close to uncovering their identity.

NINE

IT WAS A PERFECT MORNING to be on the lake. And gliding over the calm water as the sun crested the tree-lined shore was exactly what she needed to soothe her frayed nerves on this barely post-dawn Sunday.

Knees bent, shins vertical, back straight, Lindsey leaned forward and breathed deep as she dipped her blades into the water, pushed with her legs, and propelled the scull forward. Once the seat slid back and her legs were flat, she lifted the blades from the water and swung them behind her. Relaxing her upper body and arms, she bent her knees and let the seat slide forward again.

Dr. Oliver had been right. Getting back into her routine did help restore a sense of normalcy to her life. Thank goodness Mother Nature had cooperated with warm, windless weather ideal for sculling.

As she skimmed over the surface of the lake, Lindsey exhaled, the tension melting from her shoulders. The rhythmic cadence of the strokes calmed her even more than her session three days ago with Dr. Oliver. And while the text from Heidi canceling Thursday's cooking slot had been bad news for her budget, the welcome reprieve from returning to the scene of the crime more than compensated for the lost income.

The sun inched up another notch, the trees casting long shadows on the serene lake in the early morning light. Best of all, she had the expanse to herself. There would be more lake traffic later, once the chilly sunrise temperature rose to the predicted low seventies, but at this hour no sound broke the stillness save the soft dip of her blades and the occasional honk of a goose.

Should she extend her session today? Do an extra lap or two of her usual route? She could always attend the later service at her church. And afterward, thanks to the additional exercise, she could afford to splurge on a sweet treat from—

Whoa!

Her pulse stumbled as one of the blades came to an abrupt stop, violently rocking the scull.

Reflexes kicking in, she summoned up every ounce of her skill to rebalance and keep herself from ending up in the lake.

Once stable, she repositioned her blades and gave the water a sweep, searching for a clue about what had happened.

Other than the ripples from her near-capsize, nothing marred the glassy surface.

Lindsey furrowed her brow.

Had she hit a submerged object? Run into a school of the Asian carp that had evaded capture during the 2018 attempt to vanquish the invasive species from the lake?

Whatever the cause of her strange upset, it had ruined her tranquil interlude. The calm that had settled over her was evaporating as quickly as the thin layer of early morning mist hovering above the surface of the water.

So much for extra laps. The prospect of a comforting cup of hot chocolate in the safety of her own condo was much more appealing and—

The scull rocked again, harder than the first time. And not because she'd hit anything. She wasn't moving.

What in the world?

Before she could attempt to steady the scull, it tipped hard to the right, dumping her into the cold, numbing water.

Not good.

Adrenaline kicking in, she pushed back toward the surface, brain morphing into emergency mode.

While her cold-weather rowing attire offered more than sufficient protection in her scull, it provided none in water hovering in the low-fifties range. Hypothermia was a very real danger. At best, she had eight to ten minutes to get aboard and stroke to shore.

Not a problem, Lindsey. You've practiced getting back into an over-turned scull ad nauseam, done it on many occasions during your rowing career. You've got this.

With that encouraging mantra looping through her mind, she crested the surface. All she had to do was step on the rigger, flip the scull back over, reset the handles, and—

A vise wrapped around her ankle and yanked, giving her no chance to do more than catch a quick gasp of air before the water closed over her again.

She kicked against the restraint, fighting to release her foot as she was tugged downward.

It held fast.

Heart racing, she tried again.

No luck.

Whatever had clamped onto her ankle continued to drag her deeper—and her small amount of reserve air wouldn't last long.

Quashing the instinctive urge to keep struggling toward the surface, Lindsey forced herself to switch direction, pushing downward through the dark water, toward whatever had latched onto her foot. At this early hour, the sun was too low to mitigate the always poor visibility in the lake water, meaning she'd have to work blind.

But she could feel.

And as she bumped into a solid object and tried to free her ankle from whatever was holding it, what she felt was . . . hands?

How could that be?

Lindsey peered through the murky water, but only a bulky, shadowy outline registered as her lungs began to burn.

She had to breathe.

Now.

Unless she freed her ankle in a matter of seconds, she was going to drown. And after all she'd been through, that wasn't how she wanted to die.

She reached down again, but all at once the hands clenched around her ankle released their hold.

Relief surging through her, she shot toward the surface, inhaling water as her lungs caved a millisecond before she broke through to fresh air.

Treading water, she coughed and searched the lake for her scull.

It was ten feet away, upside down.

She swam toward it and grasped the edge, trying to process the bizarre scenario as she hacked up lake water.

Failed.

A shiver rolled through her, and she forced herself to focus on the immediate danger. Namely, hypothermia. She had to get out of the water and back to shore ASAP.

Following the rote procedure she'd learned long ago, she righted the scull. With both oar handles in her left hand, she clasped the opposite deck edge with the other, scissor kicked, and pulled her hips up and over the edge. After retaking her seat, she scanned the water.

The placid surface offered no hint of the trauma that had taken place a dozen feet down minutes ago.

Lindsey grasped the oar grips, maneuvered the scull in the direction of the boathouse, and picked up her rhythm again. Or tried to. But a severe case of the shakes left her strokes jerky rather than smooth. Besides, it was hard to concentrate on technique after coming within a heartbeat of death.

Again.

Right on the heels of her close encounter with James Robertson's killer.

She almost lost her grip on the oars as that connection registered.

Was it possible the killer had somehow learned her name? Could they have decided to dispense with her in case she remembered a pertinent piece of information that would help the police identify him or her?

Or was she jumping to conclusions? Being overly dramatic? After all, the hands had released her.

Someone fully briefed on the case would be able to provide the best answer to her questions.

Someone like the lead detective.

As the dock came into sight, Lindsey squeezed the oar grips. If she never saw Jack Tucker again, it would be too soon.

But who else could she talk to? The cops in this municipality would file a report if she called them, perhaps poke around the lake and ask a few questions. But they had no connection to the Robertson case, nor any clue as to whether a dangerous leak may have occurred.

Only Jack Tucker could provide that kind of insight.

So as a matter of self-defense, she'd have to touch base with him. Like it or not.

Definitely not.

LINDSEY BARNES WAS CALLING him at—Jack checked the cell he'd set on the bathroom vanity—seven thirty on a Sunday morning?

Did that mean she'd remembered a pertinent detail about the killer?

He exited the shower, secured a towel around his waist, and snatched up the phone. "Tucker here. How can I help you, Ms. Barnes?"

"I'm sorry to bother you on a weekend." A tremor ran through her stilted apology.

He tensed. "No bother. What's up?"

"More like what's down."

It was too early for riddles, especially after tossing most of the night over the lack of progress in the Robertson case.

"Sorry. You'll have to explain that."

He listened while she gave him a quick recap of her experience at Creve Coeur Lake, frowning at his reflection in the bathroom mirror as she wound down.

"At first, I thought maybe I'd hit something under the surface. But when it happened again, and then hands grabbed my ankle and pulled me down, I knew it had to be deliberate." Her voice hitched again. "So I wanted to ask you if someone involved in the investigation could have let my name slip."

Jack took a moment to digest her story. Another to grasp why she'd asked that question.

"You're wondering if Robertson's killer could be targeting you."

"I know it seems off the wall, but why else would someone do that to me?"

He pinched the bridge of his nose.

First a misplaced car. Now an attack by an underwater phantom.

Was it possible the trauma from nine days ago had affected

her mind? Could she have simply run into a submerged obstacle, panicked when she'd ended up in the drink, and imagined all the rest?

"I know my story sounds crazy." Her voice grew taut, defensiveness vibrating through it. "But I also know there were fingers around my ankle. And I don't think the attack was random."

Jack maintained an even tone as he replied, composing his response with care. "No one could survive more than a few minutes in a lake at this time of year unless they were suited up for scuba diving. Are you thinking this person was lying in wait for you under the water?"

Maybe if he put the scenario she was describing into words, she'd realize how far-fetched it was.

"Like I said, I know my story is bizarre. But what other explanation could there be for what happened?"

He could think of a few. None of which she'd appreciate.

"You *have* been under a lot of stress." If there was a more diplomatic way to phrase his reservations about her story, it eluded him.

The sharp intake of breath on the other end of the line spoke volumes about her reaction to that comment, as did her glacial tone. "I'm sorry I interrupted your weekend. I'll let you get back to—"

"Hold on a sec." He pulled another towel from the rack and began scrubbing his hair. She was the only one who'd seen Robertson's killer, and alienating her in the midst of that investigation wouldn't be smart. "Are you absolutely sure about what happened?"

"Yes." No hesitation.

Jack sighed.

So much for his quiet Sunday agenda of church followed by a relaxing afternoon meal with his siblings.

"Where are you?"

"In my car at the boathouse next to the lake."

"Are you hurt?" That was the first question he should have asked. An obvious lapse, now that his brain was clicking into gear.

"No."

Not physically, perhaps, but the catch in her voice suggested she'd taken an emotional hit from today's episode, whatever the cause.

"Are you warm and dry?"

"Yes. I ch-changed in the locker room."

Smart. She didn't need a case of hypothermia on top of the rest of her trauma—real or imagined.

"Are there any other people around?"

"A few are starting to show up."

"Lock your doors and keep your phone in hand. I'm going to get a few eyes on the lake perimeter. Watch for me in twenty minutes and call again if anything happens that concerns you."

"All right. Thanks."

The line went dead, and Jack flew into action. In six minutes flat he was dressed, shaved, and jogging toward his car, phone pressed to his ear as he connected with his sergeant, who could get officers on-site fast. If they didn't canvas the area ASAP to see if anyone had spotted suspicious activity around the lake, the opportunity to find potential witnesses would be lost.

That call completed, he put the car in gear and set his cell on the seat beside him as it pinged with a text notification.

He picked it up again while he pulled out of his driveway.

A message from one of the undercover officers watching Pop, including a photo.

This guy doesn't fit the homeless mold. He and the subject are at Al's Diner.

Jack pulled over, enlarged the somewhat grainy photo that had been taken on the sly, and homed in on Pop's companion.

The man was in profile, a cap pulled down over his hair, but there was no mistaking his identity.

It was ex-homeless veteran Chad Allen.

Bingo.

And the link fit. Pop had been on the streets for years. It was very possible his path had crossed with Allen's and the two had struck up a friendship.

If so—and in light of Allen's connection to the Robertson murder—the obvious conclusion was that he'd given Pop the jewelry. Payback, friendship, concern for the man's welfare . . . there could be any number of motives for the gift.

Only Allen could provide that answer.

Whether he would cooperate remained to be seen, but that had to be the next order of business. Not a trip to Creve Coeur Lake.

He put his fingers in motion, returning the text.

Pop's companion still there?

No. They talked for a couple of minutes and he took off. Seemed upset.

No doubt after Pop told him he'd been questioned and passed on the message that law enforcement wanted the name of his generous friend.

Jack pulled away from the curb and stepped on the gas.

It was possible Allen would run, but with a new wife at home, odds were he wouldn't bail.

In fact, he could be headed home now to warn her there were storm clouds ahead.

After thanking the undercover officer, Jack punched in Lindsey's number.

She answered on the first ring, and after explaining that officers were en route, he got to the real reason for his call.

"I'm going to have to bail on the lake reconnaissance. A

solid tip came in on the Robertson case, and I have to follow up on it. I'll stay in the loop with the officers at the scene, though, and touch base with you later to take a statement."

"Okay."

But it wasn't. As they signed off, her inflection suggested she thought he was humoring her, had dismissed her story as one of those reports that had to be investigated even though everyone knew from the outset nothing substantive would be found.

That wasn't true. Well . . . not exactly. While he might have a few doubts about what had transpired this morning, it was clear Lindsey didn't. And nothing in their encounters to date suggested she was less than stable.

Nevertheless, it might be prudent to do a bit of research on the previous traumatic incident she'd alluded to. Anyone subjected to too much stress could end up having emotional and mental issues. It would be foolish to discount that possibility.

Or the possibility she could have deeper psychological issues with no relation to recent or past incidents.

Like the kind that had plagued his mother.

Gut twisting, Jack mashed his lips together and pressed harder on the accelerator.

That was ancient history. He should let it go once and for all. Allowing those memories to color his perceptions of others was a mistake. Not everyone who had mental lapses was sick.

On the other hand, there was nothing wrong with a healthy dose of caution based on experience. It was called self-preservation.

So while he'd give Lindsey the benefit of the doubt despite the two recent incidents that had implausibility written all over them, some doubt was wise.

And he'd also have plenty of it on hand when Allen came home and found a St. Louis County homicide detective waiting to talk to him.

TEN

AS THE FAINT RING OF THE DOORBELL penetrated her restless slumber, Dara forced her eyelids open. Peered at her watch.

Eight fifteen.

Who would come calling at this hour on a Sunday morning?

Whoever it was, Chad could deal with them. He was up already, if the faint aroma of coffee wafting through the cracks in the closed bedroom door was any indication. While he'd abandoned their sleep-late Sunday morning ritual now that he was spending his nights on the couch, this was one small luxury she wasn't giving up. Even if sleep had been elusive since the Robertson murder.

She burrowed back into the pillow. She could spare another half hour under the covers before she had to get ready for the second service at church.

Ten seconds later, the doorbell rang again.

Heaving a sigh, she pushed herself to a sitting position, shoved her hair back, and groped for her robe at the foot of the bed. Apparently Chad intended to ignore the summons, perhaps assuming it was another pushy reporter. But the harassment from the press had tapered off over the past week, so that didn't seem likely.

The bell pealed again as she trudged down the hall.

"All right already." She muttered the comment as she passed the kitchen doorway and scanned the room.

No sign of Chad.

Nor was he in the living room. The couch had been reconfigured from a makeshift bed back to its usual role.

Huh.

Where could he be?

She continued to the front door, pausing by the peephole to squint through the fish-eye lens.

A clean-cut, respectable-looking stranger stood on the other side.

As he leaned forward to press the bell again, she scuttled back. Bit her lip.

The guy was persistent. And he didn't show any signs of leaving until someone responded.

Better answer and find out what he wanted.

She moved back to the door and pulled it open a couple of inches, leaving the chain on the lock.

The man smiled. "Ms. Allen?"

"Yes."

After giving her robe a quick once-over through the meager crack, he pulled out a small holder, flipped it open, and aimed it her direction. "Sorry to wake you. Detective Jack Tucker, St. Louis County Police. Is your husband home?"

Pulse skittering, Dara flicked a glance at the street behind the man.

The parking spot Chad had claimed last night in front of their apartment was empty.

Why?

"No. I'm sorry. He's, uh, not here."

"Do you know when he'll be back?"

How could she, when she didn't even know he'd left or where he'd gone?

"No."

"Do you mind if I wait for him inside?"

Yes, she did. But how could she say no without adding to any suspicions this detective already harbored about her husband?

"I guess that would be okay." She closed the door and slid the chain free of the lock, her brain shifting into high gear. She had to warn Chad. Give him a chance to prepare for the unpleasant surprise waiting for him in their living room.

"Thanks." The detective entered as she eased back to give him access.

"Um . . . why don't you have a seat?" She motioned toward the couch in the tiny living room. "Would you like a cup of coffee?" That would give her an excuse to retreat to the kitchen, grab her cell from the charger on the counter, and escape to the bedroom to call Chad.

"No, thank you. I stopped for a caffeine fix on my drive here." Flashing her another smile, he claimed a seat on the sofa.

"I think I'll get a cup for myself and change. I, uh, like to sleep in on Sunday. That's why I'm wearing this." She plucked at the edge of her robe.

"No problem."

"I'll be back in a few minutes."

"Don't hurry on my account." He propped an ankle on a knee, his casual posture suggesting this was a friendly visit.

But it wasn't.

Something else had happened to implicate Chad in the Robertson murder.

Something bad.

She knew that as surely as she knew her husband had secrets he hadn't shared with her since this nightmare began.

He'd have to share them now, though. Didn't matter what he told this detective. He couldn't pretend to her anymore that everything was fine. She wouldn't let him. She was done waiting for him to initiate a conversation on the subject.

Dara slipped into the kitchen, snatched her phone out of the charger, and slid it in her pocket. Coffee was a low priority compared to calling Chad, but she filled a mug anyway before escaping to the hall.

Just as she reached the bedroom door, the front knob rattled.

Chad was home!

She spun around and sped back to the living room.

The detective stood and faced the door as her husband pushed through. "Good morning, Mr. Allen."

Chad reared back as if he'd been struck, panic spiking in his eyes.

"The detective arrived a f-few minutes ago, Chad." Dara took a step forward as she tried to keep breathing in a room that suddenly felt airless and claustrophobic.

Their visitor's demeanor remained calm and impassive. "I have a few more questions for you, Mr. Allen."

"I told you everything I know the day of the murder." He fisted his hands at his sides.

"I'm here today to talk about a more recent development. The stolen jewelry you gave your friend Pop."

Her husband's face lost several shades of color, and he groped for the edge of the open door.

Dara's stomach coiled into a knot. "Chad? What's going on?"

"I don't know." He closed the door.

"Who's Pop?"

Chad didn't answer her question—but the detective did.

"He's a street person, Ms. Allen. A Vietnam vet whose real name is Henry Finn. Your husband met him at Al's Diner this morning."

Dara looked at her husband. "Is that true?"

110

"Yes." He responded to her, then refocused on the detective. "But I never gave him any jewelry."

"I have the bracelet he tried to pawn." Detective Tucker maintained a conversational tone. "It belonged to the victim's wife. He said it came from you."

"I didn't steal it—and I didn't give it to Pop."

"What's your relationship with him?" Their uninvited visitor pulled out a notebook.

Chad's Adam's apple bobbed. "You mind if we sit?"

"Not at all." The detective reclaimed his chair.

"Dara, do you . . . do you want to join us?" Chad twisted toward her.

She looked at the man she'd married, felt the almost-palpable fear radiating from him, and heard the real questions he was asking.

Did she believe in him? Trust him? Was she willing to stand beside him through whatever ordeal lay ahead? Or was she going to assume the worst and turn her back on him when he needed her most, as so many other people in his life had?

Dara drew a shaky breath.

Maybe she was being foolish. Her father would think so. But she'd lived with this man for nine months. Loved him with her whole heart. Learned about the demons that had plagued him, about all he'd overcome to start a new life. Knew him better than she'd known many people who'd been part of her world far longer. And her intuition said that whatever trouble he was in wasn't of his making.

Slowly she walked over to him and placed her hand in his.

He clung to her fingers, the gratitude in his eyes tightening her throat as he tugged her down beside him and drew her close.

The detective positioned his pen over the notebook. "Tell me about Pop."

Chad let out a slow exhale. "He saved my life on the street.

Literally. It's a rough place, and early on I was out of my element. He stepped into an altercation that could have left me dead. Everyone on the street knew and respected him, and the other guy backed off. After that, Pop sort of adopted me. Taught me the ropes. Helped me survive. I owe him a debt I can never repay."

"Except with stolen jewelry."

"No!" Chad's posture stiffened. "Like I said, I don't know anything about that."

"He said it came from you."

"He told me that this morning." Chad's grip on her fingers tightened, and Dara squeezed his in return. "I assume you had a tail on him. That's how you found me."

"Yes."

"I don't know who passed that jewelry on to him. All I can tell you is it wasn't me."

"Why would someone pretend it was?"

"Maybe the real murderer wants to throw suspicion on Chad." Dara leaned forward. No one had asked her to participate in this conversation, but she couldn't remain mute while someone insinuated that her husband had committed a vile crime.

Chad nodded. "That's my take too. Who better to pin a murder rap on, right? A former homeless person who was on the premises the day of the crime." He scrubbed a hand down his face, dejection radiating from him. "The perfect fall guy."

The detective didn't weigh in on that comment. "How often do you visit Pop?"

"Every couple of weeks."

Dara stared at Chad.

That was news too.

His gaze swung toward her. "I have to keep tabs on him, Dara. I usually run down on my lunch hour and give him a few bucks outside the soup kitchen where he eats. Or I stop by the encampment on the river after work. The last two Sundays, I've taken him to Al's early for a decent breakfast. I never told you any of this because I didn't want you to worry about me being in a dicey area of town."

Dicey area of town.

Could that be where he'd gotten the bruise on his upper arm? The one he'd tried to hide from her?

Tempted as she was to ask that question, she clamped her lips together. Voicing it in the presence of law enforcement wouldn't do her husband any favors.

The detective tapped his pen against his notebook. Regarded them both for a moment. Rose. "That's all I need for today. I may be back in touch as the case progresses."

She and Chad stood too.

"I'll show you out." Dara walked over to the door in silence, closing it behind the detective after he exited. Then she turned and faced her husband. If he wanted her trust from this stage forward, he had to be honest. Stop keeping secrets. "How did you get the bruise on your arm?"

He blinked—but didn't respond.

"I heard you tossing on the couch one night and came in to check on you." She positioned herself behind the side chair the detective had occupied, wrapped her fingers around the top of the back, and held her breath.

A mix of indecision and fear flared in Chad's eyes, but in the end he answered her question. "The morning of the Robertson murder, I went down to the encampment early. Someone must have seen me slip Pop a few dollars, because while I was walking back to my car, a guy jumped me. I guess he assumed I had more cash on hand. I managed to fight him off, but I fell on the concrete. I would have told you about it, except the timing with the murder stunk. I was afraid you might think I got injured in a fight with the dead guy."

The very possibility that had crossed her mind.

But there was no point in admitting that to Chad. Not if she believed his story.

And she did.

The police, however, would be less likely to accept his explanation. So keeping the bruise secret was smart.

As for the fact that he'd been jumped, if it had happened once, it could happen again.

That was almost as scary as his circumstantial implication in the murder.

She came out from behind the chair and walked over to him. Wrapped her arms around his waist and laid her head on his chest. "I know you care about this man, Chad, but you could have been killed that day. Isn't there a safer way to keep in touch with him?"

"I gave him a throwaway phone today. That will let me set up future meetings at the diner instead of looking for him at the encampment or soup kitchen. I'll be careful, Dara. But I can't cut him off."

"Couldn't you convince him to leave that life behind, like you did?"

"I've tried, but it's the only world he's known for too many years." He buried his face in her hair. "I'm sorry I've shut you out. But I was afraid you'd . . ." His voice rasped, and he swallowed. "I don't want to lose you, Dara. These past months with you have been the happiest of my life. They've felt so much like a dream that I keep expecting to wake up and discover that everything's fallen apart, like it always has."

"That was then, Chad. This is now. You've turned a corner. We'll get through this together as long as you keep talking to me. And loving me."

"I'll always love you. No matter what." He squeezed her tight.

She squeezed back.

But that "no matter what" caveat didn't leave her feeling warm and fuzzy. Nor had he promised to keep talking to her.

Was there more he hadn't told her?

Possibly.

Yet wrapped in his embrace, it was hard to nurture doubts. In his strong arms, she felt safe and hopeful and encouraged.

Whether that mood would last remained to be seen. The detective may have left for today, but until the Robertson case was solved, Chad would remain in his sights. And unless the police identified the person who'd passed that bracelet on to Pop, supposedly on her husband's behalf, a former street person who'd been working at the scene of the murder would stay at the top of their prime suspect list.

Which didn't bode well for her and Chad or their future together, despite her reassurance moments ago.

ELEVEN

"THANKS FOR THE UPDATE, SARGE."

Pressing the end button on his cell, Jack crossed to the kitchen cabinet beside his sink.

Now that his boss had confirmed what he'd expected to hear—that the lake reconnaissance had produced nothing—there was no reason to report back to Lindsey in person. A phone call would suffice. Their conversation from this morning gave him all the material he needed for his report.

He withdrew a glass, filled it with OJ, and surveyed the shelves in his fridge. All the ingredients were on hand for the chicken cordon bleu and chocolate mint squares he'd promised to make for the sibling gathering he was hosting today. If he started to work on the meal now, it would be ready to serve by one o'clock, as promised.

But if he squeezed in a church service and paid Lindsey a visit instead, Bri and Cara would have to make do with far less ambitious fare.

He swigged his juice.

Church and family always came first—unless work intruded. Thankfully, his sisters understood the demands of a job that didn't have regular hours and often disrupted plans.

That wasn't the case today, though. He didn't have to give Lindsey priority this morning.

Yet considering how upset she'd been earlier, and taking into account all she'd been through over the past nine days, passing on the results of the lake reconnaissance face-to-face would be a thoughtful gesture.

Give it a break, Tucker. You just want another chance to try and figure out why she took such an instant dislike to you.

Scowling, Jack gulped down the remainder of the juice and set the empty glass on the counter with more force than necessary.

Okay, fine. There would also be a personal motive for his visit. Her puzzling antipathy bugged him, and the detective in him hated unsolved mysteries. There had to be an explanation for her attitude, and it wasn't a crime to want to ferret it out. Besides, it wouldn't hurt to try and get a few more insights into the South Carolina incident she'd referenced.

Decision made.

He'd forgo cooking, squeeze in church, and pay her a visit. The pan of lasagna in his freezer that he always kept on hand for emergencies would have to suffice. Cara and Bri would forgive him for the change in menu if he explained that duty had called.

He didn't have to tell them Lindsey's enmity was also eating at him.

An hour later, after putting the lasagna in the oven on low heat, dashing to the midmorning church service, and alerting his star witness in the Robertson case that he'd like to drop by, he pulled up in front of her condo and checked his watch.

In one hour, he had to be back at his house to welcome his sisters. Shouldn't be a problem. What he had to say to Lindsey wouldn't take long.

But hopefully long enough for him to do a little probing

and identify the burr under her saddle about a certain police detective.

As he circled his car and strode up the walk to her unit, Lindsey pulled open the front door, brow knitted, her baggy sweatpants and oversized fleece sweatshirt screaming comfort clothes.

Once he got close, she cut to the chase. "Did the officers find anything?"

He ascended the two steps to her porch, pausing at the top to give her a quick once-over.

Near as he could tell, she wore no makeup. Her hair was combed straight and tucked behind her ears, the slight frizz suggesting a recent shower. The shapeless wardrobe gave no hint of any curves underneath.

How could a woman who'd done zilch to enhance her appearance for his visit, who'd given him the cold shoulder during each of their encounters, have the power to make his fingers tingle and his pulse pick up?

Go figure.

"Well?"

Whoops.

Her annoyed prompt must mean his attempt at a subtle perusal had been less than discreet.

He refocused on the professional purpose of his visit. "No. They didn't find anything."

She sank back against the doorframe and massaged the bridge of her nose. "I can't say I'm surprised, but I *am* bummed. Without even a tiny shred of proof, my story has all the credibility of a Loch Ness monster sighting."

At least she was under no delusions about the difficulty of establishing the legitimacy of her story. With no evidence to validate what she said had happened this morning, the scenario was a hard sell.

He tried to dredge up a modicum of hope, however flimsy,

to lift her spirits. "It's possible a piece of corroborating information will turn up."

Her get-real look said she knew how improbable that was. "You never answered my earlier question about whether my name might have slipped out."

So she wasn't letting go of the theory that she'd been set up this morning at the lake.

"Unlikely from the PD. Our crew is tight-lipped. But you've told a number of people about your involvement, right?"

"Only friends and people I trust."

"Who may have told other people. So it's possible the killer knows your identity."

"But you think that's a long shot."

"I try not to rule anything out during an investigation."

"A diplomatic way to say I'm grasping at straws." She eased back. "Are we finished?"

"I still have to take a formal statement."

"I already told you the whole story."

In other words, she'd rather not invite him in.

Too bad.

Disappointing his sisters with an impromptu menu was only justified if he got a few answers during this visit.

"Like I told you at the Robertson house, sometimes new information emerges in a retelling."

She huffed. "I doubt that will happen—but come on in." She pulled the door wide and motioned toward a living room that felt larger than it was, thanks to a vaulted ceiling and light, neutral décor accented with spots of vibrant color.

Nice.

The warm, inviting contemporary space was the kind of room that said welcome after a long day.

He walked over to an upholstered chair, waiting to take his seat until she dropped onto the couch across from him and tucked her stockinged feet under her.

"Before we get to the statement, I want you to know that the officers at the park stopped in all the parking lots around the lake and talked to everyone they saw on the perimeter. It wasn't a token effort. We take all crimes-against-persons reports seriously."

"Despite your doubts."

He wasn't going to pretend he didn't have any. The astute woman across from him would see right through that claim.

"A healthy dose of skepticism is valuable in my line of work." He pulled out his notebook. "Why don't you walk me through what happened again?"

She repeated the story she'd told him earlier, including her contention that someone had grabbed her ankle. But in the retelling, her tone was a bit less definitive.

Interesting.

"Are you thinking there may not have been another person involved after all?" He stopped writing to assess her.

"I was certain I felt fingers around my ankle." She spoke slowly, forehead wrinkling. "But your comment on the phone about stress made me start to question my perceptions. I mean, I have to admit that the premise of a scuba diver lying in wait is bizarre. Plus, the past week or so has been more than unsettling. First a murder, then my car gets mysteriously moved. Add in South Carolina, and I—" She snapped her jaw shut, snatched up one of the throw pillows on the couch, and hugged it to her chest. "All I know is something strange happened at the lake, and I don't have a logical explanation for it. That bothers me."

"Understandable. No one likes unanswered questions."

"Speaking of unanswered questions—did your tip this morning lead to anything helpful with the Robertson case?"

Not a topic he could discuss.

"That remains to be seen." But her reference to South Carolina was about the best opening he was going to get to probe for details, and hearing the story from the source would be more informative than whatever his research unearthed.

As if sensing the direction of his thoughts, she shifted on the couch, keeping a tight grip on the pillow. "Are we done?"

"With the statement."

She gave him a wary look. "What else do we have to talk about?"

Her attitude toward him, for one thing.

But the incident in South Carolina could offer important insights about her mental acuity and her reliability as a witness if she did begin to remember helpful information regarding the killer she'd seen.

Best to begin there.

"What happened in South Carolina?"

Her shoulders stiffened, and she moistened her lips. "That's not relevant to my life here."

"Maybe it is."

"How?"

"I don't know, but it's my job to ask questions. To dig deep. You mentioned a grocery store shooting once. I can research the case and get the essentials, but I'd rather hear your version."

"I don't like to talk about it." A film of sweat broke out on her upper lip. "It's taken me hours of counseling to get past the repercussions."

His antennas went up.

"With a psychologist?"

Her eyes narrowed. "Yes. Both in South Carolina and here. But that doesn't mean I have deep-seated psychological issues. My problems stem from trauma. I went to a professional for a psychological injury, just like I'd go to an MD for a physical injury."

"I get that. And I admire the fact that you recognized you needed help and were proactive about getting your life back on track."

That was true. Yet lingering repercussions of trauma could impact her value as a witness in the Robertson case, especially if she began to have notable lapses in memory or to imagine danger where none was present.

He closed his notebook. "I can research the South Carolina case if necessary." In light of what she'd shared, pushing her to elaborate on that experience right after another upsetting incident wouldn't be kind. Neither would digging for clues about why she disliked him.

Eyeing him, she squeezed the pillow she'd mashed against her chest. "I haven't talked about it in any detail except with my therapist in South Carolina and Dr. Oliver here. And the local police there."

"I can appreciate how difficult it is to revisit bad memories." More than she'd ever guess.

He started to rise.

"But I can give you the topline, if that would be helpful."

He froze.

Nothing in her guarded features offered a clue about why she'd had a change of heart, but if she was willing to talk, it would be foolish to stop her.

He sat back down. "That would save me time."

She dipped her chin in acknowledgment.

Yet second after second ticked by as he waited for her to begin, the silence broken only by the muffled hum of a lawnmower pushed by someone who must prefer mulching leaves to raking them on this almost-balmy fall day.

Jack stifled his frustration.

She wasn't going to follow through on her unexpected offer.

Not surprising, given how reluctant she'd been all along to discuss South Carolina. He'd have to resort to research and hope—

"I was in the produce section when the guy s-started shooting." Lindsey's choppy voice was so low he had to lean close to hear her. "There was chaos around me. People were running, screaming . . . bleeding." Her breath hitched, and a shudder rippled through her.

It took every ounce of his willpower to ignore the powerful and unprofessional urge to move beside her and fold her hands in his. "Witnessing that kind of carnage can take a huge toll."

"It was worse than th-that. I was more than a bystander. I ended up being the gunman's hostage."

Jack bit back a word he never used. Took a long, slow inhale. The kind that usually calmed him in stressful situations.

Didn't work today.

The woman sitting across from him had dealt with more trauma in the past twenty-one months than most people faced in a lifetime. And in South Carolina, she hadn't just witnessed violent bloodshed. She'd been a victim herself.

If anyone had a reason to freak out, perhaps experience psychological issues, it was her.

"I'm sorry." He gentled his voice. "I've been involved in those kinds of investigations, talked to the victims. Recovering from an experience like that can be a slow process." And being a witness at a murder scene wasn't going to help her regain her balance or heal.

"That's why I got counseling. I couldn't deal with the terror or the nightmares."

"Did the cops determine a motive?"

"Yes. The shooter was a disgruntled former employee out for revenge on the manager who fired him, and he didn't hesitate to aim his gun at anyone who got in his way. A clerk, several shoppers, the security officer at the s-store. I was hiding behind a display of tomatoes when the cops arrived, and he dragged me out. Pointed his gun at my head and threatened to k-kill me if they didn't let him leave. I remember the tomatoes smashing onto the floor around us. There was red everywhere. Like b-blood."

Jack leaned forward, hands clasped. "Did they let him leave?"

"No." She began to shake. "They tried to talk to him. Brought in what I assume was a hostage negotiator. But he k-kept getting more and more agitated. When he pressed the gun to my temple, I was sure it was over. Then all of a s-sudden, he took it away, and a shot went off. I waited for everything to go black, but instead he collapsed b-behind me."

"A sniper got him?"

"No."

Meaning the man had turned the gun on himself, leaving Lindsey unharmed.

Yet she'd come within a hair's breadth of death, just as she had at the Robertson house.

Amazing that she was still functioning after two such traumatic incidents so close together. Not to mention her bizarre experience today.

"I'm sorry you had to go through that." Not nearly adequate, but a hug was out of the question.

"I survived." She lifted an unsteady hand and tucked her hair behind her ear. "But it left scars no one can see. The first few days afterward, I took dozens of showers, but I never felt like I could get all the b-blood off. And the nightmares . . . they never stopped. Waking or sleeping."

A bead of sweat trickled down her temple, and her respiration grew erratic. Like she was beginning to hyperventilate.

Could be a panic attack coming on. The symptoms were all there.

As he well knew.

Though such attacks were in the past now, they remained vivid in his memory.

"Sorry." Her breath came in short gasps as she confirmed his conclusion. "Panic attack. This is . . . why I don't talk . . . about South Carolina. Haven't . . . had one . . . in a while."

124

"Tell me how I can help."

She closed her eyes. "Xanax . . . in kitchen cabinet . . . by the sink."

A common med for anxiety symptoms.

"I'll get it for you."

Instead of responding, she focused on her breathing, using a common technique to dispel panic attacks. Inhale on a prescribed count, hold it for a second, exhale on the same count.

It was obvious she had the routine down.

As she fought to regain control, he hurried to the kitchen and checked the cabinets beside the sink. One pill bottle was tucked beside the salt and pepper shakers, and he pulled it out. Read the label.

Bingo.

He searched through another couple of cabinets until he found a glass, then moved to the water dispenser on the fridge.

While he waited for the glass to fill, he glanced at the photo affixed to the door with a magnet. A beach scene, with a smiling Lindsey looking more relaxed than he'd ever seen her.

But as his gaze flicked to the woman standing beside her, his pulse stumbled.

Clair Arnold and Lindsey had been friends?

Close friends, if the sole photo on Lindsey's refrigerator was of the two of them.

And if they'd been close, it was not only possible but probable that Clair had mentioned him to the woman sitting in the next room.

The woman whose manner toward him in every encounter had been frosty at best.

A muscle in his cheek ticced.

Clair must have told her about the recommendation he'd made that had led to her death, and the strong encouragement he'd given her to pursue it.

Liquid spilled over his hand, and he yanked the glass away from the waterspout, gut knotting.

A mess on the floor, and a mess in his heart.

Clenching his teeth, he tugged a length of paper towels off the holder on the counter and sopped up the spill.

He'd come here hoping for a few pieces of information about South Carolina and a clue that might help him get a handle on why Lindsey disliked him.

What he'd gotten was far more than he'd bargained for.

A story that had shaken the usual rock-solid, stoic composure he'd cultivated to survive in a field where blood and bodies abounded, and a photo that had fanned to life the simmering guilt he'd been plagued with for three long years.

He disposed of the damp paper towels, picked up the bottle of pills and the glass of water, and crossed the room.

Game plan?

Confirm Lindsey was okay, then make a fast exit before he said or did anything that would further alienate the traumatized woman in the next room who'd somehow managed to pique his interest and breach his defenses without even trying.

He had a lot to process before they had any further conversation.

And with Bri and Cara due to arrive soon, this wasn't the time to try and think through the ramifications of everything he'd learned today—or work out what he could say to Lindsey that would make her blame him any less than he blamed himself for the death of her friend.

TWELVE

THAT HAD BEEN WEIRD.

As Jack's car disappeared down the street, Lindsey frowned after him from inside the front window.

What had carved those deep grooves above his nose as he'd delivered her pill and water? Why had he gone from solicitous to distracted in a heartbeat? What had triggered his fast departure?

Weirder still?

Her sudden case of motormouth about South Carolina.

Massaging her forehead, she wandered back to the couch. Sank into the cushions.

What on earth had prompted her to talk about that experience with a man she didn't even like, when it was hard enough to discuss it with someone she felt comfortable confiding in, like Dr. Oliver? Or her therapist in South Carolina.

It made no sense.

Except . . . there was something about Jack Tucker that instilled trust, hinted at a compassionate heart. The man also exuded honesty and integrity and decency.

She punched the pillow she'd gripped during her tell-all session and shoved it into the corner of the couch.

It wasn't hard to see how a woman could fall for the handsome detective. Or why Clair had extolled his virtues during the four months they'd dated.

So maybe he was a good guy in general. But wanting a person to be someone they weren't was flat-out wrong.

And in Clair's case, it had also been deadly.

Swallowing past the sudden tightness in her throat, she stood. Grocery lists for the week weren't going to make themselves, and thinking about Jack Tucker—or trying to analyze her talkativeness this morning—was a waste of energy.

Her phone trilled as she entered the kitchen, and she veered toward the counter.

Madeleine.

Perfect.

A chat with her friend should help settle her nerves.

"Good morning, Lindsey." Madeleine returned her greeting in her usual cheerful manner. "I missed you at services and thought I'd check in. Did your rowing session run long?"

Lindsey blinked.

How had Madeleine known she'd gone sculling? As best she could recall, they hadn't discussed her Sunday plans during their last conversation.

"Um . . . a little longer than usual. Did I mention I was going out to the lake this weekend?"

A couple of beats passed.

"I'm not sure. But don't you always row on Sundays?"

"During the season, but we're kind of past that now. I didn't go to the lake the last two weekends."

"Well, I couldn't imagine you not rowing on such a beautiful day. Though I expect it was chilly this morning, wasn't it?" Her friend's tone remained conversational.

"Yes." Lindsey shivered despite the midday sun that was bathing the world outside the window in warm, golden light.

Which was crazy.

Why would she suddenly have misgivings about someone who'd never been anything but kind to her? After all, Madeleine knew she stretched out the rowing season as long as possible, weather permitting. Even if she hadn't mentioned lake plans for this weekend, it would be logical for her friend to assume she'd work in a session, given the warm temperatures.

There was no reason for Madeleine's question to stir up doubt.

Yet uncertainty appeared to be her lot today. Thanks to Jack Tucker's skepticism, she was also beginning to doubt whether someone had grabbed her ankle this morning.

Could she be losing it? Starting to come unglued? Was a breakdown in her—

". . . Chad and Dara, so I called them too."

Quashing her resurging panic, Lindsey tuned back in to the conversation. "Sorry. I got distracted for a minute. What did you say?"

"Chad and Dara weren't at church, either. I called Dara a few minutes ago. She didn't give me any details, but they had a very upsetting morning. The detective on the Robertson case paid them a visit."

Lindsey leaned back against the counter.

So that was why Jack had bailed on lake reconnaissance.

"Did she tell you what he wanted?"

"No. All she said was that he was following up on a new lead. Now I'll let you get back to whatever you were doing. I'm glad you were able to work in a rowing session this morning. I hope it relaxed you."

Hardly.

But Lindsey kept her comment more generic. "Rowing has always been my happy place."

Until today's experience had forever hosed her go-to scene for visualization exercises.

"We can all use one of those. And if the mild weather holds for a few more days, you may get in another session or two. Take care, and I'll talk to you soon."

Lindsey remained by the counter after the call ended, weighing the phone in her hand as she tried to quell the uneasiness rippling through her. To steady a world that suddenly felt off-balance.

Could her unsettled state be a delayed reaction to the frightening events of this morning, or had everything that had happened to her over the past twenty-one months taken a more serious toll on her mental stability than she'd thought?

Mounting evidence pointed toward the latter. Unless her mind was beginning to play tricks on her, why would she doubt a close friend like Madeleine or turn what may have been nothing more than an unfortunate accident into a sinister attack that perhaps had no basis in reality?

Fingers trembling, Lindsey set the cell on the counter as tendrils of fear twined around her windpipe, cutting off her air supply.

Another panic attack was looming.

No!

She wasn't going to let all the bad stuff that had happened mess with her mind. Whatever was going on, she'd get through it. And it wasn't as if she was in this alone. Dr. Oliver was in her corner.

In fact, why not call him now? He was always available to clients, and she could also set up an appointment for tomorrow or the next day. They'd talk this out, and she'd be fine. She would *not* lose her grip on reality.

As long as nothing else happened to rattle her world.

"I TOLD YOU not to bother me on weekends. This better be an emergency."

At the curt greeting from Matthew Nolan, Eric Miller swiped the sleeve of his T-shirt across his forehead and walked to the end of the deck behind his house, keeping watch on the door. This was not a conversation he wanted his wife to hear.

"There's been a new development."

"I'm listening."

"Robertson's wife came into the office Friday. Met with all the honchos. I got a memo this morning that she wants a complete report on all financials by the end of the month."

"So?"

"So there are discrepancies if anyone digs deep, as you know."

"A financial report isn't an audit."

"It could come to that. Apparently she intends to play a much bigger role in the company than anyone expected. She also wants to be briefed on pending deals. That would include the strip mall you're after."

Nolan was silent for a moment. "What's she like personally?"

"I don't know. She's always kept a low profile."

"Is she qualified to run the business?"

"I have no idea."

"If she plays as rough as her husband did, I'm not going to be happy." Nolan's voice hardened. "We may have to get aggressive in our efforts to dissuade her."

A wave of nausea rolled through Eric, and he tightened his grip on the burner phone. "I don't have the stomach for those kinds of games."

"It's a little late for second thoughts. You're already in this one. Here's what I want you to do. Find an excuse to talk to the wife on her next visit. Size her up and report back. In the meantime, I'll work my law enforcement connections, see if I can get more details about what the murder witness saw or heard. Let's hope she wasn't there during my phone conversation with Robertson . . . or doesn't start to remember details if she was. Otherwise, she could be a problem. Thanks to the wife, I'm already on the cops' radar. I don't want any more hassles—or anyone breathing down my neck and watching my every move."

A bead of moisture trickled down Eric's back, between his shoulder blades. The Sunday temperature was warm, but fear, not heat, had activated his sweat glands.

"I need my money, Nolan."

"Do your job, and you'll get it. The simple solution is to convince the wife the strip mall isn't a smart deal. One more thing. In the future, let's use texts. No chance of anyone overhearing that kind of conversation."

Nolan ended the call, and Eric slipped the cell into his pocket, fingers quivering.

He wasn't cut out for subterfuge.

But there was only one way to end this nightmare.

Get the man what he wanted.

Best case, James Robertson's wife would be easier to work with than her husband had been, Nolan would get his coveted strip mall, and the witness to the murder wouldn't know or remember anything that could come back to haunt them.

Worst case?

He wasn't even ready to think about that.

"WHAT HAPPENED to the chicken cordon bleu?"

"Change in plans." Jack responded to Bri's question as he peeled back the foil from the pan of lasagna. "I had to work this morning."

"Bummer. Your lasagna is amazing, but I was all geared up for chicken." Cara peeked into the other oven in the double set. "However, if that's Mom's green bean casserole, you're vindicated."

"It is."

She offered him a melancholy smile. "I love when you make that. It's almost like Mom is still with us."

The very reason his menus often included the casserole that had been a staple at family dinners until Mom died a year ago.

"I wish she *was* still with us. Dad too." Bri dipped her chin and adjusted a fork that was slightly askew in one of the place settings.

Jack dished up the first generous serving of lasagna and handed the plate to her. "They are."

"It's not the same." Bri sniffed.

His throat tightened, and he resorted to the wisecrack strategy he employed whenever his emotions got unruly. "Hey. No crying in my lasagna. It has plenty of salt already."

Bri made a face at him. "Ha-ha."

"At least you have someone new in your life." Cara directed that comment to their sister, then focused on him. "You want me to put the green beans on the table?"

"Yes. Thanks."

"There's someone out there for you too." Bri took the second plate he held out.

"Maybe."

Bri gave him a familiar look. The one that said "Let's work together to encourage Cara."

"You're only thirty-three, kiddo. It's not like you're over the hill." At Bri's eye roll, he shrugged. "What?"

"Your diplomatic skills leave something to be desired."

"I was just stating a fact. Thirty-three isn't old. You found someone, and you're thirty-four. The senior among us." As she liked to point out when it suited her, despite her mere six-month advantage over him.

"But I have issues." Cara set the casserole on the table and dug a serving spoon from his utensil drawer.

Bri jumped back in without giving him a chance to respond.

"I do too. We all do. Comes with the territory if you're a kid from a rough background. We're just lucky we got the best foster parents in the world, and that they adopted us. If I met a guy who could look past *my* problems, you can too."

"Mine are different than yours. But you may be right. Jack's older than me and he hasn't found anyone yet either."

"Don't be too sure about that." Bri relieved him of the last plate and set it on the table.

"What does that mean?" Cara paused, spoon in hand.

"Nothing. Let's say grace." He took his seat, bowed his head, and launched into a longer-than-usual blessing, tacking on a silent prayer that his siblings would drop the subject of romance.

"He met someone who interests him." Bri spoke the instant he finished the blessing.

So much for the plea he'd directed heavenward.

"Yeah? Tell me everything." Cara picked up her fork and aimed it at him.

"There's nothing to tell. I'm not dating anyone at the moment."

"Bri?" Cara turned to their sister for more information.

"I won't dispute our brother's statement, since I've never known him to lie, but I'll stick by my claim that he's met someone who's caught his eye."

"Who is she?"

"He'll have to answer that one. I'm sworn to secrecy because it's case-related."

Cara's head swiveled back toward him. "Okay. Spill it."

"There's nothing to spill."

Bri speared a green bean. "When's the last time you saw her?"

She *would* ask that question.

"Seeing someone in connection with an investigation doesn't qualify as a social call."

"Unless you fabricate a work excuse to contact her." Bri

arched her eyebrows as she chewed. "And you didn't answer my question. Telling."

His sisters knew him too well.

"I'm not in the market for romance." He shoveled in an extra-large forkful of lasagna.

"Why not?" Bri pinned him with the penetrating stare she usually reserved for fire scene investigation work.

He pointed to his mouth and continued to chew. Slowly.

"You're stalling." Bri angled toward Cara. "As a renowned historical anthropologist with keen insight into human behavior, what's your take on our brother's avoidance tactics?"

"I think that question is more the bailiwick of a psychologist."

At the mention of a psychologist, Jack stopped chewing as an image of Lindsey materialized in his mind.

"That got his attention." Bri tapped her index finger on the table, watching him. "The case you were called out for this morning wouldn't have been the Robertson murder, would it?"

He swallowed the mushy lasagna, since there was nothing left to chew. "I can't comment on an in-progress investigation."

"I'll take that as a yes—and an answer to my earlier question." Expression smug, she went back to eating.

"Does that mean this woman you like is related to a murder investigation?" Cara's gaze zipped back to him.

Their younger sister might think she had deficiencies that handicapped her in the romance department, but her intellect and instincts were second to none.

"This discussion is over. Don't forget to save room for dessert."

"I always have room for Mom's chocolate mint squares." Bri took a second helping of green beans. "I'm glad one of us makes them on a regular basis."

"Sorry. Not on the menu today. I ran out of time. But I have ice cream and sundae fixings."

"No chocolate mint squares?" Cara's face fell. "That was going to be my treat of the week."

"I promise I'll bake them for our next lunch. But I'd be happy to give you the recipe if you don't want to wait that long. It wouldn't hurt to expand your culinary repertoire beyond soup and omelets, you know."

"Why bother? We have a ton of great takeout places in Cape. Cooking isn't my thing."

"Trust me, we know. I almost broke a tooth on those ribs you made last spring."

"They weren't *that* bad."

Jack hiked up an eyebrow.

"Okay." She raised her palms in surrender. "I'll concede they were on the crunchy side. But I'm too busy to hone my cooking skills."

"If you're interested in finding a guy, you know what they say about the way to a man's heart."

"Oh, puhleeze." Bri set her fork down with a clatter. "You of all people should know cooking isn't gender specific. Would *you* care whether a woman you liked could cook?"

Another image of the personal chef who'd captured his fancy materialized in his mind.

"He's off in la-la land again." Cara cocked her head.

"Uh-huh. Maybe he's wondering if this woman he's interested in can put a decent meal together."

No need to wonder about that.

Besides, his interest in her had nothing to do with her skills in the kitchen.

"Could we change the subject, please? Cara, why don't you fill us in on the plans you mentioned for a research project?"

"Shall we let him off the hook?" His younger sibling deferred to their sister.

"I suppose we'll have to. He's not going to talk anyway.

And I've been wanting to hear more details about your plans too. The hints you dropped sounded fascinating."

Cara was more than happy to expound on the project she hoped to undertake during her fall sabbatical. It seemed there was a remote estate in southern Missouri that was home to journals written in an arcane French dialect only the reclusive owner could decipher, which Cara believed would contain a treasure trove of anthropological data. She was in the process of securing the owner's participation and applying for fellowships.

Jack listened with one ear while he mulled over next steps with Lindsey.

Based on that photo on her fridge, it wasn't hard to deduce the source of her antipathy toward him.

How to mitigate it was far less clear. Because the simple truth was that if he hadn't encouraged Clair to venture beyond her comfort zone, she'd still be alive.

He chased a lone green bean around his plate.

After four months of frequent dating, he should have realized the whitewater rafting outing he'd encouraged her to sign up for during her vacation would be too much of a stretch. Sweet as she was, she hadn't had an athletic bone in her body. In truth, much as he'd liked her, their leisure interests were polar opposites. Outdoor activities for him, needlepoint and afternoon tea for her.

In hindsight, it was clear a long-term relationship hadn't been in the cards for them and that it had been wrong to suggest she broaden her horizons with an activity more suited to his interests than hers.

He stabbed the bean, but instead of eating it, he laid his fork down.

Encouraging her to go whitewater rafting had been as misguided as someone privy to his background suggesting he go rock climbing, knowing it could be a recipe for disaster.

As the rafting had been for Clair after she'd fallen out of the boat, hit her head on a rock, and been dragged under the rapids.

The lasagna in his stomach hardened into a rock.

What had he been thinking?

And how was he ever going to make peace with the guilt that—

". . . lost him a while back."

At Bri's comment, he refocused on the conversation. "I've been listening." Sort of. "Those journals seem like they would be of more interest to a linguist than someone with your background." A shot in the dark, but if an arcane language was involved, his comment shouldn't be too far off base.

"Huh." Cara considered him. "Maybe he *was* listening."

"Nah. He's just good at faking it." Bri gave a dismissive wave. "You want to tell us what you were really thinking about—or can I guess?"

Instead of answering her question, he shifted his attention to Cara. "You ready for a sundae?"

"Yes. And for the record, if you *have* met someone, I hope it works out for you."

"I hope it does too. When the right woman comes along." He stood. "Bri, you want a sundae?"

"Yes. My sweet tooth will be satisfied, even if my curiosity won't." She heaved a theatrical sigh, rose, and began to clear the table. "If you do get serious about this woman, tell me we won't be the last to know."

"You'll be at the top of the list. But don't hold your breath."

"I don't know. I sense romance in the air."

Jack snorted. "Blame that on Marc."

"For what it's worth, I get the same vibes. And there's no Marc in my life." A hint of wistfulness threaded through Cara's words.

Jack gave her shoulder a squeeze. "Don't give up hope."

"No worries. Hope springs eternal and all that. But I'm fine either way. I mean, I have a wonderful life and a career I love and a fantastic family. What's to complain about, right?"

"Right." Nevertheless, there was much to be said for having someone to come home to at night. Or so he'd been thinking lately. "Three sundaes coming up."

During the remainder of his sisters' visit, the conversation transitioned to more neutral topics, their usual lighthearted banter and teasing a welcome interlude in what otherwise had been an emotional roller coaster of a day.

By the time he walked Bri and Cara to the door later in the afternoon, his mental state was much more upbeat.

Yet as he doled out hugs, waved them off, and turned to face his empty house, his dilemma came roaring back.

What could he say to Lindsey that would convince her to forgive him for the role he'd played in her friend's death?

THIRTEEN

"SORRY FOR SCHEDULING ANOTHER after-hours Monday appointment, Dr. Oliver. This is getting to be a bad habit."

"Like I told you last week, Lindsey, being here for clients during a crisis is part of my job." He handed her a bottle of water and took the seat he always claimed. "Tell me about the upsetting experience you mentioned on the phone."

"It's going to sound off the wall." Pulse picking up, she wrapped both hands around the bottle of water. "Crazy, almost."

He offered her an encouraging smile. "Trust me, I've heard more than my share of unusual stories. Crazy is too strong a word for most of them."

"Mine may be the exception."

"I'll give you my honest opinion after you share it with me. Fair enough?"

"Yes." After taking a swig of water, she launched into a condensed version of the lake incident and the doubts that had begun to infiltrate her mind about the accuracy of her perceptions.

Throughout her account, his expression remained neutral, giving no indication of his reaction.

When she finished, he tipped his head and studied her. "That's a very scary story."

"Because someone attacked me, or because the attack could be a figment of my imagination?"

His brief hesitation wasn't reassuring.

"Primarily the former. In the eighteen months you've been seeing me, I've never picked up any indication of compromised mental processes. That said, however, repeated stress *can* take a toll."

She frowned as her fingers tightened on the water bottle, producing a harsh crinkling sound in the quiet office. "I don't think the police detective is certain about my mental soundness after all the bizarre turns my life has taken of late."

"Let me ask you this. In your own mind, is there any doubt about where you left your car last week, or that a hand grabbed your foot at the lake?"

"No on the car. I'm not absentminded, and I remember parking it by the basketball hoop. The lake situation is a little different. I couldn't see much in the murky water. All I know is that whatever latched onto my ankle felt like fingers."

"It couldn't have been a submerged object?"

"I don't think so. My foot didn't just get caught. I was pulled down. Hard. I thought I was going to . . . to drown."

"Yet you didn't." He tapped his pen against his tablet. "Whatever—or whoever—this was, released you."

"Yes."

"Why?"

One of many questions she couldn't answer.

"I have no idea. I can't explain anything that happened yesterday. All I know is I ended the day very unsettled, questioning myself, and on the cusp of a panic attack."

Faint furrows scored his forehead. "You haven't had one of those in months. Not even after finding yourself at a murder scene."

"I know."

"When and where did it come on?"

She set the water bottle on the table beside her and wiped her palms down her slacks. "At home. After I told the detective about the South Carolina shooting."

His eyebrows peaked. "I thought you avoided talking about that incident."

"I usually do."

"What prompted you to discuss it with the detective?"

"I'm not certain. I'd referenced it in passing during one of our conversations, and when he came to take my statement about the lake, he asked me about it. I tried to put him off, but he said he was going to research it anyway. In the end, I decided to save him the trouble." Not a lie, but there had been more to her motivation than that—even if she hadn't pinpointed exactly what.

One more mystery to add to her growing list.

"I have to say I'm surprised."

"That makes two of us."

"Why did the detective care about South Carolina?"

"He wasn't specific. I got the impression he doesn't like to leave any stone unturned in an investigation. Plus I'm his star witness in the Robertson case. Not that I've been much help."

"He could be hoping you'll remember more."

"That's true. But other than the shoe brand I mentioned at our session on Thursday, no other details have come to mind. Do you think I could still remember anything helpful?"

He gave a slight shrug. "The human mind can sometimes surprise us, although memory does tend to become less reliable over time."

"So if I do happen to remember another detail or two, they might not be accurate."

"That's possible."

She sighed. "It probably doesn't matter if I do. After all that's happened, I think Detective Tucker will be inclined to take anything I say in the future with a grain of salt."

"I'm not worried about his perceptions. Only yours. Let's focus on you, and how you've been feeling now that you've had more than twenty-four hours to think about what happened. Any panic attack issues today?"

"No." She picked up the water again and rotated the bottle in her fingers. "But I'm starting to feel paranoid. I even began wondering whether I could trust a friend who called not long after the panic attack." She filled him in on her conversation with Madeleine.

He listened without speaking until she finished. "After you thought through the logic of her assumptions, did you still have doubts about her?"

"Not as much . . . but I couldn't shake them entirely. And that's not like me. I'm not the type to overreact or see threats where none exist. But I'm starting to feel like I need to keep looking over my shoulder."

"That sounds more like hypervigilance than paranoia to me. I often see it in people suffering from PTSD. Given all your recent trauma, a manifestation of hypervigilance wouldn't surprise me. I would expect it to eventually subside, like the panic attacks did."

"Except I came close to having one yesterday."

"Triggered for a logical reason. And you managed to contain it before it got out of control."

The knots in her shoulders loosened a hair. "So do you see any major cause for alarm in my mental state?"

Another hesitation.

"Not yet. If any more odd situations come up, we can reevaluate. At this point I'd suggest you continue to follow your usual schedule. That will help restore a sense of normalcy and balance to your life. You may want to avoid the lake for a couple of weeks, until you feel more settled, but don't neglect your exercise routine."

"I'm not planning to go back to the lake until next season, anyway. The weather's supposed to change tomorrow, and I'm not a cold-weather rower. I'll use my rowing machine on Wednesdays and Fridays for the winter and start my day with a run the rest of the week."

"Excellent. A predictable pattern will help you regain a sense of control. How did you sleep last night?"

"Not great."

"Understandable after what happened."

"I tried my usual relaxation techniques, but none of them helped. And I've been tense all day today too." Thanks not only to the lake incident, but to the mystery of why she'd opened up to Jack Tucker about South Carolina and why he'd taken off so fast afterward.

"Why don't we do a visualization? I have a new one I can walk you through that's been effective for most people."

"At this stage, I'll try anything."

Lindsey eased back into the cushions, closed her eyes, and let herself travel to the garden Dr. Oliver described. She took in the expanse of colorful blooms as the grass tickled her bare toes, touched the velvety softness of the rose petals, inhaled their sweet fragrance, listened to the trill of a cardinal.

By the time they finished, her tension had melted away.

"Better?" Dr. Oliver smiled.

"Much."

"Shall we schedule another appointment for later in the week? I know we'd decided to scale back to monthly visits, but in light of all that's happened, it may be wise to see each other more often for a while."

"I agree. I'll call tomorrow and see if Margie can find me a slot during regular office hours."

He stood. "If you have any problem scheduling, let me

know. And remember, if anything comes up, don't hesitate to call."

"I appreciate your accessibility."

"Always. Take care, and I hope you sleep better." He opened the private exit door.

"I'm sure I will."

She walked down the hall, her footsteps silent on the carpet in the professional building that was quiet at this hour, since most occupants were gone for the day.

Almost too quiet.

A shiver snaked through her, and she looked over her shoulder. Shook her head.

Must be the hypervigilance Dr. Oliver had mentioned. Not that caution was bad—as long as it didn't morph into paranoia. But he didn't seem overly concerned about that, nor about her mental state in general.

It was unfortunate Detective Tucker wasn't as convinced her mind was sound.

But what did it matter? Unless she remembered another relevant detail about James Robertson's killer, there would be no justification for further contact. And after his fast escape from her condo yesterday, he wasn't likely to seek her out.

Which was good, given her feelings about him. After all, while he exuded professional competence, he also came with a ton of baggage as far as she was concerned. And that wasn't a complication she needed in her life.

Yet as she hurried toward her car in the November darkness, the notion of not seeing him again didn't offer much solace.

Odd.

But whatever the explanation for that reaction, she'd get over it. If she never had to talk about the Robertson case again it would be too soon. And what were the odds another incident like yesterday's would bring them together?

Slim to none, which suited her fine. She could do without any more excitement in her life for the foreseeable future.

After sliding behind the wheel of her car, she locked the doors and tossed her purse onto the seat beside her.

Going forward, she'd follow Dr. Oliver's advice. Stick with her routine. Keep everything as normal as she could. Try not to worry about her mental state.

And hope nothing else happened to rock her life as that unseen force had rocked her scull in the early morning hours yesterday at Creve Coeur Lake.

THIS WAS HIS CHANCE.

Eric braced as Heidi Robertson exited her husband's office early Tuesday evening, long after most of the employees had left for the day and hours after she'd met with the key leadership for a briefing on financials and pending deals.

Fabricating an excuse to extend his day hadn't been difficult, even if it was out of pattern. But she didn't know anything about his usual work schedule, so this aberration wouldn't raise any red flags with her. And hanging around, waiting for an opportunity to talk to her alone, was about the only way he'd be able to get a handle on her personality along with a few insights into her business acumen, as Nolan had directed.

"Good evening, Ms. Robertson." He stepped forward as she strode toward the exterior door.

She paused, faint parallel creases denting her forehead. "Good evening."

He introduced himself and explained his role in the company. "I wanted to express my condolences on the loss of your husband."

"Thank you." She opened her purse and pulled out her keys.

"If there's anything I can help you with here at the office

while you get up to speed on the business, please let me know."

"I appreciate that." She glanced at her watch.

Not the most friendly person he'd ever encountered—but she'd just lost her husband, and people manifested grief differently.

If he didn't get her talking, however, he'd only be able to offer impressions, not information. Insufficient for a man like Nolan.

"I, uh, hope the police find answers for you quickly." An awkward segue, but it was the best he could come up with on the fly.

"They haven't found anything yet." The creases on her brow deepened. "Our chef was in the kitchen, but the only detail she's remembered hasn't been helpful."

What detail was that?

Did it have anything to do with the conversation between Nolan and Robertson?

If there was a diplomatic way to ask that question, it eluded him.

"I'm sorry to hear that."

"Well, I suppose she could remember more." She jiggled her keys. "Your name came up in the meeting this morning, in reference to a strip mall my husband was interested in acquiring. I believe you've been doing the due diligence on it, correct?"

"Yes."

"I'd like to go over the financial analysis with you Thursday. I'll be here part of the day. It seems to be an attractive opportunity. The balance sheet is impressive, and the income stream has been steady."

His pulse skittered.

That news wouldn't please Nolan.

Nor would he be happy to hear that Heidi Robertson appeared to have a decent mind for business.

"It does look solid on paper, but there are a few liabilities that don't show up in the numbers."

"Let's talk about them on Thursday. Have a nice evening." She continued down the hall.

He remained where he was until the door closed behind her, debating next moves.

Should he text Nolan?

Sweat broke out above his upper lip, and he swiped it away.

Why not wait until after he met with their new CEO? A quick conversation in the hall didn't provide much basis for evaluation. It was possible she wasn't as savvy about business matters as their brief exchange suggested.

Yet as he returned to his office to get his coat, Eric faced the truth.

Heidi Robertson wasn't an airhead trophy wife, as the office staff had joked when James married her eight years ago after his spouse of thirty-four years died of cancer.

She was smart—and from all indications more than capable of stepping into her husband's shoes. Perhaps all along, despite the low profile she'd kept, she'd been his trusted partner on the business front too. In fact, she might be as ruthless as he'd been. Potentially worse, since James had become more hard-hitting and less lenient about mistakes after his marriage.

None of which boded well for Nolan's plans to get the strip mall. Nor did it provide an incentive for him to pay off the insider who was supposed to smooth the path for a deal of a lifetime that seemed less and less likely to happen.

Meaning Nolan could resort to more drastic measures to beef up his odds.

Eric exhaled a shaky breath.

All he could do was hope that come Thursday, whatever case he built would convince Heidi to write off the strip mall and finally get him out of the corner he'd painted himself into.

FOURTEEN

DARA WAS A MESS.

As Lindsey circulated among the students during the final minutes of her Tuesday Cooking on a Budget class, she kept tabs on the younger woman.

Losing your grip on a container of pasta and sending the tiny shells flying every direction could happen to anyone. That was a one-off. But dropping the whole batch of take-home menu sheets while handing them out to the class? And the worry etched in Dara's features?

She was seriously stressed.

"Let me help you." Lindsey crossed to her and bent down, gathering up the wayward papers.

"I'm sorry." Dara kept her chin down as she issued the tear-laced apology. "I shouldn't have come tonight."

"Of course you should. Can you stay for a few minutes afterward? I have tea in my satchel. There's nothing more soothing than a cup of peppermint tea after a rough day."

"I don't know." She bit her bottom lip. "Chad will be worried if I'm late."

"Why don't you call him? I'll be happy to walk you to your car if he's concerned about your safety."

"I guess I could do that." She motioned toward the papers Lindsey had collected. "I'll finish passing those out."

Ten minutes later, after the rest of the class had departed, Lindsey dug out two bags of tea from her satchel and held them up. "The perfect antidote to stress. I could use a cup myself."

"Are you sure you don't mind staying late?"

"Not at all." She pulled mugs from the cabinet, filled them with water, and motioned to a pair of stools against the wall. "Why don't you move those over to the prep island and I'll join you as soon as the tea is ready?"

Dara complied, but she remained standing as she angled away and spoke in a low voice on her cell, the staccato tap of her foot another indication of her anxiety.

At the *bing* from the microwave, Lindsey removed the mugs, circled the island, and claimed a stool. She smiled as Dara ended the call. "Chad okay with the delay?"

"Yes." The other woman perched on the edge of the adjacent seat and gripped her mug with both hands.

Taking a sip of tea, Lindsey appraised her over the rim of her mug.

Had law enforcement—in the person of Jack Tucker—paid the newlyweds another call? Was that why Dara was upset? Or was this residual anxiety from his Sunday visit?

Whatever the cause, would a sympathetic ear help her decompress?

Only one way to find out.

"I've been wondering how you and Chad are doing." Lindsey chose her words with care, maintaining a conversational tone. "For me, it's been tough ever since the Robertson murder. I've been super frazzled. It doesn't help that the police haven't solved the crime yet, either."

"I know." Dara tucked her hair behind her ear and stared into the reddish-brown brew. "Have the cops been bothering you much?"

"On and off. I remembered one detail about the killer, and they're hoping I'll remember more." No reason to mention the bizarre lake incident that had prompted her latest interaction with law enforcement.

"They've been bugging us too. The main detective came by on Sunday."

Lindsey kept her manner nonchalant. "Why?"

Fingers trembling, Dara lifted the cup. "I think they still suspect Chad."

"Without evidence, suspicions won't amount to anything."

Dara swallowed. "They have some evidence. But it's all circumstantial."

That was news.

"I don't think circumstantial evidence would give them sufficient grounds to press charges, if that's worrying you."

"I hope not. But all the attention is making our life pretty miserable." Her voice caught, and she dipped her head.

Pressure built in Lindsey's throat, and she touched Dara's shoulder. "What does Chad say about all this?"

"Not much. That's part of the problem." She let out a shuddering breath and peeked over. "I really need to talk to someone, but I don't have any close friends here yet."

"I think of you as a friend. And I'd be happy to lend an ear if that would help."

Dara chewed on her lower lip again. "Will you keep everything I tell you in confidence?"

"Yes. I promise."

While Dara took a tiny sip of her tea, indecision tightening her features, Lindsey waited. Pushing would be a mistake.

At last the other woman spoke. "You know Chad's background, right?"

"The basics."

"It sort of sets him up for suspicion, you know?"

"Does he have a record?"

"No, but a former street person is always going to raise red flags if they get connected to a murder."

"You mentioned circumstantial evidence. Do you feel comfortable sharing anything about that with me?"

"Yes. As long as you keep it to yourself."

Lindsey listened as Dara filled her in on the earring the police had found on the running board of Chad's truck and the stolen bracelet—supposedly from Chad—that his homeless friend had tried to pawn, prompting the most recent visit from Jack.

Hard as she tried to maintain a neutral expression, Lindsey struggled to hide her dismay. While none of what Dara had relayed was incriminating, it would definitely bump Chad higher on the suspect list even if he denied any knowledge of the circumstances in both cases.

"Chad explained it all to the detective, but I don't know if he believed him." A tear trickled down Dara's cheek.

"Suspicions don't count. Under the law, you're innocent until proven guilty." All true, but that sort of evidence would result in intense and upsetting scrutiny. "You don't think Chad's homeless friend may have been trying to set him up, do you?"

"No." She launched into an account of their relationship. "But I didn't know any of that until Sunday. I didn't even know Chad was staying in touch with this man. He said he kept it a secret because he didn't want me to worry about him going down there."

A man under suspicion, a wife in the dark, a detective on the hunt.

What a mess.

No wonder Dara was jittery.

Lindsey inhaled the soothing mint aroma rising from her mug before she spoke. "How do you feel about Chad not telling you he was visiting his friend?" Best to phrase it like that than flat-out ask if she believed her husband's story.

152

Dara exhaled. "Kind of . . . betrayed, I guess. And blindsided. I mean, I get that he was trying to protect me, but a man and wife shouldn't keep secrets from each other, should they?"

"Probably not in most cases, but it does sound as if his intentions were good."

"Yeah." Dara scrubbed a finger against a blemish on the stainless-steel prep counter. "But I keep wondering . . . if Chad didn't tell me about his friend, what else hasn't he told me?"

"About the case?"

"Or anything." Moisture pooled on her lower eyelids, clumping her lashes. "I love him, Lindsey, and I've always trusted him. But I . . . I don't know what to believe anymore. I think he's being honest with me, but there's this little twinge of doubt I can't get rid of. And that's wrong, isn't it? I mean, I shouldn't have any doubts, should I?"

Lindsey took a sip of tea. If only Dr. Oliver were here. He'd know how to advise a troubled young bride.

But maybe Dara wasn't seeking advice. She might just want to vent, to speak the fears she'd been bottling up inside. Verbalizing concerns often helped relieve stress, as she knew firsthand. And a few words of reassurance wouldn't hurt, either.

"I don't think you should beat yourself up about this, Dara. You and Chad have had a lot thrown at you these past couple of weeks. When your world is turned upside down, it's normal to begin questioning everything. Has Chad ever done anything until now that made you doubt him?"

"No."

"Do you feel safe with him?"

"Yes." Zero hesitation. "And I know he loves me."

"Then it may be best to give him the benefit of the doubt. Everyone makes mistakes. Not telling you about his trips downtown, no matter how well-intentioned, could have been one of Chad's. Maybe the best thing you can do is put that aside and move forward from here. Letting an error in judgment forever shape your image of someone might be as big of a mistake as misguidedly keeping secrets. One that could change your relationship permanently."

Some of the tension in Dara's features dissipated, and the corners of her mouth rose a smidgen. "You know what? That's exactly what I needed to hear. My brain kept getting more and more muddled as I tried to think this through. You were able to be impartial about it and cut past all the doubts that were cluttering up my head."

"Sometimes it helps to get a third-party opinion."

Dara picked up her tea and drained the mug. "Thank you for the tea and the chat."

"My pleasure. Shall I walk you to your car?"

"Why don't we walk out together?"

"I'm going to stay and do a final touch-up here. I don't want the Horizons cooking classes to lose their happy home."

"I could stay and help you."

"Thanks, but you should go home to that new husband of yours. I'll bet he's counting the minutes until you arrive."

"He did say he'd be waiting for me." A tiny dimple dented her cheek.

"Good man."

"Are you sure you'll be okay here by yourself?"

"No worries. I do this every week."

After Dara gathered up her coat and notebook, Lindsey walked out with her and gave her a hug.

Dara squeezed back. "Thank you again for tonight—and for caring."

"Like I said, I consider us friends. I'll call in a few days to see how everything is going."

Lindsey stepped back as Dara got in her car, waving as the

other woman drove toward the exit. Then she returned to the kitchen and did a fast, final cleanup.

Once the space was pristine, she put on her coat and picked up her satchel. Thank goodness the past two days had been normal. Her early morning runs had been invigorating, every item on her grocery lists had been available during her shopping trips, and she'd picked up a new client. Not a bad way to begin the week.

The only dark cloud on the horizon was a return trip to the Robertson house on Thursday. But it was either that or lose a steady, well-paying client, and her business was too new to justify dropping someone because the thought of returning to the traumatic scene turned her stomach.

She'd get through it, though.

Satchel in hand, she trekked to the door, locked it, and pulled it shut behind her as she stepped outside.

From within the small pool of illumination cast by the security light, she scanned the dim, deserted parking lot as Jack Tucker's description of the area from the day he'd driven her here to retrieve her car echoed in her mind.

No, it wasn't the best part of town. But she'd never worried much about that before. And she wouldn't start tonight. Alertness usually prevented trouble, and she was always mindful of her surroundings.

Walking toward her car at a fast clip, she kept a sharp eye on the lot, the hypervigilance Dr. Oliver had mentioned kicking in.

But no one was about on this chilly night.

As she approached her Focus, however, a car swung into the lot, its headlights arcing across her. Pulse accelerating, she shaded her eyes from the blinding glare and picked up her pace.

Thankfully, it seemed the driver had no nefarious purpose

in mind and was using the lot to execute a U-turn. The car did a three-sixty and rolled back out to the street.

Left once again in semidarkness, Lindsey leaned against her car and blinked to clear the spots from her vision. Just as she'd done the day of the murder, when a shaft of sunlight from the roof window above the island where she'd cowered had pierced her eyes.

She took a steadying breath as those moments replayed in her mind.

Her vision had been compromised for a few seconds as she'd eyed the vase she'd hoped wouldn't have to double as a defensive weapon. But it had started to clear as the killer bent down to pick up the piece of dropped jewelry—and the sleeve of their jacket had pulled up briefly to reveal part of the forearm.

She closed her eyes. Tried to call up that image.

There had been color on the patch of exposed skin. A bruise, perhaps? Except it had had a more defined shape, hadn't it? Like a . . . tattoo?

Or had she imagined that? After all, she'd had no more than a quick glimpse, and the lingering sunspots in her vision could have played tricks on her eyes.

But what if they hadn't?

What if what she'd seen had been real?

Should she tell Jack about this?

Mind racing, Lindsey slid behind the wheel of her car. Locked her doors. Started the engine.

Telling him could be risky. He already had doubts about her reliability. In this case, even *she* wasn't certain about what she'd seen—if it had been anything at all.

Maybe she ought to think it through, wait until morning to settle on a course of action. If she passed on any more dubious information, her credibility as a witness would be shot.

As would her credibility, period. Jack would write her off as a delusional woman who'd succumbed to too much stress.

For whatever reason, the loss of personal credibility with him bothered her more than the idea of him dismissing her value as a witness.

She pulled out of the parking lot and aimed her car toward home.

It was too late in the evening to analyze that odd reaction, especially after listening to Dara's dilemma and doing her best to offer counsel and support.

Besides, in light of the younger woman's predicament, her own quandary paled in comparison. She wasn't dealing with a new husband who could end up being accused of murder.

So she'd sleep on the situation and decide tomorrow how much, if anything, to tell Jack.

Assuming she didn't wake up as uncertain about the accuracy of the new memory that had surfaced as she was about what had really happened at the lake.

FIFTEEN

A CALL FROM LINDSEY BARNES.

Jack's mouth bowed.

That was a midweek treat, even if he still had no idea what to say to her about his culpability in Clair's death.

He detoured into the empty headquarters break room, put the cell to his ear, and greeted her.

"Good morning, Detective. Do you have a minute?"

"Yes. How can I help you today?"

"I have some . . . pass . . . may be . . . the case."

He squinted at a scuff mark on the wall. "Sorry. You're breaking up. Can you say that again?"

". . . range, so . . . unreliable reception . . . different area."

"I'm missing most of what you're saying." But if it was related to the Robertson case, he needed to hear it.

"Why don't . . . text, or I could . . . afternoon? I'm on . . . client's house."

Jack blew out a breath.

So much for the wonders of technology.

"If this is about the Robertson case, I'd rather not wait." Because at the moment, they were dead in the water with that investigation. "Are you in your car?"

"Yes, but . . . spotty . . . towers."

"Where are you?"

It took three tries, but he finally managed to decipher her location. Naturally, it was one of the worst areas in the city for cell coverage.

But she wasn't far from the Windsor Tea Room, and if she hadn't been there before, she might enjoy stopping in while she shared whatever she had to tell him.

"If you can spare a few minutes, I could meet you to discuss this."

". . . shopping early, so . . . give you half . . ."

"That works." Whatever she'd said, he'd *make* it work. "You're close to a spot that has quiet corners for conversation." He gave her the name and address. "Did you get that?"

"Yes."

"I can be there in twenty minutes."

"Okay . . . you then."

Jack pocketed the phone and pulled out his keys. While he'd keep his fingers crossed that whatever information she had was helpful, he'd also find a way to bring up Clair during their discussion. It would be disingenuous to pretend he hadn't seen the photo and put two and two together. Now that he understood the rationale for Lindsey's antipathy, he had to try and clear the air.

Keys in hand, he swung around to find Cate watching him.

"Morning." She lifted her Starbucks cup in salute and took a sip.

"Morning."

"Where's my chocolate mint square?"

Oh yeah. He'd promised to bring her a piece of the dessert he'd planned to bake on Sunday.

"I didn't get around to making it. Duty called."

"I heard about the lake caper."

The office grapevine was alive and well.

"That, plus a lead on the Robertson case."

"I heard about that too. Anything surface to corroborate the lake story?"

"No."

"Strange situation. Like the car incident."

"Yeah." If she was expecting him to say more, or speculate about Lindsey's reliability, she was out of luck.

"So you're off to a tearoom, huh?"

Oh, man. He'd never hear the end of this.

"They happen to have excellent food."

"I know. I've been there. I'm surprised *you* have."

"One of my sisters wanted to go to afternoon tea for her birthday." Otherwise he'd never have ventured inside. But they'd had heartier fare in the display cases up front, which had been more his style than the bite-sized delicacies he'd shared with his sisters. And there'd been a few guys in that section of the shop.

"Ah. Mystery solved." She took another sip of her java. "Your star witness ought to appreciate the traditional British tea fare, given her profession."

How much of their conversation had she overheard?

"We're not going to tea. She's in that neighborhood, and she has more information to pass on. It was a convenient meeting place."

"She couldn't share this information by phone?"

"Bad connection."

"Uh-huh."

He jingled his keys. "If what she's got is about the Robertson case, I'm not waiting until she has better cell service to find out."

"I agree we could use a break on that one. And I hope this rendezvous has a more definitive outcome than the lake situation. Of course, if nothing else you'll be able to enjoy a treat."

"True. They have great scones. Or I may get something heartier and call it lunch."

Cate's lips twitched. "I wasn't referring to food."

"What's that supposed to mean?" He planted his fists on his hips and gave her his most intimidating interrogator glower.

It had zero impact. "You're the detective. Figure it out."

"You know what? You're as bad as my sisters."

"I've met your sisters. I'll take that as a compliment. Good luck today—on all fronts." She lifted her coffee again and sauntered out of the break room.

He mashed his lips together as she disappeared into the hall.

Insinuations about his interest in Lindsey were getting old. From Cate *and* Bri.

But he ought to let them roll off his back. Until the Robertson case concluded, his dealings with Lindsey would remain professional—except for whatever explanation he was going to give her about Clair.

A subject that deserved his full and undivided attention during the drive downtown.

Unfortunately, he was no closer to figuring out a game plan twenty minutes later as he pulled up on the side street beside the tearoom and parallel parked behind Lindsey's Focus.

He'd have to wing it and hope for a burst of eloquence when an opening came up to broach the subject.

Inside the door he paused to scan the shop.

Lindsey had claimed a table for two in the corner of the front window, and at this late-morning hour they had the dining area almost to themselves. The only other customer was seated much closer to the display counter, giving them privacy.

Ideal for the conversation they were about to have.

Lindsey raised a hand in greeting, and he moved across the room to join her.

"Have you been here long?" He stopped beside the table.

"About ten minutes. I ordered a pot of the house blend. I hope that's okay."

"Fine. What can I get you to eat?"

"I have a piece of shortbread coming. All of their sweets are excellent, but if you're in the mood for more substantial food, I can recommend the Cornish pasty or sausage roll. The scones are delicious too."

"You sound like a regular customer."

"I wouldn't go that far, but I have a couple of clients in this area, and if I have a few minutes to spare, I like to stop in for a cup of tea. It's calming on a hectic day."

"Let me put in an order and I'll be right back."

"Don't rush on my account. My shopping today went faster than expected, and the groceries are fine in the cold car."

Despite her reassurance, he placed a quick order for a Cornish pasty and returned just as a server delivered their tea and Lindsey's shortbread.

"Go ahead and eat." He motioned to her snack. "They said it would take a few minutes to warm mine up."

"I can wait." She hefted the teapot and set about filling their cups, shooting him a quick glance. "I don't think what I have to say warranted a trip downtown for you."

"It was hard to tell from the broken conversation, and any lead at this point is worth whatever effort it takes to get."

She set the pot down. "Should I assume there hasn't been much progress with the case?"

"It's still high on our radar, and we're investigating a few persons of interest, but there have only been a handful of significant developments."

"I doubt my new piece of information will fall into that category." She sipped her tea. "I understand from Chad's wife that he may be one of your more serious persons of interest."

He picked up his cup. "What did she tell you?"

"About the earring wedged in the running board of his truck and the bracelet he supposedly gave his homeless friend to pawn. She's very upset."

"Justifiably so. That's compelling evidence."

"Also circumstantial—and convenient."

"Did she say that?"

"No. That's my take. Don't you think the notion that someone could be trying to set Chad up is credible?"

"I haven't ruled anything out." Truth be told, the evidence implicating Chad Allen didn't quite ring true, as Cate had noted the day of the murder.

"I'm glad you're keeping an open mind. I can't see Chad being involved in robbery, let alone murder."

"But someone out there is, and it's my job to find them. Why don't you tell me your new information?"

She broke off a bite of shortbread but didn't eat it. "I remembered something else about the killer."

His pulse kicked up a notch.

That was the best news he'd had all week.

"Tell me about it."

He listened as she described her experience in the parking lot last night, and the memory it had prodded loose.

"Here's the thing." Her brow puckered as she pressed a finger against a crumb from the broken piece of shortbread. "I was half-blinded from the sun. I think I saw what I described to you, and I think the mark on the arm was a pattern rather than random markings. Like a tattoo. But all I had was a fast glimpse. It's possible my eyes were playing tricks on me."

He tapped a finger against the tabletop. "I can see how it could be hard to determine whether the markings were a pattern with only a quick look, but are you also suggesting there may have been no markings at all?"

"I don't know what I'm suggesting." She sighed and pinched the bridge of her nose. "With all the confusing experiences I've had lately, I feel shell-shocked. I was going to wait to tell you about this until I was sure, but I hated seeing Dara so upset last night. I decided to share it with you on the off chance it would help identify the culprit and take some of the pressure off Dara and Chad."

The server delivered his food, buying him a few seconds to digest Lindsey's news.

If the killer did, in fact, have a tattoo, Lindsey's information could be very helpful. If what she'd spotted wasn't a tattoo, less so. Assuming she'd seen anything at all.

"You're wondering if what I've told you has any basis in reality, aren't you?" She popped a piece of the shortbread into her mouth, her posture taut.

Whatever other deficiencies she may have, her ability to read people was top-notch.

"I'm weighing the probabilities."

She offered him the facsimile of a smile. "That's a tactful way to put it. Do they teach diplomacy in detective school along with interrogation skills?"

"No. But according to my sisters, I would have benefitted from a class or two on that subject."

As that admission spilled out, he frowned.

Why on earth had he mentioned his family? It had no relevance to the topic at hand.

Whatever his motivation, the information seemed to intrigue her.

"How many sisters do you have?"

"Two."

"Older or younger?"

"One of each. Bri's six months older, Cara's six months younger."

Lindsey's forehead knotted. "I'm having trouble with that math."

Oh yeah. Anyone who didn't know his background would be confused.

"We're foster siblings. Our foster parents took us in after we were pulled from bad situations. They ended up adopting us." And that was all he was going to say on the subject. He'd already told her more than he told most people. "Let me ask you a few questions about what you saw on the killer's arm."

She hesitated, as if she wanted to delve deeper into his personal history, but in the end took his cue. "Okay."

"Which arm was it on?" After pulling out his notebook and pen, he bit into his pasty.

"The right."

"How big was it?"

"I don't know. It started about three inches above the wrist and disappeared into the coat."

"What color was it?"

"Dark blue or black."

"Any other colors?"

"Not that I could see."

"Can you give me any idea about the shape? Focus on the outline."

Her eyelids fluttered closed, as if she was trying to visualize the mark, but at last she shook her head. "I can't call up any detail. I do have an appointment with my psychologist later this afternoon, though. Do you want me to see if he has any techniques that could help me remember more—or determine if what I saw was even real?"

"It couldn't hurt." He closed his notebook and continued to eat while he processed all Lindsey had told him.

If what she'd seen was real, and if the killer did have a tattoo, this could be a huge break.

But those were two big ifs, especially in light of her bizarre experiences last week.

Maybe her psychologist would be able to dig out a few details that were buried in her psyche, however.

"Would you like to talk to Dr. Oliver?"

At her quiet question, he cocked his head. "Why?"

"He can give you his read on my mental stability."

"I never said I doubted it."

"You didn't have to." She finished the last of her shortbread, brushed the crumbs off her fingers, and reached for the purse she'd slung over the back of her chair. "In your shoes, I'd have plenty of doubts too."

When she rose, he tossed his napkin onto the table and stood. He'd vowed to tell her about Clair before this meeting ended, and if he didn't speak up fast, she'd be out the door.

"Can you give me ten more minutes?"

She remained by the table. "Aren't we done?"

"With business."

Her fingers flexed on the strap of her purse, her expression wary. "What does that mean?"

He took a steadying breath, trying to dispel a sudden case of nerves.

He could use her Dr. Oliver about now. The man was no doubt excellent at mediating true confession sessions and calming stormy waters.

"I've been wondering since the day we met why you've given me the cold shoulder. I think I figured it out Sunday." He fisted his hands at his sides and braced. "I saw the photo of you and Clair on your refrigerator door. She never told me your last name, or I'd have made the connection sooner."

Lindsey inhaled sharply, her features slackening as comprehension dawned. "I should have realized you'd seen that."

"I'd like to talk to you about her."

The sudden shimmer in her irises ate at his gut. "Did you know we were best friends?"

"Yes. I also understand why you'd blame me for what hap-

166

pened to her. If it's any consolation, I blame myself too. And nothing I've done for the past three years has helped ease that guilt. All I'm asking you to do today is listen. You don't have to say anything."

The sudden faint indentations on her brow telegraphed her indecision.

If she bolted, he'd let her go and hope that once the shock wore off, she'd reconsider and be more receptive when he broached the subject again.

With every second that ticked by, his hopes diminished. She wasn't ready to—

"Ten minutes." She retook her seat.

Shifting gears, he sat again too and plunged in. "I assume Clair told you about me?"

"Yes." Her features hardened. "In case you didn't know it, she was falling in love with you."

The pasty he'd eaten congealed in his gut. "I began to suspect that in hindsight, but we only dated for four months."

"It doesn't always take long to know when you meet the right person."

"Is that personal experience speaking?" The question was out before he could stop it.

Interestingly, she didn't take offense.

"No. That's what I've observed."

"Is that how it was with your parents?"

She stiffened. "You want to waste your ten minutes talking about my parents?"

Huh.

She was fine with a question about her love life, but she didn't want to talk about her parents.

There was a story there. And not a happy one, if he was reading her body language correctly.

But that was a subject for another day.

"Sorry. I'll stay on topic. Clair was a lovely person, and I enjoyed our dates, but it wouldn't have worked between us long term. We were too different."

"If you knew that, why did you encourage her to go white-water rafting? Surely you knew after months of dating that those kinds of activities weren't her thing."

"Yeah, I did. And I wish I had a good answer to your question." He raked his fingers through his hair. "By that point, I was beginning to wonder if we had enough in common to sustain a relationship. But I liked Clair a lot. I guess I hoped that if she was exposed to more adventurous activities, she might enjoy them. That if we could find more common interests, there might be a future for us. But in hindsight I realize that was a mistake. When I talked to her parents at the funeral, I took full blame for what happened. I would have told you that too, but in the crush of people at the service, we never connected."

A muscle beside Lindsey's eye twitched, and she turned toward the window that offered a view of the gray urban landscape on this cold day. "I wasn't there."

It took a few seconds for her hoarse comment to register. Once it did, he had no idea how to respond.

She turned back to him. "Did you know I was supposed to go to that dude ranch with her?"

He searched his memory. Came up blank. "She may have mentioned it in passing, but if she did, it didn't register."

"Well, I was. We'd signed up for it months before. I was excited about the horseback riding and hiking and learning how to fly fish. She was looking forward to reading by the infinity pool, the gourmet meals, and the spa."

"Why didn't you go?"

"I'd been saving up for an intensive five-week Le Cordon Bleu seminar in Paris. The session I wanted to take wasn't offered that often. Not long after Clair and I booked our trip, I found out the course was being held in a few months—and it overlapped with our trip. Clair encouraged me to go, said we could change our plans, but we would have lost a lot of money. So I talked her into going alone." Distress etched her features. "I shouldn't have bailed on her. If I'd been there, I would have tried to convince her to skip the rafting rather than push herself beyond her comfort level—or I'd have gone with her."

Jack exhaled.

It appeared he wasn't the only one with regrets.

Hers, however, were far less deserved than his.

"I think your guilt is misplaced. I'm the one who suggested she give whitewater rafting a try. And I'm guessing that if she cared about me as much as you say, she may have done it to please me."

"That's my take too. But me backing out of our trip was also a factor."

He swirled the dregs of his tea, a few fugitive leaves clinging to the side of the cup. "What-iffing and second-guessing doesn't change anything. But for whatever it's worth, I'm sorry I ever mentioned it to Clair."

"I'm sorry you did too. It's better to accept people as they are than try to change them."

The sudden hurt deep in her eyes suggested that comment wasn't just about Clair. That there was a personal component to it.

What was Lindsey's story?

Not a subject he could broach today, with the clock winding down on his allotted ten minutes.

"I agree. And for the record, that was out of pattern for me. If I had it to do again, I wouldn't encourage Clair to go rafting. I'm sorrier than I can say for the loss of your friend, and I understand why you'd hold that against me. But I hope at some point you can forgive me for my mistake."

She searched his face, then dipped her chin and pulled out her keys. "Thank you for sharing all that with me."

No offer of forgiveness—but that would have been too much to hope for while she was still digesting his confession.

"Since we may need to have more conversations, I thought it would be better to address the issue. Try to clear the air between us."

"I appreciate that." She stood, and he rose too. "I'll talk to Dr. Oliver and see what he thinks about the memory that surfaced. If I have anything worthwhile to report, I'll text you."

"Thanks. I'll walk you out."

"Don't bother."

"It's not a bother. My mom taught me to always escort a lady to her door—or her car."

The corners of Lindsey's lips rose a hair. "Clair said you were a gentleman."

"Mom would have been pleased to hear that."

She tipped her head. "Past tense?"

"She died a year ago."

"I'm sorry." Compassion softened her features.

"Thanks. Losing Dad was hard enough, but when your second parent dies . . ." He swallowed past the tightness in his throat. "There's a finality to it, an emptiness, that's hard to deal with. Do you still have both your parents?"

"No. My dad died twelve years ago. No siblings, either. I was an only child."

"At least you have your mom."

"Yeah." She averted her gaze and walked toward the door, leaving him to follow—and wonder about that less-than-warm response. Must be issues there.

He reached beyond her to pull the door open, inhaling a sweet, spicy scent that fit this personal chef whose orbit had intersected with his.

As they parted at her car and he watched her drive away, that appealing aroma lingered in the air. Like thoughts of the intriguing woman who'd known too much trauma in her life and apparently had skeletons in her closet, just as he did.

Perhaps one day she'd tell him about them.

For now, though, he'd simply be grateful for her willingness to listen to what he'd had to say, and hope their paths crossed again soon.

But for reasons that didn't involve murders, missing cars, boating accidents—or danger of any kind.

SIXTEEN

"GOOD MORNING."

At the greeting from behind her in the Robertson kitchen, Lindsey spun around, sending a handful of grated cheese spewing over the countertop and onto the floor.

Heidi stood in the doorway. "Oh, I'm sorry. I didn't mean to startle you."

Trying to rein in her galloping pulse, Lindsey gripped the edge of the granite behind her. "No worries. I was, uh, lost in thought."

Not a lie. She'd been replaying her session with Dr. Oliver yesterday and thinking about her tearoom exchange with the detective who was beginning to dominate her thoughts.

"I don't want to disturb you, but I was hungry for the first time in two weeks and decided to scramble an egg or eat some yogurt before I go to James's office." Heidi sniffed and pulled out a tissue. "To be honest, I was also lonely. The house feels so empty and quiet."

Lindsey's throat tightened. Her client might not have been the warmest person in the past, but tragedy could shake anyone's world, leave them feeling vulnerable—as she knew from

172

personal experience. It wasn't difficult to empathize with someone going through that ordeal.

"Why don't I make you an omelet?"

"Won't that interrupt your cooking?"

"No. I'm at a stopping place. I can put everything on hold for ten minutes." She gathered up the grated cheese littering the floor and counter and tossed it in the trash as she responded.

"Well, if you're certain . . ." Heidi slid onto a stool at the island. "Thank you. And I also appreciate your willingness to continue on as my personal chef. I know it has to be hard to come back here after . . . after everything that's happened."

"I don't like to disappoint people, or renege on commitments." Lindsey crossed to the fridge and removed a carton of eggs, along with a container of mushrooms.

"Admirable traits. Ones that sometimes seem in short supply in today's world." Heidi rested her elbows on the granite countertop and linked her fingers. "At least the lead detective on James's case appears to be dedicated to his job. But I don't think the police are making much headway." She sighed.

"I wish I could have been more help." Lindsey sliced a few mushrooms and put a pat of butter in a small sauté pan.

"I'm sure you told them everything you know."

"Yes, but it wasn't much."

"Detective Tucker mentioned the shoe brand you noticed."

"As far as I know, that didn't lead anywhere. But I did remember one other thing." As she added the mushrooms to the sizzling butter, she described the mark she'd seen on the person's arm. The same information she intended to share with Dara later today when she called to check in with her. Hopefully that would help relieve her mind about Chad.

Heidi's forehead crimped. "That could be an important new detail. Have you told the detective?"

"Yes." She whipped up eggs, milk, and chives and poured the mixture into another pan.

"What did he say?"

"He listened, but I have no idea where it will go from there—if anywhere."

"Why wouldn't he follow up? He struck me as conscientious. I can't imagine him not investigating a lead like that."

"Unless I remember more about it, there's not much to investigate. Besides, I've had a couple of . . . strange . . . experiences over the past week that haven't helped my credibility." Enough about that. "Would you like a cup of coffee with your omelet?"

"I already have a cup. James kept a small coffeemaker in his office. He liked to have his caffeine close at hand." A tear brimmed on her lower lashes. "Sorry. I can't get used to the fact that he's g-gone."

"I can't begin to imagine how hard this must be for you." Lindsey continued to put the omelet together by rote, adding the mushrooms and folding the eggs over at the appropriate stage of doneness.

"It's like a nightmare that—" She stopped and withdrew her phone from the pocket of her slacks. Checked the screen. "Sorry. It's James's office. I have to take this." She stood.

"Shall I bring your omelet to the study when it's ready?"

"Yes. Thank you." She put the phone to her ear and greeted the caller in a businesslike tone.

Lindsey finished the omelet, walked it down the hall, and set it on the burnished desk in the study after Heidi motioned her in with a distracted wave, obviously more interested in the call than the food.

After exiting quietly, she retraced her steps to the kitchen and continued preparing the dishes Heidi had selected for this week's menu, her mind only half on the task.

Strange how life worked.

Like . . . what were the odds that she'd have been in this kitchen at the very time the killer was here? Or that the detective assigned to the case would be the man who'd captured Clair's heart? Or that her hostility toward Jack Tucker would not only begin to soften, but morph into . . . attraction?

And that's what it was, whether she wanted to admit it or not.

She sprinkled chopped garlic into the olive oil marinade for the salmon entrée, the pungent aroma swirling around her.

Truth be told, it was hard not to like a man who was willing to admit his mistakes. Who acknowledged culpability and felt guilty about errors in judgment. Who came across as dedicated and conscientious, as Heidi had noted. Who radiated integrity and honesty.

As she stirred the marinade, her comment to Dara on Tuesday about how everyone makes mistakes replayed in her mind. As did her suggestion that the younger woman put Chad's transgression aside and move forward. That it wasn't wise to let one error in judgment forever shape your image of someone.

Lindsey winced as she added a splash of lemon juice to the marinade.

If she believed what she'd told Dara, she'd give Jack a second chance. Accept that a person who made a bad judgment call wasn't necessarily a bad person.

Just as she wasn't a bad person, even if she'd put her selfish desires above her commitment to Clair and the trip they'd planned. A choice she'd regret for the rest of her life, as Jack had confided he'd regret his.

But dishing out advice was a lot easier than following it.

She set the salmon fillets in the marinade, put them in the refrigerator to steep, and moved to the next menu item on today's prep schedule.

Yet as she went through the motions, her mind remained on Jack.

She ought to report back to him about her session with Dr. Oliver—not that there was much to report. He hadn't been able to help her remember more about the mark she'd seen.

But while she had Jack on the phone, perhaps she could summon up the forgiveness he'd asked for. His remorse seemed real, and it would be hypocritical to offer Dara advice she wasn't willing to follow herself.

Yes, that would be the ethical and charitable course.

And she'd follow it.

As soon as she gathered up her courage—and corralled the butterflies that took flight in her stomach whenever an image of the tall, handsome detective flitted through her mind.

FILE FOLDER IN HAND, Eric stopped outside James Robertson's office, where the man's wife was waiting for him to discuss the pros and cons of the strip mall project.

Hopefully, he'd built a sufficient case to convince her it was a bad deal.

If he hadn't, reporting back to Nolan wasn't going to be fun.

Squeezing the folder, he knocked on the door.

"Come in."

He pushed through.

Heidi Robertson was seated behind James's desk, glasses perched on her nose as she read a document in front of her. She spared him no more than a quick glance, then waved him into the chair across the broad mahogany expanse. "I'll be with you in a minute."

He took the seat she'd indicated, waiting while she scribbled on a yellow legal pad beside her.

At last she looked up. "Sorry. I wanted to jot a few notes before I shifted gears."

"No problem."

"Let's talk about the strip mall opportunity." She pushed the folder in front of her aside and replaced it with another one. Flipped it open. "After our brief conversation in the hall on Tuesday, I gave these financials another review. I didn't see any red flags." She scanned the sheet he'd provided. Took off her glasses. "You mentioned liabilities. Tell me about them."

Heart hammering, he opened his own file. "Location, for one. Crime statistics in that area have been trending upward for the past few years."

She frowned. "I'm familiar with that part of town. It doesn't trigger any alarm bells."

"The numbers don't lie." Although data could be manipulated to support any position, if you knew how to frame it.

"You have reports to back that up?"

"Yes." He withdrew a sheet and passed it across the desk, keeping his features neutral. Unless she dug in deep, they appeared to paint a less-than-rosy picture.

She put her glasses back on, and for two eternal minutes, while sweat trickled down the side of his neck, she pored over the sheet he'd handed her.

Finally she set the paper on the desk and removed her glasses. "I'm not certain this is worrisome. There's been no increase in violent crime, just a bump in minor vandalism and shoplifting. From what I hear in the news, that's happening everywhere. Crime is rising, period. How do these statistics compare to trends in other areas of town?"

The moisture in his mouth evaporated.

She was much shrewder than anyone in the company had given her credit for. Almost a clone of her husband.

"I, uh, was more focused on running the numbers in the vicinity of the mall."

"Do the same for a few other similar areas and let me know

what you find." She folded her hands on the desk. "Anything else?"

"Yes. The structure is overdue for cosmetic updates, and the systems are older." He extracted another sheet from his file and handed it to her. "I ran a few of the costs we could expect to incur over the next five years."

Once again, she settled her glasses on her nose and examined the paper. "Is this based on a physical inspection of the property?"

"Yes."

"Did my husband see this?"

"No. We hadn't yet had an opportunity to discuss it."

She perused the financial analysis sheet again, the creases on her brow deepening. "A steady increase in income stream may justify these kinds of expenditures. Are any of them urgent?"

"The infrastructure won't fall apart tomorrow if no investments are made, but the mall is showing definite signs of age and wear. Image matters for retailers that want to attract higher-end customers." He did his best to sound matter-of-fact rather than desperate.

"Hmm." She slipped both of the sheets he'd offered into her project file. "Let me think about this. Is that all?"

"There's one more factor to consider—the mix of properties we own. We're already heavy in retail. If we want to maintain a diversified portfolio, we should think about bumping up our holdings in one of the other sectors. We have a reasonable amount of industrial and multifamily residential, but we're light on office buildings." He handed her his last sheet.

"I would think that would be a benefit, given the work-from-home trend spurred by Covid." She gave the paper a cursory skim.

"If the trend continues. Many businesses prefer to have their people on-site."

"Except in tight labor markets, employees have a great deal of power. I'm not hearing many of them clamoring to fight rush hour traffic or spend unproductive hours every week commuting. James and I had talked about that." She cleared her throat, sniffing as she slid the last paper into the file. "I'll take everything you've said into consideration. Thank you for your work on this."

He was being dismissed, with no resolution to his dilemma and no clear indication of whether she shared her husband's rabid interest in adding that particular strip mall to the company portfolio.

"If I can be of any other help, let me know." He stood.

"I will." Her cell began to vibrate on the desk, and she checked the screen. "I have to take this. It's the detective handling James's case."

"I hope he has positive news."

"He may. There's been a development I want to discuss with him. Our chef has remembered a new detail. If you'll excuse me." She picked up her cell and gave him a pointed look.

He dipped his head and retreated, slowing his pace as he walked toward the door and cocking his ear in the direction of the desk. But her volume was too low for her words to be intelligible.

Nevertheless, this meeting had been bad news all around.

As far as he could tell, the arguments he'd put forth against the mall hadn't persuaded her. And the witness was remembering more and more.

He scratched his arm as he walked back to his office.

Nolan wasn't going to be happy about any of this.

Meaning it was very possible he'd have more unpleasant tasks to pass along to a certain CPA who was already in a very precarious position.

"THAT'S GREAT NEWS." Phone to ear, Dara sat at her kitchen table, relief coursing through her at Lindsey's news about the killer's tattoo. "That should get Chad off the hook."

"I hope so. I only got a quick peek, though. But the more I've thought about it, the more certain I am there was a mark of some kind on the person's arm. I'm going to tell that to the detective too. How are you doing otherwise?"

"Better since you and I talked on Tuesday. We do all make mistakes, and Chad is sorry now he didn't tell me about Pop. He's also being more open, even though that's hard for him."

"I'm glad to hear that. You'll be at class next week, right?"

"Yes." The back door opened, and Chad stepped through. Dara smiled and lifted a hand in greeting.

"I won't keep you. I'm sure you're in the midst of dinner prep. I'll see you Tuesday."

"Thanks for calling."

As she pressed the end button, Chad shrugged out of his heavy work coat. "Smells good in here."

"We're having beef stew." She crossed to him, and he wrapped her in his arms. "Ooh! Your fingers are cold!"

He tightened his grip. "You can help me warm them up later."

At the husky note in his voice, a little thrill zipped through her. "I think that could be arranged."

After a few moments, he released her to hang his coat on a hook by the door. "Who was on the phone?"

"Lindsey. She had news."

Chad listened as she told him about the mark or tattoo.

"What do the police think?"

"She didn't say, but it has to be a positive. I mean, you don't have a tattoo or a mark of any kind on your arm. This should clear you."

"I don't know, Dara." He rubbed his forehead. "They could

still think I was involved. As an accomplice or something. Like a lookout while my partner robbed the place."

Her spirits deflated. "No one's mentioned anything about two people being involved. Why would you jump to that conclusion?"

"I know how cops think. They've connected me to the crime already with circumstantial stuff, so if I'm not the killer, they're still going to wonder if I'm linked to the crime."

Was that true—or was he overreacting?

"Maybe not, Chad. It's not like you have a record or have ever had any trouble with the police."

He pulled her close again, his grip fierce. As if he was holding on for dear life. "I like your optimism. I wish I had it."

"I have enough for both of us."

After a few seconds, he drew back and offered her a smile that seemed forced. "I'm ready for that stew."

"Coming right up."

She served their dinner, and though they focused on more pleasant topics during the meal, the underlying tension was almost palpable.

For if Chad's take on the situation was correct, they weren't out of the woods yet.

SEVENTEEN

IF HER OUTSIDE ROWING had to be put on hold until the lake warmed up again in the spring, running wasn't a bad second choice to start her Sunday. Especially on a crisp, clear morning with the dawn glow lingering on the horizon.

Leaves crunching underfoot, Lindsey rounded the corner and picked up speed on the path that wound through the county park adjacent to her neighborhood. A major selling point when she'd purchased her condo.

No one was about yet at this early hour on a day many people liked to sleep in, but she wasn't alone. Ducks paddled on the lake beside her, squirrels scampered about hiding their winter stash, and a cardinal overhead greeted the awakening world with a musical trill.

Peace.

Utter peace.

Exactly what she needed after all that had happened since this month began, and a perfect prelude to set the mood for church attendance later.

Despite the overdose of trauma during the past couple of weeks, she had much to be grateful for as Thanksgiving approached. Including an invitation from Madeleine to join the eclectic group the Horizons director always gathered together for the holiday, comprised of people who might otherwise spend the day alone.

Of course, she could have gone to Boston. But if past experience was any indication, Mom would work until late Wednesday, make reservations at a high-end restaurant for their Thanksgiving meal, and escape to her home office to catch up on work emails in the waning hours of the day.

Not the jolliest of holidays.

Staying here had been smart. Madeleine's party would be much—

"No!"

Lindsey jolted to a halt as a woman's cry echoed in the still air from the other side of a cluster of pine trees up ahead.

Pulse quickening, she peered that direction in the murky light.

Two forms were visible through the branches. A gray-haired woman in casual attire, holding tight to what could be a purse, and another taller person, who was pulling on it.

A mugging?

At this hour?

As Lindsey tried to digest that, she groped for her pepper gel and started forward, nerve endings tingling. A confrontation with a mugger hadn't been on her morning agenda, but—

She gasped as the attacker shoved the woman to the ground. Pulled out a knife. Raised it above his head and—

Lindsey stumbled. Slammed her eyelids shut as bile rose in her throat.

The woman had been stabbed!

Struggling to breathe, hands shaking, she opened her eyes and fumbled for her phone.

Dropped it.

Choking back a sob, she bent to pick it up, glancing toward the man as he raised his hand again.

"No! Stop!" The anguished plea was out before she thought through the ramifications.

The attacker swung toward her. Hesitated. Brought the knife down once more on the figure that now lay unmoving on the ground.

Then he pivoted and sprinted her direction.

Sweet mercy!

Heart thumping, Lindsey squeezed the cell and began to run away as fast as her shaky legs allowed. Cold air hurtled past, but the chill on her cheeks was nothing compared to the icy fear coursing through her veins.

Please, Lord, let me get out of this alive!

That desperate entreaty came from the depths of her soul as she risked a quick peek over her shoulder.

The person with the knife was gaining on her.

Blood pounding in her ears, she increased her speed, using every muscle she'd developed over a summer of rowing as she searched her surroundings for anyone who might be able to help.

But as usual on cold Sunday mornings, she had the park to herself.

Except for the person chasing her, who wasn't likely to show any mercy to an innocent runner if they'd been willing to stab a defenseless older woman for her purse . . . or whatever she'd been carrying.

So unless she outran the attacker, or a County park ranger happened to cruise through on a security patrol, she could very well end up a statistic.

Like the woman bleeding on the ground among the pine trees.

JACK TOOK THE TURN onto Lindsey's street on two wheels, tires squealing.

Too fast. Too dangerous. Not his usual style.

Gripping the wheel, he eased back on the gas pedal as her condo came into sight, several local police cruisers parked in front.

There was no reason for haste. She was safe inside, surrounded by law enforcement officers and vehicles. He'd heard her voice. The panic constricting his windpipe was illogical.

But until he saw her and was able to make sense of the message she'd left him after calling 911, logic was elusive.

He parked behind one of the cruisers, strode toward her unit, and displayed his creds to the officer standing outside her door.

After a quick scan of the ID, the man motioned him in.

As Jack opened the door and stepped inside, Lindsey's head whipped his direction. She was seated on her couch. Same place she'd been sitting the day she'd told him about the South Carolina incident. Same pillow hugged against her chest.

And she was in worse shape than she'd been while fighting off an imminent panic attack. All of the color had leeched from her complexion, and despite the distance separating them, the tremors rippling through her body were obvious.

"Sorry for the delay. I was at the early church service, phone silent, when your message came in. I got here as fast as I could." He closed the distance between them and sat beside her. "Are you okay?"

She tried to push up the corners of her lips. Failed. "I've had better days. In fact, I've had better months. But I p-probably shouldn't have bothered you. There are plenty of people here."

"It was no bother. Did anyone take a statement?"

"Yes, but no one's come back to tell me if the woman is a-alive."

"I'll see what I can find out in a minute. First, walk me through what happened." Details had been scant in her semi-hysterical message.

He listened as she described the horrifying scenario she'd stumbled into, resisting the urge to reach for her hand and enfold it in a comforting clasp—until she began taking in short, choppy puffs of air, her shaking intensified, and a film of moisture broke out on her forehead.

No way could he ignore such clear distress signals.

Disregarding professional protocol, he edged closer and tucked her ice-cold fingers in his.

She didn't pull away.

"Do you want me to get your medicine?"

"No." She swallowed, clinging to his hand. "Just give me a few minutes to concentrate on my breathing."

He remained silent while she struggled to rein in the looming panic attack, waiting until her shaking subsided and her respiration normalized to speak. "I think you licked it."

"Yes. Thanks for the loan of your hand."

"Anytime." He cleared the huskiness from his voice. "There's an officer outside the door. You're safe. If you're comfortable staying here alone, I can try to get an update."

She nodded. "Please. I want to know what happened to that poor woman."

After giving her fingers a quick squeeze, he crossed the room and exited the condo.

Out in front, a number of officers were talking by one of the cruisers, a County park ranger among them.

He joined the group, introduced himself, explained the reason for his presence, and got straight to business. "What do we have?"

"I was first on the scene." An older guy who came across as a seasoned veteran spoke up. "I knew Ms. Barnes was safe and locked in her condo, so I went directly to the park to investigate." He hesitated.

Jack frowned when he stopped. "And?"

The man shrugged. "I couldn't find anything."

A faint alarm began to beep in Jack's mind. "What do you mean?"

"There was no indication of any sort of altercation or injury in the area Ms. Barnes directed us to."

"Are you certain you were in the right spot?"

"I verified it with dispatch, and Russo double-checked with Ms. Barnes after she arrived." The man indicated a female officer in the group. "She was taking the statement."

"We did spread out after more officers arrived, to cover a wider area." This from the ranger. "No one spotted anything out of the ordinary. No blood. No tamped-down foliage. No other witnesses who've come forward. It's weird."

No weirder than the lake or car incidents.

Yet as far as he could see, Lindsey's mind was sound.

But his birth mother had been able to fool people too.

As the yellow alert in his mind turned red, the flame of attraction that had sparked to life for Lindsey began to sputter.

The last thing he needed was another delusional woman messing up his world.

Maybe Lindsey's mental processes were fine, and there was a logical explanation for all that had happened. But until that explanation was found, it would be foolish to risk his heart.

The wise course was to tamp down any personal feelings and play it safe while the situation got sorted out.

"Can one of you show me the area in question?"

"I'll be happy to." The ranger inclined his head toward his car. "Why don't we drive? It will be faster."

Jack didn't argue.

Five minutes later, the man led him to a small cluster of pine trees. The area was marked off with crime scene tape, a lone officer on duty.

Jack scrutinized the scene from all angles outside the cordoned-off area. Moved inside for a closer look.

After fifteen minutes, he reached the same conclusion as the other officers.

As far as he could see, there was nothing here to indicate a woman had been stabbed.

It was possible a County crime scene tech might spot something—and the area would remain secure until that could be arranged—but if he was a betting man, he'd lay odds that even eagle-eyed Hank would come up blank.

Time to go back and tell Lindsey the bad news.

A chore he did *not* relish.

"WHAT DO YOU MEAN, they didn't find anything?" Lindsey stared at Jack, who'd taken the chair across from the couch instead of rejoining her. Bad vibes wafted toward her.

"There's no evidence to validate your story."

"But . . . what about blood? I saw the knife. I saw the man stab her!"

"We didn't find any blood."

She tried to wrap her mind around that news, but it wouldn't compute.

"I don't understand. I mean, she was wearing a coat, so I guess the blood could have been absorbed. But she had to be hurt. How could she have gotten up and walked away? And assuming she somehow managed to escape, why wouldn't she have called for help? Reported the crime?"

"I don't have an explanation for that."

Yes, he did. She could see it in his eyes—and it made her sick to her stomach.

He thought she'd imagined today's attack. Had perhaps also put an unwarranted sinister spin on the lake incident. Forgotten where she'd parked her car the night it disappeared. That all the pressures she'd faced over the past year and a half had pushed her over the edge. That she was hallucinating and no longer had a grasp on reality.

Was he even starting to wonder whether she'd seen anyone at the Robertson murder scene? Speculating that everything she'd relayed may have been a figment of her imagination?

Truth be told, and hard as it was to admit, she was also beginning to wonder about her sanity.

Because if she were viewing this from the outside, she'd be thinking along the same lines as Jack.

Her throat tightened, and she swallowed.

She needed to talk to Dr. Oliver.

Bad.

"So what happens next?" She clenched her fists until her nails dug into her palms.

"One of our crime scene techs will go over the scene. And we'll be on the lookout for any reports of an attack. We'll also check with area hospitals to see if any stabbing wounds show up in the ER."

At least he hadn't dismissed her claims outright and was planning to follow up.

But his skepticism was clear. Meaning her credibility was compromised.

"I'd appreciate being kept in the loop if anything turns up."

"Goes without saying." His tone was pleasant and professional, but the caring note that had warmed it earlier while he'd held her hand had evaporated.

Another punch in the stomach, though it was hard to blame him for his caution.

Nevertheless, disappointment didn't absolve her from granting him the forgiveness he'd asked for with Clair.

"Before you leave, I wanted to tell you that I've thought about everything you shared in terms of your relationship with Clair, and I no longer have any bad feelings toward you about what happened. I think we both made mistakes that led to a terrible outcome, but I don't think Clair would want us to beat ourselves or each other up about that for the rest of our lives."

An odd mixture of relief and regret rippled across his features. "I appreciate that."

"I also wanted to let you know I asked Dr. Oliver whether he could help me try to remember more details about the markings on the killer's arm. I even suggested hypnosis. But he said that doesn't work very well as a memory-recovery method. While it can help a person recall additional information, the memories tend to be a mix of accurate and inaccurate details, and witnesses usually can't tell which are true and which are fabricated."

"Thanks for asking him about it. That lines up with what I've learned on the job." He rose.

She stood too. "For the record, Dr. Oliver hasn't raised any serious red flags about my psychological health."

While this latest incident could change his opinion, until he told her otherwise, her statement was true. And letting Jack leave thinking she was crazy was unacceptable.

"Will you talk to him about what happened today?"

"Yes."

"I'd like to know what he says, if you don't mind passing that on."

"I can do better than that. I can waive client/doctor privilege and give him permission to talk to you." That was a risk, but if it boosted Jack's confidence in her reliability, it was worth the chance.

Faint creases appeared on his brow. "I don't want to invade your privacy."

"But you do need a credible witness. One a doctor of psychology can vouch for."

He studied her. "I'll tell you what. Talk it over with him. If you both agree to that plan, I'll consider it."

"That's fair."

"Is there anything else I can do for you today?"

Trust me. Believe in me. Look at me again with warmth and compassion and perhaps something more.

But she said none of that.

"I'll be fine."

He hesitated, as if tempted to say more, but in the end he turned away and walked toward the door. On the threshold, he paused. "Call if anything else comes up."

She managed to coax her mouth into a tiny, wry smile. "Let's hope nothing else does. But at this stage, I have no idea what to expect next."

"It's been a roller coaster, no question about it." His lips flattened.

"Except there's no amusement in this amusement park." Her voice caught on the last word.

The parallel lines embedded above his nose deepened. "Watch your back."

"More so now than ever."

With a dip of his chin, he stepped outside, closing the door behind him.

Lindsey crossed the room and twisted the lock, then moved to the window to watch as he paused to talk to two of the officers before continuing to his car. Less than a minute later, he pulled away from the curb and disappeared down the street.

And quite possibly from her life, unless she could assure him that his witness in the Robertson case wasn't losing her mind.

Time to call Dr. Oliver and see if he was going to be an ally in that effort—or if what he had to say after today's incident would only add fuel to Jack's suspicions.

EIGHTEEN

"YOU BEAT ME HERE AGAIN."

As Bri greeted him and claimed her usual seat for their bi-weekly Tuesday night dinner, Jack set his cell on the table. "I was in the area for a case follow-up and finished early. No point going back to the office. I can do email anywhere."

"I hear you." She hung her purse on the back of her chair and inspected him. "You look tired."

Not surprising. That's what happened when you tossed for two nights in a row and only clocked a handful of hours of sleep, thanks to an unsolved murder case and a personal chef in whom you'd taken far too much personal interest.

"Work's busy."

"Yeah?" She didn't seem convinced. "Work's always busy. What else is going on? Is there a new development with the Robertson case that's causing you to lose sleep?"

"Not exactly."

Their server arrived before Bri could respond, but as soon as he took their order and left, she morphed back into inquisitor mode.

"Explain that."

Naturally she'd home in on his vague answer.

IRENE HANNON

He picked up the basket of rolls and held it out. "Have one."

"I'd rather have an explanation." She took a roll anyway, her expression growing speculative. "I'm thinking your insomnia is related to your witness."

He tried not to gape at her.

How on earth did she do that?

More importantly, how much should he share with her? She *was* a clear thinker, and he could use a sounding board at this stage. Plus, since she already suspected he was attracted to Lindsey, what did he have to lose by getting her take?

"Give the lady a gold star." He took a roll.

"I knew it." She leaned forward. "She's gotten under your skin, hasn't she?"

"Let's just say I find her intriguing."

"There are worse places to start a relationship."

"Our relationship is professional."

"I wouldn't expect anything less—for now. Doesn't mean more can't develop. Like with Marc and me."

"This is a whole different scenario, with very different obstacles."

"Such as?"

Jack shook out his napkin. Draped it across his lap.

How much could he say without giving away secrets he'd never shared with anyone? Not Mom or Dad. Not his sisters. Not the counselors who'd tried to help him after he entered the foster program.

But his background was a big stumbling block with Lindsey, so he'd have to touch on it without going into detail.

"There was an incident Sunday." He gave Bri a quick recap of the report Lindsey had called in, as well as the other strange situations she'd encountered and the tense standoff she'd been pulled into in South Carolina.

His sister exhaled as he finished. "Wow."

193

A gross understatement that didn't come anywhere close to capturing his feelings.

"It's a boatload to deal with. For her and for me."

Twin grooves appeared in Bri's forehead. "So let me clarify. The incident in South Carolina happened. That's documented. The murder happened. There's a body. But there's nothing to support her claims about the car or lake or stabbing, correct?"

"Yes."

"Huh." She focused on a spot over his shoulder, her brain clearly working overtime. "I think I see the problem. You like her, but you're worried she's having a mental breakdown."

"Or worse."

"What could be worse?"

He shrugged. "She could have psychological issues, period. Maybe long-standing in nature, which have been exacerbated by recent events."

"Does she come across as unstable?"

"No. But everything that's happened has thrown her for a loop. I think she's beginning to question her grasp of reality."

Bri snorted. "Who wouldn't, if they'd gone through everything you described? Has she gotten any professional help to deal with all that?"

"Yes. Here and in South Carolina."

"That's a positive sign. It means she recognizes she's in over her head."

"The thing is . . . what if she does have ongoing issues—and always will?"

Bri tapped her two index fingers together. "You're thinking of your birth mom, aren't you?"

He tried not to let his shock show. "Why would you ask that?"

"Come on, Jack. We grew up in the same house. Even though you never talked much about her, and Mom and Dad were close-mouthed, I could read between the lines. I don't know what she did to you, but I always assumed it was bad. And I also got the sense it was way outside the realm of normal child abuse—if the terms normal and child abuse can be used in the same sentence. That she may have had psychological issues."

Good luck to any arsonist who tried to put one over on his smart, perceptive sister.

"She did." And he wasn't going to offer any details about them. Now or ever. "That's not a place I want to visit again."

"It's also problematic for your case, isn't it? I mean, if your witness is unreliable, anything she remembers about the killer will have to be taken with a grain of salt, right?"

"Yes."

"A double whammy." She leaned back. Folded her arms. Pursed her lips. "Have you considered talking to her therapist? With her permission, of course. Just to get a better read on her mental state?"

"She offered that."

"Take her up on it. An unbiased professional opinion may help you get a handle on whether her issues are trauma-induced or longer-term in nature."

"It feels like an invasion of privacy."

"It isn't if she offered. Get over the guilt complex." She leaned forward again. "What's *your* take on her stories about the car and lake and stabbing?"

He picked a loose crumb off his roll. Mashed it between his fingers. "I think she thinks they happened."

"What if they did?"

He peeled the squashed crumb off his skin. "There's no evidence in any of those cases to support her claims."

"But they could have happened, right?"

"The car and lake, possibly. The attack in the park? Doubtful. I had our best crime scene tech go over the area. Hank found nothing."

"Maybe someone didn't *want* him to find anything."

He narrowed his eyes as her meaning registered. "Are you suggesting the attack may have been staged?"

"I'm trying to think outside the box. That said, I admit the notion of a setup is bizarre. Out in left field. A stretch. But is it possible? Yes."

Jack stared at the salad the server set in front of him and declined a sprinkling of pepper. There was more than enough spice in his life already.

While Bri conferred with the man about changing a side for her order, Jack ran her idea through his mind.

It was kind of crazy—but her approach was rational. When investigating any case, a competent detective took all possibilities into account, no matter how off-the-wall they were.

As he should have done in this case. *Would* have done if he hadn't let personal feelings for a witness and his own history interfere with his usual sound judgment.

If nothing else, why not take Bri's advice and meet with Lindsey's psychologist? If the man's verdict raised no red flags, it might be time to devote serious brainpower to his sister's theory.

"Does your silence mean you think I'm losing it too?" Bri arched her eyebrows at him as she dug into her salad.

"No. I think your idea may have merit. At the very least it gives me food for thought."

"Excellent. While you chew on that, let's concentrate on the food at hand. I'm starved after working through lunch today, thanks to a new case that landed on my desk."

He listened as she described the probable arson scenario, but his star witness remained top of mind.

It was hard to believe someone would move her car, go scuba diving at Creve Coeur Lake, and fake an attack in a park. That was extreme.

But if you'd committed murder and were afraid the sole witness could remember an incriminating detail, you might be willing to push the envelope to discredit that witness in order to save your hide.

It was a definite stretch—perhaps even grasping at straws—but if Lindsey's psychologist gave him a positive report, he wasn't going to discount any theory that provided a rational explanation for the strange experiences she'd had since this case began.

"LINDSEY, I'M SORRY we couldn't get you in sooner. We've been slammed with one crisis after another this week." Dr. Oliver joined her in his office, closing the door behind him.

"No worries. I'm getting to be a nuisance, aren't I?"

"Never." He took his seat and set a large mug of coffee on the table beside him.

She did a double take. "I don't think I've ever seen you drink coffee." Or anything other than water during their sessions.

"A rare exception to my no-caffeine rule. I was here twelve hours yesterday and it will be the same today. I needed an energy boost. Tell me what's going on."

"More of the same."

"Explain that."

As she gave him the rundown on what had happened Sunday, he sipped his coffee, expression unreadable.

When she finished, he set his mug down. "I can see why that would be very disturbing for you, both the experience itself and the lack of evidence to support your story. Are you certain the police investigated thoroughly?"

"Yes. The detective on the Robertson case called in the crime scene unit. He sent me a text yesterday to let me know they came up blank. I think his confidence in my reliability is plummeting." She fidgeted in her seat. "To tell you the truth, mine is too."

"You don't think what happened on Sunday was real?"

"It felt real. But if it happened the way I thought, wouldn't there have been some evidence? A few drops of blood, minimum?"

"That would be a reasonable expectation."

"So what's going on? Am I losing it?" She braced.

Eternal seconds crawled by as he mulled over her question.

When he at last responded, his tone was slow and measured. "I have to admit I'm a bit baffled. Nothing in our interactions up until now suggested to me that you had any deep-seated psychological issues. Nor did any of the case notes your therapist in South Carolina provided. However, we do have to factor in your recent ordeal at the Robertson house. You've had a lot to deal with over the past twenty-one months, and repeated trauma can take a toll."

"Could it make me imagine things that aren't real?"

"As a byproduct of trauma alone, that would be unusual. Stress can intensify symptoms of psychotic disorders, and it sometimes plays a role in hallucination episodes in a number of those illnesses, but I'm not seeing anything to suggest bipolar or delusional disorder. Likewise for schizophrenia. We could be moving toward PTSD, though. Tell me how you're doing emotionally. Are you feeling depressed?"

"A little. But wouldn't it be normal to be a bit down, with all that's been happening?"

"To some degree. If it gets worse than that, you need to let me know."

"I think I'm more anxious than anything else. I mean, I can't believe I imagined what happened Sunday. Or at the lake. The experiences are vivid in my mind. And I'm functioning fine in every other area of my life. Why would these two anomalies occur? And what if it happens again?"

"Did the police give you any opinion about your reports?"

"Not directly. The only one who's talked with me at any length about them is Detective Tucker. He hasn't said he has doubts about my mental stability, but that's what I'm picking up. Which brings me to a question. If I gave you permission, would you be willing to talk with him? Offer him a professional opinion about my psychological state?"

"May I ask why?"

She squirmed in her seat. That was a question she wasn't prepared to fully answer . . . but if she couldn't share her feelings with Dr. Oliver, who *could* she share them with?

"Two reasons. First, I don't want him to discount me as a witness in the Robertson case. If he does, nothing I remember will be of any use to him in solving the murder. But I also . . . well, he's a very nice man. I would hate for him to discount me on a personal level, either."

Dr. Oliver's lips flexed. "You like this man."

"Yes."

"Under those circumstances, I can see why his skepticism would be troubling. Yes, I can talk to him. He's welcome to call or come by. And I promise you I won't tell him anything I haven't told you."

Not altogether reassuring, but she wouldn't renege on her offer to Jack.

She forced up the corners of her mouth. "You did say not long ago that you didn't see any major cause for concern in terms of my mental state."

"True—but I do think we should be watchful. Should you continue to have these experiences or any new symptoms develop, I want to hear about them immediately. I don't like the trend line I'm seeing. If the depression worsens, or your anxiety intensifies, I want you to call me and I'll consult with your primary care doctor to discuss potential medications to help you over the hump."

She wrinkled her nose. "Medication would be a last resort for me. I don't even like taking it for panic attacks."

"Understood. It's just one other tool we have in our arsenal. Shall we end with a visualization?"

"I'm not certain that's necessary tonight. Talking with you was a huge help. And as the last client, I don't want to extend your already long day any longer than necessary."

"Are you sure?"

"Yes." She picked up her bottle of water and her purse. "I'll have Detective Tucker reach out to you. Thanks for your willingness to talk to him."

"Not a problem."

He walked her to the door, and Lindsey picked up her pace down the hall toward the exit.

Thank goodness Dr. Oliver hadn't been alarmed by her story about what had happened on Sunday. Nor did he seem to think it necessarily indicated a mental breakdown.

But he knew her far better than Jack Tucker did. While a discussion with a credible source like him couldn't hurt, there was no guarantee it would dispel all—or even most of—Jack's doubts. Not after the recent bizarre events.

Truth be told, it didn't dispel all of hers, either.

She pushed through the outside door, cringing as a blast of cold air stung her cheeks.

Trying to prove what had happened at the lake was an exercise in futility. If someone had grabbed her ankle, all they'd had to do was swim away without leaving a trace. But why had there been no evidence of the stabbing in the park? What had happened to the woman? Why hadn't she reported the crime? How come the man with the knife had stopped pursuing the jogger who'd witnessed his crime?

Nothing added up.

Yet despite the lingering doubts lurking in the corners of her mind, with each passing day she was more and more certain that scenario hadn't been the figment of an overactive imagination. It had happened.

The dilemma was how to prove it.

She slid behind the wheel and put the car in gear.

Maybe she ought to venture back to the park. Poke around herself. It was possible the County crime scene unit had missed something, wasn't it?

Not likely, Lindsey.

She blew out a breath.

Fine. It was a long shot. But what could it hurt to take another look around after her two cooking gigs tomorrow? There were always a few walkers in the park in the afternoon. Probably more than usual, with many people starting their long Thanksgiving weekend. It wasn't as if she'd be there by herself again. And she'd keep her pepper gel at the ready.

Worst case, she'd find nothing and end up exactly where she was now.

But sitting around passively while people questioned her sanity was getting old.

At least she could make an attempt to find one tiny piece of proof that would help convince Jack his key witness in the Robertson case wasn't coming unglued.

NINETEEN

WHAT WAS LINDSEY DOING in the park in the middle of the afternoon?

Jack paused as he rounded the curve on the path that led to the scene of the supposed stabbing three days ago.

She was slouched on a bench under a towering oak that sported a few withered leaves clinging to their grip on life, fixated on the small cluster of pine trees where she'd said the attack happened.

Stay or go?

It wouldn't be difficult to beat a hasty retreat—but he ought to let her know he'd followed up on her text and had a conversation with Dr. Oliver. While the psychologist had thrown in more caveats than the lawyers who wrote those voluminous, eye-glazing terms of service agreements you had to sign for almost everything in today's risk-averse world, he'd been more cautious than negative about Lindsey's mental acuity.

As for the strange situations she'd found herself in? He'd had no definitive explanation for those.

But Bri's theory was gaining traction in his mind.

And it might be time to share that theory with Lindsey. Reassure her he was keeping an open mind and hadn't written her off as a nutcase—the conclusion she'd reached on Sunday, if he'd read the hurt in her eyes correctly as he'd left her place.

He resumed walking, greeting her from several yards away to warn her of his approach.

Despite his attempt to mitigate the startle factor, she jumped to her feet, spun around, and aimed a container of pepper gel his direction.

He halted and lifted his hands. "Hold your fire."

Color surged on her cheeks, and she lowered the canister. "Sorry. It doesn't take much to spook me anymore."

"Understandable. May I?" He motioned toward the bench.

"Sure." She shoved the container into the pocket of her coat, sat, and scooted to the end.

He took the other side, leaving plenty of space between them. "What are you doing here?"

"I could ask you the same question."

"I wanted to take one more walk around the area where you saw the attack."

"Me too." She expelled a breath. "It was a wasted effort. I didn't spot anything helpful. Nor did being back here trigger a memory that would lead to proof it all happened." She cocked her head and regarded him. "I'm surprised you revisited the scene, though. I assumed you had total confidence in whoever went over it."

"I do, but I like to dot all the i's and cross all the t's. Especially when I have a feeling something's been missed."

"Like what?"

"I don't know. But a colleague had a theory." Not a precise description of his relationship with Bri, but close enough. If he told Lindsey he'd been discussing the case with his sister, he'd have to explain why. "It's a stretch, but I'm not discounting it." He gave her the highlights.

Lindsey stared at him. "You think someone would go to all that trouble just to undermine my credibility?"

"I can't rule it out. You're the only witness in the Robertson killing, and desperate people do desperate things. Someone who's trying to evade a homicide charge may fall into that camp."

Her expression spelled skepticism in capital letters. "I don't know. It seems like a *very* long stretch." A cold gust of wind barreled past, and she turned up the collar of her coat. "But speaking of credibility, did you talk to Dr. Oliver?"

"Yes. Early this morning. He was cordial and answered all of my questions." No reason to mention all his caveats.

"Did he tell you enough to convince you I'm not hallucinating?"

"Hallucination was never mentioned. He gave me a quick tutorial on the effects of repeated trauma and stress, and it was obvious he thought your issues were related to those kinds of factors rather than any sort of psychosis. So I'm comfortable with—"

A flying object shot over his head, and he ducked.

"Sorry, mister." A boy of eleven or twelve trotted over, gaze fixed on the branches of the oak tree above the bench. "My Frisbee's stuck. Can you get it for us?" He waved to two other kids who were running toward them.

Jack looked up. A plastic yellow disk was wedged into a branch of the tree ten or twelve feet up.

His heart began to pound. "I'm, uh, not sure I can reach it even if I stand on the bench."

"You could put your foot on that branch." The boy indicated one that was accessible from the bench and would give him the height he needed to get the Frisbee.

He started to sweat. "Climbing trees isn't safe."

"Yeah, I know. My dad told me that. He made me promise never to do it. But you're a grown-up. Nobody can tell *you* not to climb a tree."

He swallowed. Hard.

"Maybe I could help."

At Lindsey's soft comment, he looked over to find her watching him, her gaze curious—and discerning.

She'd picked up on his discomfort and was trying to give him an out.

He couldn't ask her to climb a tree, though. How chivalrous would that be?

On the other hand, the thought of taking his feet off terra firma sent a chill through him far colder than the frosty air nipping at his cheeks.

"We can do this." Without waiting for him to respond, she stood and stepped up onto the seat of the bench. "If you'll spot me, I'll have it down in a jiffy. And I promise to do my best not to fall and squash you." She flashed him a smile.

Hard as he tried, he couldn't get his lips to curve up in response.

Instead, he rose and positioned himself beside the bench next to her. "Be careful."

"My middle name."

She stepped up, onto the back of the bolted-down bench, and grabbed a sturdy branch to the left. Once she had a firm grip on it, she hoisted herself up onto the limb the boy had indicated. The Frisbee came loose with one tug, and she sent it sailing down before lowering herself back to the seat of the bench.

"Thank you, lady." The boy grinned up at her.

"Happy to do it."

Jack held out his hand to assist her down, and she took it in silence, descending to the ground mere inches away from him.

"One crisis averted. I wish all of them were as simple to fix." Her tone was light, but her eyes continued to probe.

At least she hadn't asked him why he'd let her do the climbing, despite her obvious curiosity.

"So do I."

She played with the zipper on her jacket. "Well . . . I have to get busy on the dessert I'm contributing to tomorrow's dinner, so I best get at it. And I know you want to take a look around here. I should head home."

"Did you walk over?"

"No. I drove. I used my rowing machine this morning, which is more than sufficient exercise for today." She eased back a hair. "If you get cold out here and want to, uh, stop in for a cup of hot chocolate after you're finished, feel free. I also have coffee, but my hot chocolate is legendary." She displayed a dimple he'd never noticed. Or maybe she'd just never given him that kind of smile before. "No need to commit now. See how you feel after you're done. And if you decide to pass, happy Thanksgiving."

"You too."

"Thanks." She lifted her hand and took off at a fast clip for her car.

He watched her go, mulling over the tempting idea of detouring to her condo for a cozy get-together over hot chocolate.

Could there be a better prelude to Thanksgiving?

But if he accepted, would she expect an explanation for his odd reluctance to climb up and pluck the boy's Frisbee from the tree?

And if she asked him about it, what would he say?

Shoving his hands in his pockets, he wandered toward the copse of trees where the alleged stabbing had taken place. The odds of finding any evidence to substantiate Lindsey's claims were about as dismal as the odds of him finding a cure for his fear of heights.

And until a few minutes ago, he'd also have classified the odds of him sharing the cause of that phobia with anyone as equally dismal.

Somehow, though, the thought of giving Lindsey a peek into

his background wasn't as stomach churning as he'd expected. And the explanation for his change of heart was simple. The appealing personal chef had gotten under his skin, as Bri had already discerned.

So since Dr. Oliver had seen more evidence of trauma than psychosis, it might make sense to begin opening up a bit in anticipation of the day when this strange and unsettling chapter was behind them and they could move on to a more personal relationship.

He stopped at the edge of the trees to assess the scope of his reconnaissance task, then began a methodical if informal grid search of the area, as he'd done on Sunday. Hoping for more productive results this go-round.

What he found or didn't find here, however, had no bearing on his decision about whether to take Lindsey up on her invitation. That involved a leap of faith with no basis in empirical evidence. It was all about the heart. And trust. And laying the groundwork for the future.

It was also heavily contingent on whether he could dig deep for the courage to dredge up his terrible memories and reveal to her the source of the scars he'd never shared with a living soul.

HE WASN'T COMING.

Quashing a pang of regret, Lindsey poured the filling over the crust in the springform pan, slid her contribution to tomorrow's dinner into the oven, and set the timer.

Now what?

Pie.

Why not make a pie too? Focus on baking instead of dwelling on the handsome detective who, sad to say, didn't appear interested in her despite his chat with Dr. Oliver.

Doing her best to think pleasant thoughts about the holiday

dinner tomorrow at Madeleine's, she preheated her second oven, mixed together the crust ingredients, rolled out the dough, and fitted it into a pie pan. After crimping the edges, she pricked the bottom all over with a fork and brushed it with an egg wash.

No doubt Madeleine already had someone lined up to bring a pumpkin pie, but was it ever possible to have too much pie? And Thanksgiving was all about leftovers anyway, so—

Ding dong.

Lindsey's heart lurched.

Had Jack decided to take her up on her invitation?

Wiping her hands down her apron, she hurried toward the front door and peeked through the peephole.

The blue-eyed detective stood on the other side, wind ruffling his hair, cheeks ruddy from the cold.

Her pulse tripped into double time.

He must be interested after all.

Or perhaps he'd found a piece of evidence to validate her claim about Sunday's attack.

Either would be welcome news.

Taking a calming breath, she opened the door.

The corners of his mouth rose. "Is the hot chocolate offer still valid?"

"Of course. No expiration." She moved back to allow him to enter. When a gust of wind followed him inside, she closed the door behind him. Fast. "Did you find anything?"

"No. I didn't really expect to, but hope springs eternal. I considered doing a second pass, but after the wind picked up and the temperature dropped, I had hot chocolate on my mind."

"I'll have it ready in a jiffy. May I take your coat?"

"Thanks." He shrugged it off and handed it over.

Lindsey opened the coat closet in the foyer, inhaling the faint, masculine scent emanating from the cold fabric as she slipped the jacket onto a hanger.

Whew.

She took longer than necessary fitting the garment into the closet, giving her cheeks a chance to cool down.

When she turned back, his killer smile remained in place. "It smells good in here."

Yeah, it did.

But he must be referring to the aromas wafting from the kitchen.

"Cheesecake's baking."

His eyebrows peaked. "Cheesecake for Thanksgiving?"

"I take it you're a pumpkin pie traditionalist?"

"Guilty as charged. But I like cheesecake too."

"This one has an Oreo crust and chunks of Oreos inside."

"Sold. I'd forfeit pumpkin pie for that any day."

"I could save you a piece." Now where had that come from? It sounded like she was angling for another excuse to see him.

Oh well.

The truth, indiscreet as it could be, had a way of slipping out.

But his next comment suggested he was fine with the idea of another social meetup. "If there's any left, I'll take you up on that. So is your baking done for the day?"

"Not quite. I decided to make a pie too. Why don't we go into the kitchen and I'll finish that up while we drink our hot chocolate?"

"That works."

He followed her to the back of the condo but remained standing while she pulled out a saucepan.

"You can sit." She motioned to one of the two stools at her counter.

"My parents had a rule. Nobody sits till everybody sits. Put me to work."

"I like that as a general rule for families, but guests are exempt."

"Not this one."

He wasn't budging.

Kind of nice, really.

"Well . . . if you insist." She handed him a container of unsweetened cocoa powder. "Measuring spoons are in the drawer to the right of the sink. Sugar canister is on the counter above. You can add two tablespoons of cocoa and two tablespoons of sugar to the milk."

"Got it."

She measured two cups of milk into the saucepan and set it on medium heat.

While he completed his task, she pulled a bag of chocolate chips and a bottle of vanilla extract from another cabinet.

Once the milk was warm, she whisked in the chips and vanilla until the chips had melted.

"And now for my secret ingredient." She pulled out a bottle of peppermint schnapps from the cabinet under the sink. Added a splash.

"Aha. You're a mint lover."

"Can you think of a more perfect combination than chocolate and mint?"

"As a matter of fact, no. My mom's recipe for chocolate mint squares always gets rave reviews. I'll save you a couple next time I make them."

Another excuse to see each other again.

This day was getting better and better.

After stirring the hot chocolate again, she poured it into two mugs and topped it with whipped cream. "Enjoy."

He took a sip, which left him with an endearing white mustache. "Amazing."

Tapping her upper lip, she handed over a paper napkin. "One of the downsides of whipped cream, but so worth it."

"I agree." He wiped off the residue and motioned to her piecrust. "Are you going to blind bake that?"

She blinked.

He was familiar with blind baking?

While a fair number of men knew their way around a kitchen, most in her acquaintance stuck to the basics.

"Yes." She picked it up off the counter and slid it into the oven. "You seem to be familiar with some of the intricacies of baking."

"I learned to cook long ago. By necessity. These days I do it for fun on weekends. Nothing on the scale of a professional like you."

"Why did you have to learn to cook?"

He took a slow sip of his hot chocolate. "It's a long story. I don't mind telling it to you, but why don't we finish your pie first?"

We?

He wanted to help with that too?

A little shiver of pleasure rippled through her at his offer, which was odd. Cooking solo had always been her preference.

But the idea of having a partner in the kitchen was suddenly oh-so-appealing.

"If you're certain you want to help."

"I wouldn't have offered if I didn't."

"Okay. Then let's do this." She sampled her own hot chocolate and positioned the recipe for him to see. "I'll put the pumpkin, brown sugar, and eggs on the counter. You can measure them and whisk everything together while I get the rest of the ingredients out."

"Sounds like a plan."

As he went to work and she began collecting the spices, cream, and milk, it was clear Jack was at home in the kitchen. She didn't have to tell him to pack the brown sugar, or remind him to be precise in his measurements, or show him how to whisk.

"You're good at this." She pulled the cream from the fridge and started back to the island.

He hiked up one side of his mouth. "Thanks. That's quite a compliment, coming from a pro. How did you become a chef, anyway? Did you follow in the footsteps of someone in your family?"

She froze at the innocent but loaded question.

While Madeleine had gleaned bits and pieces of her background, only Clair knew the whole story.

Yet all at once she was tempted to share it with the handsome detective whose calm demeanor, quiet competence, and caring manner had helped her navigate the turbulent waters that had roiled her life these past three weeks.

But should she, at this early stage of their relationship?

Or was her less-than-rosy history with her parents best kept under wraps until a stronger foundation of trust had been established?

TWENTY

APPARENTLY THE FOLLOW-IN-THE-FOOTSTEPS question he'd thought was innocuous had been anything but.

As Lindsey's shoulders stiffened, Jack stopped whisking. "Sorry. I didn't mean to tread on sensitive ground."

She continued to the island and set the container of cream on top. "No need to apologize. I just don't talk much about my family situation."

"I can change the subject. Why don't we—"

"No. It's okay." She exhaled. Faced him. "I can give you the highlights. Or lowlights, to be more precise. Cooking isn't a family tradition. My dad was in international finance and my mom's the VP of marketing for a Fortune 500 company."

When she named the firm, he hiked up his eyebrows. "Impressive."

"Yeah, it is—and Mom and Dad had similar career aspirations for me. Law or medicine were their suggestions, given my excellent grades. But I didn't have the stomach for blood, and law bored me. After some mega battles, I agreed to get a business degree. One year into the corporate world, though, I knew I couldn't spend my life doing that kind of work. I wanted a more creative outlet that fed my soul as well as my body. Hard as I tried, I couldn't be the person Mom and Dad wanted me to be. So I quit my job and went to culinary school."

"How did your mom feel about that?" Because her dad would have been gone by then if he'd died twelve years ago, as she'd told him.

She turned aside to rummage through a drawer. "She wasn't happy." There was a world of hurt in her voice.

His heart contracted. "She didn't support your choice, did she?"

"No." Lindsey kept her back to him as she withdrew a large stirring spoon. "As Mom made clear, she didn't send me to a high-priced college so I could flip pancakes or be a scullery maid."

Jack cringed. "I'm sorry." Not close to adequate, but it was too soon for the hug he was tempted to give her.

"Thanks. But I did fine. After I graduated, I landed a job at a high-end restaurant in South Carolina. I planned to work on that side of the business for about ten years, then venture out on my own. The grocery store incident accelerated my timetable."

"How did you end up in St. Louis?"

She swiveled back toward him, her features schooled into a neutral expression. "I'd visited Clair on several occasions after she got her job here, and I liked the town. It seemed like it would be a good fit."

"Has it been?"

"Yes. Except for everything that's happened in the past three weeks, I've enjoyed living here and establishing a business."

"All of the bad stuff will be behind you eventually."

"It can't happen soon enough to suit me." She set the spoon on the island, pulled the piecrust from the oven, and returned to the counter that separated them. "Ready for me to add the rest of the ingredients?"

They were done talking about her parents.

Yet from the condensed history she'd provided, her life hadn't been a bed of roses on the family front, either.

And it helped explain why she'd been angry with him for urging her best friend to do something that didn't reflect her interests or personality.

He gave the contents of the bowl another quick whisk and pushed the mixture toward her across the island. "Have at it."

It took only a couple of minutes to stir in the remaining ingredients, but he did a double take as she measured the last one. "You put pepper in pumpkin pie?"

The corners of her lips tipped up. "A secret ingredient shared with me by one of the pastry chefs I used to work with." She measured out an eighth of a teaspoon, blended it in, and poured the filling into the crust.

Once the pie was in the oven, Lindsey set a timer and motioned to the stools at the counter. "Shall we sit? The cheesecake has to bake at least another half hour, and the pie will take close to an hour."

Uh-oh.

She was expecting him to keep his promise to explain the comment he'd made earlier, about the necessity of learning to cook.

His pulse picked up.

While he'd intended to follow through, a sudden wave of doubt crashed over him. His story wasn't pretty, and who knew how she'd react?

Cradling her mug in her hands, Lindsey remained silent. She didn't push. She simply waited for him to get comfortable with the idea of sharing confidences—or not.

He had seconds to make a decision.

Honor his promise to tell her more about his background, or succumb to a case of cold feet and flee?

Yet she'd opened up to him. Didn't he owe her the same in return? Especially if he wanted this relationship to progress?

Just do it, Tucker. You'll have to tell her at some point, and if your background turns her off, you may as well know now rather than set yourself up for heartbreak later.

That was true.

But how did you launch into a tale you'd never told a single soul?

WHATEVER JACK'S SECRET, he'd changed his mind about sharing it.

Curious as she was about his earlier cooking comment and his odd reluctance to rescue the boy's Frisbee in the park, it would be unkind to press the issue. Best to give him an out.

Lindsey pushed up the corners of her mouth. "Maybe sitting isn't the best idea. I expect you have chores to take care of the day before the holiday, like everyone else does."

His eyebrows dipped into a V, and when he spoke, his words were slow and careful. As if he was weighing each one. "I do have to make a green bean casserole for dinner at my sister's tomorrow. It was a staple at every family holiday gathering for as long as I can remember. One of Mom's specialties. My foster mom's, that is. My birth mother . . . Lorraine . . . she didn't cook much."

Was that an opening? Did he want her to ask a few questions, help guide him along whatever path he wanted to go down?

She slid onto one of the stools and approached with caution. "That fits with what you mentioned earlier, about learning to cook out of necessity."

"Yeah." After a nanosecond of hesitation, he circled the

island and took the stool beside her, resting an elbow on the countertop as he angled toward her. "I learned to forage from a very young age."

"How young?"

He gave her a taut shrug. "As far back as I can remember, to some degree. More so after I was seven. Lorraine was an indifferent mom at best, a terrible one at worst." His fingers curled into a ball, and a muscle ticced in his jaw. "She had huge, unpredictable mood swings and delusions. She always thought someone was trying to break into our apartment, and she'd tell me to watch the door. If I got distracted, she'd fly into a rage and punish me. I don't remember when that started, but the pattern was well-established by the time I was four."

Shock rippled through her. "That's far too young to be given any sort of responsibility."

"Not according to Lorraine."

Lindsey wasn't certain she wanted to hear the answer to her next question, but she asked it anyway. "How did she punish you?"

A subtle quiver rippled through him. Easy to miss if she hadn't been watching closely. "She'd drag me up to the roof of our apartment, dangle me over the edge, and threaten to drop me." His voice hoarsened, and he cleared his throat. Swallowed.

Lindsey stopped breathing.

How did a person survive that kind of abuse and grow up to be normal, aside from an understandable fear of heights?

"Where was your father during all this?"

"I have no idea. He was never part of my life. There's no father listed on my birth certificate."

"And no one knew about the abuse?" She gently rested her fingers on top of his clenched fist.

He looked down at their connected hands. "My grand-mother caught her doing it one day when I was five. Not

long after that, she moved in with us, and life got calmer—
and safer. She watched out for me. Loved me. Cared for me.
Showed me the only kindness I'd ever known. She died when
I was seven, but those two years with her saved me."

"Did your mom go back to punishing you after she died?"

"Not with the roof routine. I was big enough at that age
to fight her off. So she stopped taking care of me. I subsisted
on cereal and canned goods, learned to do my own laundry,
cleaned my own room. That's when I vowed someday to learn
to cook so I never had to eat cereal again."

Jack's story was even more of a nightmare than what she'd
been living through these past three weeks.

"How did you end up in foster care? Did someone finally
report your birth mother?"

"No. She abandoned me the summer I turned eight. Left
one day and never came back. For two months, I lived alone,
eating from garbage cans after the food in the apartment ran
out."

An eight-year-old left to survive on his own?

Unbelievable.

"Your neighbors didn't notice what was going on?"

He barked out a mirthless laugh. "Where we lived, everybody kept to themselves. These weren't the type of people
who wanted anyone to know their business."

"So how did foster care enter the picture?"

"We got thrown out of the apartment. Turns out Lorraine
hadn't paid the rent for months. An eviction notice came, but
I couldn't read all the big words. The first I knew about it
was when I came home one day after scavenging for food and
found the front door locked and all our stuff on the sidewalk."

Merciful heaven.

The story kept getting worse and worse.

"What did you do?"

"I panicked. Not because I was on my own. I was used to

that. But Gram had a gold claddagh pendant her father had given her mother on their wedding day in Ireland. Gram treasured it. She kept it in a box of cough drops in her dresser where Lorraine wouldn't find it and hock it, but once in a while she'd take it out and show it to me. Thankfully, no one who'd gone through the broken-down furniture on the sidewalk had bothered with the cough drops. The pendant was still there."

A little, motherless boy who suddenly had nowhere to live but who cared more about a sentimental item from his grandmother than where he would sleep that night.

Her heart melted.

She took a sip of her hot chocolate, swallowing past the lump in her throat as she struggled to hold on to her composure. "So if the apartment was locked, what did you do? Did you ask someone to call the police?"

"No. Lorraine had always told me to stay away from them. She said they caused problems. So I went to the church at the corner and knocked on the door of the house beside it. A priest answered. He fed me and assured me the police weren't my enemies. He also stayed with me through the whole ordeal with the patrol officer and the woman from Social Services who showed up. By the end of the evening, I was with Mom and Dad. And I never left."

Lindsey let out a slow breath. "I can't believe everything you went through as a child. Most people who'd experienced all that wouldn't have gone on to live a normal, productive life."

"I wouldn't have, either, if it hadn't been for Gram, and then Mom and Dad. But those early years messed with my mind for a long time. Part of me thought it was my fault Lorraine was the way she was. That I'd failed her somehow, and that's why she left. Why she punished me."

"Oh, Jack." She twined her fingers with his. "None of that

was your fault. It's obvious your birth mother had psychological issues."

"I realize that now. From the research I've done, I suspect she had schizophrenia or bipolar disorder. But coming to grips with that was tough. And I've never overcome my fear of heights. Other than that, though, I gradually settled into a more normal life, thanks to Mom and Dad. From the day they took me until the day they died, they did everything they could to make up for my rough beginning." The last word rasped.

Thank God he'd been placed in a loving home. Otherwise, Jack could easily have ended up on the other side of the law.

"I'm glad your story had a happy ending."

"I am too. Sadly, not all foster kids are as lucky. That's why I take a week of vacation every year and volunteer at Camp Gideon. Have you heard of it?"

"No." But kudos to him for his willingness to help others.

"It's a summer camp for kids like me, started by an ex-army pilot who was also in the foster program. It's about forty-five minutes west of St. Louis. Kids from backgrounds like mine need a leg up, and Rick does a great job creating a memorable and positive experience for them."

"I doubt he could do it without volunteers like you."

Jack lifted one shoulder. "I believe in paying it forward." He looked again at her hand resting on his while several silent seconds ticked by. "You know . . . I've never told that story to anyone."

Her heart stumbled. "Not even your parents?"

"No." He lifted his head and his gaze locked onto hers, its intensity short-circuiting her lungs. "But I'm glad I told you."

"I'm glad too." Her response came out in a whisper.

"I also want to thank you for telling me about the situation with your parents. Your mom in particular."

"It pales in comparison to what you went through."

"Hurt is hurt. And it's always worse when it comes from a family member." He eased his hand free and slid off his stool. "I should go. Your desserts will need your attention soon, and I have a casserole to make."

She stood too, despite her reluctance for this confidence-sharing session to end.

He followed her to the foyer, slipping his arms into his coat after she removed it from the closet. "I hope you enjoy your holiday."

"You too." But pleasant as her day at Madeleine's would be, spending it with the detective who'd just offered her a window into his soul would be much, much better.

A timer began to beep.

"Your cheesecake calls." Jack's lips curved up.

She shifted her focus to them.

They were very nice lips. Firm, but with a hint of softness that suggested his kisses would be—

"Lindsey?"

She yanked her gaze back to his eyes, where heat had begun to simmer. "Cheesecake. Right." She fought down the warmth threatening to spill onto her cheeks. "Burnt cheesecake from a chef would be a major faux pas."

"Unless she had an excuse for being distracted." Without breaking eye contact, he lifted his hand and trailed a finger down her cheek, sending a tingle through every nerve in her body.

Oh, man.

She grabbed the edge of the closet door and held on tight.

"Are you—" Her voice cracked, and she tried again. "Are you flirting with me, Detective?"

"No. I don't flirt. I believe in sending direct messages." He maintained the skin-to-skin contact for another moment, then withdrew his hand. "Happy Thanksgiving, Lindsey."

"You too."

"I'll be in touch after the holiday. But if anything comes up in the interim, call me."

"Okay." It was all she could manage.

As she continued to cling to the closet door, he let himself out, the soft click of the lock behind him prompting her to tiptoe over and peek through the sidelight.

At his car, Jack stopped at the door and lifted a hand in farewell.

Huh.

If he was that certain she'd be watching, she must have sent a boatload of I'm-smitten clues.

But who cared? They'd entered new territory today, and the future was brighter now that much had been explained. Like his fear of heights. And his understandable reluctance to get involved with anyone who might have mental issues similar to his birth mother's. Plus, a deep-seated fear of desertion could also make him cautious about entering into any relationship.

His touch at their parting, however, suggested he was fast putting any reservations behind him.

One more blessing to be grateful for this Thanksgiving week.

The only thing that could make tomorrow's holiday even happier?

Solving the Robertson murder case and an end to bizarre incidents like the ones that had upended her world over the past three weeks.

Unfortunately, a vague niggle of unease as she watched Jack drive away left her with an unsettling feeling that they weren't out of the woods yet.

Where do we stand?

Proceeding according to plan.

We may have to get rid of her if she
remembers anything else.

> Shouldn't be necessary. We've made sure her
> credibility is compromised, and the carpenter
> is still a prime suspect thanks to the planted
> and pawned jewelry. I don't want any more
> killing.

Like I've said, we could set it up to come
across as a suicide or an accident. After all,
she's been under a lot of strain.

> Easier said than done.

I have confidence we can pull it off, just like
we've pulled off everything else. Is the tattoo
gone?

> Getting there. It isn't fun.

It's less painful than going to prison. That
tattoo should have been gone long ago
anyway. When can we get together?

> Safer to wait until this is over.

I'm getting impatient. This is dragging on
much longer than I expected.

> If there hadn't been a witness in the kitchen
> that day, we'd be home free. Have to go.
> Schedule is full this afternoon.

You're always busy.

> Goes with the territory. Life will be less crazy
> after this is over.

If getting rid of Lindsey Barnes will speed up
that outcome, I'm in.

I'll keep that in mind. Happy Thanksgiving.

Not as happy as it could be.

There's always next year.

Hold that thought. And keep Lindsey in your
sights. We're too close to our goal to let
anything—or anyone—stand in our way.

TWENTY-ONE

IT WAS PART OF A name.

Wrenching her eyes open, Lindsey bolted upright in bed. Groped for the switch on her bedside lamp. Squinted as soft light flooded her room at this post-midnight hour.

The mark on the arm of the person who'd killed James Robertson *had* been a tattoo. The image of it that had replayed in her mind as she slumbered was real. She could call it up just as clearly wide awake.

While most of it had been hidden by the sleeve of the long coat, two letters had been visible when the person reached down to pick up the dropped piece of jewelry that had come to rest mere inches from her hiding place.

An *e* and a *y*.

The swirl at the end of the *y* had curved back up over the letters and disappeared into the sleeve of the coat.

She had to tell Jack.

But not at this hour. Her news could wait until tomorrow. Perhaps shared over the piece of cheesecake she'd saved for him from Thanksgiving dinner two days ago.

Wouldn't that be a pleasant end to the long holiday weekend?

Mouth curving up, Lindsey eased back under the covers as the wind outside whistled past, rattling the shutters. Hopefully the meteorologists were wrong, and the snow in the forecast would pass St. Louis by. If they did get dumped on, that could put a damper on a visit from Jack.

But not on her news—and waiting to tell him in person wasn't an option. So first thing tomorrow she'd give him a call, whether a personal visit was in the offing or not.

And if new information kept surfacing, there might be enough fragments at some point to piece together a solid lead for the police to follow.

An outcome that would please everyone involved.

Except the killer.

HIS FAVORITE CHEF was on the line.

Smiling, Jack grabbed his cell off the counter as he finished pouring his first cup of Sunday java. "Morning."

"I didn't wake you, did I?"

"No. I always get up with the sun. How was your Thanksgiving?"

"Lovely. How about yours?"

"Very pleasant. Bri outdid herself. I think she was trying to impress her new boyfriend and his grandmother."

"Did it work?"

"Near as I could tell. If someone made a feast like that for me, I'd sit up and take notice."

"Duly noted. Moving on to other topics, I have news."

He sipped his coffee while she filled him in on her latest recollection, waiting until she finished to speak. "That will be very helpful if we can ever identify any suspects besides Allen."

"How can Chad still be a suspect? He doesn't have a tattoo."

"Whoever did this could have had an accomplice. Allen was in a perfect position to act as a lookout."

"Then he fell down on the job, because I got past him. If he was watching the door, wouldn't he have tried to divert me?"

Hard to argue with that.

"I agree we can rule him out as the killer—and likely as an accomplice."

"He and Dara will be relieved to hear that. By the way, there's a piece of Oreo cheesecake in my fridge with your name on it."

He gave the snowy scene outside his window a regretful scan. "If we weren't in the midst of a blizzard, I'd run over for it. As it is, I'm even forgoing church."

"Join the club. No worries on the cheesecake. It will keep in my freezer for months."

"I don't intend to wait that long to claim it."

"Nice to know. So I guess we're both in hibernation mode for the day. Let's hope the streets are clear by tomorrow, though. I have a busy week ahead."

"Busier than usual?"

"Mm-hmm. Heidi Robertson asked me to cater a lunch on Tuesday for the employees at her husband's company. Or her company now. A thank-you to them for helping her get up to speed on the business. I had to work that into my schedule in addition to my usual clients. What does your week look like?"

"Also busy. But less predictable than yours. Crime doesn't happen on a schedule."

"Maybe you'll get a new lead on the Robertson case."

If only.

"We can hope, but at the moment the details you're re-membering are it."

"No pressure there."

"None intended. In terms of the tattoo, I'd like to hook you up with one of our sketch artists to try and recreate what you saw. There are a few tattoo databases out there, and it's possible we may get a hit."

"Sure. Have them give me a call."

"I'll try to join you for the session if I can." Not customary, but he'd take any excuse he could get to see Lindsey.

"That would be great."

In the background, the beep of a timer echoed. "It sounds like you've already been working in the kitchen." He wandered over to the window.

"I got up early too. Once that image came to me in the middle of the night, it was hard to get back to sleep. Instead of lying there staring at the ceiling, I decided to put the hours to productive use and get a jump on the food I'm making for Tuesday's lunch."

"I won't keep you then. Expect a call from one of our forensic artists tomorrow. And slot me into your busy schedule for that piece of cheesecake. Maybe later in the week, if both of us are available."

"I'll pencil you in for Thursday or Friday."

"That'll work. In the interim, watch your back."

"Trust me, I've been looking over my shoulder for weeks. And as you know from personal experience, I always have my pepper gel at the ready."

"Stay with that program until we get this case solved."

"That's my plan."

Much as he hated to end the call, she had chores to attend to and he had case reports to bring up to date. Not the most exciting task on this snowed-in Sunday, but he might as well make constructive use of the downtime, as Lindsey was.

"I'll talk to you soon."

As they said their goodbyes and he ended the call, Jack gave the landscape outside his frosted window a sweep. The white curtain of falling flakes obscured the view, hiding all details of the terrain beneath a mantle of white. It was easy to see how settlers on the plains back in the 1800s could get lost and freeze to death while walking between their house and their outbuildings during a snowstorm, despite the fact that all the clues to guide them were close by if only they could see for a few brief seconds through the concealing snow.

A spot-on analogy for the Robertson case.

Surely there were more clues out there that would lead them to the killer. Perhaps within touching distance. All they needed was a break.

But unless they got one soon, whoever had shot James Robertson was literally going to get away with murder.

"*EXCELLENT JOB, LINDSEY.* Thank you for working this into your schedule."

At Heidi's comment, Lindsey turned toward her in the Robertson Properties conference room, where the thank-you lunch was winding down. "I was happy to do it. The menu wasn't complicated, and I was able to prepare a lot of the food while I was snowbound over the weekend. Plus, my afternoon client yesterday canceled, which gave me some breathing space."

"However you managed it, everything was delicious. And the treat was much deserved after everyone's efforts to help me get a handle on things here." She surveyed the employees who were milling about, sampling the gooey butter cake squares and triple chocolate brownies. Sighed. "It's hard to focus on business, though, when all I can think about is James—and the questions that remain about his . . . his death." Her voice caught, and she pulled out a tissue. "Sorry. Hard as I try to be businesslike here at the office, sometimes I slip."

"I'm sure everyone understands." She started to reach toward the woman to give her arm an encouraging pat. Dropped her hand. Heidi wasn't the touchy-feely type. "I know the police are working hard to answer all your questions. And I'm also remembering more details that may prove helpful."

Heidi dabbed at the corner of her eye. "About the person you saw in the kitchen?"

"Yes. I know now that the mark I saw on their arm was a tattoo. I remembered two letters, below the sleeve of the coat. I met with a forensic artist from the police department yesterday afternoon, who was able to reproduce what I saw." Too bad Jack hadn't been able to join them, as he'd hoped. But an armed assault took precedence over a drawing session.

"Did the police think that would be helpful?"

"It's possible. The case detective said there are tattoo databases out there, but I think it will be more useful if they identify a suspect on their own and then see if that person has a tattoo."

"I suppose any new clue is positive news, no matter how . . . oh, Eric! May I borrow you a minute to talk about that strip mall opportunity?"

Lindsey glanced behind her. A fortyish man holding a gooey butter square in one hand and a can of soda in the other stood a few feet away.

"Sure."

"Lindsey, will you excuse me? I have a pending business decision, and I haven't had a minute all morning to meet with Eric."

"Of course. I'll refill the brownie plate."

As she moved away, Heidi motioned the man into a corner of the conference room, where the two conversed in low tones.

Lindsey continued to the small adjacent kitchen and began removing the plastic wrap from the last tray of brownies.

Stepping into her husband's shoes had to be tough for Heidi, but she seemed to be rising to the challenge. And maybe the work was a blessing in disguise, if it kept her from dwelling on—

Her phone began to vibrate, and she pulled it out.

Dara.

A twinge of guilt nipped at her conscience.

Why hadn't she carved out a few minutes to call her with the definitive news about the tattoo? Putting the young bride's mind at ease should have been a priority.

"Hi, Dara." She closed the door to the conference room, muffling the laughter and conversation. "I've been thinking about you and Chad. How are you doing?"

"Chad's fine. I've got the flu."

Good grief. What else could happen to the newlyweds?

"I'm sorry to hear that. How sick are you?"

"I have a hundred and two temperature and I feel like I've been hit by a truck. I was calling to let you know I won't be at class tomorrow night."

"Is there anything I can do for you?"

"Keep your distance. I wouldn't wish this on my worst enemy."

"I hear you. I do have a piece of news that may cheer you up a little." She relayed the story about the tattoo again. "So Chad should be off the hook."

"I don't know." Dara didn't sound convinced. "He said even if the mark you saw did turn out to be a tattoo, the police could think he was an accomplice."

Jack's exact take.

"I don't believe that. And I don't think the police are giving the partner theory much credence, either."

"That would be a relief. The pressure is keeping Chad awake at night. But I know he wasn't involved."

Dara's tone was confident. As if she'd put all doubts about her husband to rest. Which was heartening.

Unless he really was somehow involved.

Lindsey frowned as that scurrilous suspicion infiltrated her mind.

Where had *that* come from?

Never in their acquaintance had Chad done anything to suggest he was less than trustworthy. Jack might have to keep doubts front and center in his job, but she wasn't going to let his professional mindset color her view of the world. Her judgment about people had always been sound. Besides, they knew Chad wasn't the killer. He didn't have a tattoo. And her rationale for nixing the accomplice notion was logical.

Chad hadn't been involved in the murder.

"Hold on to that thought, Dara, and take care of yourself. I'll email you the recipes from tomorrow's lesson."

"Thanks, but don't rush. I won't be doing any cooking for the next few days."

Lindsey cracked the door to the conference room and surveyed the table. She ought to be able to gather up enough leftovers for a couple of meals. It wasn't as if Heidi would take the extra food home, anyway. Her tastes leaned more toward nouvelle cuisine than the Waldorf chicken salad sandwiches and cheddar potato soup entrees served today. But she'd clear the donation with the woman anyway. Now that Chad was off the suspect list, Heidi wasn't likely to mind sharing leftovers with him and his sick wife.

"I'll tell you what. Why don't I drop off some food for you and Chad later this afternoon? I'll ring the bell and leave it on the porch."

"I don't want to put you to any trouble."

"It's no trouble. I catered a lunch today, and not all the food was eaten. If you or Chad need anything else, let me know."

"Thank you so much. Madeleine made the same offer when she called earlier today. She sent a bunch of leftovers home with us on Thanksgiving too. I don't know what I would have done these past few weeks without the two of you."

"That's what friends are for." No surprise that the Horizons director was keeping tabs on Dara and Chad, or that she'd invited them to Thanksgiving. The woman's generosity was boundless and spilled over far beyond her commitment to the nonprofit organization she'd founded.

"I owe you two big-time."

"No, you don't. Just pay it forward." As Jack continued to do with his volunteer work at the foster camp.

"I'll do that." Weariness etched her voice.

"You rest. Tell Chad to watch for the food later."

After they said goodbye, Lindsey slid her phone back into her pocket and continued unwrapping the brownies, setting aside four for Dara and Chad in case the hungry horde in the conference room devoured all of them.

Should she pilfer one for Jack too?

No.

The cheesecake in her freezer ought to be sufficient to entice him to visit again—if seeing her wasn't adequate incentive.

But based on their parting last Wednesday, there was plenty of motivation with or without a culinary treat.

Until the Robertson murder was solved, though, he'd no doubt confine any romantic inclinations to a simple touch. He was too much of a pro to mix business and pleasure.

The question was, when would the case wind down?

She picked up a piece of broken brownie and popped it in her mouth, but the rich, chocolaty taste didn't sweeten her outlook.

Yes, a few details buried under the trauma in her memory were emerging, but eventually that well would dry up. If the case remained active and unsolved, how long would it take Jack to decide it was acceptable to put it on the back burner and move romance to the front?

Longer than she'd like, probably.

So all she could do was hope more clues surfaced, and that this case would be closed soon without anyone else getting hurt.

We have a problem.

        What's wrong now?

Lindsey's remembering more—including the
last two letters of the tattoo.

        The tattoo is being taken care of.

Not fast enough.

        You need to calm down. She hasn't
        remembered anything that can hurt us.

What if she does?

        She won't. And her credibility is already in
        question. It can become more questionable if
        necessary.

I think it's necessary now.

        Let's be patient.

I'm tired of being patient. Why don't we just
get rid of her?

        I don't want any more killing.

That's not my first choice, either, but if it has
to be done, it has to be done.

        We're not there yet.

If we wait too long, we may be sorry.

        Trust me on this, okay? I've got it under
        control.

You said that about the setup at the house,
and look where we are now.

That was a fluke. No one knew Lindsey would show up.

Whatever the reason, we have a mess.

We're fine. I promise.

You've promised a lot of things, but I'm still waiting for most of them to happen. I'm tired of skulking around in the shadows. I want this over.

It will be soon.

• • •

Hello? You there?

• • •

Message received. You're not happy. But please don't do anything rash. We're too close to the finish line to take risks. Let's discuss next steps together. One foolish mistake could put all our plans in jeopardy. Sleep on that thought tonight, and we'll talk tomorrow. Okay?

• • •

TWENTY-TWO

THIS COULDN'T BE HAPPENING.

Not again.

Lindsey stared at the spot where she'd parked for the cooking class, a dozen yards from the door.

It was empty.

Squeezing the strap on her tote, she scanned the dark lot as the cold wind battered her face, the mounds of snow from the storm last weekend hunched like malevolent white specters on the black asphalt.

Nada.

Her car was gone. No question about it.

Keeping an eye on the empty expanse, she retreated to the church hall, slipped back inside, and locked the door.

Now what?

She could call the police—but what if her car was parked around the corner, like it had been last time? They'd really think she was nuts if she reported it missing again.

Should she make a circuit of the streets on the perimeter of the church property, see if she could locate the car herself?

But what if she did find it? Was she supposed to simply drive away like this had never happened? Tell no one?

No. That would be foolish. For two reasons.

First, this wasn't the best neighborhood to be wandering around in at night, even armed with pepper gel. And second, if this was another attempt to undermine her integrity as a witness, to convince her and the police she was losing her mind, someone ought to know.

Someone like Jack.

She pulled out her cell. There was a risk in telling him, of course. It could erode the credibility she'd built up with him, renew his doubts about her memory of the events related to the murder as well as her potential as a romantic interest.

But someone had taken, or moved, her car. There was zero doubt in her mind about that.

Bracing, she tapped in his number.

He answered on the first ring. "Hi. I was just thinking about you."

On any other cold night, the warmth in his tone would have chased the chill from her bones. But who knew how he was going to react to her news?

She leaned back against the wall. Closed her eyes. "You're never going to believe this."

"What's up?" His manner switched at light speed from easygoing to dead serious.

"I'm at my cooking class. My car is gone again."

Silence as he digested that.

"You mean it's missing?"

"Yes."

"Where are you now?"

"In the church kitchen."

"Is anyone else there?"

"No."

"Stay put. I'm on my way." There wasn't a trace of skepticism or here-we-go-again frustration in his response.

"I hate to bring you out on such a cold night. Maybe I should take a stroll around the block, see if the car is parked on the perimeter like last time. I could keep my phone in hand and call you if I have any issues."

"No. I don't want you wandering around that neighborhood at night. I'll be there in fifteen minutes. Don't go outside. Lock the door and get your pepper gel out."

His grim, clipped tone must mean he was convinced her claim was valid.

Relief coursed through her, and she sank onto a stool, pressure building in her throat. "Thank you. Not only for coming but for not dismissing my story like I'm sure your colleagues did after the first incident."

"There have been too many odd episodes in the interim. And in the past few weeks I've gotten to know you. Even without consulting Oliver, I don't see any evidence to suggest all of these strange events are a figment of your imagination. Sit tight and watch for me."

The line went dead.

Taking a long, slow breath, Lindsey put her phone away, got out her pepper gel, and took up a position by the window that offered a view of the parking area.

Twenty-five minutes later, a car swung into the lot. When it stopped, the lights flicked off and Jack emerged.

She met him at the door.

"Everything okay?" He gave her a once-over.

"Fine."

"Did you see anyone in the lot while you waited for me?"

"No."

"Sorry it took me so long to get here. I circled the block before I pulled in. Your car's around the corner, next street over. I didn't want to leave until a patrol officer got there. He'll stay by it until I come back."

She pinched the bridge of her nose. "This is getting ridiculous."

"I can think of a stronger term." A muscle clenched in his cheek. "I also have news. While I waited for the officer, I took a close look at the car. There's a small streak of what appears to be relatively fresh blood on the car door near the handle. Could it be yours?"

"No. I haven't cut myself since the day James Robertson was killed. A nasty encounter with a knife while I was dicing at my next customer's house. I should have followed your advice and gone home instead of trying to carry on with my schedule. But that cut healed."

"Then we may have captured the perpetrator's DNA." He pulled out his cell. "I called my boss to have him get a CSU tech down here. I want the car gone over by an expert, and I want a blood sample sent to the lab ASAP. I also plan to knock on a few doors, see if anyone saw anything helpful."

"Does that mean you and my car will be here for the foreseeable future?"

"Well into the night, I imagine. Would you like me to have someone drive you home?"

Thanks to her full plate tomorrow, including a session with Dr. Oliver, she ought to accept. Even if hanging out here came with the bonus of a few hours in Jack's company.

"I do have a busy—" Her phone began to vibrate, and she pulled it out.

Madeleine.

The woman's timing was impeccable.

"Give me a minute."

"No rush." Jack strolled a few feet away and began scrolling through messages.

"Hi, Madeleine."

"Back at you. I just wanted to check in and make certain you didn't run into any glitches at the church because of the change in day for the class."

"No glitches with the church. A little glitch afterward."
She explained what had happened.

"You've got to be kidding me."

"I wish I was. I called the case detective, and he's going to
have one of their crime scene people come down to go over
the car. Maybe the blood he found will give them a lead."

"We can hope. If your car is stuck there, do you need a
ride home?"

"The detective offered to line one up for me."

"Why don't I pick you up instead?"

Tempting as it was to accept her offer instead of hitching a
lift with a stranger in a patrol car, it wouldn't be fair to drag
Madeleine out on a cold night like this when an alternative
was available.

"I don't want to bother you again."

"It's the least I can do, considering all the hours you've
donated to teaching classes for me."

"I appreciate it, but the church isn't exactly in your backyard."

"It is tonight. I was at a gallery opening for a showing by
a friend of mine not too far from the church, so I'm in the
neighborhood. Watch for me soon." She ended the call without
waiting for a response.

Lindsey slid her phone back into her pocket and swiveled
toward Jack. "My friend Madeleine is in the area and will
pick me up."

"That works." He rejoined her. "I can give you a lift back
here in the morning."

"I'd appreciate that. How long will it take to run the DNA?"

"In general, best case is twenty-four hours. I'll push hard
for a rapid test, though. As soon as I have it, I'll run it through
our databases and see if we can find a match."

"What if you don't?"

"We hang on to it. My gut tells me that whoever the blood

240

on your car belongs to is either Robertson's killer or has a close link to the killer."

"Your colleague's theory about someone trying to discredit me as a witness by pulling bizarre stunts is becoming more and more credible."

"After tonight, I'd say it's passed the theory stage. Whoever has been targeting you has done an excellent job covering their tracks—until tonight. Leaving blood behind was a big mistake. We'll run your DNA too to rule out a match, but if you don't have any cuts, it doesn't belong to you. I'll call you tomorrow to set that up."

Headlights swung into the lot, and Lindsey picked up her satchel. "Madeleine's here."

"I'll walk you out." He pushed open the door, and a frigid blast of wind pummeled them. "Sorry."

"Not your fault." A shiver rippled through her. "Who expects winter this early?"

"Welcome to St. Louis. By tomorrow it may feel like spring again." He angled his body to shield her while she pulled the door closed and double-checked the lock, then took her arm as they circled Madeleine's car. "I'll be in touch as soon as I know anything."

"Thanks again. For everything."

He closed the scant distance between them, a swirl of his subtle but potent aftershave tickling her nose. "My pleasure." The dim light shadowed his features, but the warmth in his husky voice was impossible to miss—and helped take the chill out of the night air.

Heart doing a happy dance, she slid in after he opened the door. Set her satchel on the floor while he closed it. "Thanks again, Madeleine. It was lucky you were close by." Her greeting sounded as breathless as if she'd run a fifty-yard dash.

"Providential." Her chauffeur watched Jack return to his car. "That's the case detective?"

"Yes."

"I like how he took your arm."

"He's, uh, very polite."

"Also very hot."

Lindsey clicked the seat belt into place, keeping her chin down. Thank goodness the darkness hid her flush. "I noticed."

"You'd be dead if you didn't. And I got the impression it was mutual. The body language between you two was telling."

Sheesh.

Was she that easy to read?

"He's very nice."

"Why do I have a feeling that's an understatement?" Though Madeleine's grin was hidden by the shadows, it spilled over into her inflection. "But hey. I'm rooting for you. It's not easy to find hot men who are also polite and nice. Yours truly can attest to that. I'm sorry for the circumstances that brought the two of you together, but God works in mysterious ways. Wouldn't it be amazing if all the weirdness happening in your life leads to romance?"

Madeleine moved on to other topics, suggesting her question had been rhetorical, but yeah. It would be amazing.

Best of all?

The odds of it happening appeared to be more and more in her favor with every passing day.

And now that the killer or someone connected to the killer had made a mistake, they might be one step closer to finding the identity of the person who'd committed the terrible crime in the Robertson kitchen—and turned her life into a living nightmare ever since.

***

HE WASN'T GOING to be happy if he found out about this.

But hopefully he wouldn't.

After all, the cut wasn't terrible. And as long as they continued to keep their distance, he wouldn't see it. At the rate things were going, it would be healed long before they had another in-person visit.

Unfortunately, however, it was deep. A candidate for stitches under other circumstances. But a visit to an urgent care center was out of the question. There could be no record of this injury.

At least the glove had caught most of the blood, once it was back on. Taking it off had been a mistake, but operating that stupid electronic signal device with gloved fingers had been impossible.

Besides, who knew Lindsey had a cracked taillight with a jagged edge that could snatch a muffler? Extricating the fabric had been tricky, and the clock had been ticking on the signal capture. Haste, it seemed, didn't just make waste. It also led to mistakes . . . and a case of follow-up jitters.

At least a scotch and soda would alleviate the latter. It would also take away the lingering bone chill from this frigid night. There ought to be enough booze left in the emergency reserve bottle for tonight. Tomorrow, the stash could be restocked.

Beneath the bandage, the cut began to throb, and blood started seeping through the gauze. Again.

A word slipped out that wasn't fit for polite company, but who cared? No one was around to hear it.

Wasn't there a rule about elevating wounds above the heart to control bleeding and swelling?

Worth a try, once the scotch was in hand.

And if lady luck deigned to smile after the cut stopped bleeding and the booze was gone, maybe sleep would come.

But the best cure for insomnia?

An end to the police investigation.

So if tonight's incident didn't convince the police Lindsey was crazy, there was only one step left to take.

Together, they had to make sure Lindsey stopped remembering.

Permanently.

Whether he liked it or not.

TWENTY-THREE

"ARE YOU SURE YOU'RE ALL RIGHT, Dr. Oliver?" Lindsey frowned at the therapist as their session wound down. "You're flushed again."

He offered her a strained smile. "Much as I hate to admit it, I've been feeling progressively worse this afternoon. In hindsight, I should have cut the day short. But I don't like to let clients down."

"People would understand if you got sick. There's a nasty flu bug going around."

"It doesn't feel quite like the flu or I wouldn't have continued to see clients all day. Maybe it was something I ate. If I'm still under the weather tomorrow, though, I'll have to reschedule my Friday clients. Fortunately, you're my last appointment of the day. After this, I plan to go home and crash."

"Why don't we cut our session short? In case you do happen to be coming down with the flu, I should keep my distance." Because if she didn't cook, her income flow would dry up. There was no paid sick leave for personal chefs—one of the downsides of working for yourself. A bout with the flu would deplete her bank balance and disappoint the clients who counted on her.

"If you don't mind, I think that would be advisable for both our sakes. I'll alert Margie about our shortened session so she can adjust your bill."

Lindsey waved that aside. "I'm not worried about a few dollars after all the nights you've stayed late to see me over the past few weeks."

"No. Fair is fair. If I don't give a full hour, I don't charge for a full hour. Is there anything else we should talk about before we both call it a day?" He closed his notebook.

"I don't think so. I'm just glad whoever moved my car last night made a mistake. It proves to me—and the police—that the other incidents were real too. I can't tell you what a huge relief that is."

"I'm sure it is. I know how worried you were that all the trauma had taken a serious mental toll." He pulled out his handkerchief and mopped his brow. "And now, it's time for this doctor to heal himself. I think my temperature is spiking."

Lindsey picked up her purse and stood. "I'll let myself out. Take care of yourself."

He rose too, much more slowly. As if pushing himself to his feet took supreme effort. "I'll try."

"Is there anything I can do for you?" While he never talked about his personal life, from the few comments Margie had made, he didn't have much, if any, family. And an ex-wife wasn't likely to be waiting in the wings to run emergency errands in case of illness.

"No, thank you. I'll be fine. Nothing a few aspirin, plenty of liquids, and rest won't cure."

"Well, my offer stands if you change your mind."

"Thank you."

"I'll see you next week." She left the office, crossed to the door, and exited into the hall.

As she headed toward the main entrance of the professional building, she turned her phone back on and scrolled through messages.

No voicemails, but there was a text from Jack.

> Sorry, but I have to cancel on the cheesecake
> tonight. Got pulled into a double homicide.
> Will be working very late. Rain check
> until tomorrow? Also, none of the nearby
> residents saw any suspicious activity around
> your car. DNA came back too. No match in
> databases. Still handy to have when we round
> up a suspect. Talk to you soon.

When, not if. At least he was staying optimistic.

But as she bundled up to brave the winter chill outside, her spirits drooped.

Wherever the killer was on this cold, inhospitable evening, they were probably gloating that despite the evidence they'd left on her car last night, and despite the fact that her credibility had been restored, the police were as baffled as ever about who'd murdered James Robertson. Neither of the clues she'd remembered had led anywhere, and without a match in the databases, last night's blood sample wasn't much use—which the killer no doubt knew when they bled on her car.

She exhaled and pushed through the outside door.

While it was possible another tidbit or two would surface from the depths of her mind, the odds there would be enough to identify the perpetrator were minuscule.

Bottom line, the police were no closer to finding out who was behind the murder than they'd been on day one.

Lindsey exhaled, a frosty cloud of breath forming in front of her face.

How galling to think that someone who had murdered in cold blood could be sitting in front of a cozy fire or enjoying a gourmet dinner with nary a care in the world, basking in the assurance they were home free.

A very real possibility.

And at this point, nothing short of a miracle was going to bring the culprit or culprits to justice.

HE DID NOT WANT to take this call.

But she or her lawyer would bug him all weekend if he didn't.

Vibrating cell in hand, Anthony Oliver locked the hall door behind Lindsey and dragged himself back to his desk.

A stiff drink, antibiotics, and peace of mind. That's what he needed.

The first two he could manage. The third? Not so much.

He carefully lowered himself into his chair and answered the call from his ex-wife. "I asked you not to disturb me during office hours."

"Office hours should be about over. It's late. Just like your alimony payment is. In case you've forgotten, yesterday was the first of the month. No deposits were made in my bank account."

As if he didn't know that.

But it was hard to pay the exorbitant amount she'd stiffed him for when the so-called sure-bet investments his broker had talked him into continued to nosedive.

"The money will be in your account by Monday." Somehow. Some way. Liquidating tanking stocks wasn't ideal, but if that kept his ex off his back and bought him more time, it was worth it. His money troubles should be over soon.

Unless his partner in crime continued to make mistakes.

Anger flared in his gut at the stupidity of last night's stunt, but he held it in check, just as he had when he'd learned the news. He'd deal with that complication after this call.

"You're late every month, Tony."

He pulled out his handkerchief again. Patted his forehead. The aspirin alone weren't cutting it anymore. He needed antibiotics.

"I'm doing the best I can. I don't make a fortune."

"You do very well."

"Not as well as I used to. A therapist who can't even salvage his own marriage loses credibility—and clients. My reputation took a hit after the divorce. People assumed that if I couldn't solve my own problems, I couldn't help them solve theirs. Rebuilding my practice has been slow going."

"You should have thought of that before we broke up. If you'd cared half as much about me as you do your clients, we'd still be together." Her whiny petulance grated on his nerves, as always.

"I couldn't be with you twenty-four seven, like you wanted. One of us had to work. And I was tired at the end of the day. I have a demanding job intellectually and emotionally."

"As you never failed to remind me."

Anthony started to respond to her sulky comeback. Stopped. They'd been over this territory ad nauseam. It was impossible to reason with her.

"You'll have your money Monday."

"I better. You owe me, Tony."

"Not anymore. You've been bleeding me dry for three years."

"It's those speculative stocks that are killing you."

"I only got into those because you and your fancy lawyer are soaking me for every penny you can get." How had he lived with this sniping woman for fifteen years while she spent money like there was no tomorrow? And now she'd driven him to the verge of bankruptcy. Between the hit his practice had taken after the divorce, the obscene amount she'd been awarded in the settlement, and the increasing debt he was sinking into as he tried to maintain his lifestyle, he'd be flat broke in six months.

That's why his plan had to succeed, despite last night's blunder.

On the plus side, the police wouldn't be able to trace the blood—as far as he knew.

"You never were good with money, Tony."

"You were certainly good at spending it." He bit back another retort. Getting into a shouting match would accomplish nothing. "This conversation is over."

"Fine. It's not a joy to talk to you, either. I'll watch for the deposit on Monday."

The line went dead.

Slowly he lowered the cell to his desk. Picked up the tepid bottle of water he'd sipped during Lindsey's session. Forced himself to take a long pull. Adding dehydration to his woes would be foolish.

As soon as he psyched himself up, he'd call—

A knock sounded, and Anthony lifted his arm to swipe at his forehead again. Winced. "Yes?"

Margie cracked the door. "Sorry to interrupt. Anything else you'd like me to do before I leave for the day?"

"Find a cure for the flu?" May as well go with that diagnosis. It was convenient if not accurate.

She cocked her head. "I thought you looked a little green around the gills at lunchtime. You should go home and rest."

"Next on my agenda. Could you contact my clients for tomorrow and reschedule them?"

"Of course. Do you mind if I do that from home? I have to pick up my daughter at ballet."

"Fine by me. I'd rather you avoid any germs I'm spreading." Not that there were any germs to spread.

"I won't argue. The flu can knock you flat. Take care of yourself, and let me know how you're doing in the morning."

She closed the door behind her, and Anthony pulled out his burner phone. On to the next call. One that would require much more finesse than the last one. Difficult to manage if you weren't in top form and were seething with anger, but it couldn't be put off. Loose cannons had to be dealt with as fast as possible.

He punched in the number.

She answered on the third ring. "This is a surprise. I thought we were confining our communication to texts."

"That was the plan. But this is an emergency. Let's not use any names during our conversation." He took a calming breath. "I heard about the car incident."

Silence.

He waited.

"I suppose your client told you. Did you have a session today?"

"She left a few minutes ago."

"I did tell you I was tired of waiting. And I miss you. We were supposed to be able to get together by now. Move on to the next part of our plan."

"If we hadn't had an unexpected complication, we'd already be there."

"We can get rid of that complication."

"I don't want any more killing. Once was bad enough."

"What if she keeps remembering things?"

"There can't be much more to remember. I was covered head to toe. I'm more worried about last night. They found blood on her car. Yours, I presume."

"Yes. I cut my finger. But my blood isn't in any database. I've never had a run-in with the law, served in the military, or submitted a sample to any of those genealogy places. That tattoo of yours is a bigger problem. You should have gotten rid of it after you divorced Shelley."

"No names, remember?" He rested his arm on the desk, grimacing as the sensitive skin and pus-filled blisters stretched beneath the bandage under his long-sleeved dress shirt. Combined with fever and joint pain, those symptoms suggested infection—and the over-the-counter hydrogen peroxide cream hadn't had any effect. Thankfully, his doctor had been willing to prescribe an antibiotic after a phone consultation. For an infected cut, not a tattoo.

"Fine. I stand by what I said."

"I'm getting rid of it now."

"You-know-who has already seen part of it. Can't you speed up the process?"

"No. The skin has to heal for four to six weeks between each treatment. We're off the subject. I called to talk about our plan, and sticking with the program. Last night could have caused big problems."

"I was careful. I covered up, and no one saw me." She shifted into cajoling mode. "Oh, honey, don't be mad at me. I just want us to be together."

"I do too." He summoned up every ounce of his acting skills, putting as much sincerity into his voice as he could. She had to believe he loved her as much as she loved him. Otherwise, he'd lose his ticket to financial security. "But we'll have a whole lifetime together if we're patient and let this play out. I wish we didn't have to deal with the witness complication, either, but another killing will increase the risk."

"Not if it looks like an accident or suicide."

"Suicide is no longer an option. The blood from last night gives her previous stories credibility, which would bolster her confidence, not demoralize her and lead to suicide. An accident would require careful planning."

"You're an excellent planner."

He tamped down his annoyance. "I'll tell you what. I'll think about it and come up with a plan we can implement if necessary." Which would be never, as far as he was concerned. But if that concession appeased her in the short term and kept her toeing the line, it was an easy offer to make. "How does that sound?"

"Better than nothing." She sighed. "Why does love have to be so complicated?"

"I think it's the nature of the beast. Keep hanging in and we'll get through this."

"Can we at least talk now that you've broken radio silence?"

"Texts are still safer." If she was getting restless, however, an occasional call might help keep her in line. "But why don't I call you on Saturday night? We'll have a phone date."

"I suppose that will have to do. It's hard to get romantic over the phone, though."

"If we talk about all the things we're going to do once we're together again, it could get downright racy."

A soft, throaty chuckle came over the line. The one she liked to use in their private moments. "I'll hold you to that."

"You may. Until then, we're going to play it safe, right? No more risky stunts."

"No more stunts."

"Good. Watch for my call at nine o'clock Saturday night."

"I'll be waiting." She gave him a smooch over the line.

Rolling his eyes, he reciprocated. "Happy dreams."

"That's a given after hearing your voice. Love you, honey."

"Love you back. Good night." He stabbed the end button. Scowled. Slammed a drawer shut.

Women were more trouble than they were worth.

But he'd come too far down this path to backtrack. And he'd earned the payoff, even if he'd continue to pay a price for it well into the future.

Summoning up his energy, he pushed himself to his feet, circled his desk, and retrieved his coat from the closet. As soon as he picked up his antibiotic, he was going home and crashing. If the drugs kicked in, maybe by tomorrow his fever would be down and the pain in his arm would subside.

He shook his head in disgust.

Getting a tattoo to please Shelley was more proof of the folly of love. Or infatuation. Or whatever he'd felt for her long ago that had faded to nothing as the years passed.

Anthony eased his arm into the sleeve of his coat, flinching as the fabric put pressure on the bandage covering his sensitive skin—and trying not to think about the painful sessions yet to come over multiple months and the long drive to Columbia each time to minimize the risk of being recognized.

He settled the coat on his shoulders and exhaled.

The only positive on this cold, stressful night?

Despite the slipup with the car that had ruined all the work they'd done to cast doubt on Lindsey's mental health, and despite her resurfacing memories, there was virtually no chance the police would ever be able to pin James Robertson's murder on him.

After all, he had an airtight alibi, thanks to the professional conference he'd attended in Clayton that day. People constantly slipped in and out of sessions to take client calls, so no one had paid any attention when he'd left soon after one began and came in late to another after he returned following the lunch break.

And no one had seen him at the vacant house next to the Robertson place that had provided perfect cover. It had been a simple matter to cut through the bushes separating the properties, let himself in, and wait for the victim to come home.

Everything would have gone like clockwork if Lindsey hadn't shown up.

He muttered a word he would never use in front of clients

as he stepped out of his office suite and locked the door behind him.

If he was lucky, everything would quiet down and there would be no reason to take another life.

But an unnerving sixth sense told him his luck was running out . . . and that Lindsey's days were numbered.

TWENTY-FOUR

"READY TO CALL IT A NIGHT?" Cate clapped a hand over her mouth to cover a yawn. "I'm beat."

"I hear you. I've been going nonstop since sunrise." Jack twisted his wrist to see his watch. "That would be eighteen hours ago, give or take."

"I'm in the same boat. Unless you can think of anyone else to interview tonight, I say we're done."

"No one who can't wait until tomorrow. As far as I can see, this has crime of passion written all over it." Jack scanned the scene in the suburban home where the tragedy had unfolded. The two bodies had been removed, and the betrayed wife who'd apparently sought revenge was in custody. Every interview had painted a picture of a love triangle gone awry.

"I agree. We'll compare notes in the morning." She pulled a knit cap over her ponytail. "Midmorning. I'm sleeping in."

"You're the lead on this one, you set the schedule. And that works for me. I wouldn't mind clocking an extra hour or two myself after our late night."

"Speaking of late nights—did all of this interrupt your plans for the evening?" She swept a hand over the scene, where the CSU techs continued to work.

"Nothing that can't be rescheduled." The only upside to cancelling tonight's cheesecake rendezvous with Lindsey was that he still had it to look forward to.

A definite spirit-lifter.

"I get the feeling your plans would have been a whole lot more pleasant than this."

Jack flattened the slight bow in his lips. Nothing got past Cate. His fellow detective and Bri were cast from the same mold. "Anything would be more pleasant than this."

"True." Cate perused him for a beat, then moved on to a different topic. "I heard about the blood on the Robertson witness's car. Maybe that will lead somewhere."

"Not yet. There wasn't a DNA match in the databases."

Cate's eyebrows peaked. "You got DNA run already?"

"The lab did a rapid test for me."

"What strings did you have to pull to make that happen?"

He hiked up one side of his mouth. "I borrowed a page from your playbook. You know how Hank likes your sister's baklava? Someone in the lab is partial to my chocolate mint squares and was willing to work through lunch with that as an incentive."

"Bribery."

"Kindness." His grin broadened as he parroted her words back to her from their conversation weeks ago about Hank. "What can I say? I'm a nice guy."

"Hmph." She pulled out her gloves. "It's a shame your effort to expedite the process didn't lead to a match in the system."

"It may confirm a suspect as our killer down the road, though."

"You're an optimist. If you want my opinion, that case will die on the vine unless your witness remembers something else useful."

"That could happen."

"Keep the faith. Whoever killed Robertson needs to be

behind bars. Let's regroup on this one tomorrow and hope the wife ends up confessing."

"Now who's being optimistic?"

"At least I have a suspect."

"I will too, one of these days."

"In the meantime, go home and get some sleep. See you tomorrow." She fished out her keys and strode toward the door.

Jack followed more slowly.

The truth was, Cate was spot-on. The Robertson case was cold, and getting colder by the day. Their few breaks hadn't produced any usable leads, and as Oliver had reminded him during their chat, the more time that passed, the less likely Lindsey would remember anything—and the less reliable her memory would be if she did. That wasn't a negative assessment of her mental stability. It was a fact. Memories had a tendency to fade and become fuzzy.

So unless the killer made another mistake or they got a lucky break, the Robertson murder seemed destined for the cold case file.

MAYBE SHE WAS BEING PRESUMPTUOUS.

Frowning, Lindsey braked in the circle drive in front of Dr. Oliver's house as darkness fell, leaving the world in shadows.

The chicken and broccoli casserole she'd put together for him last night after their session, stored in a cooler in her trunk, was a thoughtful gesture—but did a home delivery to your therapist cross a line between professional and personal?

She surveyed the upscale, contemporary house. While not as glitzy as some of the homes she visited as a personal chef, it was at the high end of the housing spectrum. Obviously well-established psychologists with a solid client base made big bucks.

Not that she begrudged him a handsome return for his

work. Heck, anyone who helped people get through tough stretches deserved to live in a mansion as far as she was concerned.

It was clear, though, he had the means to order a meal from any restaurant in town and have it delivered by one of the many services that had sprung up during the Covid era.

However, the food was in the trunk and she'd veered far off her usual route to do a good deed. As long as she was here, she could apologize up front for invading his personal space, hand over the casserole, and make a fast exit.

It would be hard for anyone to find fault with such a kind gesture, right?

Mind made up, Lindsey slid from behind the wheel, scooped the casserole from the cooler, and ascended the steps that led to the front door.

A muted, musical echo sounded in the house after she pressed the bell, and she tucked herself into the recessed doorway to avoid the biting wind while she waited for a response.

And waited.

And waited.

Drat.

He must be sleeping. Or in the bathroom. Or perhaps his condition had worsened and he'd gone to the doctor.

Peeking out from the alcove, she surveyed the porch. It was cold enough to leave food outdoors, but unless she could find a secure spot, an animal might get to it before Dr. Oliver did.

And a parade of raccoons across his porch wouldn't endear her to—

The door rattled, and she stepped back.

Problem solved.

The therapist peered at her, bleary eyed, from the dim interior. "Lindsey?"

"Yes. Sorry. Did I wake you?"

"I was going to get up anyway." He blinked, as if to clear his vision. "What can I do for you?"

"I don't want to invade your turf, but I brought you a casserole for when you're feeling better." She lifted the container. "The heating instructions are on top."

"That was very kind of you." He leaned forward as she held it out, but as he took it and straightened up, he swayed.

Lindsey surged forward and grabbed his arm to steady him, her pulse picking up. He must be really sick. "Maybe you should sit down. Or I'd be happy to drive you to an urgent care."

"Thank you, but I'll be fine."

Fine didn't come close to describing his wan appearance.

"At least let me help you to a chair." Getting up close with flu germs was a risk, but walking away from someone in obvious need of assistance was wrong.

He hesitated. "I can get to a chair, but a walk to the kitchen may be beyond me. If you could put this in the refrigerator for me, I'd appreciate it." He held out the casserole.

"I'll be happy to."

As she took it, he retreated a few steps and sank onto a chair in the foyer. "I'll be okay after I sit for a minute and clear the sleep from my brain."

Not based on the flush in his cheeks and the beads of sweat above his upper lip, but she'd already butted in more than she should have by showing up at his door uninvited.

"Is the kitchen in the back of the house?"

"Yes." He waved a hand that direction.

She dispensed with the chore fast, giving his fridge a quick inspection as she slid the casserole inside.

A few containers of takeout leftovers, eggs, juice, jam, cold cuts. Not much else.

Her casserole would come in handy after all.

Back in the foyer, she found him standing again, one hand

braced on the back of the chair. "Thank you for stopping by. I'm sure the food will be delicious."

"You're welcome." She paused. "Is there anything else I can do for you before I leave?"

"No. I don't want to delay you. You probably have plans for the evening."

"Not until later."

"Still, I don't want to give you my germs. Whoever you're meeting tonight will be nervous about catching the flu if you stay too long."

"No worries on that score. No one even knows I'm here. But if you don't need anything else, I'll head out. You look like you should lay down again, anyway."

"I think I will." He started to turn toward the door to let her out. Lurched sideways.

Again, she sprang forward to grasp his arm.

With an agonized moan, he yanked it back and cradled it against his chest, every ounce of color vanishing from his already pale complexion.

"Oh, I'm so sorry. I didn't mean to hurt you." If he had body aches that bad, he needed medical attention. "Here, let me help you over to the chair again." She moved closer. "Why don't you lean on me?"

"No." He lifted his arm, palm forward. "I can manage."

She halted, her gaze shifting to a dark mark on his forearm when his sleeve rode up, an oddly familiar scent swirling around her.

Funny that she'd never noticed his aftershave during any of their sessions. He must reserve it for—

All at once, she froze. Sucked in a breath.

This was the same subtle scent she'd smelled that day in the Robertson kitchen. The one that had mingled with the odor of charred bread. Faint and indistinct then, but clear as a bell now.

And was that a tattoo on Dr. Oliver's arm?

As the pieces clicked into place with the same ominous, measured cadence of an executioner's footsteps, Lindsey's heart stuttered.

Anthony Oliver, the prominent and respected psychologist, was James Robertson's killer?

No.

Impossible.

Wasn't it?

LINDSEY HAD FIGURED IT OUT.

Stomach knotting, Anthony bit back a curse.

He should have shut the door in her face. Never let her come in.

Now it was too late.

Meaning his partner in crime was going to get her wish.

Lindsey would have to be eliminated.

"Um . . . I think I should be going, Dr. Oliver. I, uh, don't want to risk getting the flu." A combination of panic and incredulity etched her features.

He grasped her arm as she edged away. "I'm afraid I can't let you leave, Lindsey."

Fear flared in her irises. "What are you talking about?"

But she already knew. He could see it in her eyes.

"I think you've figured out the puzzle. I don't know exactly how, but it doesn't matter. You've forced my hand."

Her complexion paled. "What does that mean?"

"I think you can figure that out too."

Summoning up every ounce of his dwindling strength, he pulled her purse off her shoulder and tossed it aside. Dragged her down the hall, to the linen closet where he stored his valuables when the housecleaners came.

She put up a formidable fight. There was power in her

arms and legs, the muscles honed from her fitness regimen and rowing. Not difficult to counter if he was in peak form, but he was far from that today.

Even with the surge of desperation-fueled adrenaline that gave his waning energy a temporary boost, it took every ounce of his strength to deflect her blows and subdue her enough to shove her inside and lock the door.

"Hey! This is crazy." She began pounding on it. "Let me out! You'll never get away with whatever you have planned."

Yes, he would.

As soon as he developed a plan.

But he wasn't in this alone. Two heads would be better than one, especially when one of those heads was fuzzy, thanks to a raging fever.

Ignoring Lindsey's hammering and her shouted demands for release, he pulled out his burner phone and walked down the hall toward his bedroom, away from the noise.

She answered on the second ring. "You're a day early. I thought you weren't going to call until—"

"We have a problem." He explained it in three clipped sentences.

The word she uttered burned his ears. "I knew she was going to be trouble. Didn't I tell you we should get rid of her?"

"I hoped it wouldn't be necessary. Now that it is, the question is how."

"You said you were working on a plan."

"I was going to. But the tattoo's infected. I'm not operating at full capacity."

Her tone changed from agitated to solicitous in a heartbeat. "Oh, Anthony. How bad is it? Do you need to see a doctor?"

Yeah, he did.

But that wasn't going to happen.

"You know I can't risk having anything about a tattoo on medical records."

"I'll take you somewhere out of town. An urgent care. You could give a fake name and pay cash." Alarm raised her pitch.

"Urgent care centers require IDs." An ER might work, but they didn't have time for an out-of-town drive tonight to reduce the risk of someone recognizing him. "I have antibiotics. I'm hoping they kick in. We have a bigger issue to deal with at the moment than a sore arm."

"Do you have a fever?"

He had to get her back on track.

"Yes. It's not that high, but I do have a bit of brain fog. We need to focus on the more immediate crisis. Any suggestions?"

"Let me think for a minute."

In the silence that followed, he sank onto the edge of his bed.

She'd be pacing right now, her brain processing at warp speed. When it came to subtle conniving, she was in a league by herself.

"I have an idea."

"I'm listening."

As she spelled it out, his sluggish brain searched for flaws in her rationale.

None jumped out.

While it would be easier to simply kill Lindsey here and dump her body somewhere, the cops would assume a death with no other obvious motive was related to the Robertson situation. This way, there would be no concrete evidence to prove that theory.

And the idea to use Lindsey's propensity to do good deeds against her—like delivering food to people who were ill—was ingenious, if chilling.

For an off-the-cuff plan, it wasn't half bad.

"Do you think you're up to this?"

At her question, he wiped the sweat off his forehead with the sleeve of his shirt. "I'll have to be."

"Rest until I get there. I'll move as fast as I can."

"Bring the dark car."

"I don't like that one."

He reined in his temper. Like they had time in the midst of this mess to worry about vehicle preferences. "Put up with it for tonight. Turn off your lights on the approach and pull behind the house. I'll watch for you and meet you in the garage. Cover up completely and tuck your hair under a hat."

"I know the drill. Believe me, I'm not taking any chances at this point."

She should have thought of that Wednesday night.

But he left that unsaid.

"Glad to hear it. I'll follow you to the drop site, then we'll come back here until we leave for the final destination. Are you certain there won't be anyone there?"

"Yes. We'll have the place to ourselves."

He stood. Began to pace. "I wish it hadn't come to this."

"I do too. But I can't see any way around it, can you?"

Unfortunately, no. Not if he wanted to avoid going to prison for the rest of his life.

"I guess not."

"It will be fine, Anthony. She's a troubled young woman who was never going to have any impact on the world anyway. Not like you or me. And after all we've both been through, we deserve a happy ending with each other."

No, they didn't—not that it mattered. Besides, however this played out, there would be no happy ending in his future.

"I'll see you soon."

"Try not to worry too much. We've got this. Once she's out of the picture, we'll be safe. Love you, hon."

"Love you too." As the lie spilled past his lips, he pressed the end button.

The next few hours would be taxing if he was operating at

full capacity. In his present state, he was in for a rough ride physically and emotionally with Lindsey. She was a fighter, or she wouldn't have survived all the traumas that had plagued her. It would take both of them to pull off the final deed.

A wave of nausea washed over him at the prospect of another killing, but he swallowed past it. Second thoughts and regrets were useless. He was in too deep to escape.

But getting rid of Lindsey wasn't ideal. The police would be suspicious. Especially that detective she'd taken a fancy to. If they set it up right, though, and left no clues behind, no one would be able to prove it was anything but another example of his client's propensity to be in the wrong place at the wrong time.

Yet there were any number of ways this could go south. No matter how careful they were, the margin for error was high.

Too high.

So until they pulled this off and emerged unscathed, he wasn't going to take anything for granted.

Nor was he going to dwell on the innocent woman in his closet, whose luck in escaping deadly situations was about to run out.

TWENTY-FIVE

WHY WASN'T LINDSEY answering the door?

Frowning, Jack aimed the face of his watch toward her porch light.

Seven thirty on the dot. The time they'd agreed on earlier in the day, after she'd told him she had an errand to do tonight on her way home.

Strange.

If she was running late, she would have let him know. She wasn't the type to leave someone waiting.

He pressed the bell again.

Thirty seconds passed.

No response.

A niggle of unease rippled through him.

If she was home, something was wrong.

Leaving the quasi-shelter of the porch, he turned up his collar and circled around to the back of the condo. It took some maneuvering to get a line of sight through the window to her security keypad in the laundry room, but once he did, the red light was visible.

Her system was armed.

She wasn't home.

His unease ratcheted up.

He pulled out his cell. Tapped in her number. Waited as it rang . . . rang . . . rang . . . rolled to voicemail.

Slowly he slid the phone back in his pocket.

Now what?

Chin tucked into the collar of his coat as he pushed into the cold wind, he returned to the front of the unit. Hesitated. Continued to his car.

There was a remote possibility she'd been delayed and wasn't in a position to answer her phone or send him a text.

But that didn't feel right.

In fact, it felt all wrong.

Doing his best to quash a rising wave of panic, he slid behind the wheel and tried to think through next steps.

He could try to locate her phone, but that would take both a court order and precious time. It might also be overkill.

If she didn't show up within fifteen minutes, however, he was getting the legalities in the works.

Jack started the engine, cranked up the heat, and pulled out his cell. Maybe her friend Madeleine had heard from her.

A quick search of the internet for the Horizons organization that sponsored the cooking class Lindsey taught yielded the director's last name. Further digging produced her address. After that, it was a simple matter to get her number through the national cell directory.

She answered three rings in, sounding harried.

After he introduced himself, he explained the reason for his call.

"No, I haven't heard from Lindsey since the car incident on Wednesday night. Hold one sec. It's a bit noisy where I am." The background din faded while he waited for Madeleine to speak again. "Tell me what's going on."

"I don't know. I was supposed to meet her at her condo at seven thirty, and she hasn't shown."

"That's not like her." A thread of worry wove through her voice.

"I agree. I'll wait another few minutes, then move on to next steps. You're certain she didn't mention anything to you about an errand this afternoon?"

"Yes."

"Do you happen to know who her last client was today?"

"As a matter of fact, I do. She cooks for a family in Frontenac named Martino. They have a friendly dog, and she told me once she likes to end her workweek by playing with it for a few minutes before she leaves."

It wasn't much, but it was more than he'd had five minutes ago.

Jack ended the call, found a phone number for a Martino in the exclusive suburb Madeleine had referenced, and put a call in.

A woman answered, and he got straight to business after introducing himself.

Unfortunately, Lindsey's client didn't have much to offer.

According to her, Lindsey had been ready to leave when she got home about 5:30 and hadn't lingered to chat.

Jack ended the call and skimmed his watch again. Tried Lindsey's cell once more.

It rolled to voicemail.

He texted her.

His message went unanswered.

No more waiting.

He called Sarge.

It didn't take long to convince his boss to make a court order to get her cell location a top priority. Not in light of all that had happened over the past month to their only witness in the Robertson case. Sarge also promised to get a BOLO alert in the works for her car.

Everything that could be done was being done.

Yet as Jack set the phone on the seat beside him, he knew deep in his bones it wasn't enough. That while the previous pranks directed against Lindsey had been focused on inflicting mental rather than physical damage, the intent had changed.

This time, the endgame wasn't deception and distress.

It was death.

BRUISED TEMPLE THROBBING where it had connected with a shelf when Dr. Oliver shoved her into the closet, Lindsey squeezed her fingers into tight fists and tried to keep breathing.

It was impossible to know how long she'd been confined in the suffocating blackness, but at least she was safe for the moment.

All bets were off once the door opened again, however.

And when that happened, she had to be ready to defend herself.

But how?

It was the same question she'd been asking herself over and over once the shock had begun to wear off about the identity of James Robertson's killer. The same person who'd been trying to push her over the edge of sanity these past few weeks.

While that still wasn't computing, it was impossible to deny the reality.

Once again, she felt along the shelves, searching for something—anything—that could be put to use as a weapon.

But there was nothing in here other than towels and sheets, based on the textures of the fabrics. Metal hangers that had the potential to inflict damage were hard to find in linen closets. How in the world could she fashion the plush towels and four-hundred-thread-count sheets filling the shelves into a weapon?

Wait.

Shelves.

AKA wooden planks.

If they weren't nailed in place, could she remove one and use it as a flat bat? If she came out swinging, that might give him pause. Maybe distract him enough to let her gain the upper hand.

Mights and maybes didn't make for great odds, but it was the only plan that came to mind.

Swiveling around until her back was to the door, she swept the sheets off one shelf and dumped them on the floor. Felt around the sides.

Yes!

The shelf was just resting on supports. She could remove it. Better yet, each was comprised of two boards. Handling a smaller board wouldn't be as unwieldly.

She lifted the front board and drew it toward her. Once it was clear of the supports, she tipped it and let one end slide down until the board was vertical.

Then she pivoted and faced the door.

It was impossible to know how this was going to play out, but she wasn't going down without a fight.

A fight with her trusted therapist.

She exhaled.

The whole scenario was surreal.

Why on earth would Dr. Oliver kill James Robertson and steal jewelry? A man with a thriving practice, who lived in a house like this, couldn't need money.

It made no sense.

But whatever his motive, it had to be powerful. Nothing less would induce him to commit murder.

And if he'd killed once, he wouldn't hesitate to do so again. *Would* do it again, now that she'd discovered his secret. Letting her live would destroy him. That's why she had to charge out of this closet the instant it opened like she had nothing to lose.

For in truth, she didn't.

Unless she escaped, before this night was over, she'd be as dead as—

She froze.

Were there voices on the other side of the door?

Gripping the shelf, she pressed her ear to the wood panel.

Yes.

Though the sound was muffled, two people were talking.

Jack had been right. The killer did have an accomplice.

Her spirits tanked.

Two against one reduced her already slim odds.

But she had to give it her best shot. No knight on a white horse would be charging in to rescue her. While Jack would be worried if she wasn't home for their cheesecake date, he wouldn't have a clue where to look for her. Dr. Oliver was a smart man. He'd know her phone could be used to locate her and would have turned it off by now.

She was on her own at this point—except for God.

So while she waited for the next act to unfold, she prayed for the same things she'd prayed for that day in the South Carolina grocery store.

Courage. Fortitude. And deliverance.

AT THE VIBRATION on his hip, Jack stopped pacing in his living room and yanked out his phone.

Sarge.

"Court order came through. We've located her phone." In typical fashion, Sarge cut to the chase without any greeting.

Fine by him. He had no patience for niceties after more than an hour of snowballing anxiety.

"Where?"

Jack narrowed his eyes as his boss gave him the location. Same street Chad Allen lived on.

That couldn't be a coincidence.

"She's still not answering." Jack strode toward the door, snatching up his coat en route. "I tried again five minutes ago." And every five minutes since his first call.

"City's dispatched an officer to the location."

"I'm on my way there too. Will you let me know what they find?"

"Yes."

"We should alert the officer to stay clear. We may want our CSU people on this."

"Already done."

Jack ended the call as he continued to the garage. Once behind the wheel, he accelerated toward the city at speeds that weren't exactly prudent.

Ten minutes into the drive, his phone vibrated. Sarge again. He put the call on hands-free before answering. "What have we got?"

"Not only her phone, but her car."

"What about Lindsey?" He braced for bad news.

"MIA. The phone is lying on the street at the back of the car. The trunk's half-open."

His stomach somersaulted. The facts added up to a grab. Unless . . .

"I assume the trunk's empty?"

"Except for two large coolers."

The ones she must use for food transport.

"Is CSU on the way?"

"Yes."

"I'll be there in less than five minutes."

"You looking for anything in particular?"

"No, but I have people I want to talk to." He explained the proximity to Allen's house.

"Weird coincidence."

"Or not."

"I hear you. Keep me in the loop."

"Goes without saying."

Jack completed the drive in less than five minutes. Lindsey's car wasn't parked in front of Allen's apartment, but it was close.

There had to be a connection.

He parked and jogged toward the officer. "You see any activity since you've been here?" He scanned the area as he spoke, the few overhead streetlights giving the scene an eerie glow.

"No."

Jack pulled on a pair of latex gloves. Looked inside the two coolers.

One of them contained a foil-covered disposable container.

A delivery, perhaps?

He moved to the side of the car. Flashed his phone light inside. No sign of her purse there or on the ground.

Another indication she'd been snatched.

Leaving the officer to keep watch over the car, he sprinted down the street to the Allens' and took the steps to the front door two at a time.

Dara Allen answered after three rings, her husband behind her, their expressions wary.

"I'm not here about the Robertson case." Best to make that clear fast or they weren't going to be receptive to his questions. "I'm trying to locate Lindsey. Her car was found parked down your street. Was she expected here—or have you seen her?"

Dara's forehead wrinkled. "No to both. She dropped food off for us Tuesday afternoon when she found out I had the flu, and she called yesterday to see how I was, but I haven't seen or talked to her since. Is she missing?"

"She's not with her car, and her cell phone was found on the ground. There's a casserole in her trunk. Could she have been dropping off more food?"

"It's possible. That's the kind of person she is. But last time she called to tell me she was coming. I don't think we're on her usual route, so I'd be surprised if she came without checking first to make sure someone was home."

It was hard to argue with that logic, but why else would she be on their doorstep with a casserole if not to do a good deed?

"Is there anything we can do to help?" Chad joined the conversation.

"Not at the moment, but if you hear from her, I'd appreciate a call. Or you can ask her to call me." He fished out a card.

Chad waved it off. "I have your contact information already. We'll let you know if she gets in touch."

"Thanks." He left the apartment and retraced his steps to Lindsey's Focus.

A crime scene van had arrived, and a tech was already gloved and ready to go.

The man greeted him. "Am I looking for anything special?"

"Clues to help us figure out where the driver is and who took her."

"You think she was abducted?"

"Her phone was on the ground and the trunk was half-open when I arrived. Her purse is also missing."

"Got it. I'll see what I can find."

Jack handed him a card. "I'm going to knock on a few doors. Call me if you spot anything significant."

The tech offered a salute and got to work.

An hour later, after ringing the bells of every apartment that had a line of sight to Lindsey's car, he was nowhere. Residents either ignored his summons, weren't home, or had seen nothing.

He circled back to the car.

The tech straightened up from the trunk as he approached. "Any luck?"

"No. You?"

"No trace evidence, if that's what you're asking. I did find one thing that may be helpful. The driver's seat was pushed back. Unless the owner is very tall, she wasn't driving."

That put a whole different spin on the situation.

The obvious conclusion from the setup was that Lindsey had been abducted while removing a casserole destined for the Allens from the trunk.

But she wasn't tall—so if she hadn't driven the car here, that conclusion was toast.

Had she even been *in* the car when it had been parked here?

And if not, why drop her car here and set the stage for what appeared to be an abduction?

His brain began to spin as he spoke to the tech. "Go over every inch of the car."

"SOP—which means I'll be here another hour. Minimum. I should have worn my long underwear."

Biting as the cold was, it was hard to feel sorry for anyone complaining about the weather when Lindsey could be—

"Is there a problem here?"

At the question, he swung toward the sidewalk.

A bundled-up older man with a knit cap pulled over his ears and forehead had stopped a few feet away, a puppy straining at the leash he held.

Jack walked over to him. "We're trying to find the owner of this car. Do you live around here?"

"One block over." He waved to the south. "I'm out here every couple of hours with the pup. It was my wife's idea to get a dog, but she doesn't like walking her at night in the cold. Who knew a puppy had to do its business so often?" He leaned down and gave the pooch an affectionate pat. "I saw a woman park this car during my last circuit."

Jack's pulse picked up.

Was he finally getting a break?

"Can you describe her?"

"No. It was dark, and she was dressed like I am with a hat and a muffler wrapped around her face. Maybe her heater didn't work."

Or she didn't want anyone to be able to identify her.

"You certain it was a woman?"

"Well . . ." The man tightened his grip on the leash as the pup strained forward. "I couldn't swear to it in a court of law, but it looked like a woman. She was tall, though. Taller than most women. Her head was close to the roof."

Supporting the tech's comment about the seat being pushed back.

"What time was this?"

"Oh, about seven fifteen, I guess."

More than two hours ago.

Not good.

A lot of bad stuff could happen in two hours.

"Is there anything else you can think of?"

"There was one other sort of odd thing. When I got to the end of the street and turned the corner, Missy here"—he motioned to the dog—"found a tree she liked. While I waited, I glanced back. The driver got out, walked around to the back of the car, then came down the street like she was in a hurry. About fifty feet from the corner, she stopped by another car and got in on the passenger side."

"What kind of car was the other one?"

"I don't know the make. I'm not into cars. If it runs and gets me where I need to go, that's all I care about. But it drove by me as it turned the corner, and I noticed it was a dark sedan. Couldn't see the people inside, though. The windows were tinted. But it looked expensive."

"Did you by chance notice the license plate?"

"I did. The first two letters happened to be my wife's initials—NL. Norma Lewis. They jumped out at me."

Jack took out his notebook and began jotting down the information the man had passed on. "And your name is?"

"Dick."

He asked a few more questions, got the man's contact information, and tucked his notebook away as his fingers started to grow numb. "You've been very helpful, Mr. Lewis."

"I hope you find the owner of that car. Hate to see crime in our neighborhood."

"If more citizens like you stepped forward, the streets would be safer." He took out another card. "Please give me a call if anything else comes to mind."

"I'll do that. Now I should take this little lady home before we both get frostbite. Good luck."

"Thanks."

But as the man continued down the street, Jack knew it would take more than luck on this cold night to find Lindsey.

While an abduction would have been bad enough, there was an elaborate plan in the works here. As there had been at the lake and in the park and at the church.

The big difference was that in those cases, Robertson's killer had been trying to make it appear as if she was losing her mind.

Tonight they were setting her up to lose her life.

TWENTY-SIX

SOMEONE WAS COMING.

Pulse accelerating, Lindsey eased back in the closet where she'd been listening with her ear pressed against the door for who knew how long. Yet hard as she'd tried, she hadn't been able to decipher a single muffled word. It would have been helpful to have a clue about what was in store for her. But her role was the same, no matter what.

Attack with every ounce of her strength.

Muscles tensing, she lifted the shelf and prepared to charge out fighting.

"Lindsey, we're unlocking the closet." Dr. Oliver's voice came through the wood panels, grim and no-nonsense. "I have a gun pointed at the door, and you already know I won't hesitate to use it. Once I tell you to open it, come out and walk toward the living room. Do you understand me?"

"Yes." But she wasn't going to follow a single instruction. He wouldn't shoot her in his house. There would be blood everywhere. For someone who'd been meticulous every step of the way about covering his tracks, it would be out of character for him to leave proof she'd been on his property, thereby linking him to her death. He wasn't going to use a gun in his house.

But despite any precautions he might take in his home, the strands of hair she'd plucked out by the roots and tucked into every nook and cranny in the closet were waiting for the County CSU to find. So were the spots of blood she'd smeared under several of the shelves after shoving up the sleeve of her sweater and pricking her arm with a loose thumbtack she'd found on the floor in a back corner.

If she died tonight, Jack wouldn't rest until he found her killer—and all the clues she'd left should be enough to put Dr. Oliver and his accomplice away forever.

Small consolation if she lost her life, but at least justice would be done.

A key was inserted in the lock, and her heart stuttered.

This was it.

Time to charge out, swinging.

The instant the lock stopped rattling, she twisted the knob, shoved the door open, and thrust through with all her might.

A woman yelped as the edge of the door connected with a solid object.

Woman?

As she tried to digest that, a bright light pierced her eyes.

"Grab her legs!"

She raised the shelf and swung toward Dr. Oliver's voice.

But as she lunged toward him, someone tackled her ankles and she went down.

Hard.

Before she could catch her breath, a body slammed against her back, pinning her in place. Hands mashed her cheek to the floor. The shelf was wrested from her grasp.

In seconds her plan had been reduced to rubble.

The light flipped off, and she found Dr. Oliver crouched

down, inches from her face. He wasn't holding a gun but a loop of rope.

"Very smart, Lindsey. You figured out I wouldn't shoot you in my own house, didn't you? I do have a gun, but that would leave too much blood. Strangulation is much cleaner." He forced the loop over her head, despite her attempt to writhe away. Cinched the knot around her neck. Gave it a tug.

Her air supply was immediately restricted.

She tried to reach for it with the hand that wasn't trapped under her body, but he pressed a knee to her arm.

"If you don't behave, we'll finish the job here and dump your body elsewhere. Keep that in mind. Put your hands behind your back." He pulled out a length of cording and passed it behind her. "Tie her hands. Cooperate, Lindsey, or this will keep getting tighter." He demonstrated by tugging again, squeezing her windpipe even more.

Gasping for air, she followed his instructions. At the moment, she wasn't in any position to launch another attack. All she could do was buy herself every possible minute to try and find another window of opportunity to get the upper hand.

Once her wrists were secured—and none-too-gently—Dr. Oliver retreated a few feet, keeping a firm grip on the tether around her neck. The pressure on her back diminished as his accomplice slid off. "Stand up."

It wasn't easy to do with a throbbing head and bound wrists, but somehow she managed to get upright, using the wall for support.

"Maybe we should scrap our plan and finish this now, then dump the body. She hurt me, Anthony."

As the familiar voice spoke behind her, cold and riddled with anger, shock rippled through Lindsey.

No.

It couldn't be.

Slowly she swiveled toward the living room, trying in vain

to think of some explanation for this bizarre turn of events. Surely her ears had deceived her.

But they hadn't.

From ten feet away, Oliver's accomplice was watching her.

It was Heidi Robertson.

***

THE CSU TECH WASN'T HANK, but he was thorough. Yet he'd come up with a big fat zero other than the prints he'd lifted from the Focus, which would no doubt be identified as Lindsey's.

Jack forked his fingers through his hair as hot air blasted from the vents in his car.

The partial plate the witness had seen wouldn't help him with MULES. You had to have a complete alphanumeric sequence to run a plate through the Missouri Uniform Law Enforcement System portal. A better resource was the Missouri Information Analysis Center. They could cross-reference the letters he had with a variety of databases, then try to match those results with whatever other information was provided. Like the description of a dark sedan.

Worth trying, but the twenty-four to seventy-two hour turnaround wasn't going to help him tonight.

And his gut said tomorrow would be too late.

He slammed the heel of his hand against the steering wheel and muttered a word he rarely used.

If there was even one tiny clue to follow up on, he'd be all over it. But there wasn't.

This was as difficult to unravel as the Robertson case.

No surprise, since the two were related and had likely been masterminded by the same person.

Whoever that was, they were smart and meticulous and careful. The only lapse had been the blood on Lindsey's car.

But without a match in the database, that hadn't helped anyway.

He turned the heat down and scanned the street again.

Was it possible someone else had seen a helpful detail but hadn't answered the door earlier? Should he make another circuit of the neighborhood, call in reinforcements? Sarge would assign more people if he asked.

Trouble was, there wasn't much for anyone to do except knock on doors, and he'd done that once.

Couldn't hurt to do it again, though. See if any of the people who hadn't responded to his knock before were willing to talk to him now. What else was there to do on this Friday evening he'd planned to spend with Lindsey?

He reached for the door handle as his cell began to vibrate. Paused to pull it out.

Dick Lewis.

Had he thought of another fact or two he wanted to pass on?

Jack put the phone to his ear and greeted the man.

"Sorry to bother you, Detective, but I was just telling my wife about what's going on over on the next block, and she said we had a little excitement on our street earlier too. While she was getting ready to run over to our daughter's, she glanced out the window to see if Missy and I were coming back yet from our walk, and she saw a car sideswipe an SUV parked across the street from our apartment. She said it was about seven fifteen. I think it was the car I saw."

That seemed like a stretch.

Jack stifled a sigh and shut off the engine. "Why do you think that, Mr. Lewis?"

"It was a dark sedan, and the timing fits. My wife knows cars, and she said it was a BMW. The owner of the SUV came out of the building across the street as it happened, and he tried to chase after the car. It took off, but he called the police.

I don't know if our neighbor got a license plate, but you may want to check."

That would be a huge break if it was the same car.

A big if, though the timing was promising.

"Why didn't your wife tell you any of this earlier, Mr. Lewis?"

"She was already gone when I got home with Missy. She didn't get back from our daughter's until five minutes ago."

It was a long shot, yes—but if that's all you had, you went with it.

"I appreciate the tip. I'll follow up."

"Always happy to help keep our streets safe."

"What's the name and address of the SUV owner?" It could be faster to talk to the man directly rather than try to track down the patrol officer who'd taken the report.

"We don't know him. He hasn't lived here long. But I know which apartment is his."

Jack jotted the information down as Dick recited it.

"Thanks. I'm on my way."

After running a quick search to get a name to go with the address, Jack slid from behind the wheel and rejoined the CSU tech, who was about ready to leave. "I have one more small job for you. Around the corner." He explained what had happened. "I'm hoping there's paint from the other vehicle on the damaged car."

"City may already have a sample."

Jack gave him a get-real look.

The tech lifted his hands, palms up. "Fine. I get it. With all the other crime downtown, a sideswipe is small potatoes. I'll follow you over."

Jack returned to his car, put it in gear, and drove around the block.

He parked in front of the long row of flats that lined the street, wedging in behind an older-model SUV sporting a long scrape along the side. The CSU van claimed a spot farther down the street.

"I'll alert the owner to what's going on." Jack motioned toward the apartment as the tech joined him. "No need to wait around after you're done here. I could be a few minutes. And it's getting colder."

"Tell me something I don't know."

Leaving him to his task, Jack walked up the steps to the porch of the flat and rang the bell.

A mid-twentyish man answered, and Jack did yet another introduction and explanation.

"So you think this car was also involved in another crime?" The man peered toward his vehicle, where the tech was working.

"It's possible." The wind whistled past.

"You want to come in? It's a cold night."

"Thanks." He crossed the threshold, into a space that smelled of pizza, beer, and bachelor pad. "I'm hoping you were able to see some of the license plate."

"I did better than that. Like I told the other cop, they hit my car just as I came outside. They braked for a minute, and I ran down the steps. I waved at them, but they either didn't see me or didn't choose to stop. I pulled out my cell and got a picture as they drove off. It's grainy, but you guys may have tools to clean it up. I sent it to the other cop, but I could give it to you too."

"That would be helpful." Jack recited his cell number while the guy worked his phone, and a few seconds later a ping announced its arrival.

"You think I can get them or their insurance company to pay for my repairs?"

"A photo is gold." Jack clicked on the image. Enlarged it. The picture was grainy and difficult to read without any enhancements, but the first two letters did appear to be N and L.

Yes!

The long shot had become a sure bet.

"That's what the other cop said. But he wasn't certain about the cleanup or how long it would take."

A hit-and-run sideswipe without injuries wouldn't necessarily be a priority, but when it had a connection to someone whose life was in danger, it got bumped to the top of the list.

"Because this is related to another case, I'll have someone on it ASAP."

"Wow. Thanks a lot."

"We'll be in touch." He headed for the door.

"I hope you solve the other case too."

"We'll do our best."

He let himself out. The CSU tech was already gone, sample in hand. Less important now that they had a license plate, but it wouldn't hurt to rack up supporting evidence.

At the moment, he was more interested in having the County computer folks work their magic on the photo.

Thankfully, he'd stored the number of a primo one in his phone after she'd cleaned up security camera photos for one of his cases six weeks ago. If she was home, she ought to have access to a few tools that would be helpful.

He scrolled through to her number and placed the call.

Two rings later, she answered.

"Emma, Jack Tucker. You helped me with a case a few—"

"Hey, Jack. I remember. What can I do for you?"

"I'm sorry to bother you on a Friday night, but I've got a rush job." He explained what he had.

"I'll be happy to take a look at the photo. Send it over."

"Do you have access to what you need at home?"

"Doesn't matter. I'm at the office. Yours isn't the only hot case."

Did anyone in law enforcement work regular hours?

"I need this as fast as you can do it. A life may be at stake."

"Understood. Send it over and I'll get right on it."

"Thanks. It's coming as we speak." Jack ended the call and sent her the image.

Then he pointed his car west, toward headquarters.

Not that he didn't trust her to ratchet this up on her to-do list, but everyone thought their case was urgent. It would be harder to put his aside if he was breathing down her neck.

Literally.

Besides, without any other leads to follow up on, he may as well be at the office. What would he do at home except pace and worry?

Because unless his instincts were way off, Lindsey's life was hanging in the balance.

And so was his future.

For as Lindsey had told him early on, it doesn't always take long to know when you meet the right person.

While their acquaintance was short, deep inside he knew she was that person. The one who was destined to play a major role in his future.

If she survived the night.

TWENTY-SEVEN

"WALK INTO THE LIVING ROOM, Lindsey."

Dr. Oliver's directive registered at a peripheral level as she gaped at Heidi, but it wasn't until he tugged on the rope and tightened her noose that she managed to get her feet moving.

This was becoming more bizarre by the moment.

What was the connection between these two?

Why would Heidi want to kill her husband?

How had she convinced Dr. Oliver to help her?

No answers came to her as she stumbled toward the living room.

But at least Dr. Oliver had nixed Heidi's suggestion that they finish her off here.

"Stop."

She paused at his command.

"Anthony, honey, are you all right?"

Honey?

Another jolt ricocheted through her.

Heidi and Dr. Oliver had a romantic relationship?

"I could be better. The police are going to be looking for my car."

"Oh, sweetie, don't worry about that. There are dozens of

fender benders in the city every day, and the cops down there have bigger fish to fry than trying to track down a hit-and-run with no injuries."

"What if someone saw what happened?"

"It was dark, and half the streetlights were out. No one could see much from a window, and it's too cold tonight for anyone to be wandering around outside."

"A body shop will know the car was in an accident." Dr. Oliver sounded seriously rattled.

"Relax, Anthony. You can lease a car for a couple of months and let yours sit. At that point, tonight will be ancient history. Tell them someone sideswiped *you* while the car was parked on the street."

Heidi's tone was soothing. Placating. Caring.

The voice of a woman in love.

A far different version of Heidi than the woman who demanded that staff park behind her garage to keep riffraff out of view.

Lindsey gritted her teeth.

How she rued the day she'd taken a job at the Robertson house after the client Dr. Oliver had referred to her had in turn put her in touch with Heidi.

"I don't know."

"Anthony, trust me, it will be fine. But I'll take the wheel on this trip. You shouldn't be driving with such a high fever."

"I don't like all the calls that detective made to her phone. He'll be looking for her."

Lindsey's ears perked up, and a surge of hope shot through her.

They had to be referring to Jack.

Multiple calls meant he was worried and perhaps already in search mode.

Unfortunately, there wasn't much chance he'd think of Dr. Oliver.

"He has no idea where she is. You said she told you no one knew she was planning to stop here."

"You know . . . we probably shouldn't talk about all this in her presence."

Heidi gave a mirthless laugh. "Why not? It isn't like she's going to have the opportunity to tell anyone what she hears. You ready to go?"

"I don't know." Agitation and uncertainty wove through his words. "None of this feels right."

Was Dr. Oliver having second thoughts about their plans?

If so, that could work to her advantage.

"That's because you're sick. We're going to get you looked at as soon as we finish this unpleasant business, even if I have to drive all night to take you to an ER where no one will recognize you. Let's get her out to the car."

A resigned sigh filled the silence, followed by a ripping sound. "I guess we don't have any choice at this stage. Use this first."

After a few seconds, Heidi appeared in front of her, a length of duct tape in her hand.

Before Lindsey realized her intent, Heidi slapped it against her mouth and pressed the ends against her cheeks.

No amount of twisting and turning deterred her from the task, and the increasing pressure of the noose put a damper on too much struggle.

"Let's go." Heidi picked up a hat from the couch and tucked her hair into it. Then she slipped her arms into a coat and wrapped a muffler around her neck.

"Hold this while I put my jacket on." Another tug on the rope as Dr. Oliver spoke.

Heidi disappeared behind her, their handoff producing only a tiny window of relief for her lungs.

They were getting ready to take her somewhere to dispose of her.

Somewhere that would have no link to them.

Her time was running out.

But what was she supposed to do with a noose around her neck, her hands trussed, and a gag muffling her voice?

A sudden tsunami of fear stole her breath just as effectively as the rope.

Summoning up every ounce of her self-discipline, she fought it back.

There might yet be an opportunity to break free. Dr. Oliver was sick, and he didn't seem enthusiastic about the task ahead. Heidi didn't have the advantage of muscle power honed from years of running and rowing.

Lindsey balled her fingers.

She'd find a way to make another attempt.

They were *not* going to defeat her. At least not without a fight.

"I'm ready." Dr. Oliver spoke again.

"Wait. Let me get the hat."

A few seconds later, a knit cap was pulled onto her head from behind. Latex-enclosed fingers appeared in her field of vision as Heidi pushed her hair inside.

"There could be a few strands lying around here." Dr. Oliver sounded increasingly nervous.

"We'll vacuum when we get back. Okay. We're all set."

"Walk toward the kitchen, Lindsey." Dr. Oliver prodded her.

She did as he directed, legs stiff.

Heidi moved ahead, opening the door to the garage and preceding them into the spacious triple-bay attached structure that housed two dark sedans.

"Follow Heidi to her car." He jiggled the rope, as if urging a horse to pick up its pace.

Lindsey's step faltered as Heidi stopped by the car and shook out a very large garbage bag.

Were they going to kill her here after all? Put her body in a bag and dump her somewhere?

"Keep moving." Dr. Oliver prodded her again from behind.

She didn't budge.

He pulled the rope taut, cutting off her air supply, and she let out a strangled gasp.

"I said move."

She stumbled forward.

At the back of the car, Heidi raised the bag. Slid it down over her body as the tether around her neck went slack.

Blackness engulfed her.

A few seconds later, cording was lashed around her ankles.

Lindsey choked back a sob.

Her odds of survival were plummeting.

Without her hands or feet or voice, she was helpless to launch a counterattack.

"Sit in the trunk, Lindsey."

No.

She wasn't going to go willingly to her death.

"This is ridiculous." Heidi spat the comment out.

An instant later, a hard shove sent her tumbling backward. She fell into the trunk, her head connecting with hard metal as she toppled in.

Bright pinpricks of light cascaded across her dark field of vision as her legs were lifted, the bag was pulled down over her feet, and a cinching sound echoed in the trunk as the drawstring was secured.

"Don't worry. The bag has plenty of air for the short time you'll be in it." This from Dr. Oliver.

He was reassuring her she wouldn't suffocate? The same man who'd put a noose around her neck?

It was ludicrous.

If the situation wasn't so dire, she'd laugh at the absurdity.

But laughter was the last thing on her mind.

The trunk lid slammed shut, sending a vibration through the car.

Moments after that, car doors opened. Closed. The engine was turned on. The car began to roll toward an unknown destination.

Based on Dr. Oliver's comment, it wasn't far.

And wherever it was, that's where she'd meet her end.

Unless she could outsmart them . . . or overpower them . . . or Jack figured out where she was and sicced law enforcement on them.

None of which seemed likely in light of the formidable odds stacked against her.

Pressure built in her throat as a wave of despair crashed over her.

How could it end like this, after everything she'd been through? Everything she'd survived? Especially now that she'd met a man who could very well be The One?

You're giving up, Lindsey. That's not like you. You're a fighter. This isn't over till it's over. Think! Come up with a plan of attack. Maybe they'll win in the end, but don't let them steal your spirit along with your life.

As that silent pep talk echoed in her mind, anger began to build inside her.

No matter the odds, she wouldn't go down without a fight. At the very least, she'd make their job more difficult. Inflict injury of her own on them if she could.

Her brain began to click into gear, the left side taking over.

First, to do anything, she needed her hands. Freeing them had to be her top priority. If she could loosen the cording around her wrists, have her hands available, she'd be in a much stronger position to resist. Even if they intended to throw her into a lake or river while she was in this bag, having the use of her hands would give her the ability to perhaps open the bag and swim out.

Second, if their plan was to get her out of the bag at their final destination before finishing her off, they'd either have to carry her or free her ankles so she could walk. In his current physical condition, Dr. Oliver didn't appear to be up to toting anything over fifty pounds for any distance. Freed ankles would also work to her advantage.

Third, she should leverage the element of surprise. Let them think her hands were still secured when they hauled her out of the trunk. Catch them off guard once she was ready to launch her strike.

So as the car wove toward its destination, Lindsey got to work.

And if she succeeded, the two people who'd already killed an innocent man in a surprise attack would get a surprise of their own when their latest intended victim threw a few roadblocks on their path to murder.

THAT WAS FAST.

As Emma's name flashed on the screen of his cell, Jack greeted her. "I didn't expect to hear back from you in less than fifteen minutes."

"I bumped you to the top of the queue, as promised."

"I owe you."

"Bring me a few more of those chocolate mint squares and I'll call it even."

"You got it. Were you able to decipher the plate?"

"Yep." She rattled it off. "I also ran it for you, since I assumed that would be your next step. It belongs to an Anthony Oliver."

As Jack tried to digest that startling piece of news, his car began to drift, forcing him to do a fast course correction.

Anthony Oliver?

Lindsey's therapist?

That was crazy.

And yet it made perfect sense in a warped way. Who would better know someone's vulnerabilities—and how to exploit them—than the psychologist of the patient being targeted?

But that also meant he was either Robertson's killer or the accomplice.

This was getting weirder by the minute.

Why would he get involved in such a sordid mess?

And who was the woman who'd been in the car with him earlier tonight?

"Detective Tucker?"

He refocused on the conversation. "Yes, I'm here. You just solved one of my cases. Expect a whole plate of mint squares. Do you have an address for the vehicle?"

"Yes." She recited it.

"Thanks. I'll be in touch."

Without waiting for her to respond, he punched the end button, called Sarge, and gave him a fast rundown. "I know we have to get a court order to search his house and office, but I'm going in under exigent circumstances while we wait for that to come through. Can you get officers there fast? Quietly, in case Oliver's home."

"I'm on it. How far away are you?"

"ETA ten minutes." That was another lucky break. The man lived in Clayton, minutes from headquarters.

It appeared the tide of this case was turning at last.

Now all they had to do was find Lindsey before it was too late.

"They'll be waiting for you. Go get him, Tucker."

"That's my plan."

He ended the call and sped down I-64, exiting two minutes later and barreling toward the posh neighborhood Oliver called home.

As Sarge had predicted, two patrol cars were already parked a few doors down from Oliver's dark house when he arrived.

The officers met him as he approached.

"We have a potential abduction situation, so let's proceed with caution." Jack inspected the residence. "I'll ring the bell while you two do a walk-around. If he isn't home, we may have to go in uninvited."

The two officers split up and circled the house from opposite sides while he approached the front door and pressed the bell.

Two rings later, there was still no response.

He followed the officers around to the back, where they were examining the patio door.

"Find anything?"

"Nothing that raises any alarms." One of them straightened up. "We're trying to determine the easiest way to get in. I flashed a light in the back window, and it doesn't appear his security system is armed."

"Any cars in there?" Jack motioned to the rear-entry garage, which boasted a narrow horizontal panel of windows near the top of each door.

"One. It matched the license plate dispatch gave us. And it appears there's damage on the side of the vehicle."

"The door next to the garage will be quicker to breach than this one." The other officer stood too. "One kick ought to do it."

"Let's give it a try."

He strode over, the two officers falling in behind him.

Rather than wait for one of them to do the job, he twisted sideways and smashed his heel below the lock. The door splintered. A follow-up kick sent it flying.

They were in.

"One of you stay out here. The other, come with me." He pulled out the booties and gloves he'd grabbed from his glove compartment and handed a set to the officer. "I don't think anyone's here, but be prepared for trouble just in case."

"Got it." The officer donned the equipment and pulled out his pistol.

Jack did the same and pushed through the door. Flipped on a light.

It was a laundry room that provided access to both the kitchen and garage.

"Let's check the house first."

After calling out Oliver's name in case the man happened to be home, Jack took the lead, turning on lights as they moved from room to room.

Nothing in the kitchen raised red flags.

The living room appeared to be undisturbed.

Everything in the foyer was pristine.

Jack started down the hall.

Stopped.

A closet door at the end was open.

He put his feet in gear again, halting a yard back.

Major red alert.

In one fast scan, he took in the pile of sheets on the floor inside and the missing half shelf. Moving closer, he flicked on the flashlight he'd brought from his car, homing in on a brownish crimson spot on one of the sheets.

It was blood.

Lindsey's.

He knew that as surely as he knew there would be a lot more of it unless he found her fast.

Heart pounding, he fumbled for his cell and got Sarge on the line again.

His boss listened to his download before speaking. "We need his phone records. Also a location on his cell, assuming he hasn't turned it off. I'll coordinate that. Does he have a second car?"

"Unknown. But the damaged BMW is in the garage."

"We'll check on a second vehicle and get a BOLO alert

issued if he owns another one. I'll also have the CSU send a van over there."

"We need to find out if there's any family we can talk to. Office staff too. I can dig into that after I finish the walk-through here. I'll also have the officers who are here knock on the neighbors' doors."

"Sounds like a plan. I'll get our people on the intel piece."

The line went dead, and Jack put his phone away.

While he'd do a full circuit of the house and garage, his gut told him he'd already discovered the main clues visible to the naked eye. The CSU folks would doubtless unearth additional evidence during their thorough examination of the scene, however. It was also possible the door-to-door canvas would yield another helpful hint or two, though in neighbor-hoods where houses were often shrouded behind landscaping designed to offer optimal privacy, witnesses were generally difficult to find. Family, friends, and staff interviews could fill in blanks too.

But all of that would take time.

Time Lindsey didn't have.

She'd already been missing for hours, and people with bad intentions didn't stretch out their risks any longer than neces-sary. Especially smart ones.

And Oliver was smart.

Smart enough to perhaps stay one step ahead of the law, as he had throughout this whole ordeal.

But he'd made mistakes tonight, like the one last week with the blood on Lindsey's car. Either he was getting rattled, or circumstances had pushed him into a course of action he hadn't had an opportunity to plan to the nth degree, as he'd done for the lake and park setups.

If they were lucky, Oliver would keep making mistakes. Continue leaving them a trail to follow.

If he didn't?

Jack tamped down an uncharacteristic wave of panic as the answer to that question came through loud and clear. Letting fear undermine his professional composure and usual meticulous thinking would be a mistake. He had to stay at the top of his game.

Lindsey's life depended on it.

And as he continued his walk-through of Oliver's house, he prayed for one more break that would lead him to the woman who was fast claiming his heart—in time to save her life . . . and their future.

TWENTY-EIGHT

EVERYTHING WAS GOING SOUTH.

As the car rolled through the darkness, Heidi behind the wheel, Anthony wiped a hand down his face.

Maybe the fever was messing with both his brain and his nerves, but despite the impressive plan his partner had come up with on the fly, he couldn't shake the specter of disaster hovering over him. Seat-of-the-pants had never been how he operated. Meticulous planning paid off, as evidenced by the success of the original car incident, the lake attack, and the staged mugging.

But there'd been no time for planning after Lindsey showed up at his door on a mission of mercy.

He looked over at Heidi in the dim car.

If she was nervous, it didn't show. Her hands were relaxed on the wheel, her attention fixed on the road ahead as she tooled toward their destination.

As if she'd sensed his gaze, she glanced at him. "How are you holding up?"

"Physically, okay."

"You getting cold feet about this?"

"I don't like killing."

"She left us no choice, honey. Besides, you didn't seem all that squeamish about getting rid of James. I guess love is a powerful motivator." She reached over and touched his leg, the sudden warmth in her voice in stark contrast to the coldness of her comment about her husband.

"That's true." He tried to mask his revulsion as he spoke the lie. Love had nothing to do with Robertson's murder. Not on his end, anyway.

He turned away and stared out the side window into the darkness.

In hindsight, the irony of his situation with Heidi would be almost humorous if the stakes weren't so high.

But he hadn't known her history the night he'd been trolling for funding sources at a society function after his divorce and tagged her as an easy mark. After chatting her up, it had been obvious her love for Robertson was based on dollar signs, and that any feelings she may have had for her husband in the beginning had faded after eight years of marriage to a workaholic. She'd been ripe for the plucking.

Just as James had been when Heidi had targeted the lonely widower at the health club where she'd worked as a receptionist. With no children in the picture, she'd seen a clear path to easy street. A secret she'd shared with her new paramour after confiding that her previous husband had squandered all their money and left her for another woman, pushing her to find a new love interest with deep pockets.

The same way he'd viewed her, once his own money problems began.

A perfect illustration of what goes around, comes around.

The only glitch with his plan? She'd had a prenup that precluded her from getting any of Robertson's fortune if she initiated a divorce.

By the time he'd found out about that complication, he'd done his snow job too well and she'd fallen for him. Hard.

She hadn't cared about giving up Robertson's money—until he'd told her his own funds were limited.

And thus was hatched the plan to eliminate her husband.

Greed was as powerful a motivator as love.

"See? I told you it would be deserted."

Anthony tuned back in to his surroundings, giving the industrial area a sweep as Heidi killed the car lights and swung into an empty parking lot.

"Are you certain there's no security?"

"Yes. The employee who mentioned it to me a couple of days ago as a potential acquisition said it was abandoned and in such disrepair the owners didn't even bother to lock it anymore. He said it's being sold as a tear-down." She drove around to the back of the structure, where the car would be hidden from the view of any passersby.

"Why would he recommend that you buy this place?" He gave the somewhat seedy surroundings another inspection. "It isn't exactly prime real estate."

"It doesn't have to be for the self-storage facility he proposed we build. But I plan to nix the idea. That's not a business I want to be in." She braked. Scanned the building. "However, if someone robbed Lindsey and abducted her, they couldn't find a more ideal spot to finish her off."

Her matter-of-fact manner turned Anthony's stomach.

Thank goodness the car was too dark for her to see his expression of disgust.

How could he ever have pretended to care for this woman?

How would he pretend in the future?

He swallowed past the bile rising in his throat.

Much as he needed money, could he really follow through with this killing just to salvage the prestige and high-end lifestyle he'd become accustomed to?

Especially when Lindsey was the intended victim.

James Robertson had been a stranger, but he knew the

young woman who'd come to him for counseling. Had grown to care for her, as he cared for all his clients.

Yet if he didn't see this to completion, he'd go to prison for the rest of his life—which could be of short duration if he got the death penalty.

A trickle of sweat that had nothing to do with his fever snaked down his temple.

He was stuck.

At this point, his scheme wasn't just about financial survival.

It was about survival, period.

And there was no way out.

Lindsey had to die.

THE CAR HAD STOPPED.

Lindsey's pulse accelerated as she continued to wiggle her wrists, doing everything in her power to loosen the cording that bound them. There was definitely more slack than there'd been at the start of this car trip, so her skin hadn't been rubbed raw in vain. But was it sufficient to let her pull her hands free when the moment of truth came and she made whatever play the situation afforded her?

Unknown.

Yet she couldn't risk doing much more. If the cording fell off too soon or drew the attention of her captors, it would tip them off to her plan.

The hum of the engine ceased, and her lungs stalled.

A few seconds later, the doors opened.

Half a minute after that, the trunk latch disengaged.

"Untie her feet while I check the door." Heidi's muffled voice came through the metal. "I'll be back in a minute."

A slight creak indicated the lid had been lifted.

The drawstring by her feet was loosened, and Dr. Oliver

grabbed her ankles and pulled her toward the back of the trunk until her legs were dangling outside. He grasped her shoulders and sat her up, shielding her head with his hand. Like he cared about hurting her.

One more factor she might be able to leverage in her favor.

If only she could talk to him while Heidi was gone. Plead her case.

But talking probably wouldn't produce favorable results, anyway. Action would be her salvation, if she could find the right opportunity.

"I'm going to stand you up, Lindsey." He sounded out of breath. "Lean against the car for support if you need to."

The next instant, she was heaved upright. Once she got her balance, he pulled the garbage bag up and over her head. The hat came with it, and her hair tumbled down.

While he bent to cut the cording around her ankles, she gave the area a fast appraisal as a cold wind whistled past.

They were parked beside what appeared to be a deserted industrial building. No lights pierced the darkness of the parking lot, nor were there any other vehicles visible. In the distance, outlines of other structures created hulking shadows against the night sky, and faint, random pools of illumination dotted the gloom. None close enough to shed light on the nefarious activity taking place here, however.

Any hope of nearby help evaporated.

She was in this alone, armed with nothing but her wits to pit against two cold-blooded killers, at least one of whom was armed.

But her feet were free, if slightly numb, and with one tug, her wrists would be liberated too.

She hoped.

The question was, when should she make her move? Out here, in the open, where she might be able to disappear in the night if the circulation returned to her feet and she could run without stumbling—or inside, where there could be places to hide and objects that could function as weapons.

Before she could come to a decision, Heidi returned.

"The door's unlocked, as expected. Let's go inside and finish this. It's too cold to stand around out here."

Dr. Oliver took her arm and towed her toward the building, Heidi's ominous words ringing in her ears.

Finish this.

The end was near.

So if a window of opportunity didn't open soon, she'd have to create one.

Or in a handful of minutes, she'd be dead.

"*I STILL DON'T SEE* why we had to swing by here at this hour. This neighborhood gives me the creeps."

As Eric stopped in front of the empty warehouse he'd suggested Robertson Properties consider acquiring, he put the car in park.

It was hard to blame his wife for complaining about the detour. The area was beyond dicey.

But she could indulge him after the impromptu celebratory dinner he'd sprung on her now that the company had passed on the strip mall and his payment from Matthew Nolan had hit his account this afternoon. Stopping by off the clock to check out the potential purchase he'd recommended would demonstrate his commitment to the company and help build job security.

Heidi Robertson came across as the type who would appreciate and reward employees who went the extra mile.

"I told you, hon. I'll earn brownie points with my new boss when I tell her I drove by tonight."

"Seems like a waste to me. Won't you have to come back in the daylight to see the inside?"

"At some point, if she decides to proceed. But she'll be impressed that I swung by to get a first impression."

She gave the structure a dubious inspection. "It's pitch dark. What can you see?"

"Not much. That's why this will be quick. I just want to be able to tell her I took a look. One circuit is all I have planned."

"Well, let's do it and get out of here."

Eric put the car in gear again and drove toward the corner of the building. Continued along the side. Paused as he circled around back.

"I thought you said the building was empty." His wife leaned forward and peered at the dark sedan parked near the door as a faint light flashed inside the windows spaced along the top of the structure.

Huh.

That didn't seem right.

According to the material he'd reviewed on the property, no one should be here.

"It's supposed to be." He flipped off his lights as the illumination inside vanished. If someone was trespassing, they were likely up to no good—and calling attention to his presence could put him and his wife at risk. "I'm going to drive by the car. Write down the license while I read it off."

"Why? Can't we just leave?"

"Humor me, okay?"

"I don't like this, Eric. It feels dangerous."

"I'm only going to stop long enough to get the license information, and I'll keep the doors locked. You ready?"

"As ready as I'm going to be." She rummaged through her purse and extracted a pen and piece of paper.

"Here we go." He continued forward, lowered his window, and stopped beside the back of the car. Aiming his cell at the license, he turned on the flashlight and read off the plate.

"Got it."

After setting his phone on the console, he continued around the building and drove a block away. Stopped.

"Now what?" At his wife's query, he picked up his phone again.

"I'm going to report what at the very least is a trespassing violation."

"Maybe they're not trespassing. That was an Audi, Eric. Why would someone who owns such an expensive car trespass?"

Good question.

But a better question was, why would someone who owned an Audi be in this neck of the woods at this hour of the night?

Something suspicious was going on back there.

"I don't know. I'll let the police figure that out." He tapped in 911.

The operator answered at once, and as Eric reported what he'd seen, his lips tipped up.

How providential that he'd decided to swing by here on a whim tonight to build credibility with his boss.

Not only would Heidi be impressed by his diligence, she'd be grateful he'd interrupted what could be an illegal activity on property that might be destined for the Robertson portfolio.

And who knew?

If he was lucky, she might even give him a raise.

TWENTY-NINE

AS FAR AS HE COULD SEE, other than the spot of blood on the sheet in the closet, there wasn't anything in Oliver's house to suggest Lindsey had been here.

Nor was there anything in the garage.

Jack fisted his hands on his hips and gave the structure one more three-sixty.

Even if there was a piece of evidence confirming Lindsey's presence, however, it wouldn't help him figure out where she was now.

Time to touch base with Sarge and—

His phone began to vibrate, and he pulled it out.

Speak of the devil.

He put it to his ear. "You find anything? Because I have zip." He didn't attempt to hide his frustration.

"Yes. I have a location for Oliver's phone. I'll text it in a minute. Here's where it gets interesting. The whereabouts of his cell coincide with a report that was called in a couple of minutes ago about suspicious activity at an empty warehouse in the county, just outside the city line a few miles north of your location."

Jack's pulse picked up.

That was the best news he'd had all night.

He took off at a jog for his car. "Tell the responding officers to hold back until I get there. If Oliver took Lindsey to a place like that, the situation could go downhill fast. We have to assume he's armed." And cornered people weren't always rational.

"I passed that along once I saw the connection. There's more. The citizen who called this in provided the license plate of the car he saw parked behind the warehouse. Get this. It belongs to Heidi Robertson."

What?

Jack's pace faltered.

Heidi Robertson was with Oliver?

What in the world was that all about?

He picked up his pace again. "I'm trying to make sense of that."

"We can sort it out later. First priority is keeping your witness alive. I'll put a hostage negotiator on standby. Keep me apprised."

"Will do."

Jack ended the call and sprinted toward his vehicle.

The connection between Heidi and Oliver was a mystery. One that would take a while to untangle.

But if Oliver had been behind all the incidents designed to undermine Lindsey's mental integrity, he was eminently suited for the job. He knew her history—and could use that to cast doubts on the credibility of any details she might remember about the killing.

It was diabolically clever.

It was also beyond sick.

A man who had chosen a profession dedicated to helping people deal with traumas had instead created one for a patient in order to save his own neck, causing untold mental anguish.

But why had he decided to end her life rather than continue his campaign of subversion?

Another question without an answer.

For now, though, the when and the how were more important than the why.

Jack waved over one of the officers assisting at Oliver's house and gave him a fast recap. Then he slid behind the wheel of his car, checked the location in the text from Sarge, and hit his flashing lights. He'd shut them off once he got close to the warehouse, but they'd allow him to maneuver through traffic faster. At this hour, flooring it, he ought to arrive in less than ten minutes.

Yet every minute counted when someone's life was in danger.

And being one minute too late could mark the difference between life and death.

THE DANK COLD in the cavernous warehouse seeped through Lindsey's sweater, and she shivered as Dr. Oliver propelled her forward, into the shadowy space lit only by the moonlight filtering through the large perimeter windows at the top of the high walls.

"This spot is as good as any." Heidi, in the lead position, spoke over her shoulder as she paused to examine the space.

Lindsey's heart stuttered.

The end was near.

Beside her, Dr. Oliver's labored breathing either indicated illness or anxiety—or perhaps both. "I'm not certain I can pull the trigger."

At least one of them still possessed the remnants of a conscience.

"I know it will be hard, but she left us no choice, Anthony."

"Shooting is dangerous. Guns can be traced."

"It has to be found first. We can toss it in the river before we go back to your place. Or we could go with the noose.

That would be quieter. And there's a perfect spot for it." She motioned upward, to the metal catwalks crisscrossing the building below the rafters.

Dr. Oliver gave them a slow perusal. "No. Hanging is too painful and traumatic. But a fall from up there would be quick—and I wouldn't have to watch the impact."

Lindsey stared at the two of them, stomach churning.

They were debating murder options as if this were a discussion about which item to order from a restaurant menu.

What was wrong with these people?

"Fine with me. Why don't you give me the gun while you take her up?" Heidi crossed to Dr. Oliver, and he handed it over. "I think there's access to the catwalks over there." She motioned toward the side of the building and began walking that direction.

Stall, Lindsey! Buy yourself time to collect your thoughts and come up with a plan.

Letting her instincts guide her, she bent over and began to fake a heaving motion.

"Heidi! Wait!"

At Dr. Oliver's command, the staccato click of the woman's heels on the concrete floor stopped . . . then drew closer again. "What's wrong with her?"

"I don't know. She may be trying to throw up. Trauma can induce nausea. If she aspirates vomit with her mouth covered, she'll choke to death."

"Problem solved."

"Heidi!" His sharp rebuke ricocheted off the walls. "That's a terrible way to die."

She shrugged. "No matter how she dies, the end result is the same."

At the woman's cavalier response, the roiling in Lindsey's stomach intensified—making the risk of throwing up very real.

Dr. Oliver didn't respond, but his grip on her arm tightened. As if he was angry. Then he ripped off her gag, taking layers of skin from her lips with it.

She moaned and sagged against him at the shocking sting.

But the burning pain was worth it to get her voice back.

"Let's do this." Dr. Oliver's tone was resigned.

Heidi started forward again, toward the metal stairs that led to the catwalk.

Though Lindsey tried to resist, Dr. Oliver dragged her along. She continued to writhe in his grasp as they approached the stairway, using the gyrations to hide her struggle to free her hands. Apparently she hadn't worked the cording quite loose enough.

At the foot of the steps, Heidi turned and waved them up. "I'll follow you as far as the first landing after you're up." She leaned in close, her face inches away as she lifted the pistol, her eyes hard and cold. "Don't try anything foolish, Lindsey. Anthony may not want to use this gun, but I will if I have to."

She moved aside, and Dr. Oliver spoke. "Don't make this any harder than it has to be, Lindsey." He kept his voice low and close to her ear while he forced her up the steps, as if he didn't want Heidi to hear. "I'm sorry it came to this. It was all supposed to be so easy. We were going to build a circumstantial case against the carpenter. Enough to put the spotlight of suspicion and law enforcement attention on him, but insufficient for a conviction. You weren't supposed to be in the kitchen that day."

Was he seriously trying to apologize as he led her to her death?

This was surreal.

"I don't understand how you can do this to me. I trusted you." She continued to tug at the cording.

"I know. And I'm sorry to betray that trust. But when push comes to shove, life is all about number one."

"Not for everyone."

"With few exceptions, that describes the vast majority of people." He stopped at the landing, chest heaving.

"Everything all right, Anthony?" Heidi's question floated up from below.

"Yes. Catching my breath."

Lindsey worked harder on the cording. If she could keep him talking, maybe she could buy herself an extra minute or two.

"It was your aftershave, you know."

"What?" He squinted at her.

"That's how I knew it was you. I smelled it in the kitchen the day I found the body. I smelled it again at your house tonight."

"It wasn't the tattoo?"

"That clinched it, but the aftershave was my first clue."

He gave a soft, mirthless laugh. "Proof that the devil truly is in the details. I never wore it to the office. Some clients have an aversion to certain scents. But I used it that day for the conference I attended—my alibi, if ever one was necessary. Who knew it would come back to haunt me?" He propelled her upward again. "Keep walking."

Below them, the tap of Heidi's shoes against metal indicated she was climbing up to the landing.

"I, uh, didn't know you were a scuba diver." The cording was getting looser. In another minute or two, she should be able to free her hands.

If she had that long.

"Years ago, but I still had all the gear. It's gone now."

Naturally.

He wouldn't leave anything lying around that could connect him to a crime.

They were approaching the top of the catwalk.

She had to make her play soon.

"And you staged the mugging."

"Yes. With Heidi. My planning was meticulous until she blew everything by moving your car again and leaving her DNA as evidence." Anger scored his words.

One more piece fell into place.

The biggest remaining question was why he'd launched this scheme to begin with.

"If you love her, why didn't she just divorce her husband so you two could be together? Why did you have to kill him?"

He snorted. "Love didn't have anything to do with it. It was all about the money. And killing him was the only way to get it." He forced her onto the catwalk at the top of the steps.

Dragging her feet as much as possible, she continued to work on the cording as he pushed her forward over the narrow grating. "Please, Dr. Oliver. You don't have to do this."

Finally! She had the wiggle room to pull her hands free.

"Sadly, I do." He tightened his grip, halting their progress. "May as well stop here."

Heart thumping, she peered down into the cavernous warehouse.

Heidi was about fifty feet away and down a level, no more than a dim outline in the murky interior.

Perfect.

If she could elude Dr. Oliver, get off the catwalk, and hide in a dark corner, they'd have a hard time finding her. They wouldn't risk using their phone lights to search. Not after Dr. Oliver had gone ballistic when Heidi flicked hers on for a brief minute while they got the lay of the land. As he'd told her, a light inside a deserted warehouse could arouse suspicion and perhaps prompt a call to the police. They couldn't take that chance.

As he began loosening the noose around her neck to remove it, her pulse vaulted into the stratosphere.

As soon as the rope was off, that would be her window.

And as she prepared to rip her hands free, she prayed for the strength to overcome her adversaries and survive this night.

JACK KILLED HIS LIGHTS and pulled up beside the three cruisers that were parked in the shadows on the warehouse property. A fourth one swung in as he braked.

Sarge had called in plenty of reinforcements.

Good man.

As Jack got out of his car, the officers joined him.

After giving them a rapid briefing, he encompassed all of them with his question. "Any of you know this property?"

"I've driven through here on patrols."

Jack turned to the fortysomething officer who'd spoken. "Do you remember how many access points there are?"

"I think there are two loading docks on the left side and two in the back. I know there's a door in the front, and as best I can recall there's another one next to the loading docks in the back. But I can't swear to any of that. I wasn't here to take inventory."

"Understood." The man had recalled far more than *he* would have from a routine patrol circuit. "According to our tipster, the car is in the back. I'm going to assume that door is the one most likely to be open."

"Are the subjects armed?" This from a young cop. Perhaps fresh from the academy, based on the adrenaline pinging off him.

"That would be my expectation. Have weapons in hand and flashlights ready. Be prepared to use the flashlights to startle or illuminate on command. Keep them off unless I tell you to use them. I want one person at the loading docks on the left and one by the door here in front in case anyone tries to escape through those exits." He tapped two of the officers as he spoke, then turned to the remaining men. "You two come with me. We're going in slow and silent while I assess the situation. Any questions?"

Head shakes all around.

"Let's do this."

He took off at a trot for the back of the building, pistol at the ready, nerve endings tingling.

If fate was kind, he wouldn't have to use his weapon.

But if that's what it took to save Lindsey's life, he'd pull the trigger in a heartbeat.

And he'd do it without a single regret.

THIRTY

NOW!

With a mighty yank, Lindsey jerked her wrists apart.

The loosened cording gave way, freeing her hands.

Thank you, God!

After giving Dr. Oliver a shove, she swung away and took off across the grated floor of the narrow, rusted ramp that offered a dizzying view into the bowels of the building.

Unfortunately, the element of surprise didn't last long.

"Anthony! Go after her!"

As Heidi's command bounced off the walls of the empty building, Lindsey picked up her pace. But it was hard to move fast in the dark on a surface that didn't feel any too steady.

Despite his less-than-optimal physical condition, he pounded after her on the metal platform, shaking it even more.

It was everything she could do to remain upright as she ran on the vibrating grate beneath her feet.

But she managed to keep her balance—until the toe of her shoe caught in a loose piece of grating and she stumbled.

The next instant, Dr. Oliver grabbed her arm.

"Anthony! Push her over! Be done with this!"

At Heidi's cold, callous words, anger swelled inside Lindsey.

She hadn't come this close to escaping to fail. If someone was destined to be pitched over the side, it wasn't going to be her.

Swinging around, she went into attack mode.

She pummeled Dr. Oliver with her free fist. Dodged his blows. Writhed in his grasp after he latched onto her other arm. She fought him with every ounce of her strength as they bounced back and forth between the side railings on the ramp suspended high above the unforgiving concrete floor of the warehouse.

"Stop resisting . . . Lindsey." He panted the command, clearly winded by the exertion. "I'm stronger . . . than you are."

Maybe when he wasn't sick.

But his skin was burning up.

And he also had an Achilles' heel.

She latched onto the arm with the tattoo. The exact spot that had caused him to yowl in pain earlier when she'd touched him there.

It had the same effect this time, and he jerked free, raining curses on her.

Blocking out his vile obscenities, she prepared to bolt and take her chances with Heidi's gun. It held a limited number of bullets, and unless the not-so-grieving widow had a superb aim, shooting in the dark would only waste ammunition.

But Dr. Oliver lunged at her before she could swivel around.

Somehow she managed to sidestep a full body slam on the narrow platform. But as she angled sideways to avoid him, he connected with her shoulder, tipping her off-balance.

A second later, he crashed into the railing headfirst, knocking a section of the rusted metal out as he fell to the ramp and lay unmoving, one limp arm hanging into the abyss.

Tremors ricocheted through the walkway from the impact, and Lindsey tottered. Tried to latch onto something. Anything.

Failed.

She pitched toward the gap in the railing, groping in empty air for a handhold as she fell toward the blackness, her scream echoing like a death knell in the silent, tomb-like warehouse.

THE WOMAN'S SCREAM changed everything.

"Scrap the previous plan. We're going in fast." Heart pounding, Jack opened the door and dashed into the warehouse ahead of the two officers who'd accompanied him.

It was hard to see much in the darkness, but blindly sweeping flashlight beams around would pinpoint their location and put a bull's-eye on them.

Fortunately, the click of rapid footsteps on metal helped him home in on the action.

A person was running up the steps to the catwalk. Too tall to be Lindsey, too thin to be Oliver.

It must be Heidi.

He scanned the length of the walkway suspended high above the floor of the warehouse, squinting at the metal structure as he tried to—

His lungs froze.

Lindsey was hanging from the edge of the ramp. Holding tight for the moment, but she wouldn't be able to maintain her grip long if she was injured.

Above her, someone lay motionless. Had to be Oliver.

"We're moving in." He nudged the officer next to him. "Find a secure spot fast that offers cover and shine your light at the person climbing the steps." He turned to the other officer as the first one melted into the darkness. "I want light on the two people on the catwalk the instant I give you the word. Let's go."

As they ran forward, a spotlight picked out the figure on the stairs.

Jack stopped as the woman swung around and shaded her eyes.

Identity confirmed.

It was Heidi.

He lifted his Sig Sauer and called out. "St. Louis County Police. Drop your weapon."

Instead of complying, she raised a gun and aimed it his general direction.

Didn't she realize she made a perfect target in the spotlight?

"Drop your weapon. Now!" Jack held steady, aiming for her center mass. He had no time for games, not with Lindsey's life literally hanging in the balance.

A shot rang out, pinging off metal behind him as the recoil jolted Heidi.

She was shooting blind.

The odds were she wouldn't hit anything—but she could get lucky. And she'd been warned.

Jack squeezed the trigger once. Twice.

Her gun clattered to the warehouse floor below her as she crumpled and slid down the steps.

He didn't spare her a second look as he spoke to the officer beside him. "I want light on the catwalk. Get the other officers in here. Call for ambulances. Follow me up as soon as someone else can take your place with the light." He sprinted for the metal stairs. "Hold on, Lindsey. I'm coming." His shouted entreaty reverberated through the structure.

At the base of the stairs, he glanced up . . . and up . . . and up to what lay ahead.

A flimsy, grated floor. Rusted railings. A staircase with a landing that didn't look any too solid.

All very high up.

He broke out in a cold sweat as his stomach began to churn. His worst nightmare had just come to life.

What if his latent vertigo reared its ugly head? What if he lost his balance or became disoriented or—

"Jack! Hurry! I'm slipping!"

At Lindsey's panicked plea, he gritted his teeth.

He could do this.

He *would* do this.

Fixing his gaze on the solid surface beneath his feet, he bounded up the metal treads, stepping over and around Heidi where she'd come to rest on the landing as he continued upward. Once on the catwalk, he steadied himself with one hand on the railing and kept his Sig at the ready as he raced toward Lindsey, doing his best to ignore the quiver in the grating beneath his feet . . . and the quiver in his legs.

As he approached the spotlighted area, he gave Oliver a quick inspection.

The man lay sprawled on the grating, unmoving. He appeared to be breathing, but as far as Jack could see, he posed no imminent threat.

After shoving the man's legs aside, Jack holstered his Sig and dropped flat on his stomach on the grillwork above Lindsey as more light flooded the area. Locking his feet around the closest railing supports, he reached down and grasped her forearms, keeping his focus on her rather than the chasm stretching below. "I've got you, sweetheart."

"My hands . . . are slipping."

"I won't let you fall. I promise."

"You shouldn't . . . be up here. It's too . . . high for you."

She was worried about *him* after almost plunging to her death?

His throat clogged. "I'm fine." Not even close, but he'd get through this—even if the warehouse was beginning to spin around him.

"Don't . . . let me go."

"Never. That's a promise."

In more ways than one.

The other officer joined him, and he switched back into his official voice. "Grab her right arm. Let's pull her up on the count of three."

Ten seconds later, Lindsey was standing on the walkway in the circle of his arms, tremors rippling through her body as she clung to him.

Or were the tremors his?

Didn't matter. She was safe, and as soon as they were back on terra firma, he'd be fine.

That couldn't happen fast enough to suit him.

"I can't believe you found me." The erratic breath from her choked, whispered words fluttered against his neck.

"It was close. Too close. Let's get off this catwalk." He gently extricated himself from her clasp and helped her skirt around Oliver.

"Is he . . . is he alive?" She edged past the man's prone form.

"I think so." He directed his next comment to the officer. "Stay with him until the paramedics get here."

They had to sidle past Heidi too as they descended. Keeping a firm grip on Lindsey, he guided her around the slumped body.

"Is she . . . is she dead?"

Jack glanced down at the officer who'd descended to the floor after giving her a cursory assessment. The man shook his head.

"Yes. Hold on to the railing while we go down this last stretch. I'll be right in front of you. I won't let you fall."

He maneuvered himself ahead of her and followed his own advice with the railing. With the stiffening evaporating from his legs, he needed the support as much as she did.

At the bottom, he turned and helped her down the last

couple of steps. "Let's get you checked out." The paramedics had arrived, and he put his arm around her as he guided her toward them. Not his usual protocol on the job, but when the woman you were falling for had almost died, the rules didn't apply.

"I'm fine, Jack." She held back as he tried to urge her forward. "I don't need medical attention."

"I'd rather hear that from an expert. Humor me?"

She sighed and offered him a tiny lip flex. "It's hard to say no to a person who saved your life."

As she leaned into him, he led her toward the paramedics.

One of them sized her up as they drew close, then set up a stair chair. The kind another team was already carrying toward the steps to transport Oliver off the catwalk.

Smart move.

No way was Lindsey going to let them put her on a stretcher.

"You're my first patient of the night." The fortysomething guy smiled as they approached, his relaxed, affable manner no doubt designed to calm injured and sick people who were also stressed and scared. "Have a seat." He tapped the chair.

She lowered herself onto it gingerly. As if she hurt all over.

After hanging from a catwalk, that wouldn't be unexpected.

But what other injuries did she have?

Jack dropped to his haunches beside her, scrutinizing her in the illumination from the lights the medical team was setting up as he twined his fingers with hers.

To put it kindly, she was a mess.

Her temple was black-and-blue, her lips were raw and puffy, and when she pulled up the sleeves of her sweater to display her bruised and bloody wrists in response to a question from the paramedic, his stomach kinked, fermenting the anger already brewing there.

Given Lindsey's physical injuries, plus the emotional trauma she'd been put through, it was hard to feel even one iota of remorse for taking Heidi out.

As for Oliver—assuming he survived, they ought to lock him up forever.

Jack remained silent while the paramedic took vitals, flashed his penlight in Lindsey's pupils, and asked a ton of questions. But he didn't relinquish his grip on her hand.

"How hard did you hit your head?" The paramedic examined the bruise on her temple.

"Hard enough to see stars. But I hit the back of my head harder."

"Show me where."

She touched a spot near the middle.

As soon as the man began to feel it, she winced. "Ouch."

"Sorry." Nevertheless, he continued probing. "That's quite a goose egg. Did you lose consciousness?"

"No."

"The ER docs may want to image that."

"No." Her posture stiffened. "I don't have any concussion symptoms."

"No headache?"

She gave a shrug of concession. "Other than a headache."

"What about dizziness, nausea, light or sound sensitivity, confusion?"

"No."

"Any neck pain or weakness or tingling anywhere?"

"No."

"I can treat your abrasions here, but with two bumps to the head, it may be smart to be evaluated for a brain injury in the ER."

"That's not necessary. I'll be fine."

"Lindsey." Jack squeezed her hand and rejoined the conversation. "Why don't you let them take you to the hospital? If there's any damage, waiting could be a mistake."

Indecision flickered in her eyes. "I hate causing you any more worry, but I really want to go home, Jack." Her voice hitched, and moisture pooled on her lower lashes. "I can call 911 if any symptoms develop."

After all she'd been through, it wasn't hard to understand why she'd crave the comfort of familiar surroundings.

He looked at the paramedic. "In your opinion, how dangerous would it be if she went home?"

The man regarded her. "My official recommendation is to go to the ER. That said, I'm not seeing any strong evidence of a serious brain injury, and the risk passes after about four hours. I don't think the danger would be too high if someone stayed with her until the early hours of the morning, and she followed up with a doctor who has experience in concussions within a few days."

"I'll stay."

"Jack." Lindsey touched his hand. "I can't ask you to do that."

"You didn't ask. I volunteered." He dug deep for a smile, but it eluded him. "Besides, I need to take your statement and I'd rather do that somewhere more comfortable than here or in an ER—and after we both clock a few hours of sleep. Deal?"

The shimmer in her eyes intensified. "Thank you."

He brushed a few tangled wisps of hair off her forehead. "My pleasure."

"If that's the decision, let me clean you up so you can get on your way." The paramedic went to work.

Jack left her in his care while he stepped away to call Sarge with an update on both the situation in the warehouse and his plans for the remainder of the evening. Well, some of his plans, anyway. The taking the statement part, not the staying with Lindsey overnight part.

"That'll work. I've tapped Cate to assist at the scene." As Sarge spoke, she came through the door.

Jack lifted a hand in greeting, and she veered his direction. "She just arrived."

"Fill her in and get out of there."

"You don't have to twist my arm. I'll touch base with you again in the morning."

As he ended the call, Cate joined him. "I hear the Robertson case has been solved."

"Yeah." He gave her a rapid-fire briefing. "CSU should be here soon."

"I figured that. Officers are securing the perimeter." She regarded Lindsey. "Tough night for her."

"Beyond tough. Closer to fatal. If we'd been even a few minutes later . . ." His voice roughened at the thought of how close he'd come to losing her.

Cate continued to regard Lindsey, her mouth set in a grim line. "I know what that's like."

Yeah, she did, thanks to her own near-death experience at the hands of a ruthless killer during her undercover days.

He swallowed. "And that's on top of all the other trauma she's had."

"I hear you. Take her home. I've got this covered."

"Thanks."

He didn't linger to chat with Cate. Instead, he returned to Lindsey's side.

The paramedic added a final piece of tape to the bandage around one of her wrists and stood. "She's all yours."

That had a nice ring to it on this otherwise harrowing night.

"Ready to go?" He held out his hand.

Weariness etched her features as she grasped his fingers. "More than."

As he gave her a gentle assist up, she shivered.

No wonder.

The sweater she was wearing didn't provide near sufficient warmth in the damp, dank structure.

He should have noticed that sooner.

In one quick movement, he shrugged out of his jacket and draped it around her shoulders.

"I can't take this." Her protest was halfhearted at best as she snuggled into the warmth. "You'll get cold."

"I'll be fine as far as the car. And I'll crank up the heat when we get there. Let's go." He slid his arm around her and led her out of the building, into the strobing lights piercing the darkness from multiple cruisers. After tucking her into the front seat of his car, he circled around to the driver's side.

As he slid behind the wheel, she shifted toward him. "How in the world did you find me?"

"Why don't I give you the short version tonight and fill in all the details tomorrow?" He turned on the engine and put the car in gear.

She clapped a hand over her mouth to cover a yawn. "I'll settle for that."

Somehow he managed to condense the nerve-wracking last few hours into a handful of sentences as he drove away from what could have been another murder scene.

Would have been if he'd arrived a handful of minutes later.

The mere thought of tonight's other possible outcome sent a chill coursing through him that had nothing to do with the cold night air.

When he finished, she expelled a long, slow breath. "It sounds like fate was on our side."

"Or a higher power."

"I like your take better." She let her head drop back against the seat. "Is it all right if I close my eyes for a few minutes?"

"You have not only my permission but my encouragement."

Silence fell in the car save for the hum of tires on the pavement, and within five minutes she'd fallen into a deep sleep.

No wonder.

She had to be exhausted physically and emotionally.

So once he got her home, he'd hustle her to bed, rack out on her couch while she slept, and keep one ear tuned throughout the night in case her real-life nightmare came back to haunt her dreams and she needed the comfort of a caring hug.

THIRTY-ONE

WHAT WAS THAT DELICIOUS AROMA?

Stomach rumbling, Lindsey blinked her eyes open and inhaled long and slow.

When had she last eaten? Lunch yesterday?

Yes.

A lifetime ago, in light of all that had happened since then.

Amazing that she'd slept the night through with nary a bad dream.

But Jack's promise to stay close as he'd tucked her in had given her the peace of mind to enjoy a long, restful, dreamless sleep. And now, with sunshine peeking around the edges of her blinds, and her bedside clock reading eight thirty, the events of the past fifteen hours felt more like a horror movie than reality.

The aches and pains radiating throughout her body as she threw back the covers and swung her feet to the floor, however, were stark evidence of how real it had all been.

And how close she'd come to never seeing another dawn.

Quashing that chilling thought, she pushed herself to her feet. Winced. Hobbled into the bathroom on unsteady legs.

Stared in shock at the bruised face and puffy lips reflected in her mirror.

More proof that last night's trauma had been all too real.

And no amount of makeup was going to disguise the purple hues mottling her skin or the swelling around her mouth.

May as well accept that she wasn't going to win a most-photogenic contest for a while. But a quick shower and change of clothes ought to help her *feel* more normal at least. And if the enticing aroma wafting through her condo was any indication, her stomach was in for a treat. Jack obviously hadn't been kidding when he'd said he liked to cook.

Ten minutes later, in clean leggings and a sweatshirt, she finger combed her damp hair as she emerged from her room and wandered down the hall toward the kitchen.

On the threshold, she paused.

Her knight in shining armor wasn't wearing a helmet or chain mail today. On the contrary. His hair was rumpled, his slacks were creased, and his shirt was wrinkled.

But he looked every bit as noble and gallant as those legendary knights of old.

As if sensing her perusal, he turned from the stove. While his smile warmed her, it couldn't disguise the grooves beside his mouth and the fine lines radiating from the corners of his eyes that spoke of worry and exhaustion and stress.

"Good morning." He moved the pan off the burner. "How are you feeling?"

"A little sore, but otherwise okay."

"What's the verdict on your head?"

"No problems. The only souvenir of my close encounters with hard objects is a dull ache." She leaned a shoulder against the doorframe. "How much did you sleep? My couch wasn't designed for anything but short naps."

"Enough." Without giving her a chance to dwell on that

obvious fib, he swung the spotlight back to her. "You look rested."

"I didn't wake up once."

"That's what I thought. I didn't hear a sound from your room all night. Are you hungry?"

"Very."

"Have a seat. When I heard you moving around, I shifted into high gear."

"You didn't have to make me breakfast."

"Believe me, cooking in a kitchen as well-stocked as this isn't a chore." He crossed to the oven and pulled out a tray of biscuits.

She gaped at the source of the tantalizing aroma that had nudged her awake. "Are those homemade?"

"Is there any other kind?" He flashed her a grin. "It's my mom's recipe. She always made them for breakfast if someone needed a pick-me-up or we had something to celebrate. I decided this morning qualified on both scores for us." He set the tray on a cooling rack. "Go ahead and sit." He walked over to the table and pulled out a chair for her.

She slid onto it, watching as he put the biscuits in a basket, dished up scrambled eggs, and set a fruit parfait in front of her. "Wow. I'll be spoiled. In light of my profession I probably shouldn't admit this, but my usual breakfast is a bagel and cream cheese."

"Mine too. But it's Saturday, the Robertson nightmare is over, and we have a whole future to look forward to." He joined her at the table. "Do you mind if I offer a blessing?"

"By all means."

He took her hand, and though she dipped her chin and tried to pay attention as he gave thanks, the warmth of his strong grip seeping into her skin was a major distraction.

"Dig in." He released his hold as he passed the basket of biscuits.

She took one and slathered it with butter. Bit into the tender, flaky goodness. Sighed. "These are fantastic. You can make them for me anytime."

"Count on it." He locked onto her gaze with an intensity that played havoc with her respiration. But a moment later, he lowered the wattage and motioned to her plate. "Why don't we table personal matters until we finish breakfast and I take your statement?"

"That seems reasonable." Otherwise, the flutter in her stomach would render eating impossible. Forking a bite of egg, she shifted the conversation back to recent events. "Fill me in on the details of how you found me."

He complied as she finished one biscuit and helped herself to another. "I'm just sorry I didn't get there sooner."

"You got there. That's all that counts." She scooped up another bite of her eggs. "I still can't believe Dr. Oliver and Heidi Robertson were a couple."

He cocked his head. "You mean beyond being partners in crime?"

"That's my conclusion." She told him about the exchanges she'd witnessed and the endearments Heidi had used.

"A love triangle." He frowned as he buttered a biscuit. "That puts a different spin on motives."

"I'm not certain how much love was involved, based on Dr. Oliver's comment to me last night that it was all about the money, and that killing Heidi's husband was the only way to get it."

Jack took a sip of his coffee, his expression thoughtful. "I wonder if she had a prenup."

"That angle never occurred to me, but it would fit."

"Should be easy to confirm. As we dig into this case, I expect we'll discover all kinds of interesting personal data that will help us pin down motives for all parties."

"You think Dr. Oliver will cooperate with the investigation?"

"Doubtful. Guys like him lawyer up. But it may be a moot point anyway."

Lindsey stopped eating. "Why? Is he badly injured?"

"Not from the fall on the catwalk. His attempt to eradicate his tattoo, however, led to infection—and sepsis."

That explained the sore arm.

"Is that blood poisoning?" From the little she knew about that malady, it could kill very fast.

"Yes. The doctors aren't giving him great odds."

Exhaling, she set her fork down and rested her hand on the table. "It's all so surreal. Hard as I try, I can't reconcile the caring therapist I knew with the cold-blooded killer who shot James Robertson in his own kitchen and turned on a patient he was trying to help deal with trauma."

"Just goes to show how the upright image some people project to the world can mask a dark soul." Jack's jaw hardened, and a muscle clenched in his cheek.

"I guess you see a lot of that in your work."

"Too much. But I also cross paths with people like you, who renew my faith in the human race." He covered her hand with his, his features softening. "And my sisters are a daily reminder that good exists in this world. You'll like them."

They were veering back into personal territory.

Fine with her.

"I can't wait to meet them."

"Plan on it in the very near future. Why don't we finish up here and I'll take your statement so we can get the official business out of the way and give other, more important things our full attention?"

A trill of anticipation zipped through her, and she picked up her fork. "I'm on board with that."

Jack steered the conversation to lighter topics while they

ate, refused her offer to help him clear the table, and morphed into detective mode as he took her statement.

The instant they were done, however, he closed his notebook, stood, and extended his hand. "A scene change seems in order. Shall we go into the living room?"

Despite her protesting muscles, she pushed herself to her feet and took his hand.

He led her into the adjacent room, where the couch had been restored to its usual function, the blanket and pillow that had helped transform it into a makeshift bed neatly piled on a side chair. After settling her on the cushions, he crossed to the fireplace and flipped on the gas logs. Once the flames were dancing in the grate, he returned to the sofa and sat beside her.

Close.

Very close.

They'd definitely moved into personal territory.

He reclaimed her hand as he angled toward her. "I know last night was a nightmare for you, but I want you to know it was a nightmare for me too. All those hours I was racing around trying to find you, I kept thinking that God surely wouldn't bring someone like you into my life, give me a glimpse of an amazing future, then snatch you away before we had a chance to really get to know each other."

It appeared Jack was as straightforward in his personal life as he was when pursuing a case. No beating around the bush with this guy.

Also fine with her.

And as long as *he* was being so honest . . .

"I had the same thought."

His lips flexed. "And here I was afraid I might be rushing you. I mean, we only met a month ago." He reached over and stroked gentle fingers down her cheek.

At this proximity, it was hard not to drown in his blue eyes.

She tried to keep breathing. "You're not rushing me."

"Good to know." His gaze dropped to her mouth. "Under normal circumstances, that would be my cue for a kiss. But much as I'd like to follow my inclinations, I don't think your lips are up to the job today."

Neither did she, dang it. Just getting the food past them had been painful, careful as she'd been.

"Sad to say, they aren't. On the plus side, though, I'm a fast healer. I ought to be back in fighting—or kissing—form in a few days. I still have your cheesecake too, if you need an extra enticement to drop by again soon."

"I know that will be delicious, but I have a much more enticing sweet treat on my mind." He gave her a slow smile. "As for dropping by . . . I may outwear my welcome."

"Not possible."

"Also good to know." He lifted her hand, carefully avoiding her damaged wrist. "Since your lips are off-limits, let's try this on for size."

He raised her hand higher. Kissed the back. Moved on to each knuckle. Continued to each finger. Turned her hand over and pressed his lips to her palm.

The temperature in the room skyrocketed.

For kissing that didn't involve the melding of mouths, this was beyond potent.

And it got more potent when he edged even closer and began to trail kisses along her jawline. Up onto her cheek. Across to her earlobe.

Whew.

She tipped her head to give him better access, closed her eyes, and sank back onto the couch.

If this was any indication of his kissing power, an actual lip-lock would be off the charts.

"You okay with all this?" As he spoke the question, the warmth of his breath feathered across her cheek.

"Mm-hmm." It was all she could manage.

He dipped lower to nuzzle her neck.

Someone purred.

Good heavens. Was that her?

Jack's throaty chuckle provided the answer. "I think I found the lady's sweet spot."

"I think you found all of them—that I know of."

"Won't it be fun to discover the rest?"

At that delicious notion, a shiver of delight rippled through her. "I'm in. And once I have my lips back, turnabout will be fair play."

He eased back far enough to see her face. "I like how you think, Lindsey Barnes. In fact, I like you period."

"The feeling is mutual. And you know what? If it took all the bad stuff that's happened this past month to lead me to you, it was worth it."

A shadow darkened his features. "I like the outcome too, but not the process. I wish we could have gone straight from Day One to here and skipped all the trauma in between."

"I'll tell you what." She twined her fingers together behind his neck. "Let's do our best to forget about yesterday and focus on tomorrow. Because I see an incredible future ahead of us. Starting right now."

"To borrow your phrase, I'm in. Shall I pick up where I left off a minute ago?"

"By all means."

And as Jack went back to giving her a preview of just how exciting their tomorrows might be, Lindsey did her best to let go of all the fear and terror that had tainted her life since South Carolina. An easy task while the man she was falling in love with demonstrated how much he cared for her.

Truth be told, though, given the depth of the trauma she'd

endured, recollections of the horror would no doubt rear their ugly head on occasion in the days and months to come.

But somehow she knew that with Jack beside her, the bad memories would eventually fade away as the new ones they made together banished the darkness from her mind and filled her heart with light and joy.

EPILOGUE

"BRI LOOKS HAPPY, DOESN'T SHE?"

Somehow Jack managed to tear his gaze away from the most beautiful woman at the wedding reception—that would be Lindsey—to spare his sister a quick glance as she swayed to the music on the dance floor with her new husband.

Yes, she did. Beyond happy, in fact. More like radiant. And gorgeous.

He searched the crowd, homing in on the maid of honor. Cara was sitting off to one side, talking animatedly with the groom's grandmother. Probably about the sabbatical she was set to begin next month at that remote estate down near Potosi with the reclusive owner who'd agreed to help her with her research.

His youngest sister was gorgeous too. Also dateless. What was wrong with the men in her circle that they couldn't see past the challenges she'd overcome with such admirable grace and grit?

But that was a concern for another day.

Tonight, the woman beside him deserved his full attention.

"Don't you think so?" Lindsey nudged him.

He nodded. "Yes. I don't know that I've ever seen her happier. Or maybe it's easier to spot true happiness when you're feeling it yourself." He reached over and squeezed her hand.

She returned the pressure. "The months we've been dating have been the happiest of my life too. At this stage, the nightmare I went through feels like nothing more than a bad dream."

"I hear you. I'm glad it ended fast after the night at the warehouse. If Oliver had survived, we'd still be dealing with the aftermath."

"I know." She sighed. "On a happier note, I have good news."

"I do too." More than one piece, actually. But he'd save the best for last. "You go first."

"Dara called today. She and Chad are expecting. Madeleine and I have already talked about throwing her a baby shower."

That sounded like the woman he'd come to love. Always thinking of others.

"I'm happy for them. They had a tough stretch, thanks to Heidi and Oliver."

"But they stuck together and weathered the storm. An example for all of us." She squeezed his hand again. "Now tell me your news."

"I've been accepted for the next session of the FBI National Academy. It starts in October."

Her face lit up. "Oh, Jack. I'm thrilled for you. But I'm not surprised. When you told me County had nominated you, I knew you'd get one of the coveted spots. I mean, if they wouldn't take the best detective in St. Louis, who would they take?"

"You may be a bit prejudiced."

"No." She gave a definitive shake of her head. "That assessment is based on firsthand experience. If it wasn't for you, I wouldn't be sitting here tonight." A sudden shadow dimmed the animation in her eyes.

"Luck and God had more to do with that than my detective skills."

"I'll concede they both came into play, but you jumped on

340

every lead. Not many detectives would have pushed as hard and as fast as you did."

"I had an ulterior motive." He winked at her, doing his best to dispel the sudden pall that had fallen over their conversation. This wasn't the mood he wanted to create for the rest of their evening. "Speaking of ulterior motives, why don't we stroll out to the terrace? The heat's not too bad for early August, and the setting is romantic." He motioned to the French doors that lined one wall of the reception venue, which opened onto a large courtyard with an illuminated fountain. "I could get us each a chocolate mint square to finish the evening on a sweet note."

"I already had wedding cake—but you know I can never pass up your chocolate mint squares. I think I've gained five pounds chowing down on them since we met."

"Not that I've noticed." He gave her slinky dress with its skimpy, oh-so-alluring shoulder straps a slow, appreciative perusal. "Especially in that phenomenal outfit."

Despite the soft lighting, it was impossible to miss the slight flush that rose on her cheeks. "You have a silver tongue, Detective Tucker."

"Complaining?"

"Never. I'm all yours."

"Hold that thought."

He rose and drew her to her feet, his pulse picking up.

This was the moment he'd been anticipating for months. The brief but critical exchange that would determine the course of his whole future.

At the bank of doors, he opened one and ushered Lindsey through. "Pick a spot and I'll join you in a minute."

"There's a secluded table over there." She motioned to one tucked beside a rose trellis, not far from the fountain. "That work for you?"

"Perfect."

"I'll go claim it—not that there's a crowd to fight. It appears we have the whole terrace to ourselves."

Also perfect.

"I'm fine with that. Be right back." He leaned down and brushed his lips across her forehead.

"I'll be waiting." After rising on tiptoe to give him a discreet return kiss on the cheek, she strolled toward the table, the hem of her dress swishing around her legs.

Jack lingered to watch as she paused beside a rosebush and leaned down to smell the blossom, his throat tightening.

How blessed he'd been the day this special woman had walked into his life, adding joy and light and laughter to his world. A world he'd thought was more than adequate as it was.

But what a difference love made.

It brightened. Illuminated. Warmed. Filled the empty place in his soul he hadn't even known existed.

And if all went well in the next few minutes, that love would grace all his tomorrows for the rest of his life.

SOMETHING WAS UP.

As Lindsey claimed a chair at the table for two and Jack disappeared inside, a quiver of anticipation zipped through her.

After eight months of dating, their trajectory seemed clear. Yet he hadn't so much as hinted about making their relationship permanent.

Could tonight be the night?

Maybe.

What better setting to get a person in a proposing mood than the wedding celebration of a cherished sibling?

However . . . given Jack's background, eight months might be unrealistic. Love and trust didn't come easily to him, thanks to his experience with his mother and the dregs of society he dealt with in his job.

But they were heading toward the altar, no question about it—even if a proposal wasn't on his agenda for tonight.

He came back through the door, a plate containing two mint squares in one hand, bottles of water in the other. After setting the items on the table, he sat across from her. "I didn't have a third hand. Mind sharing a plate?"

"Not at all." She picked up one of the forks balanced beside the three layers of decadence that had rocketed to the top of her favorite-desserts list after her first bite months ago. "I think it was sweet that Bri wanted you to provide these as a grand finale on her special day."

"She said it would make her feel like Mom was with us. Hard to refuse a request like that."

Another indication of the soft heart that beat beneath Jack's sometimes guarded manner.

"Shall we dig in?" She lifted her fork.

"In a minute. I have a gift for you first."

Her pulse lost its rhythm as he reached into his jacket pocket. Withdrew a small box. Held it out.

Slowly she set the fork down and took it.

This must be it.

Struggling not to hyperventilate, she lifted the lid. Removed the thick layer of soft cotton batting that covered the contents.

Oh.

Her lungs collapsed as a surge of disappointment swept over her.

It wasn't a ring.

But wait.

On second thought, this was almost as good.

The burnished gold claddagh pendant had to be his grand-mother's. The one he'd rescued from the box of cough drops in the decrepit dresser he'd found on the sidewalk the day he'd been evicted.

If he was giving her his beloved grandmother's most cherished possession, it had to mean a ring was coming at some point.

And she could wait.

Because Jack was worth waiting for.

Vision misting, she held the box reverently as she looked over at him. "This was your grandmother's, wasn't it?"

"Yes."

"I can't tell you how honored I am that you're entrusting it to me."

His eyes darkened. "I'm planning to entrust you with more than that, Lindsey." Before she could digest that, he motioned toward the pendant. "Would you like to wear it?"

"Yes."

He rose, circled behind her chair, and secured the clasp on the delicate chain, his fingers warm against her neck.

Then he returned to his seat.

What?

No kiss to go along with such a precious gift?

"Why don't we have dessert?"

She stared at him.

He wanted to eat? Now?

Was the pendant not as big a deal as he'd claimed?

Trying to reconcile his behavior with his words, she followed his lead and picked up her fork.

"Bri and Marc were leaving as I got our mint squares." He cut off a bite. "I think Marc is anxious to get the honeymoon started."

Did Jack sound a little winded?

"I expect most grooms are. Brides too." She dived into her treat. "I'm sure they'll have a wonderful trip. It was thoughtful of him to plan it around one of her bucket list destinations."

"Yeah, it was. But I hope the Pyrenees side trip after Paris won't be too taxing for her. She'll want to hike."

"I have a feeling Marc will keep close watch over her and find other sources of entertainment if she has any issues." Which she might. Though Bri had made an incredible recovery from the near-fatal parachuting accident that had shattered her femur, the incident had left her with a now almost-imperceptible limp.

"She does tend to push herself, though. Like someone else I know, who insisted on muscling through her workday after walking into a murder. All because she didn't want to disappoint clients."

"That was my stubborn streak showing—and I have the scar to prove it." She wiggled her finger at him, then went back to eating. "I should have listened to your advice that day and gone—" Her fork ran into a solid object, and she frowned down at her mint square. Poked at it with the tines.

A small flat object emerged from the pink mint filling beneath the thick chocolate icing.

What in the world?

"Something wrong?"

She waved a hand over her plate. "There's a foreign object in my dessert."

He leaned closer to inspect it. "I must have dropped it in there during the baking process. At least *you* got it rather than one of the other guests. That would have been embarrassing. What is it?"

"I don't know." After excavating it, she used her napkin to wipe off the sweet coating. "I think it's a wad of aluminum foil."

As she squeezed it, however, the shape registered.

It wasn't just aluminum foil. It was an object *wrapped* in aluminum foil.

This time, her heart did a somersault.

Fingers fumbling, she removed the wrapping to reveal a diamond solitaire flanked by more diamonds set in a beautiful filigreed gold band.

Cradling it in her palm, she met Jack's gaze across the table.

"Surprise." For a guy who was 100 percent steady and confident, his sudden uncertain smile clogged her throat. "If you're not ready for my speech, tell me and I'll tuck it away for another day."

"I'm ready." Somehow she managed to croak out her response.

He took the ring, set it on the table, and cocooned her hand in his. "You know my history, Lindsey. I've got a ton of baggage. I never expected to find a woman who would convince me to trust her with my life—and my heart. Then you came along, and I fell hook, line, and sinker. I knew almost from the beginning that you were special, and these past months have confirmed that. I love you more than words can say, and until God calls me home, that love will never waver. Every day of my life, my first and last waking thought will be of you." His voice hoarsened, and he picked up the ring. "Will you do me the great honor of becoming my wife?"

In answer, she lifted her hand.

He slid the ring on.

It sparkled in the moonlight as she flexed her finger, and she blinked to clear her vision. "I love you too, Jack. With all my heart." She touched the pendant that hung around her neck. "I figured this meant a ring was coming, but I didn't expect it the same day."

"I wasn't taking any chances. I had to ensure Gram's treasure stays in the family." He scooted his chair closer and angled it toward hers. "You didn't finish your dessert."

"A first, I know. But what was inside was even sweeter."

"I remember what you said when you ate your first mint square." Tenderness softened his features. "'This is a taste of heaven.' I'm going to do everything in my power to make certain you draw the same conclusion about our marriage every single day."

She leaned toward him and linked her hands around his neck. "I think you should seal that promise with a kiss."

A slow smile bowed his lips, the sudden heat in his eyes ratcheting up the temperature on this summer evening.

And as he pressed his lips to hers under the glittering stars, the fountain tinkling beside them while roses perfumed the air, Lindsey gave thanks.

For on that night when she'd dangled from the catwalk moments from death, her fingers slowly losing their grip, it had seemed that all her hopes for a future with this wonderful man would be dashed.

Instead, Jack had pulled her back from the abyss and they'd been granted the gift of tomorrow.

One she had every reason to believe would be filled with happy endings from this day forward.

AUTHOR'S NOTE

With every book I write, there are a number of people who help me bring my story to life. If you've been reading my novels for a while, many of the names in this note will be familiar. That's because certain people have played, and continue to play, a key role in my writing life.

On the professional side, FBI veteran and retired police chief Tom Becker remains my go-to source for law enforcement questions. When we crossed paths more than fifteen years ago while I was writing my first suspense novel, I had no idea what a blessing that meeting would turn out to be. Thank you, Tom, for helping me get the facts right year after year and book after book. I am forever in your debt.

I also want to thank the superlative team at my publisher, Revell—Jennifer Leep, Kristin Kornoelje, Karen Steele, Laura Klynstra, Brianne Dekker, and all the other dedicated staff members who work behind the scenes to make my books not only shine but get noticed in a very crowded marketplace. I am blessed beyond measure to have you as partners.

On the personal side, my husband Tom gets first billing. Read the dedication in this book, if you haven't already. That says it all. Having him in my corner through thick and thin makes all the difference as I labor to bring readers the very best stories I can write, with all the challenges that entails.

And I could never write an acknowledgment without thanking my wonderful parents. Though they are both gone now, their love continues to shine bright in my heart, lighting my way even on dark days—as it always will.

Looking ahead to 2025, book 11 in my Hope Harbor series will release in April (you can read a preview at the end of this book), and in October I'll finish up the Undaunted Courage series with Cara Tucker's tale. Her story features a remote estate, a century-old mystery, a hidden treasure, a dying language, and suspicious deaths. Get ready for a wild ride!

Until next time, happy reading!

Keep reading for a sneak peek at

Sunrise Reef,

the next book in the
HOPE HARBOR SERIES
by **Irene Hannon**!

ONE

WAS SOMETHING BURNING?

Bren Ryan stopped reading the instructions on the tube of hair dye in her hand, destined for use later today, and frowned at her reflection in the bathroom mirror. Sniffed.

A faint acrid odor with a hint of fishiness prickled her nose.

Not quite a burn smell, but close. And definitely worth investigating.

Leaving the dye on the vanity, she followed the scent, wincing as another slash of lightning strobed through the sky outside the window, followed by a boom of bone-jarring thunder.

Mercy, this was bizarre weather. Bad storms on the Oregon coast were supposed to be confined to the winter months. They never ushered in August—especially ones that went on for hours. Besides, even in the winter, torrential rain and high winds were far more common than lightning and thunder.

Whatever the cause of this uncharacteristic outburst from Mother Nature, it was certainly a dramatic beginning to her thirtieth birthday.

And perhaps it was also an omen that her decision to shake things up a bit during this new decade of her life was sound.

The smell intensified as she approached the kitchen, and she paused on the threshold. Gave the room a slow scan.

Everything appeared to be normal.

Hmm.

Could the unpleasant odor be coming from outside?

Bren crossed to the window above the sink, pushed it higher than the scant inch she'd left it cracked, and leaned over. Inhaled.

The air outside was damp but fresh.

This was weird.

She straightened up and swiveled back toward the room.

Where could the smell be—

Wait.

Was that *smoke* coiling out of the electrical socket at the end of the counter?

Heart stuttering, she dashed across the room and got up close and personal with the plate over the outlet.

The thin, vaporous wisps sinuously twisting from the prong slots were, indeed, smoke.

Which meant there was a fire inside the wall—or at the very least, smoldering wires or insulation that could soon morph into a fire unless she acted fast.

Bren grabbed her phone off the charger on the counter and tapped in 911.

After a crisp greeting, the efficient dispatcher elicited all the pertinent details and moved on to instructions. "Your fire department has been alerted. You should vacate the house and take shelter from the storm someplace safe until the crew arrives."

Bren glanced out the window toward the driveway, where rain continued to pummel her older-model Kia as dawn gave way to day. "Um . . . would my car be considered safe?"

"A structure would be preferable. Is there a neighbor who could provide shelter?"

The older couple in the next house a few hundred yards down the road would take her in if she showed up on their doorstep, but they never got up until after eight. Why ruin their morning too?

"No."

"In that case, go ahead and move to your vehicle. But keep the windows shut until the storm passes. I'll stay on the line until you're secure."

"Thanks."

Bren slid her phone into her purse, unlocked her car with the remote, pulled on the bright yellow slicker that always hung by the back door, and scurried through the rain.

Once she was behind the wheel, she put the phone back to her ear. "I'm in the car."

"Stay there until the fire crew arrives."

"Got it."

As the dispatcher severed the connection, Bren checked the time.

Six twelve.

No way was she going to make it to work in eighteen minutes. She'd be lucky to get to The Perfect Blend when the shop opened at seven, let alone early enough to help with prep and setup. Who knew how long it would take for Hope Harbor's volunteer fire department to arrive?

Dang.

From the day Zach Garrett had given her one of the two barista jobs in his new coffee shop three years ago, she'd never once missed a shift or shown up late. Reliability, punctuality, and diligence had been hallmarks of her employment.

Two of those were about to take a hit.

Sighing, she put in a call to Zach and peered at her tiny rental house through the rivulets of water sluicing down her windshield.

As milestone birthdays went, this one wasn't off to an auspicious start.

Hopefully it wasn't a preview of the year to come.

"Morning, Bren. What's up?"

At Zach's chipper greeting, Bren massaged her temple and gave him the bad news. "But I'll get there as fast as I can."

"Hey, no worries. I'll manage." His tone transitioned from upbeat to concerned. "Is there anything I can do to help?"

Her throat pinched.

Zach might be her boss, but he was also her friend. As were so many of the people in her adopted town, all of whom were more like family than the blood relations she'd left behind in Kentucky long ago.

"Thank you for asking, but at this point it's all in the hands of the fire department. I'm hoping the damage is minor and a quick fix will take care of it."

"Keep me in the loop."

"Will do. I'll get there as fast as I can."

"Like I said, I've got it covered. Nobody will get too bent out of shape if they have to wait a few extra minutes for their drink."

That was true—and another reason she'd fallen in love with this town.

"Thanks again, Zach."

"No thanks necessary. I'll see you when I see you."

Bren ended the call, set the cell on the seat beside her, and tapped a finger on the steering wheel as she waited for help to arrive, keeping an eye on her watch.

Five minutes later, a fire engine appeared down the road, the siren increasing in volume until the truck stopped in front of the house.

Not bad for a volunteer operation.

After flipping up the hood on her slicker, she opened her door and prepared to brief whoever was in charge.

The man who approached got straight to business. After a few clipped questions, he trotted off to confer with the members of the crew, who descended on her house with various pieces of equipment.

Including an ax.

Her stomach kinked.

That wasn't promising.

Nor was the muffled pounding that seeped through the frame walls minutes later.

When the man in charge reappeared and strode toward her, the grim set of his mouth telegraphed imminent bad news.

Bracing, Bren slid out of the car again, sans hood. At least the driving rain had stopped and the storm seemed to be dissipating. "What's the verdict?"

"You have an electrical fire inside the walls. Good thing you have a sensitive nose. Most people don't detect those until there's significant damage."

"Are you saying the problem is minor?" *Please let that be the case!*

"There's no visible damage, but it's hard to say what's on the other side of the drywall. It could take us a while to verify the fire hasn't spread. The wiring in the house should have been replaced years ago."

At the hint of censure in his inflection, she straightened her shoulders. "For the record, I'm a tenant, not the owner. I don't know anything about the mechanics of the house." Except that lights did tend to flicker randomly, and a few of the outlets were finicky. But every house had its quirks, right?

"Understood." His manner softened. "If you'll give me the owner's contact information, I'll apprise them of the situation. At minimum, drywall repair and wiring updates will be needed."

In other words, she'd be living in a construction zone for the foreseeable future.

Oh joy.

She passed on her landlord's information and surveyed the house. "Do you want me to hang around? I'm already late for work."

"No. We could be here another hour or two."

"Then I'll head out. If you'd lock the door from the inside and pull it shut as you leave, I'd appreciate it."

"No problem."

While he got back to business, Bren started the car, pointed it toward The Perfect Blend . . . and tried to look on the bright side.

It wasn't as if the house had actually caught fire. All of her personal possessions were safe. And if she had to live with drywall dust for a while, that was manageable. The house would still be a big step up from most of the places she'd called home over the past twelve years.

Eight minutes later, she hustled through the door of The Perfect Blend to find a long line stretching from the counter.

Zach's expression shifted from surprise to relief in a heartbeat the instant he spotted her. "I didn't expect to see you this fast."

"There was nothing for me to do at the house." She stashed her shoulder bag under the counter and slipped on her apron as she gave him a quick briefing.

"What a mess—and on your birthday, no less." He grimaced as he wiped the nozzle on the espresso machine.

"I've had worse birthdays."

"Yeah?" He eyed her as he plated a piece of cranberry nut cake for the espresso customer.

Whoops.

Talking about her past was a no-no. Only Bev at the bookstore knew any details about her younger years. And Charley Lopez, the town sage and taco-making artist who always had uncanny insights, had discerned a few facts. Other than that, she'd zipped it. Why dwell on a past she'd left behind, or let it pollute the fresh start she'd made here three years ago?

Bren called up a smile. "Ancient history. On the plus side, I caught the fire early." She turned toward the next customer in line, ending the exchange with her boss.

IRENE HANNON is the bestselling, award-winning author of more than sixty-five contemporary romance and romantic suspense novels. She is also a three-time winner of the RITA award—the "Oscar" of romance fiction—from Romance Writers of America and is a member of that organization's elite Hall of Fame.

Her many other awards include National Readers' Choice, Daphne du Maurier, Retailers' Choice, Booksellers' Best, Carol, HOLT Medallion, and Reviewers' Choice from RT *Book Reviews* magazine, which also honored her with a Career Achievement award for her entire body of work. In addition, she is a two-time Christy award finalist.

Millions of her books have been sold worldwide, and her novels have been translated into multiple languages.

Irene, who holds a BA in psychology and an MA in journalism, juggled two careers for many years until she gave up her executive corporate communications position with a Fortune 500 company to write full-time.

A trained vocalist, Irene has sung the leading role in numerous community musical theater productions and is also a soloist at her church. She and her husband enjoy traveling, long hikes, gardening, impromptu dates, and spending time with family. They make their home in Missouri.

To learn more about Irene and her books, visit IreneHannon.com. She also loves hanging out on Facebook, where she chats with readers every day.

GO BACK TO THE BEGINNING OF THE UNDAUNTED COURAGE SERIES WITH *INTO THE FIRE*

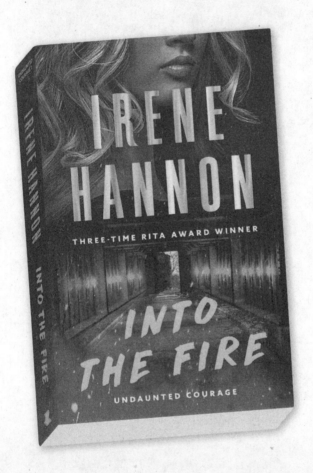

When arson investigator Bri Tucker inherits unfinished business from her predecessor, she must convince ATF Special Agent Marc Davis to help her find the missing link and track down a serial arsonist who will stop at nothing—including murder—to carry out a nefarious plan.